MW00657555

NANO

Archive 01: The City of Fire

Written by Jason Lee Crutchfield

Covert Art Designed by Matthew Burton
www.mattburton.deviantart.com

Copyedited by Randi L. Gingerich
rginger2@gmail.com

Formatted by Jonathan Pace
redmasq@redmasq.com

Dedicated to
Glenda Faye Crutchfield
and Anthea Amos

The two most influential women in my entire life.

Table of Contents

Prologue

A pitter-patter of rain fell in sheets against the landscape. The dark clouds rolling overhead rumbled like a growling beast toying with an unwary prey. Each droplet of acidic water splashing against the ground enhanced the pungent odor of soil and rusty metal. Skeletons of society lingered in the form of dilapidated houses and businesses; once thriving with life, these shells of culture sat as testimonies to the great human condition. Standing within the dark confines of one such rundown institution, I let my eyes wander over the destitute horizon of the fallen earth.

I was named Ihlia. It was not my true name, of course; the use of one's true name in the age of neurotech was tantamount to asking for a bullet in the forehead while one slept. Taking comfort in my episodes of respite, I preferred they remained devoid of unpleasant endings... or unendings as was the concern.

With every surviving human being hooked to a series of virtual intelligences and hardware, the brain was more easily hacked than a holocom, not that I ever took advantage of such handy and potentially profitable information. As I surveyed the decrepit world beneath me, I marveled at the pinnacle to which our race aspired and found genuine amusement in the fact that we fell flat on our faces at the finish line.

The history of civilization predating nanite technology involved countless wars and needless bloodshed. From the third world war to the Lunar Conflict of 2106, humanity drenched each chapter of its existence in blood. It never stopped, not even after the world ended in 2402. That was almost ten years ago.

With all the violence and destruction we mastered, humans of the past might have expected the humans of the future to usher in more inventive ways to destroy one another. Innovative developments such as the geo-guided centralized black hole fission warhead and the handheld particle disintegration cannon should have outmoded conventional firearms ejecting spiraling lead projections from the muzzle of gas-powered rifles.

I say "should have" because such technological advancements never occurred. No, for all their hype and glamour, we people of the future still felt the best way to solve a problem was to put a bullet in it, guide a missile to it, or nuke it.

Finally, on the first day of the first month marking the twenty-third century, the first nanite the size of a microchip was forged in a lab located in the heart of Tokyo, Japan. This particular machine, code named Panacea, represented the height of humanity's medical and biological achievement. A cure to virtually all ailment and injury, Panacea was surgically implanted in the brain and consisted of two parts.

The nano, or hub, acted as a rechargeable power supply

and micro computer utilizing the brain's bio-electricity to maintain and regulate the functions of the second part: the nanites. The nanites were tiny detachable components programmed by the nano hub's virtual intelligence to perform certain tasks. The number of nanites capable of docking at a single nano numbered between hundreds of thousands to millions depending on the make, model, and advancement of the implant. For Panacea, that number settled at an average two hundred fifty thousand. The unit as a whole was referred to as a nanite, implant, or augment.

Once implanted, Panacea became a symbiotic parasite feeding off the bio-electricity of its host for sustenance while providing the body with its nanites for rapid cell regeneration, correction of mutating or decaying cells, and elimination of harmful foreign substances in the body.

Many debates regarding the possible sentience and the question of whether or not the nanites were alive slowed the progress and introduction of nanites into mainstream medical markets, but the prospect of curing AIDS, cancer, and birth defects eventually overpowered such ethical jargon. Even after mainstream introduction, several conservative groups regarded the possibility of machine rebellion as grounds to forego the procedures. Once attached to the brain, however, the implant became as much a part of the host as a limb or organ.

The location of the implant on the surface of the brain was dictated primarily by its function and desired activation. Autonomous nanites were implanted in the medulla oblongata, while nanites requiring conscious activation were implanted in the frontal lobe of the cerebral cortex.

As an autonomous nanite, Panacea boasted programming capable of identifying all known illnesses, cancers, and harmful foreign objects. Updating that database involved a simple cerebral injection of a single nanite containing the data of new known threats. Once synchronized with the nano hub, the nanite uploaded the viral, mutagenic, or cancerous information to the nano for distribution to the other nanites for future use. In addition to infectious foreign objects, Panacea assisted in the rapid repair of injuries. Wounds that normally took weeks to heal could be fully closed and disinfected in moments.

While Panacea functioned as a self-activated implant, neurotech advancements eventually introduced many nanites that needed conscious activation. Such nanites required humans to educate themselves on how to utilize them as one would learn how to coordinate a new limb grafted to the body. The phrase “image training” would later be coined to describe that education.

The invention of the nanite ushered in a golden age of prosperity. Following Panacea, the question of whether humans utilized the full potential of their brains or not took on an entirely new implication. Nanites to stimulate higher thinking and advanced consciousness were introduced, and with their increased cognitive capabilities, people developed new breakthroughs in energy efficiency, waste disposal, population control, and food management.

We finally achieved the ability to live harmoniously with our planet, and for the first time since the dawn of man, we put our weapons down and enjoyed an age of true peace. People had all but evolved, moving to a state of existence globally recognized as "transcendent." Unfortunately, that peace ended not even a century later when we decided that the most transcendent way to solve a problem was to put a bullet in it, guide a missile to it, or nuke it.

Human ambition transcends all transcendence. If we learned anything from our brief respite it was this undeniable fact. Scientists developed the first nanite with combat capabilities within a century of Panacea; the world governments oversaw the development of these "secret trump cards" classified them to maintain appearances. Nanites which granted superhuman vision, speed, power, and even nanites purporting personality modification became ghost stories countries used to scare one another into pliability.

Eventually, tensions broke, and the last Global Conflict officially began in 2391. When war finally reared its ugly head, those ghost stories became a stark and horrifying reality. Nanite-enhanced super soldiers and advanced weaponry made massacre an art form. With population explosions under control during more peaceful days, the mass killing of the denizens of earth became an ironic and, in my personal opinion, hysterical problem for the enlightened human race. The advanced humanity found itself in more danger of extinction than the ignorant, barbaric version of its former self could ever boast.

The greatest punch line to the harrowing comedy of humanity, however, came as the dust settled and the wise race of man realized the folly of its self-mutilation. Several weapons of catastrophic destruction using advanced nanite technology were hidden in the repertoires of the major world powers of the time. Basically overly-powerful nuclear missiles, these weapons punched craters in the earth several miles deep and hundreds of miles in diameter utilizing nothing more than surface detonations.

Never intending to use such monstrosities even in times of war, the world leaders kept these judges of human existence called Titan Warheads slumbering peacefully in secure, highly classified bunkers never to be known by the public. Until Bradich Lesfort came along.

Under the handle Harbinger, Bradich used advanced nanite technology to simultaneously access every classified computer system in the world. He did not simply access the systems of a country or the western hemisphere; he hacked the entire world. Those Titans locked away in the high-security bunkers never to see the light of day? He not only woke them but fired them without a second's hesitation. At the time, the leaders of all the world's nations convened in a single location to end the Global Conflict that threatened to purge humanity from the planet. The titans judged that location first. After that, Harbinger obliterated every major city and several mid-populace cities without rhyme or reason.

No one ever figured out Bradich's motive for obliterating the majority of the world. As quickly as he appeared and wove Armageddon, he vanished. The fallout, several times the intensity of any conventional nuclear winter, spread across the globe within a day. It curtained the sky in an enormous cloud and completely blotted out the sun. Those not incinerated in the initial explosions faced radiation poisoning and a slow, painful end. A clear culling of humanity's remnants occurred. Those with Panacea lived; those without it died horrible deaths.

Several years later, thanks to medical and technological advancements in addition to the developments of synthetic food and commodities, what remained of earth's meager population survived in the wastelands, albeit with great difficulty. Societies sprang from the refuse of the planet and recognizable city-like developments began popping up across the globe, each with an architectural style unique to the person or people constructing it. The rare professionals trained to perform nanite surgery became a resource more precious than food and water.

Those who lost faith in humanity refused to rejoin its pathetic attempt to reestablish civilization. Instead, they succumbed to their primal desires and traveled about in gangs and packs constantly raiding the newly formed cities for supplies when the wastes failed to provide their needs or desires. Several nanite surgeons fell into this category, and after a short time bandits and thugs began sporting superhuman capabilities. In retaliation to the growing bandit threat, nanite surgeons clinging to societal standards recruited mercenaries and guns-for-hire; in exchange for their promises to protect the cities' best interests, they were promised wealth and combat augments of their own.

The cities and the wastes were quickly tagged with pet names. Representing the rise of a new age of struggling humanity, any area containing a somewhat functional society was Dawn Territory. Representing the perishing age of unreasonable ambitions and wrought with a take-all attitude, the bandit-controlled wastes were Dusk Territory. As one of the mercenaries mentioned, I pursued and protected the interests of one such town in Dawn Territory; I served as the top mercenary to Junction City, my new home following the world's destruction.

Truth be told, that mattered little to me. The work provided me contacts and leads to track down Bradich and the authority to extract that information from said contacts. That was my real goal, my only driving force since the end of the world. I wanted to find and kill that bastard with my own hands. I suppose I should have mentioned: right before donning the handle Harbinger and ending the world, Bradich betrayed and killed the only person I ever loved.

File 01: Ihlia

My chest swelled and deflated in slow rhythmic pulses as I sank one knee onto the frigid floor in front of a half-shattered window within an abandoned stone building. The darkness saturating the third level of the four-story structure strangled me in an unsettling icy grip leaving me almost blind to my immediate surroundings.

Of course, that which I desired to see was not inside the ruinous building but outside in what remained of our allegedly precious world. In fact, the longer I hid within the eerie darkness staring out into the run-down suburbs of a small, desolate town, the more I realized the strangling pressure felt more like a comforting embrace. I turned my jade eyes to the streets outside the window, and as I focused my senses, the nanite hub lodged within the temporal lobe of my brain buzzed to life, enhancing my sight by several times that of a normal human.

Each individual droplet of rain crystallized in sheets outside the window. A slow breath escaping my lips transformed into a cold mist before dissipating into the room's darkness. Long strands of my obsidian hair fanned in the crisp wind whistling in through the broken window. The breeze carried with it the decaying stench of a rotting world saturated with rust, mold, and blood. Out in the Dusk Territories, special care for aesthetic and olfactory senses simply did not rank among top priorities, and it was painfully obvious.

The scuffed black leather trench coat adorning my slender shoulders groaned quietly as I stretched trained muscles into the position necessary to steady the bolt-action rifle from which I was never separated. My left hand steadied the length of the rifle where the bi-pod would normally be attached. Careful not to poke its muzzle out the shattered window, I situated the killing utensil's stock against my right shoulder and placed my fingers against the trigger guard. With one of my nanites granting me superhuman vision, a scope was unnecessary.

Quickly factoring in the environmental conditions, I determined my effective range was roughly one mile. One mile to incapacitate the target I calculated would be traveling down the road within a few moments. I garnered my information from a reliable source, but if that old codger was mistaken...

"I'll just turn my rifle on him, instead," I inwardly mused.

As I pondered various ways to torture my old friend if his information proved useless, three distant silhouettes appeared through the curtains of acid rain that descended on the decrepit rubble of the former city. He was early. That still warranted punishment to my source, but a condescending slap to the back of the head would suffice. The target, Al Narljecht, was a twitchy, small-time gang leader for a bandit den centered in a place once referred to as Northwest Florida, a small territory set on the fringes of the world's once great nation, America.

Throughout history, America remained one of the most powerful and hated military and political forces on the planet. However, whatever reason the country suffered global scorn mattered little when it became ground zero for the global holocaust Bradich initiated. Another reason to eliminate that man's putrid existence: it was a good Samaritan act, kind of like taking out the trash. And Al Narljecht would be the perfect stepping stone on my journey.

Al's physique mocked the standard for even surviving in Dusk Territory, let alone becoming a crime lord. Those incapable of benching five times their body weight in pilfered loot and unwilling damsels usually died pretty quickly. What made Al survive, and in fact thrive in Dusk Territory to the point of assuming leadership of an entire gang, was his vast information network. Al knew many contacts both in Dawn and Dusk territories, and through those contacts he could easily exploit a city's defensive weaknesses and overstocked supplies.

In essence, Al knew where to hit, when to hit, and how to hit for the best risk to reward ratio; this knowledge attracted flocks of people to his feet willing to carry out his bidding for easy food, water, and entertainment. I was attracted more to the prospect of gathering vital information and stopping his vitals.

Given his meek build, Al never traveled alone. He

hunched at an unimpressive five feet four inches, gaining an additional illusory six inches from the towering neon green mohawk that frilled the center of an otherwise bald head. His creamy complexion and sunken eyes bordered in bright red "war paint," previously called make-up, vividly distinguished him from the dismal blandness of the surrounding buildings which were half or fully toppled and dark with aged rot. Walking on either side of the gangly crime lord, a pair of thugs with muscles bulging from a combination of rigorous exercise and strength implants splashed through puddles of sulfuric precipitation.

With steady hands I lifted the tip of my instrument and quickly trained the iron sights on the first lumbering brute's forehead. A hush fell over my surroundings like the stifled moment in a crowd just before a grand orchestra roars to life. The performance I prepared required such mastery that the waiver of but a few millimeters meant the difference between deathly silence and a standing ovation. In my particular line of work, the standing ovation would have been a most unfortunate finale.

As my perception of time slowed to a sluggish crawl, I distinctly felt the modest swell of my breasts slowly expand beneath my ragged black shirt in an elongated, drawn out breath. A single drop of water exploded into tiny translucent shards against the bridge of the unfortunate bodyguard's nose as the breath slowly hissed from my lips into a white fog. At the trough of my exhale, during the serenity of my calmest state, I squeezed the trigger.

The end of my rifle released a crack as the bullet streaked through the rain like an opening crescendo. After traveling nearly a mile, the abrupt percussion heralded the grotesque split of the target's head; against the dim, gray environment, it resembled a brightly exploding crimson fruit. The lifeless husk collapsed to the ground much to the bemuddled jerks of Al and his remaining companion. The scrawny thug's intellect instantly whirred to life; he grabbed hold of his surviving bodyguard and leapt behind him.

Still confused as to why his comrade painted a scarlet mosaic on the graveled road with bits of his own face, the second towering brute thought nothing of his leader's strange maneuver. Seeing as my performance left the bodyguard speechless, I decided to waste no time on the encore. I inhaled deeply, fluidly tugged the bolt-action lever on my rifle, and quickly replaced the ejected cartridge with a fresh, custom high caliber bullet before shifting my sights to the second hulk.

In reality, the caliber of the round was high enough to slice through the man like paper mache and find its home in the squirrelly, poorly postured crime lord, so I paid little attention to the dumbfounded behemoth and set my sights on the target behind him: Al. I fired again, and the splattered skull of the second goon mocked the first; a poor case of plagiarism in both sound and artistry. I expected to see the mutilated figure of Al crumpled to the ground after the mangled corpse of his second bodyguard dropped to the gravel. To my extreme disappointment, there was nothing.

"Blasted midget..." I cursed under my breath even as I chambered the next round. My eyes honed in on a pair of metallic claws and a bulbous nose poking from behind a granite slab that probably once served as a wall to a building. Al's weapon of choice was a pair of gauntlets that sported three jagged, toothy spikes messily jutting from the back of the hand.

Though the age of technology offered many advancements in ranged weaponry, their availability was borderline uncommon; it was not rare for a person to specialize solely in melee combat. I glanced down to the belt holding up my black, camouflaged cargo pants. On either side of my slender but supple hips rested a pair of long daggers with which I was well trained; I could understand having a contingency, but dumping my precious rifle in favor of an exclusive relationship with my blades was out of the question. No, I would maintain a swinger relationship.

When I returned my focus to the remnants of the building Al hid behind, I caught only the slosh of displaced rain as a blur zipped from that position. My inability to track Al's movements shocked me; he tore through the street in my direction with jets of water shooting up at either of his sides like an old-fashioned jet ski slicing through the ocean.

Whether a lucky guess, implanted telepathy, or

incredible deduction, Al shot behind the next stone structure just as I brought the sights of my sniper rifle to bear against the center of his forehead. My eyes twitched with a tiny pang of concern at the sheer distance he crossed during that brief moment I took my eyes off him. At least an eighth of a mile of my advantage was consumed by his unfathomable speed and my carelessness. The only explanation for that quick jolt of leg power was a nanite implant.

As the world developed and evolved nanite technology, both before and after the apocalyptic catastrophe of the Titan Crisis, new and creative implants hit the markets, legal and underground alike, almost every month. From nanites prolonging life span to ones propounding psychokinetics, the market for superhuman capabilities became as varied as those found in any comic book or novel. Many fighters and mercenaries possessed more implants than one might shake an electrocapacitor rod at.

That, however, came at a terrible risk and grievous cost. Nanites combined quasi-organic, silicon-based material with programmed microchips. As such, the nano hubs in a nanite served as virtual intelligences to accomplish the task for which they were designed. As those intelligences integrated themselves into the brain and began learning, their effects on the psyche threatened to override the sentience of the host.

That variable was factored into calculations regarding successful surgery, and an overall threshold for the safe number of implants was established. Individuals put themselves at great risk by exceeding three implants. This basic number functioned to prevent cases of a mental disorder known as hyperaugmentation; anyone suffering from hyperaugmentation was referred to as hyped by the layman.

When hyped, one began experiencing acute signs of insanity ranging from hallucinations and blackouts to dissociative identity disorder and, eventually, absolute psychosis characterized by an aggressive desire to kill... well, everything. The symptoms typically started on the less severe end of the spectrum and rapidly manifested with each consecutive implant.

A person's true threshold actually varied quite extensively from individual to individual depending on factors such as mental fortitude and will power. Those with exceptionally strong sense of self and firm wills were less susceptible to becoming hyped and as such exceeded the normally accepted threshold of three implants. Any number of implants over the threshold, however, still presented increased risk as a method to determine any individual's true threshold was nonexistent. But a method did exist to determine whether or not someone was hyped.

Al's figure twisted from behind the stone ruin, and his legs flexed beneath him. In the infinitesimal moment I beheld him, I simultaneously noted the swelling of the muscles in his thighs and the two black rings spiraling around his pupils. For every implant that exceeded an individual's threshold, a black ring would spiral about the pupil of the eyes indicating that individual's level of hyperaugmentation. The more rings in the eye, the more hyped the individual.

Normally one ring indicated occasional headaches and sleep trouble. One ring was also the point at which most surgeons denied any further implants to said individual. Alas, thugs inhabiting Dusk Territory rarely accepted "no" for an answer. They cared even less for phrases such as "It's for your own good!" In fairness, surgeons preferring the ruthless thug life in the wastes of the world rarely feigned concern for health and well-being. Before my finger could even begin applying pressure to the trigger, the cacophonous thud of Al's feet digging into the ground propelled him across the landscape like an electric current in my direction. Frantically, I attempted to hone in on his movements.

In my desperation I fired a shot which I only half-expected to find its mark, yet I still found myself cursing under my breath when it ricocheted off the gravel with a metallic whine. The obstacles littering the former city proved too difficult a handicap when combined with the nanite enhancing Al's speed. Given the nature of such quick spurts of insurmountable velocity, it stood to reason the muscle fibers in his legs were likely being shredded with each passing moment. That meant extra strain on Panacea.

After several well-timed dashes, Al rested behind a new moss-covered rock a little over a quarter mile from my nest. I was nervous. The musty odor in the room infiltrated my nostrils the same way the fear that the darkened room would become my tomb infiltrated my thoughts. I exhaled deeply, forcing the adrenaline levels to recede within my body long enough for me to regain my composure. At most, it would take Al three more dashes to reach the doorway of the rundown building. I wanted to incapacitate him in order to extract more accurate information, but my chance to keep him alive long enough to speak with him dwindled with every second.

"Al Narljecht. I had no idea you were so badly hyped. You seem to have it relatively together for someone who's supposed to have lost their mind by now." Attempting to hide my exact position at this point was meaningless. With every shot and each passing second his keen intelligence worked to evaluate the most likely perch from which I sniped. It was not rocket science, and in all likelihood Al possessed the mental processing power of a rocket scientist.

"Oh my what a beautiful voice. Why... why it almost sounds like silk rubbing against a wind chime! Ahaha! I can't wait to hear what it sounds like as I'm ripping you to pieces!" Al's voice escaped him in a twisted, bird-like eccentricity. In fact, the irony only struck me as to how closely the man resembled a scavenger bird after I heard his voice. With his stooped posture, hooked bulbous nose, towering mohawk, and talon-like choice of weaponry, Al's personification of the vulture was uncanny.

"I really have no reason to kill you. No reason yet, that

is. All I want is information and you can go about your business." I hoped the conversation would make him think. Thinking too much led to mistakes, and mistakes led to getting your brain blown out the back of your skull.

"You? Kill me? Ahahaha! I'm in stitches! Stop, stop! Hehehehe! Oh my. Interesting proposition, that one. Hm, yes, yes. And your name? You know mine, not very fair to not know the name of my... hehe... killer." His voice cracked every few words. Despite the speed and depth at which his mind processed thoughts, it seemed his composure could scarce keep pace.

"Ihlia. Ihlia Lorando. Now, where's Bradich?" I decided to get straight to the point.

"B-Bradich?! You seek Harbinger?! Ahahaha! This gets better and better! Ihlia, yes Ihlia. Seeking... Harbinger? Ehehehehe! You know he has his own agenda and doesn't take followers very easily! Most that seek to join his cause wind up in bags! Bags! Oohahaha!" I imagined Al's clawed hand flattening against his face as he tipped his head back and howled at his own jests.

"If I find him, he's the one that'll be in a bag. Mark my words." Grinding my teeth together faintly, I trained my iron sights on the area closest to Al's position. My desire to merely incapacitate him drifted closer and closer to lethal intentions.

"Hm, consider them marked. That changes things quite a bit I'm afraid. The difference between your claim to kill

Harbinger and your ability to do so are wider than the seas of old. Ohohoho! Come now, you don't need to seek Harbinger to kill you, I'll be taking care of that for you right here and now!" No sooner than the words squawked from his mouth, Al made another dash to a new cover notably closer to my sniper nest. Just as before, I was unable to even track his movements, let alone aim long enough to put a bullet in him.

"I'd much prefer if you just told me where he was so I could be on my way." Using every ounce of will in my repertoire, I stifled the urge to panic rising up in my chest like a giant lump forcing its way up my throat.

"Don't know, but I know someone who might. West of here, used to be called New York or something. Ahahaha!" The crazed cackle sloshing from his lips made me unable to discern if the madness prevented him from knowing his cardinal directions and the name of states, or if he simply wanted to confuse me. That was quite unfortunate for Al. My teetering decision to keep him alive or kill him and hope for the best toppled to the latter.

Al must have banked on his mismatched directions giving me pause because he took that moment to rocket across the remaining distance separating him from the doorway to my makeshift base of operations. I was ready. I activated a nanite lodged in my brain which, thus far, no one possessed save myself. Time slowed to a sluggish crawl. Al was leaning forward, bracing himself for the high speeds stressing his lower body. In the instant I slowed my perception, he wore a sickening grin, staring up at my window mere feet from the building's doorway.

But his grin melted in slow motion when he beheld me. Unlike before, I refrained from trying to follow his movements with the barrel of my rifle. Instead, I posted it as an unmoving sentry covering the only entrance or exit to my alcove. Al's body slowly crossed the trajectory of my aim even as my finger squeezed the trigger over the course of what seemed like minutes. His widening eyes betrayed the obvious fear of death all mortals shared even as the flash of light erupted in front of his face.

"Ohohoho shi—" Al tried to stop; his boots skidded through trails of water which he pushed up by the recoiling force of his unearthly speed. He crossed his clawed appendages in front of his face attempting to guard against the bullet that cracked from the maw of my firearm with a thunderous roar.

Like a knife through butter, the high caliber round shattered one of the claws in its trajectory and continued with a loud thud into the skull of the surprised crime lord. His body's forward momentum continued even as the force of impact sent his upper torso arching back. After turning a back flip in a forward direction, Al landed face first into the rust scented mud and slid forward before squishing to a stop at the entrance to my building.

I reached into the ammunition satchel at my side and procured another bullet before shoving the busted window open; I leapt from the third floor landing with all the grace of a feline. Al's body lay still at my feet with a swirled mix of blood and mud pouring from the chunk of his skull removed by the shot. It was unfortunate that I had grown to dislike the thug: unfortunate for him.

"New York was north, stupid asshole... Thanks for nothing," I spat the words as I chambered an extra round before draping the rifle across my shoulder in preparation for the long trek back to the nearby settlement and my home of the past ten years, Junction City.

It felt as though several moments passed, but I distinctly remembered hearing the sound only seconds after I started my journey. It was a faint sound, the familiar whisper of water being shot in a lateral direction. I pivoted my head, but it was too late. With a grotesque sound of clothes ripping and flesh giving way to steel, I felt long cold extensions pierce my back and burrow their way through folds of flesh, muscle, and organs before erupting through the front of my abdomen. I was impaled from behind by a set of three claws, and the middle one was broken.

File 02: Grave Misfortune

"You have to be joking..." The searing pain served as a blinding reminder to make sure your prey was actually down for the count. I twitched and gasped out hoarse chokes of agony as I staggered forward. The torture of those jagged claws rending through my flesh a second time when Al removed them dropped me to my knees. Immediately, Panacea went into overdrive to heal the wound. I could feel the tiny robots scurrying about and stitching together dangling innards deep within my stomach.

"Now that... was a splitting migraine! Ahahaha! But I suppose a little tummy ache is payback enough!" The enemy's chortle at my back snapped me back to reality. I possessed no time to feel pain.

I planted one foot to my side to brace myself and whirled about, swinging my rifle into position during the turn. At the end of my spin, I faced Al with the muzzle of my gun ready to finish the job I so egregiously failed. To the ever compounding misfortune of my predicament, however, the crime lord slammed the bottom of his foot into the rifle's tip as I swung it into position. With my vision blurred and nerves enflamed, my pathetic grip on the weapon unfurled, and his casual kick sent it careening through the air; it slid through several puddles before coming to a rest against a large rock in the middle of the broken road.

“Then I owe you one... because I'm having an even worse time stomaching your smell when you're this close!” I growled.

Between the metallic scent of my blood and the odor of a man who likely could not define the word “bath,” my olfactory sense was under brutal assault, and the rain pouring down our bodies only turned the foul smell into a wet, foul smell. It certainly did nothing to assist my dizziness. I was losing too much blood too quickly. Shakily, I gripped the two hilts jutting from the leather sheaths at my waist. I refused to die in such a place; I would live until I could see Bradich's eyes roll into the back of his head for the last time.

“Why you... let's see how clever that pretty little head is when it's on a roll! Ohuahaha!” Al swung his claws in an arch toward my throat. He intended to remove my head cleanly from my shoulders with a single motion. I quickly snatched my daggers from their sheaths and lifted my hands to parry his attack; the ring of my steel clashing with his indicated I temporarily avoided an untimely demise. It was certainly not the first time I had danced a passionate tango with death, but it was no easier to keep up with such a grim partner the hundredth time than the first. I simply needed to remain calm and not lose my head.

The instant our melee weapons kissed, the sparks began to fly. The combination of the situation's high tension and my special implant slowed my perception of time like a rubber band drawing close to the limit of its elasticity. Each bauble of rain hung in the air like molasses dripping from the clouds. After pulling back from my parry, Al activated his speed nanite and blurred far to my left. Though my perception slowed enough to follow the movements, it meant little as my body lacked the speed to follow suit. I desperately twisted just hoping for the chance to defend myself.

With another maddening explosion of velocity, Al passed by my figure with a demented guffaw. He cut through the air, dragging his hand behind him. The tips of his claws connected with my exposed ribs, and they hooked into place like stubborn barbs. He allowed the break-neck swiftness of his body to work to his advantage, and as he passed by, the barbs cleaved through my flesh.

I choked down painful screams and staggered back from the vicious momentum of Al's passing. Blood spewed from the gulch in my lateral muscles. His body slid to a stop several feet away before my spray of blood ever hit the ground, and seeing as I had spun to face him before the horrifying game of rip-my-skin-off, that placed him directly behind me.

I watched over my shoulder as his feet buckled against the slobbering sediment in preparation for his next dash. I wholly abandoned any hope of precision, and as his figure surged toward my back I flipped the long daggers in my palms so the blades ran down my forearms and their points protruded beyond my elbows. At the same time, I simply thrust backward and spun with no precaution given to defense. If I was to be shredded either way, then I would make sure his attacks connected only with a hefty price paid. His physical speed baffled me, but in terms of reaction and mental processing speed, I was thus far unmatched.

One of my blades connected, sinking deep into the tissue of his shoulder with enough force to skew the attack of his right arm. But his left set of claws found its mark against my chest, tearing away chunks of the ragged black shirt and bits of my favorite leather coat. More importantly, though, those claws hooked into a hunk of flesh just above my sternum; it locked us into place with our weapons crunching into skin and bone. We began grunting as our muscles shook from the strain of trying to overpower one another.

Despite my earlier accusations regarding Al's lack of any physical prowess, the reality of the situation made itself apparent during our struggle. Like me, Al possessed a Supersoldier augment. With such a nanite, appearances meant little, because the Supersoldier nanite enhanced muscular strength to the zenith of one's potential. Granted, larger muscles still meant more power, but with our frame sizes relatively equivalent, I was in no position to scoff at Al's strength.

After a few seconds, Al cackled and jerked back a few feet, the sick sound of his sinew popping as he tore his shoulder away from my dagger was joined by a rush of air as he twisted and dropped toward the ground. Placing either hand into the drenched mix of mud and loose rock, Al activated the implants in his legs just as he shifted his entire weight to his palms and bucked both legs outward in a kick much resembling a mule's.

His boots' soles found their home flat against my rib cage just below my breast line. I felt a volcano erupt within my bosom. The thunderous crack and crunch of several bones popping in time to the vehement thud of his kick acted as the catalyst for what felt like molten rock bubbling up from my core. A smoky anguish choked the very air from my lungs like ash sucking the oxygen from the air, and the parting of my lips elicited an overpowering scream like the eruption itself as my entire body catapulted backward across the muddy terrain.

The first time I bounced I could do little but gasp while my body contorted and careened further along the road. Several more of those bounces sent me in the direction of my former sniper nest. When I finally splashed to a halt in a two inch puddle of grimy water, I found myself unable to breathe, much less move. To my surprise, both daggers remained securely in my hands. The wind began refilling my lungs, and each painful inhalation brought with it the ache of splintering bones. But the pain served a purpose; it stirred me from my stupor.

With quivering hands, I planted my daggers in the ground and used them to climb to my feet. I could feel Panacea working at full capacity. Already the fatal wound in my abdomen finished slurping shut, leaving behind only a faint scar. The wounds along my ribs and chest would be stitched next, after which Panacea would take care of my broken bones. I locked gazes with the drenched, slouching figure of the unimpressive crime lord as he stalked toward me, and for the first time, I got a clear look at his skull injury.

My bullet blew the top corner of his skull apart, but his tirelessly working nanites slowly stitched it back together with each passing second. I was sure I aimed for the center of his forehead; it was hard to conceive that I missed at such range. As my confusion mounted he lifted the claws he used to impale me from behind and ran his tongue along the mix of water and blood dripping from their steel as a vicious taunt. The broken one glared at me: it was that claw!

In his attempt to block my shot, Al sacrificed that center appendage to alter the trajectory of the bullet into a part of his brain Panacea could repair! I cursed under my breath and braced myself for his assault. Then I twitched as I considered the sluggish speed at which his nanites repaired his scalp. In the time it took his nanites to make notable progress on healing his wound, Panacea fully closed three grievous injuries of my own. Why?

In the wastes, the ability to multitask was a pivotal difference between the living and the dead. I shifted my eyes back toward the darkened doorway of my former refuge. Synchronously, I began piecing together the potential reasons for his slower healing speed. I crossed my blades in front of my chest in an assumed defensive stance and decided to attempt a jab at his patience. "So Al, if your contact network is as weak as your legs I may have to go get information from your bodyguards over there," I scoffed condescendingly.

"... My legs are stronger than anyone's. My speed is that of a god! With this prototype implant, I am uncatchable. The fastest in the world! And my information network is flawless!" My goading seemed to work, but Al's severe insanity onset by hyperaugmentation made it difficult to tell for certain. For all I knew he was talking to some other invisible entity that jeered him in a similar fashion. I braced myself for his inevitable charge; I was not disappointed.

His body collided with mine as he tried to sink his claws into my torso, and that collision pushed us both into the caliginous domicile behind me. A grin slowly tugged at the corners of my lips. I realized two things almost simultaneously during the jarring impact of his frame against my own. First and foremost, my strategy was off to a successful, albeit boisterous, start. Within the small confines of the ruined abode, Al's quick bursts of speed would amount to far less than they would in the wide open battleground outside.

As his charge crushed me into the wall on the far side of the room, I quickly threw a knee between his legs. In the inky blackness surrounding us, a satisfying crunch followed by a howl of pain trumpeted my successful blow to the most sensitive parts of the male body. No matter how far humanity advanced its fighting techniques, such a well-placed blow would, certainly, always drop a man to his knees.

During my brief respite, I dashed up the flight of stairs to the next floor and spun to await my, likely enraged, aggressor. In the tenebrous confines, my sensory nanites enhanced visual and auditory perception to superhuman levels. I activated one more implant for good measure: my nightvision. Like a feline, my eyes gave off a soft, translucent glow as they pierced the pitch black corridor of the abandoned structure.

It only took a moment for Al to ascend the staircase; his eyes, tainted by a black hypnotic swirl, glowed like mine. Al, too, possessed a nightvision implant. For a moment the two of us stared, waiting for the other to twitch too soon or demonstrate uncertainty or hesitation. The very smell of frustration and anxiety mingled with the dust and hovered in the chilly air like a cloud. Al made the first move; with a berserk screech, the vulture lurched forward in the darkness and began the dance which, for one of us, would be the final curtain call.

Our weapons sang a beautiful opera only the two of us could truly appreciate. Sparks flashed at pivotal points when our weapons kissed a little too long in the darkness. In the confined space, our combat abilities were almost equal. Using the walls and ceiling, we performed a plethora of acrobatic and martial movements which boasted potent lethality against anyone untrained or unprepared. Our macabre dance carried us up two more flights of stairs over what felt like years of intensely engaging combat.

When we finally stopped, the ragged breaths heaving from both our chests betrayed our fatigue. I stood in front of the very window from which I had shot him and his comrades only moments ago. Al stood on the opposite side of the room, glaring at me with intense hatred.

“This is it, IHLIA! This is where you... hehe... where you become a pathetic little stain of blooooood! Where you become a nothing! A smear on the footnotes of my epic history! You should feel honored... ahahaha!” During our ferocious dance on the floor below, we had occasionally bypassed one another's defenses and brought steel against flesh. Our bodies dripped with rivulets of blood from various wounds inflicted by those bypasses. It occurred to me that Al failed to realize his wounds were closing far slower than mine. That realization simply confirmed the second point I discovered in that jarring tackle on the first floor.

“Sorry, Al. This is where you retire. You can't call yourself epic with such a glaring weakness.” I smirked, puffing out my chest in the most arrogant manner I could muster.

“Weakness? I have no weakness!” Al spat in a furious rage. The seething contempt peppering his tone foreshadowed his attack. With a quick burst of nanite-empowered energy, Al slammed his feet into the far wall on the opposite side of the room. Using it as a platform for propulsion, Al rocketed across the room toward me with a malevolent caw. I lifted my daggers and braced for the impact of the Al Narljecht warhead. Like a missile, he rammed his body into my own, the force of which felt like the explosive force of a nuke.

We both careened backward through the open window. The rain still fell in thick sheets against our mutilated bodies as we all but flew through the sky with the speed of a pair of shooting stars; as we descended I pushed away from him to brace for impact and tucked my body into a shape which I felt would be easy to roll with upon striking the semi-hard ground.

Despite my preparation, the landing felt like someone lifted a building and began beating me senseless with it. Somewhere between the cracking of my left arm, the snapping of my collar bone on the left side, the cries of pain from my lips, and the mockery of rolling I made while bouncing and tumbling across the gravel, I finally skidded to a halt drenched in water and covered in rust-scented mud.

With my vision blurred from the dull pain shooting through the entire left half of my body, I lifted my gaze to see Al slowly worming to his feet. It seemed he managed to land without shattering his... everything. It took several moments for the nanites to stitch my busted body together enough for me to rise to one knee. By that time, Al was hobbling toward me, coughing and sputtering with each step he took.

“Al... you're absolutely insane. You could have killed

us both!" I gasped as I forced myself to stand. My right hand gripped my left shoulder tightly; I felt that keeping it from moving might help keep it from protesting so loudly in my head.

"Ahaha... hehehe. Well, I didn't... I'm just gonna... ugh, wha?" Al paused momentarily to look down. Embedded deep in the center of his chest, only slightly off center to the left, my daggers criss-crossed through the area which assuredly contained his heart. The flow of blood gushed from the new orifice like water from a cracked dam, and his eyes twitched with the realization of what happened.

"That's right. I took the tackle on purpose so I could make sure those found their mark," I grinned at him when he gripped the hilts of my daggers. Searing pain obviously shot through him the moment he touched them, because he winced and withdrew his hands with an audible yelp.

"... And you called me crazy, hahaha! Looks like the jokes on you... I'm still alive," he retorted.

"Yes, but that's where that crippling weakness of yours comes into play. You're only barely alive because Panacea is working at one hundred percent just to maintain the functions of your heart. All your other wounds, unlike mine, won't be healing while those blades are shoved into your chest. And if you arbitrarily pull them out? You'll pull your heart out with them. There's a limit to what Panacea can do, so that's not advised." The calmness in my breath gradually returned to me as my wounds rapidly healed. Al, on the other hand, looked quite horrible.

“What's your point?” He quirked a brow as blood slowly trickled from the corner of his mouth; it was a clear sign of the blood filling his lungs.

“It's your speed nanite. It only works in tandem with Panacea. Your speed nanite supercharges your fast twitch muscle fibers, boosting them to superhuman levels for short bursts of speed. This, however, would irreparably damage the muscle... if not for Panacea.” I took a step back and regained my posture.

“So... my speed implant won't work until I get these blades out. Hehehe... clever girl. But I don't need speed at this point. I still have these claws, I could just as easily lop your head clean off with a slow swing. And you have no weapon to defend yourself.” He began hobbling forward; the drip-drop of blood cascading down the handles of my daggers left trails in the wake of his every step.

“You're mistaken on two points, Al... First, I do have a weapon.” Call it luck, telepathy, or precise prediction, but my foot thudded softly against a wooden stock laying fortuitously against a random stone in the middle of the road. We were standing at the exact place where my rifle came to rest when Al kicked it from my hands. I quickly slammed my foot down on the butt of the gun, flipping it up off the ground and into my waiting hands like an impressive skateboarding trick; the muzzle came to rest theatrically between Al's eyes.

"Secondly, no speed implant means you won't be dodging this, Al. Sorry buddy, nothing personal. Well... actually it kind of is," I murmured disdainfully. Al's eyes widened in fear, his entire body drained of the bravado exhibited only seconds prior; he was literally shaking in his boots.

"No... you can't do this! You just can't! My speed is legendary! I am legendary!" His protests rang out in perfect synchronization with the fulmination of my rifle's tip. The blood, skull bits, and brain matter were unable to pick a direction and spewed in a random assortment of patterns behind him. His body fell straight back onto the ground, and I shouldered my rifle.

"It's weird. I normally don't chamber an extra round for theatrics like I did earlier. Lucky me, don't really think I had time to reload there," I sighed softly, and as I began walking away, something gently tugged at my ankle. When I looked down, it was Al gripping the heel of my boot with pitiable desperation.

"... There's a guy to the... west in Old Texas. He calls... himself Raze. If... anyone knows where... Harbinger is..." My bullet split Al's eyes across his face, and his right one had all but exploded within the socket. Still, I could feel the piercing madness of his remaining eye even as he shared that last bit of information with me.

"Hey... I still... have a few moments... stay? It's... not

everyday... you die," he sputtered.

"Why should I? I don't exactly have any inclination to bury your corpse when you do pass on." I quirked a brow at him even as he twitched about uncontrollably. The nanites were an amazing blessing yet a terrible curse. In a situation where instant death would certainly be preferable to prolonged agony, the nanites still worked on what limited bioelectricity they received from destroyed brain tissue and attempted to tackle the impossible task of putting both the brain and their nano hub back together. Such drawn out deaths were not guaranteed but neither were they uncommon.

"I... want to hear your... story. You're pretty damn... good, hehehe... for a girl. Why... do you want Harbinger dead... so bad?" Al's single eye blinked.

"... Fine, I suppose a few minutes won't hurt. Consider it thanks for the information." I sat down on a nearby rock, crossed my legs, and secured the strap of my rifle between my breasts. As I brushed my long obsidian hair, matted by the relentless storm, behind my ear, I looked toward the sky.

"It all started on a stormy night like this one..."

File 03: A Dark and Stormy Night

"Born in an age when nanite implants were commonplace, I donned my surgical scar and received Panacea before I hit puberty. During my childhood, the Global Conflict was just beginning to ravage the world, and invading guerrilla forces targeting American coastal cities crept up in small raiding parties. They utilized advanced stealth transports to avoid detection in the dead of night; the threat posed was so severe that even parents did not dare use stories of invaders to scare their children to sleep.

Despite the constant threat of invasion, my mother and father showed me the tender loving care expected of any responsible parent. I went to school, played with friends, and for all intents and purposes led a normal life... until that night. Adulthood knocked on my door early, when at age thirteen I witnessed two hyped super soldiers hold my father down and force him to watch as they had their way with my mother.

Two memories forever burrowed into me that night as I peeked through the cracked door from inside the closet where my mother shoved me before the soldiers boisterously invited themselves into our abode. The first was beholding the torture on my parents' faces. My mother's agonized sobs and screams as they desecrated her body like their personal whore were rivaled only by the wails of my father, so full of rage and anguish that it brought me to my knees in tears.

The sounds horrified me enough, but when they transformed to deathly gurgles as the brutish soldiers nonchalantly ripped my parents' throats out with their bare, calloused hands it took everything in me to choke back a terrified scream. The second thing I remember is the stars and stripes patched onto the sleeves of their bloody uniforms. They were American soldiers.

In the middle of the night in Yordleton, my quaint little hometown in New Virginia fifteen miles from the east coast, a squad of European raiders from the Union snuck ashore intending to establish a forward base of operations in the center of my city. As though the audacious plans of our enemy didn't disregard the importance of our lives enough, my own country decided to send a response team of experimental hyperaugmented soldiers to repel Yordleton's invaders. Personally, I viewed the raiders as bogeymen shrouded in darkness that came to drag away everything I knew and loved and tear it to a bloody mess while they forced me to watch like a helpless invalid. Apparently, my countrymen viewed it as an opportunity to field test an unstable product.

The effects of hyperaugmentation are indisputably observable from contraction all the way to their more terminal stages. To assume that the government was unaware that their experimentally augmented soldiers suffered from those effects would be to assume they somehow missed the rabid mouth foam, rapid twitching, and, oh yes, the gratuitous number of black spirals overtaking their otherwise bloodshot eyeballs.

No, it was far more likely that a particular batch of soldiers subjected to novel experimentation were classified as failures due to hyperaugmentation; with the introduction of strange static voices in their heads, uncontrollable bouts of inexplicable rage, and unfettered desire to remove the limbs of anything moving, our government simply could not use them in the field. At least, not in any normal deployment. But if anything could be said of our government after squirming through several crippling economic depressions, it would be its newfound obsessive tendencies with maintaining monetary efficiency.

In all likelihood, the big wigs and movers and shakers knew the madness afflicting their volatile but costly super soldiers was uncontrollable. But what if, I'm sure they pondered, they could simply direct that madness and receive desired results? Thus, the hyped descended upon Yordleton; one could say they were released as animals rather than deployed as soldiers.

With monstrous efficiency, the American soldiers annihilated the trespassing attack force. I stress the word monstrous over the word efficiency, because the invaders' terrified screams and grotesque howls resembled something from a cheesy horror film. I could scarce differentiate the echo of the pounding rain from the splattering sounds of gore painting the town. In the end, the aggressors' demise was unable to slake the psychosis-driven bloodlust of our army, and they inevitably turned their rancor on the very town which they were sent to protect.

That night, many families shared my sorrow, forced to watch the people they loved ripped apart by the hands of our stalwart defenders dressed in familiar uniforms which, in the past, inspired feelings of relief and security. The citizens' hellish cries drowned the roaring thunder, and the metallic stench of freshly spilled blood mixed with the aroma of rainfall covering the wet landscape like a pungent spring stew. It was a conjoined, city-wide nightmare from which there was no awakening.

On my hands and knees inside the closet, hours passed with nothing but the small slit of light from the cracked doorway illuminating my face. Still in shock, it felt like decades since I last blinked or breathed; I feared either of those things would make enough noise to attract the beasts still rummaging about the prison I once considered home. I don't remember at what point I recognized the small piece of a long, familiar rectangular box poking from the top shelf in the closet, nor do I remember standing on my tip toes to drag it down. But I do remember my trembling hands fumbling with the lid and removing my father's old hunting rifle.

Several engravings ran down the length of the bolt-action rifle's metal body and across its wooden stock. None of them mattered. The only thing that mattered was steadying my shaking limbs long enough to load the thing. It felt like an earthquake racked my entire body, and as I struggled to work the chamber the way I had seen my father do it countless times before, it prematurely snapped down on my fingertip, forcing a whimper from my lips. I immediately regretted my clumsiness.

The growling racket marking the tirade of the two crazed patriots through my house ceased upon the faint squeak from my hiding place. I froze as though I had just plunged into the freezing waters of the arctic circle. The sound of slow, methodic thumping replaced their zombie-like groans and gnashing teeth as they stomped listlessly across the wooden floor toward my hideaway. The smell of blood, that before only lingered in the air like a bad aftertaste, now assaulted my nostrils with renewed fury as they drew closer step by terrifying step. Hot tears streaked quietly down either side of my face, and my hands began working by themselves to fit a high caliber round within the chamber I had fumbled with seconds prior to garnering the monsters' attentions.

Just as my heart reached the apex of its thunderous beats and my throat tightened in horror, the sounds of their advancement ceased. They began screaming lewdly at one another, and within seconds I heard a struggle which I presumed to be the two of them fighting. Anything that could possibly be broken within our home shattered in the cataclysmic hurricane of the two in-fighting hyped. The sound, while understandably inducing its own brand of fear, also served to relieve me at the prospect that they temporarily forgot about my existence.

I hugged the rifle to my chest as though it were my father personified and waited. Before long, the struggle careened onto a separate battleground which I presumed was once our kitchen. What initially began as a fight eventually became a slaughter. The sounds of one of the men changed from unbridled rage to gurgling whimpers accompanied by thrashing limbs like a child throwing a tantrum over losing a board game. The two contestants of this game, however, played for keeps.

A few moments later, a pregnant hush fell over the house. Faintly, I heard the squeaks of a swinging decoration, likely a picture frame, as it dangled from a broken string on a nearby wall. I stood and, using the tip of the rifle's barrel, pushed open the closet door. I began my slow gait into the dim light, and it struck me, then, how burdensome the weight of my father's gun felt within my shaking hands.

Outside, the rain streamed steadily in the night, painting shadows of streaking water that danced against my face and the white nightgown adorning my small frame. I crept toward the kitchen while choking back fragile whimpers. The wooden floor creaked ever so softly, and with each step I held my breath expecting one of the brutes to lunge from the kitchen.

I carefully stepped over the mutilated bodies of my parents. I dared not behold their expressions in the dim light, lest whatever resolve I had accumulated up to that point would be drained to despair. Instead, I focused my sights ahead on the kitchen doorway. The myriad of fallen lamps and dull light cascading from the ceiling fixture plastered a large man's shadow against the wall. As I approached, I distinctly heard guttural sobbing. Upon closer inspection, I saw the disfigured shadow hunched over in a contorted husk bobbing up and down in intervals synchronized with the mournful cries.

Tears dripped from the sides of my cheeks in silent rivulets. As I rounded the corner into the kitchen, I saw the two soldiers amid a broken pile of wood that once served as our dining room table. One soldier, a large African American, lay flat on his back staring at the ceiling with lifeless eyes. The deep black and purple blotches around his neck indicated that his regretful comrade strangled him to death, but at the time I was too young to know and too grief-stricken to care. The other man, a Caucasian with brown hair and a broad back, slowly turned toward me with a tear stained face and bemuddled look within his spiraling black eyes.

'I... what have I... what's happening to me? Help me, please... I...' The man shook with the same ardent fear that overtook me moments ago. His face was adorned with confusion and woe, as though the entirety of the events played out before him like a bad movie without a happy ending. His voice, still tainted by the slight ravings of madness that crafted his growls and roars earlier, cracked with a sense of innocent sadness longing for the reassurance that his unforgivable crimes were not his doing but that of a foul entity somehow separated from him.

'... You took them away. All of them. Everyone,' I meekly muttered my response and slowly lifted the rifle to my shoulder like I had seen my father do in the forest surrounding our town. Since I turned thirteen he had just begun taking me with him when he hunted, and now he would never take me again. I would never run back to the house with rabbits in tow to the mixed look of amusement and disgust on my mother's face at the prospect that such manly endeavors tainted her little lady. I would never hear their laughter again. I would never see their smiles. Even as I stood with the rifle aimed at the confused soldier's face, I tried to remember those happy faces. Instead, I saw only their visages frozen in horror.

'Wait, little girl... please, I don't know what happened... please calm down, I'm so sorry... I need help.' The man slowly stretched his hand toward me. Help? He needed help? The same man who helped himself to my mother with wild abandon? Yet he sat there on his knees daring to ask me for help? Something snapped in me, then.

I felt the color drain from my face and the sparkle of innocent youth fade from my eyes. My body, once vibrating with uncontrollable fear and confusion, steadied into an incorruptible calm. A long, deep exhale flowed from my lips as I squeezed the trigger. The resulting cacophonous kaboom simultaneously sent our bodies in opposite directions. The surprise on the soldier's face lasted only a moment before the bullet's impact catapulted him back to join his friend in the pile of debris. The soldier's face splattered into a scarlet mess that sent his body into post mortem convulsions.

The rifle shot launched me in the opposite direction against a countertop, coincidentally upon which sat a wooden contraption responsible for housing an assortment of long, sharp kitchen knives. The combined force of the rifle's recoil and my resulting impact against the counter shattered my shoulder, and I promptly slumped to a seat on the mahogany floor. My reverberating thud against the counter toppled the knives' sanctuary, but as two blades found new sheathes, one in my right thigh the other in my left bicep, I noticed a growing apathy spring to life within me.

My shadow danced and flickered on the floor with the changing light as the ceiling fixture chaotically wobbled. I felt nothing for the corpses on the ground, nor did I respond to the aching nerves in my body warning me of the hazards of the two knives impaling my figure. And I could not have cared less about the throbbing in my broken shoulder.

Instead, I found myself slowly rising to my feet. My entire body tingled with latent anticipation as I dragged the muzzle of my father's rifle behind me and walked toward the door. I could still hear the distant cries of agony and pleas for help from my neighbors over the scrape of the weapon's metal tip against the wooden floor. Though their volume and frequency declined with each passing second, they were still there. As I gripped the knob of my front door, I felt my broken bone crunch back into place as Panacea went to work. Those same nanites slowly pushed the knives from my wounds like a splinter's natural ejection from the flesh.

When I finally swung the door open, I stood as an ominous figure in the dim light. Fires had sprung from all corners of the city consuming everything they touched. The dim orange glow roared and hissed as the clouds desperately dumped their water from the heavens as though consciously trying to quell the flames. Despite the graphic scene from the bowels of hell into which my town steadily descended, I remained unfeeling. As though a part of me had broken when I fired that shot in the kitchen. While the images of my happy memories burned up like the houses in front of me casting a tingling chill of dread down the length of my spine, it was also strangely liberating like each memory was a chain wrenching itself loose from my heart.

I never blinked, but for some reason the involuntary stream of tears relentlessly poured from my jaded eyes anyway. The scene in front of me elicited no emotion. Even as several crazed shadows I assumed were hyped soldiers pounded at lifeless hunks of meat I assumed were my fellow townsmen, I felt serene. In fact, despite their madness as their attention slowly lifted with gaping anticipation at the prospect of new prey, a look of bewilderment struck them. While my matted hair and the shadow of night cast darkness across my face, the occasional illuminating bolt of lightning revealed my unmoving expression to them; I wore a twisted smile.

I knew I would die, but I did not care. I knew I would only be able to shoot one or two of them before they overwhelmed me, but I did not care. As they hunched over and prepared to charge with ferocious growls and hungry glares, I lifted my father's rifle, my rifle, to my shoulder. I decided that the first to move would be the first blown apart, and afterward I would resign myself to whatever fate decided. As it turned out, fate had something far different in mind than I did.

Before the first lunatic lunged, enthusiastic sounds of hooting and cawing exploded from a hillside near my obliterated home. The revving of several engines and grinding of tires propelled three jeeps through the sky over the side of said hill. The vehicles drew my attention and snapped me from my morbid staring contest with the hyped soldiers. The jeeps traveled in a spearhead fashion; their glaring headlights evoked hisses from the enraged hyped, who lifted their arms to shield their eyes.

The point jeep in their spearhead assortment fish-tailed into a group of soldiers and stopped directly in front of me. I watched the spray of blood and limbs with a mild numbness that steadily faded from my shattered young spirit in lieu of hope. The vehicle's driver was a large, black muscled man with a gruff face and scruffy beard. A cigar perched between his lips ended in a dull red ember from which curls of smoke rose through the spits of rain still dotting the landscape with far less fervor than the earlier storm. The other three passengers arrayed the jeep with simulated organization. Of all the members of all three vehicles, only one man stood in the back with an automatic weapon.

That figure radiated authority despite the slender cut of his frame. Long, wavy brown hair framed a chiseled face, and despite the thin manner by which he was designed, his form was carved with enviable, sleek muscles. An aura of absolute confidence emanated from his hazel eyes. Extraordinarily young, I would later find out that, at that point in time, he was twenty-three years old, yet the entire squadron obeyed his commands without hesitation. Charismatic, strong, and commanding, he looked like a pillar on which his men leaned.

'Bradich, sir, looks like we got here too late,' one of the men barked and hopped down from the shotgun seat next to the older gentleman smoking the cigar. I watched as he casually strolled to one of the staggering hyped and promptly smashed his face in with the stock of his semi-automatic rifle.

'A shame. I can only hope the spirits of those that died forgive our tardiness. Take 'em out, boys.' The man they called Bradich lifted a hand in a sweeping motion and the night sky lit up with the fire cracking sounds of automatic fire. The hyped soldiers screamed out in near unison as a hail of gunfire mowed them down like dysfunctional cattle. It was not long before one of the executioners noticed me.

'Uh oh, boss, looks like we have a survivor. She's a young one, too. About twelve, maybe thirteen.' A flashlight on the man's helmet blinded me to details, yet it also served as a catalyst that snapped me from my numb stupor altogether. I dropped to my knees, still clutching my rifle, and began to sob.

‘Yikes! Whoa, hey, stop that. Boss! She's crying, and she won't stop!’ The man looked over toward their leader who sauntered up to me with the background noise of heavy machine gun fire rattling the night air.

‘... Sorry child, we ran into traffic.’ His heartless answer should have angered me, but instead I just kept crying like the small child I was.

‘Do you want to stay here or come with us? Although I'd venture to say there's not much for you here,’ he looked around at the ruins once called Yordleton. I followed his gaze before my eyes came back to rest on his frame. He stood over me with his hand extended as though if I would only take it, my world would fill with color once more.

‘Are you serious, boss!? She's like thirteen! And what are we supposed to do with her anyway? You can't be...’ The goon's voice trailed off as I reached up and took Bradich's hand. At thirteen years old, I watched my parents die; at thirteen years old, I shed my innocence by taking my first life; and at thirteen years old, I became the youngest member of Bradich's run-and-gun mercenary group, The Bald Eagles.

Adjusting to life as a mercenary was rough at first. The shock of my parents' deaths and the grief of losing my home heavily weighed upon me in the early days traveling with the Eagles. Even in my sorrow, however, I learned much about the colorful people who became my new family. As I grew accustomed to my new life among the rough elements of the mercenary group, I found my place in the hearts of the band of misfits. Within a year, my unspoken adoption became as unshakeable as my blood ties with my late parents.

Bradich himself favored the use of twin daggers for all his melee needs, and it was Bradich himself that trained me to use mine. But after seeing my attachment to my father's rifle, Bradich introduced me to Larz who trained me in marksmanship for the next several years. Between the two of us, our sniping nests became legends told to our enemies to scare them into staying awake on watch. Ultimately, I would end up replacing Larz as the company's sole sniper when he met an unfortunate demise at the hands of an enemy marksman. Another gray day full of rain and tears, that one, but I was more prepared than when my parents were snatched from me by the maw of the Reaper, so I feel the process was healthier when we lost Larz.

Every day a new adventure shaded my life with a different color. Slowly the shell of icy trauma that took hold of my young soul cracked away, and I returned to an image of my former self. The Bald Eagles became my family; their nuances and habits peppered my life with a combination of excitement and familiarity. Though at first I was ill-received among the hardened mercenaries, their days raising me as a group strengthened the bonds we all shared on and off the battlefield. When our members died, we grieved together. When we emerged victorious and collected our bounties, we celebrated together.

Everyone, that is, except Bradich. I saw little of him during the majority of my time as a mercenary. He spent most of his time alone or with contacts preparing the next job. We worked almost exclusively for our own country, at best deviating only to take on the odd jobs from her allies. The government and military cared little for mercenaries like us, making us ideal squads to send into one-way missions. We preferred it that way, not having to worry about anything but our objective and one another.

The few times Bradich joined us in merriment or around the occasional campfire, I found him most pleasant and understood why the men surrounding him would die if he told them it was for the group's best interests. No matter what events transpired, the minute Bradich entered the group all attention swarmed to him as though he was a dazzling jewel cast among rubbish. I remember, one time, he tried to convince us that a 'bald eagle' was a bird that once served as our great country's mascot; riotous laughter erupted throughout the camp. First, the concept of a bird being bald reminded me more of dinner than something alive; second, why in the world would a featherless bird represent one of the greatest world powers?

Unfortunately, I later learned we were more like moths drawn to a vicious flame rather than Bradich being a diamond in the rough, but I'll get to that in time.

It wouldn't be until a year after joining the eagles that I first met Bradich's brother, Donovan Lesfort. Donovan was a scientist who followed the long lineage his patronage afforded him. The Lesfort family innovated and marketed the nanite implants after their original creation in Japan. They were also responsible for upgrades and the creation of further nano technology including purporting huge strides in the field of combat implants. As for Donovan, his interest and field of expertise was in the theory that nanites possessed subtle personalities; true intelligences; and, most controversially, wills of their own.

I saw him several times after that, and everything about Donovan piqued my interest more and more over the years of knowing him. Unlike his brother and the entirety of my new family unit, Donovan possessed no combat experience or prowess of any kind. As a, at the time, sixteen-year-old girl I found that to be most endearing. The prospect that there was someone I cared for that actually needed my protection nurtured a sense of usefulness and care-giving housed somewhere in my subconscious femininity that had not been completely incinerated by the flames of a male dominated group.

The kindness and patience he exuded even as he worked kindled a girlish fantasy in me that quickly deepened. It wasn't long until I realized, even in my immature state, the pangs of longing and adoration for Bradich's brother. I had fallen in love. Consequently, it was not long after that when my world's color, given to me by my new family, was once more thrust into darkness and shades of gray. This time, both literally and figuratively, the effects were permanent.

It would be a year later, as I approached my seventeenth birthday, that we accepted Donovan's request to travel to Egypt in hopes of discovering a breakthrough in his nanite theories. The events which unfolded in Cairo changed everything. It was there that Bradich... Al? Hey, Al?" I looked down to see the squirrelly crime lord's remaining eye glaze over as the bubbling sound of his last breath escaped the gaping fissure dividing his face. The dull gray sky indicated daybreak as the sun shined its rays from behind the veil of ashen fallout caused by the Titan Crisis ten years ago after the events that took place in Cairo.

"Al... it's rude to interrupt a lady when she's speaking." I shook my head and rummaged through Al's belongings. Taking the things of value, namely his pack of cigarettes, I dusted them off and slid them into the inside pocket of my trench coat.

The rain slowed to a comfortable drizzle, so I stood and examined my injuries. With Panacea's work nearly complete, I decided to begin the trek back to Junction City; it served as my residence and the location of my contact and dear friend, Doctor Oswald. In addition to providing me information in my search for Bradich, Oswald was Donovan's closest friend and the only surgeon I trusted to repair, maintain, and graft new nanites to my cortex. Notwithstanding his position as the town's leader and the man that dished out jobs and pay to mercenaries like myself, I owed my old friend a slap to the back of the head.

“Al was too early...” I remembered.

File 04: Junction City

After several hours of walking, I stood atop a hill surmounting the modest establishment called Junction City. The wind fanned my raven locks in a haphazard clutter against my dirt-smudged cheeks, and a pale smile crept up the corners of my lips as I beheld the city which I protected since Harbinger tore the world asunder ten years ago.

Its giant fortifying walls were forged by melding together various rusty steel sheets of assorted color, and enormous, old tires from ancient farm vehicles braced the walls' posterior. At the peak of the protective circumference, lines of razor wire twisted into a spiral that lined the perimeter. From an exterior perspective, the queer looking oval wall would conjure either grimaces or snickers from the unsuspecting individual. Within those walls, however, resided some of the most endearing citizens one could ever hope to meet. No matter its rundown condition, Junction City was a good a place to be as any.

For several miles surrounding the compound, Oswald ordered the rocks and hills to be leveled into flat plains. That way, approaching entities could be sighted with relative ease by one of the many sentries using telescopic scopes fitted atop high powered sniper rifles. Even as I took the first step down the hillside a mile and a half away, I already felt wary stares tracking my journey.

By the time I reached the walls, the dim gray of the afternoon shining from behind rolling fallout clouds blackened to herald the sinister night. The only lights illuminating the desolate plains were the large flood lights at the top of the city's barricade and the dazzling lightning snaking across the growling sulfuric cloud cover. The colossal gate separating the city from the myriad of threats surrounding it required two men to operate. A third remained perpetually at its peak in a state of constant vigilance. Those sentries permitted visitors entry only after a series of inquiries and searches to ensure the safety of Junction City's dwellers; needless to say, they terminated bandits and Dusk Territory advocates with extreme prejudice.

"Ihlia?" The gruff voice of the sentinel calling my name at the gate's apex brought a grin to one corner of my mouth. From my perspective outside, the watchtower loomed overhead, nestled behind those protective steel sheets. I only barely discerned the bulbous physique of one of the aforementioned sentries standing atop it. It was Bojack. The man was one of the few surviving earthlings with any pigment of color in him, and compared to the majority of men and women surrounding him, he was understandably considered black.

His hair, a wild assortment of frizzy copper and blond, surrounded his face like a lion's mane. It was difficult to tell where the fluff of his hair ended and the scruff of his beard began. His gargantuan physique towered close to six and a half feet, and it amused me to behold him within the confines of a watch tower which forced him to slouch just to avoid smacking his head against the roof. His stout body bulged with a combination of bulky muscles and a thick layer of insulating fat. Despite his overbearing appearance, Bojack was considered one of the most loveable individuals to ever grace the sanctuary of Junction City.

"Yes, Bojack, it's me. It's freezing out here, if you don't hurry and open this blasted door I think my breath will mist up the entire area," I dramatically hissed warm air against my palms before rubbing them together in mock attempts to warm them.

"Hah, that's not the weather, it's that icy heart of yours. If I let you in, it might contaminate everyone else, too." Directly behind the gate, at the post of either technologically primitive pulley mechanism responsible for swinging the giant doors ajar, I heard the muffled laughs of Bojack's comrades who were more than entertained by our jovial exchange.

"Bojack..." I allowed my voice to trail off as both my hands pressed against the slender swell of my hips and a single brow cocked skyward to mimic a threatening glare.

"All right, all right. You heard her, boys. Open the gate straight away! You know, Ihlia, you might not be so cold if you actually put some clothes on for a change. I mean look at you... what little clothes you do have are torn to shit!" The man chortled beneath his breath even as the iron door gradually opened with an ear-piercing metallic screech. As I stepped onto the other side and entered Junction City, I lifted my hand in a dismissive wave to the three gate guardians.

"Have a nice night, Bojack," I called back in a sing-song voice and ventured into the settlement twinkling with the artificial incandescence created by street lamps scattered throughout the city like flickering stars. The domiciles littering the expanse of Junction City were crafted in much the same theme as the protective walls. A typical house was comprised of incohesive junk melded into a cubical dwelling vaguely resembling the architecture of old. Inside, basic electrical capabilities were maintained by generators using synthetic fuel called "sludge" that served as the legacy of the twenty-second century's scientific achievements.

Sludge utilized most forms of refuse mixed with the synthetic formula created after years of research during the golden age of transcendent humanity. In essence, one could add a heap of trash to the synthetic formula in order to create clean-burning fuel. Coincidentally, it shared the same name, chemical makeup, and texture with the typical alcoholic beverage akin to old fashioned beer, albeit the fuel was far more potent a concentration.

Home furnishings and aesthetic decor varied from fundamental to lavish depending on the scavenging or trading talents of a house's owner. During the day, the streets filled like a busy market as men and women poured in to peddle wares. The price of an item reflected the price one was willing to pay to obtain it. Food to a man with a full belly might be worth significantly less than sustenance to the starving sack of skin and bones.

Most families in Junction City operated as an efficient unit, with one parent venturing into the wilds at dawn to scavenge for supplies or reporting for labor duties in the synthetic food production complexes. Payment for scavenging included what one could find in the old ruinous cities writhe with bandits and hyped stalking about. Payment for labor included an extra portion of food or water one could use for bartering in addition to the mandated amount for survival.

The other parent stayed behind to set up the bazaar or attend to household chores and child raising. The concern of those too lazy to work solved itself quickly. Productive individuals ate, unproductive individuals starved. The man responsible for determining the level of a man or woman's productivity was none other than the city's founder and operating nanite surgeon, Doctor Oswald.

In addition to trading for goods and services, bartering items served as payment to a town's nanite surgeon for surgeries; it proved particularly important for the prospect of raising children. Upon birth, a child would be presented to a doctor along with a predetermined stipend of goods. These goods ranged from scavenged commodities to extra or exquisite food and drink. If the payment was satisfactory, the newborn child would receive his scar, a term denoting the cranial scar caused by the initial opening of the scalp for nanite implantation.

If unsatisfactory, the child would be left to die to radiation. Unlike most doctors, however, Oswald possessed a soft heart. In all the history of Junction City, no child ever died... at least, not from radiation.

The most important nanite to be implanted was, of course, Panacea. For many newborns this would be the first and final implant, as it was the only one necessary for survival in the post-apocalyptic disaster called Earth. The surgical scar became an identifying mark, and if, perchance, the infant matured into a combatant requiring further augmentation for the sake of the city's defense, that same scar would be reopened as many times as necessary to perform nanite surgery.

As I comfortably sashayed down the vacant streets in the middle of the frozen night, the stale scent of rust and grime transmuted into an intoxicating aroma of sludge and inebriation. The only establishment with lights glaring and voices blaring, the town's local tavern, remained abuzz with business well after the darkness crept down from the heavens to lull the young ones off to sleep.

I paused for a moment and glanced up the hillside road leading to Doctor Oswald's manor; a frigid breeze whistled through the lonely void. I casually glanced back to the tavern glowing with life, laughter, and incandescent orange light. I recognized that a trip down that trail would assuredly consume several hours of irrelevant liquid distractions, unwanted sexual advances, and barbaric bar brawls, but the assured amusement resulting from such events swayed my otherwise rational logic: the tavern it was. Besides, I needed to see an old friend, and I knew that finding that old friend required only that I find the most abundant source of sludge in town.

As I shoved the squeaking metal doors ajar with nimble hands, my brain immediately hummed with biochemically induced electric pulses that awakened an implants located in my cortical folds. Every augmented human experienced the sound, though it was not so much an audible buzz, whine, or hum as it was an infinitesimal vibration pulsating within the mind itself. It became a familiar sound to which one simply grew accustomed.

The nanite which I activated happened to be the one responsible for my inhuman perception and temporal awareness. Oswald referred to it as my "Cognitive Accelerator." Apparently, no other implant existed like it in all the world. Time slowed to a crawl as though movements and reactions were stuck in a thick gelatin. While my mind raced with thoughts at normal speed, even my own body succumbed to the effect of my implant.

The ability allowed me to concoct elaborate plans, make acute observations, and account for multi-directional and rapid assaults in the blink of an eye. Actually moving my body to match those plans, accredit justice to those observations, or avoid those multi-directional and rapid assaults did not always work out, oftentimes to my harrowing misfortune. In the dull light of the tavern, however, my implant responded instinctively to a flying bottle spinning at breakneck speed directly for the front of my face upon entering the establishment.

Already the excitement was making me gush, which was exactly what the bottle would have done were it allowed to shatter against my nose and shred the entirety of my face with its impact. Behind the rotating bottle, a pair of unaware miscreants, with far too much sludge in their system for even Panacea to process, sat with faces frozen in an enraged screaming match.

The man losing the apparent argument must have decided that if his words were ineffective, perhaps his empty bottle would make a more impacting statement. Unfortunately with his drastically impaired hand eye coordination, it appeared more that he threw the bottle at the door in a pouting tantrum resulting from his inability to properly debate while drunk.

Several bystanders who had, up to that point, enjoyed the furious exchange between bar buddies, followed the careening bottle toward me with faces crawling into a position of horror. Several ladies moved their hands to cover their eyes, while the men's hands shot slowly, or so I perceived, to their mouths to cover the inevitable "ooooh!" which would satisfyingly escape their throats once the bottle mauled my face into synthetic meat. Fortunately for all those involved, I maintained a heightened state of awareness after my bout with Al.

I effortlessly tilted my head to the side and closed my eyes. Frankly, I was unsure if my body would move quickly enough to avoid its miserable fate, and I needed my eyes to remain intact. After what seemed like minutes, I felt the faintest brush of glass skim by the side of my cheek as the bottle tumbled over my shoulder toward the swinging metal door. The cacophonous smash as the glass fractured into several tiny, translucent daggers snapped my Cognitive Accelerator into deactivation while plunging the entire room into an abrupt hush.

"Oh shit..." After several seconds of quiet, a single voice punctured the silence like a comic relief. I sighed, shook my head, and sauntered up to the table where the two offenders sat frozen in horror at the realization of whose face they had almost broken. In Junction City, I was the top mercenary. A year after Harbinger destroyed the world, I helped Doctor Oswald found the town, and over the years I developed my reputation as a ruthless defender who would took any action necessary to preserve order and protect the citizens.

As I neared their table, I took visible notice of their growing terror at the thought I might reach for the rifle strapped to my back. A coy smile danced across my lips; I slapped an open palm against their table. No words were necessary. The two newly sobered men cried out, leapt up, and dashed from the tavern likely rushing to their beds to sleep off that which they hoped would turn out to be a nightmare the following morning.

“Well, guess they had enough to drink,” The words bubbled from my lips as I stared up at the remaining patrons. Like chucking a chair at a glass window, the awkward atmosphere shattered into boisterous laughter and applause. As the bar returned to usual business, I spotted a man whose countenance and posture remained steadfast during the entire ordeal. He called himself Crelyos Highwind.

Crelyos stood an impressive six feet four inches whenever he stood erect. Alas, rarity marked such an occasion. Normally, the man doubled over against his right side and shoulder, cocking his entire body in an odd slouch toward that direction. He did not look deformed, nor did it effect his gait, but it did shave a few inches from his height. His blond hair stood in carefully arranged spikes atop his head, and a constant apathetic grimace marred his chiseled jaw. His hardened body rippled with muscles forged through the endless fires of combat.

Before the Titan crisis, Crelyos served as a decorated soldier in the American Armed Forces. A deadly hand-to-hand combat specialist, Crelyos rivaled me as one of the top mercenaries in Junction City. When his fists proved ineffective or out ranged, he was a supposed dead-eye shot with the pistol he kept secure on the side of his combat boot. Aside from those facts, I knew little of the ex-soldier's past or the true extent of his capabilities. As he refused to let Doctor Oswald operate on him, a veil of mystery even shrouded his augments, but the one thing I knew was that Crelyos arrived at Junction City from far to the west. That assured his familiarity with the territories surrounding Texas.

“Ah, Crelyos, I figured I'd find you here.” After a day in the field or on watch, the two of us often found ourselves gulping down sludge together, and while Crelyos was a harsh drinking partner with a gruff voice and constant scowl, he regarded me with a sense of camaraderie and respect I imagined stemmed from his military service. In other words, he regarded me as a battle buddy.

“Go away,” His words were a fast ball aimed right for the gut, but I stood in the batter's box of his potent anger rather often, so I was used to his pitches.

“I'll buy you a drink?” I retorted as I reached into my pocket and fished out the pack of cigarettes I pilfered from Al after his demise. I motioned for the bartender, and when the short, pudgy man with a receding hairline noticed the miniature pack of smokes his eyes lit up like a child receiving a present.

“Oh thank the stars that we no longer see! Ihlia you found some ciga... hey why is there blood on it? Oh I don't care, how many do you want for the pack?” The man was wringing his hands together in excited anticipation.

With the invention of Panacea, narcotics with sticky tar build-ups classified as carcinogens ceased killing people. Panacea's healing capabilities included expunging both alcoholic and cancerous agents at an alarming rate. This was also the reason catching a buzz required one to drink the equivalent of diluted, new-age, synthesized diesel fuel.

Unfortunately for smokers, shortly after the golden age of transcendence mankind determined that reliance on nicotine and oral fixations for temporary elation simply stunted our intellectual and spiritual growth. The fall of man ushered back in those vices, but while diesel fuel remained cheap and easy to synthesize, cigarettes remained an expensive consumption of resources and time. Oswald once explained that it had something to do with the difficulty of synthesizing a tobacco substitute as it was once a natural plant, but all it really meant to me was that cigarettes were a rare and expensive commodity sought after like gold in the olden days.

"As many as it takes," I responded plainly as I gestured to myself and Crelyos. The bartender snatched up the cigarettes and went to work filling two glass bottles with oily, black sludge. By the time he turned around to present them to us, the nicotine stick sat smoldering between his lips.

"... Fine. What do you want?" Crelyos snatched the bottle and began gulping the thick ooze down his throat. I followed suit and within a moment we slammed our empty bottles against the bar top.

"I want to go to Texas," I dropped my rear onto the stool next to his and propped my elbows atop the bar.

"So go?" He quirked a brow at me with a sidelong glance. I could tell he was tracking the conversation and knew its final destination.

"I need a guide," I sank my chin against my open palms and offered him my best impersonation of a puppy-dog stare.

"Oh yeah? I need it to rain sludge for the next hundred years. Hm, that's strange, still looks like the same piece of shit wasteland it was before I said that. Imagine that." His words were a stimulating clash of humor and fury. Most people considered Crelyos an angry drunk, but that simply was not true. Crelyos was always angry.

"Crelyos, it's Bradich. I finally have a lead... and it's in Texas." I could feel my eyes shimmer with a stern passion. Crelyos knew well of my ambition; he knew the grief and heartache that plagued my otherwise emotionless core. We would be horrible drinking companions if I had not divulged at least that much during a few of my various drunken rants.

"Damn it, Ihlia. I just came from that way. I can't be movin' around back and forth like some kind of nomad." His hands lifted in apparent dissatisfaction. I knew Crelyos, however. The emergence of excuses and the softer twinge in his voice meant he was caving.

"Just came? That was over two years ago!" A soft chuckle leaked from my throat during my retort.

“Exactly, just came from there. Don't wanna go back, sorry.” He spun on the barstool until his broad back was the only part of him I remained able to see.

“Fine, if that's how it's going to be, can you at least tell me how to find a guy calling himself Raze?” I placed a hand on his shoulder in an attempt to at least evoke some sort of assistance from his stubborn demeanor. To my surprise, his entire body perked at the mentioned name, and he slowly turned to face me once more.

“You would have to go and mention him. Fine... I'll go. Pack your shit, we're leavin' as soon as possible.”

With those words, Crelyos abruptly stood and marched from the tavern into the darkness of the city streets. I had never before seen him move with such fluid purpose, and it piqued my curiosity as to the relationship between Crelyos and the man called Raze. While the prospect of pondering his past intrigued me, the pressing necessity to brief Doctor Oswald on my situation wormed its way into my head. After downing the last of my sludge, I hurried out the door and began my trek toward Oswald's mansion.

File 05: The Old Codger

Within ten minutes, I stood at the base of the steep hill leading to Oswald's home. The eerie shadows crawling along the contours of the house established a sense of foreboding; of course, the snakes of lightning slithering across a pallet of growling clouds hardly aided in dispelling that foreboding. The mansion itself stood a bastion in comparison to the town's humble construction. The melded steel sheets that formed the various walls lacked the rusted, hodgepodge colors of the common dwellings, and well-cut stone comprised the foundation of the estate.

Various cylindrical towers spiraled up from the sides of the main structure like warped appendages protruding from the body of a miserable chimera. With the entire manor powered using a handful of generators, a dull orange incandescence radiated through the many windows haphazardly thrown among the four stories. At the base of the medieval structure, seemingly ripped straight from a historical documentary, a large pair of metal doors formed the only visible entrance or exit to the giant residence.

I hissed a sigh as I gripped the thick rings welded as doorknobs to the gates. With a moderate amount of effort, I slowly pulled the squeaking iron doors ajar. Creating only enough space to allow my lithe frame passage, I invaded the doctor's abode with the stealth of a deadly predator. I engaged in the silent stalking partially out of habit, but mostly, I wanted nothing more than to scare the pants off the good doctor.

The structure's impressive interior sparkled with polished knick knacks and forgotten artifacts offered to him as payment for nanite surgery by the various scavengers of Junction City. Moth-eaten rugs of old cotton and tattered silk curtains decorated the floor and hung from the walls in a questionable artistic array. In the center of the room, a large staircase fashioned from steel and stone ascended to a balcony leading to various corridors, rooms, and tower entrances. Those rooms bore no significant purpose and simply provided flair and reminiscence of the days of old, but the towers housed many of Oswald's scientific experiments and achievements.

The room in which I stood served as the main reception hall. Small tables covered with shaggy colored cloth and crowned with cracked pottery lined the smooth walls in organized intervals. In the spaces on the wall unoccupied by pretentious decor, doors to equally extravagant, and wholly useless, rooms filled what would otherwise constitute unutilized surface area.

Within the doors on the left wall were guest rooms outfitted with as many comforts from olden days as could be salvaged from the ruins of surrounding cities. Each room possessed a grungy bed crafted from various stitched cloth and filled with random soft material collected over the years. The doors to the right served as portals to the kitchen. Within, rusty pots and pans hung from metal spikes driven into the steel walls. The cupboards, crafted from the same metal materials that dominated the architecture of the age, contained various foods.

While most were artificial starch bars or bottles of reinforcing vitamin pills, exciting cans of non-perishable food from long ago occasionally sat stacked next to the bland synthetics used to sustain society. A masterfully carved, oval concrete table claimed a far corner next to a shelf housing several bottles of purified water, and equally masterful stone stools surrounded it. Though I considered sneaking into the kitchen to grab a starch bar, I ultimately decided to forego my hunger in pursuit of Oswald.

Back in the reception hall on the back wall, on either side of the staircase, two separate steel doors leading to the same room hid within the shadows of the staircase's embossment. Moving with the skill of an assassin toward the door on the left, I wrapped my hand around the handle and pushed inward. The subtle screech as metal scraped against metal gave me only a moment's pause before I crept into the dim room. A vague orange glow, splashing dancing shadow puppets against the walls, emanated from a lamp placed atop a desk. The warm light flickered; it was designed to imitate an open flame through its artificial illumination.

Aside from the large concrete desk and expansive floor

littered with unorganized documents, several bookcases and filing cabinets lined the cluttered room. Ragged books lay scattered across the floor and strewn atop the shelves. Perhaps the last bit of paper or wood product on the planet, the neglected books elicited feelings of disappointment in me. I felt the doctor was irresponsible for treating the treasure he possessed with such blatant disregard. The disheveled room possessed little else, but along the back wall a set of stairs descended into what I knew to be a large basement.

My feathery footsteps carried me deeper into the pitch black with only the flickering glow of more lanterns designed to imitate fire hanging from pegs in the wall like eerie will-o'-the-wisps. As I neared the substratum, I heard a conversation between two people echoing up the corridor.

"Now Minette, in as much detail as possible, explain the theory for the hyped condition." The first voice was clearly male, and with its elitist drawl it clearly belonged to Oswald.

The voice that responded rang sweet and beguilingly innocent. Given its high pitch and airy tone, anyone listening would merely assume it belonged to a child. "Well Doctor, studies show that because nanites and their nano hubs utilize organic tissue combined with microcomputer virtual intelligences specifically designed with the ability to learn, the possibility exists that personalities develop within the AI once the nanites become exposed to the human neo cortex."

After pausing to take a deep breath, she continued, "At first, this personality is subtle and usually doesn't interfere with brain functions. However, as more implants are given to an individual the collective "voices," if you will, begin having adverse effects on the psyche. This usually results in typical psychosis manifestations such as dissociative identity disorder, hallucinations, and violent tendencies."

"Hm, I suppose I can appreciate the brevity of your response given our current task. Overall, the content was accurate. How do you explain the wide variety of implants and their surprising effects? Implants such as superhuman speed, titanic strength, and other capabilities?" As I listened to Doctor Oswald administer some manner of test to his assistant Minette, I rounded the corner of the base of the stairs into the room in which their conversation took place.

The old codger used the basement as his laboratory and workshop. The same flickering lights that lined the staircase descending into the basement also hung around the room's perimeter while high powered lamps focused an intense light on the various work stations. One such illuminated work station took the form of tubes filled with oddly bubbling chemicals moving from glass vial to glass vial before dripping into a mysterious beaker. The brilliant white of another light revealed a small work desk with innumerable microscopic parts and fine precision tools used to construct nanites. Finally, the last work station highlighted by a high powered bulb was the center of the room in which Oswald and his assistant stood.

A raised surgical bed sat surrounded by buzzing computers and various machines designed to read vitals and assist the doctor in his operations. Atop the bed with his scalp removed and brain exposed, one of Junction City's citizens was in for a routine checkup and nanite maintenance.

"The varying effects of nanites on the human brain stems from the unique manner in which they are created. This especially refers to some of Doctor Lesfort's, the late leading researcher and developer on controversial nanites, experimental implants. Nanites typically operate on segments of code programmed into the microcomputer designed to limit the nanites and keep them from reproducing or consuming too much bio-electricity. Doctor Lesfort, however, created a limited line of nanites that used that code to instead encourage the nanites' evolution," Minette chirped excitedly.

"Depending on the order of code and the parameters for learning combined with the aptitudes of the individuals implanted, those nanites can manifest a variety of interesting powers. From the simplicity of increased brain capacity for knowledge and understanding to more complexity such as the ability to access and infiltrate computer systems and networks, Doctor Lesfort's nanites' unique adaptation to traditional nanites has baffled modern medicine the world over!" Minette squealed.

"Yes, yes.. Doctor Lesfort, of course. That answer is also satis—" Oswald tried to commend Minette, but she hardly allowed the doctor to begin before eagerly offering more information. I mused that even if I activated my Cognitive Accelerator, I would scarce be able to keep track of her lips' movements.

"There are even speculations of supernatural manifestations of abilities such as psychokinesis which are usually attributed to the fact that we, as a species, have always possessed the potential to achieve such things but lacked the brain power to tap into them! In particular with psychokinesis, the ability to control and manipulate neutrinos into a tangible force is believed to be the cause. The nanites served to bridge that gap in understanding and capability. Why, I've even heard of someone who can channel lightning through their fingers and another who can generate magnetic fields!" Minette, the gabby assistant offering sterling responses to her mentor's distracted questions, stood atop a metal stool near the patient so she could carefully observe the operation.

Another great mystery far more intriguing to me than the nature of superhuman nanites was that woman's stature. With all her intelligence, maturity, and even physical age, Minette possessed the height and build of a child. If not for the genius she expressed in nanite surgery and the tiny swell of her breasts, discerning her from one of the merry children playing in Junction City's streets would be an impossible feat. But despite her childlike figure, Minette carried a certain charm that prevented her from personifying exaggerated youth.

Minette struggled to reach five feet tall and sported a

white lab coat over a modest dress hanging down just beyond her knees. Her hair, a vibrant, gorgeous scarlet arranged in a beautiful wavy array, framed a pleasing face covered in sun-kissed freckles. Though faded with a global lack of sun exposure, her freckles added to the sense of adorability she already expertly exuded. On the bridge of her nose, a pair of small spectacles sat in front of a pair of captivating turquoise eyes. With her lower lip clenched expectantly between her teeth, as was her habit, Minette looked to Oswald for his approval.

My abnormal mastery of stealth carried me into the heart of the room without so much as a shift in the grains of sand marring the stone floor. My target, Doctor Oswald, hunched over his patient with his back to me. The man was not physically striking save perhaps his height; he stood at six feet five inches tall with an unexemplary face and average build. His only other mentionable trait was his gleaming bald head which he spit-shined to the point of blinding radiance. A wiry brown beard started at the top of either side of his jaw and met at the base of his chin in a fluffy point. Upon his moderately lengthy nose rested a pair of glasses to assist his plain, brown eyes in their duties.

As he examined the nanites of the patient in front of him with diligent attention, he nodded in response to Minette's answer to his former inquiry, "Ah yes, yes. An answer any mentor could be proud of. Except, of course, all that nonsense about superhuman abilities. Preposterous. Nothing more than youthful fantasy of the occult," Oswald annoyedly waved his scalpel at Minette.

“But Doctor, it's true! I heard it straight from—” Minette began.

“One last question for now,” it was Oswald's turn to interrupt his assistant, “why is the anonymity of our patients, and ultimately of all living beings on this planet, so important? And hello, Ihlia. Good to see you made it home safely.”

I ceased my silent stalking with a disappointed sigh when Oswald uttered my name as a footnote to his test's final question. Despite my constant attempts to sneak up and surprise the old codger, I had thus far been unsuccessful in all ten years of our time together. The worst part was the dispassionate manner with which he continued his work as though I not only failed but never stood a chance. With a persistent pout I took my place at Oswald's side next to the miniature Minette. I folded both of my arms against my abdomen, “How do you always do that, old man?”

“Do what, Ihlia?” The doctor paused for a brief second to quirk his brow in my direction. A genuine look of confusion clothed his otherwise stoic face. Before I could retort, he lifted his hand to shush me and realization brightened his face like a scientist's “Eureka!” moment. His words escaped him in concise statements, “Distraction. Minette, answer.”

Minette's voice bubbled from her throat in her typical airy giggle. With her hand bunched into a fist near her mouth, the young assistant coughed as she prepared to recite her answer to the doctor's former inquiry. "After the creation of nanites that were capable of accessing networks, frequent incidents of neural hijacking led to identity theft, the ability to keep constant tabs on an individual's location, and in some extreme cases a hacker would utilize advanced implant technology to augment nanite behavioral programming. In effect, a hacker could steal who you were, find and kill you, or even change your brain in worst case scenarios. It was ultimately decided that a new network and a passcode would be placed on all neural networking. While the network superseded the Internet as the new highway of information, the world government applied the passcodes at an individual level."

"At birth or during their first nanite surgery, a password is hardwired into every human, particularly into the neural infrastructure surrounding the nanites. Because having a nanite implant, in essence, makes your brain partially computerized, the passcode keeps hackers from forming a direct link to your brain for purposes of tracking or worse. This passcode became a person's real name, or real identity. Unanimously it was decided that only a person's nanite surgeon would have access to this passcode and thus a person's real name. While this gives the surgeon immense power over people, it also inflicts upon them extreme accountability. If a name leaks, it can always be traced back to the acting nanite surgeon. This is also why having multiple nanite surgeons is a dangerous endeavor." Minette's matter-of-fact response was met with a sigh that bled into a satisfied but disenchanted nod.

"Yes, textbook as always, Minette. Your extravagant regurgitation inspires the vomit in us all. Of course, I am unable to discredit your evaluation as it is quite accurate. Keep up the excellent work, my dear." Oswald placed the finishing touches on his patient's brain before beginning the process of stitching his scalp back together like a toupee designed to cover his naked neurons. Oswald moved his nimble fingers like a maestro combing the darkness to elicit the desired responses from his instruments. His talents were unrivaled, and in all my years of watching him work I never once saw a patient die under his scalpel. When the final snips sealed the man's skull securely into place, Oswald stood, gripped a fluffy white towel, and began vigorously wiping the blood from his hands.

"Minette, dispose of the patient. And by that, of course, I mean escort him to one of our luxurious guest rooms and ensure that he is comfortably taking repose." As Oswald spoke the words, Minette offered a mocking salute and began rolling the surgical table across the room toward the stairs.

"Come on Mister Tilmitt, let's get you all cleaned up!" Minette's bubbly words actually sent shivers down the length of my spine.

"I hope he's not dreaming. That creepy voice would surely turn them into nightmares," I trailed off as I watched the sashay of Minette's petite hips straining to heave the wheels up and over each step. Once Oswald confirmed she was out of sight and earshot, he turned to face me and any amusement or pleasantry he feigned washed from his face like water on an oil painting.

"You would still be in the wastes had you not made progress toward your goal. I trust Al is either dead, dismembered, or both. And that self-satisfied smirk of yours, quite frankly, betrays you! So then, what did you discover and what is your next course of action?" The heavy thud of his boots echoed in the dark chambers of his laboratory as his overbearing frame hovered over me with smothering anticipation.

"Calm down, Doc," I placed the flat of my palm against his chest and pushed him back a few inches. The act required a fair amount of effort, for the doctor's muscles were reinforced by a Supersoldier implant; such physical augments were hardly commonplace among doctors, but I had never bothered to ask him why he possessed one.

Once his gleaming baldness was no longer close enough to blind me, I continued, "Before he stopped breathing, Al gave me the name of a contact living somewhere around the vicinity of old Texas named Raze. I assume he's some kind of crime lord. Most people that know Bradich are. Crelyos came from that area, so I've convinced him to guide me there. I'm sure that Raze isn't a dead end, so I don't know how long it will be before I come back, old man."

Oswald relinquished a sigh, "You know, child, this may be an inconveniently late and terribly unfair question at this point, but have you considered that this wild goose chase is unprofitable and ultimately irrelevant?" The look of desperation that washed over his face sparked a twitch from my brow. I could feel anger churning within the pit of my sickened stomach.

"Unprofitable? Irrelevant? Listen, Oswald, Donovan meant just as much to you as he did to me, so why are you okay with his killer waltzing around spitting on everything he stood for?" The words dripped from my mouth like a venomous salivation.

"I most certainly did not mean to imply I do not wish to see justice. But think about it, if you leave and something happens to make you require surgery, what will you do? Allow another surgeon to operate you? I cannot begin to express the irresponsibility of that decision considering your unique condition. Donovan made me promise to take care of you." Oswald lifted his finger to reinforce his points.

"Special condition, that's all I ever hear from you. You worry too much. I've come too far to just up and abandon my pursuit, especially now that I have the first good lead I've gotten in almost ten years!" I grunted at him. The doctor's constant state of calm managed to alleviate my anger a bit, but my resolve to pursue Bradich would not be swayed by a detail as minute as surgical monopoly.

"I'm not merely speaking of your unique Cognitive Accelerator which allows you to hyper-accelerate the chemical processes of your brain and slow down your perception of time. Though that alone will require several more years of study to fully comprehend, the fact that you possess more nanites than any other human being on record without the ill effects of hyperaugmentation is a far more important avenue of concern. If another surgeon were to open your skull and see the hardware wired to your brain..." His voice trailed off as he no doubt imagined a hypothetical surgeon selling that crucial information for enormous wealth or favor. He shook his head to and fro in disgust.

His words rang true. After the incident in Cairo ten years ago, something in me changed. According to Doctor Oswald, after a severe injury of which I remember very little and the ensuing operation to rectify my wounds, my bio-electric impulses overloaded and caused the equivalent of a short circuit in my busted brain. The nanites warped, or mutated depending on how much of the organic artificial intelligence theory in which one believed, and caused baffling effects.

Since then, the network of nanites in my cortical folds worked in perfect synchronization with my mind. As a result, it seemed that the integration of my thoughts with the nanites rendered me immune to the effects of hyperaugmentation. Doctor Oswald believed testing the limits of that was paramount to advancing human abilities and to maximize brain potential. Already I possessed more than ten implants, ranging from my Cognitive Accelerator to augments heightening each of the five senses.

"Doc, I understand, but... I just can't stop now. I'm

sorry, but I'm going. I understand if you don't agree, but I'd at least like to get a final checkup done and borrow a few supplies from you. That ammo you make for my rifle is phenomenal." I offered him my best rendition of a bittersweet smile, but it likely lacked any emotion save a minute twinkle of sadness and dread at the prospect of leaving Oswald behind. The old man grew on a person fast.

"Ihlia... I..." Minette's distant, piercing cries spiraling down the stairwell cut Oswald's words short. The tiny surgical assistant frantically called out to us from above, but her squeaky yelp interrupted her deafening shouts. Likely stubbing her toe against one of the stone stairs, Minette banged and rolled down the stairs with a vicious clamor. In the end, she spilled into the lab and skidded to a painful halt flat on her face.

"Doctor, Doctor! It's terrible! Quick! Bojack says a herd of hyped is chasing back one of our scavengers! He says it's Allen!" Her message, while discernable, certainly lacked the clarity of a person that wasn't eating cement.

"Calm down, Minette, I'm sure it's... Hyped? Allen? Oh no, Ihlia! Quickly! We must report to Bojack! I have no intention of losing another member of this city!" Oswald broke into a sprint while beckoning for me to follow. I complied without hesitation.

File 06: The Terror of the Hyped

My noir surroundings blurred across my peripherals like the fog of a dream. The only pertinent object in my vision became Oswald's stark white coat fluttering in the night's frozen winds. Within moments, we approached the jutting tower tipped with a platform that threatened to reach the heavens. The familiar buzz of my Supersoldier nanite activating sent chills along my spine as the tiny machines throttled into high gear.

My legs bulged with infused prowess for but an instant, and I slammed my feet into the earth with as much fervor as I could muster; with my newfound strength, the resulting leap rocketed me several meters into the air toward the ringed ladder leading to the perch. The rungs' cold steel bit my fingers as I clung to the ladder and, without pause, rapidly ascended it. Already the deafening sounds of rifle fire echoed throughout Junction City as I reached the top of its tallest roost. Bojack frantically fired into the distance, likely targeting the herd of hyped supposedly chasing Allen.

Allen was one of Junction City's many scavengers. With brown hair, green eyes, and plain features, Allen stood out in Junction City solely because he befriended and assisted anyone he met. Many new settlers owed Allen for their transitional ease into the city's lifestyle. But as a scavenger, Allen traversed the wastes, sometimes days at a time, to procure rare and expensive artifacts.

Allen thoroughly enjoyed his line of work and often commented that the key to the world's restoration would most certainly be found in its ruins, but at the end of the day it was Allen's wife and daughter that inspired him to seek out treasure. Providing them with a life that satisfied their every need and desire remained the strongest motivation of his excursions. Allen's dedication to the restoration of the world through his archaeological adventures, devotion as a loving husband and father, and perpetual kindness to those immediately surrounding him earned him a place in the hearts of everyone living in Junction City. Bojack was no exception, as indicated by the increasing concern that drew the very color from his darkened face.

"Bastards, I won't let them take him!" Bojack's eyes shot wide open, but while his marksmanship was marvelous, his emotional attachment to the situation shook his normally steady grip and hastened his normally patient aim. As I shouldered my bolt-action rifle and activated my vision enhancement, I quickly understood the reason for his composure's deterioration. Roughly a mile from the gates of the city, Allen desperately fled from a group of sixteen hyped. The idea that he managed to maintain distance between himself and the monsters for so long spoke volumes of his endurance... or his luck. Unfortunately, hyped lacked concepts of fatigue and common sense. They would pursue a target until killed or successful.

I felt fate and the Reaper staring through the cold, windy night like a pair of critics enjoying a live performance of a drama the ending to which they were already well aware, an ending to which I was also well aware.

"Bojack, calm down. You're not hitting anything by worrying about the scavenger," my words pierced him like icy daggers: cold but true. I recognized an immediate change in his disposition as he fought to regain control of his rampant emotions. A sense of relief washed over me as well, and together, we took aim like a pair of synchronized swimmers. As the tension peaked, my Cognitive Accelerator awakened with a hum. Together, Bojack and I squeezed our respective triggers.

The cracks echoed in unison as our bullets cut through the inky blackness toward their unsuspecting targets. Bojack's target was a grunting hyped far to Allen's left, and he fell with a short but audible shout of surprise. The projectile that spiraled from my firearm sailed over the top of Allen's head. One of the murderous beasts nipped at his heels, but with my enhanced vision and slowed sense of time, I determined that the hyped would leap at Allen to secure the kill.

My prediction proved correct as the monster soared through the air... and directly into the path of my high caliber round. With more force than that which he exerted, the hyped careened backward with a heavy crunch into the dirt. As the slow motion impact of his body indented the cracked mixture of sand and clay, the gruesome reality of the situation fortified my concerns. Allen's endurance was waning, the hyped were gaining ground too quickly, and we could not fire quickly enough.

"Bojack, we can't..." I never took my finger from the trigger, but my voice was enough to elicit a growl from the lion-like figure next to me.

"If you got time to talk, you got time to shoot." His machinations released another round into the darkness and another hyped fell, but it was not enough.

I heard the grumbling of the city folk beneath us as our gunfire roused them from their peaceful slumber. With time moving sluggishly around me, I perceived the people of Junction City with perfect clarity from the corner of my eye. Most citizens grumbled at the disturbance, and some feigned concern for whatever lurked in the dark beyond the city walls. Only two rushed out at the first sign of danger: Allen's wife, a beautiful brunette with pellucid azure eyes and a slender frame, and his daughter, a teenager sporting dirty blond locks that curled about her face, a pair of vivid brown eyes, and a developing body blossoming into womanhood. Unable to find the peaceful embrace of sleep without their loving provider, the two must have often spent their nights frantically worrying; unfortunately, for likely the first time, the situation warranted their concern.

Their faces contorted in terror as the realization sank in that the only reason for our fervent assault was the impending threat to Allen's mortal coil. Still under the effects of Cognitive Acceleration, I prepared to squeeze another futile round off to satiate Bojack's desperation, but my perception snapped back to normal when the sound of the giant metal gate slamming open broke my concentration. Bojack and I swiftly lowered our gaze to the source of the ruckus. To our astonishment, the city's gates were kicked wide open by the heavy combat boot of Junction City's most mysterious mercenary, Crelyos.

I watched in awe as he shot into the darkness like a missile. His legs gradually increased their workload to maximize his velocity. As a soldier in the American Armed Forces, Crelyos had no doubt been augmented by the Supersoldier implant. Like a multi-faceted steroid, the Supersoldier implant provided general boosts to speed, endurance, strength, and reflexes; as a mandatory implant for all military personnel, it stood to reason that Crelyos housed it in his cranium. Crelyos targeted the herd of hyped with wild abandon. I calculated his estimated time of arrival at just under one minute. I once more focused on the scavenger sprinting from his forlorn fate. The sickening dread mounting in my stomach like rising yeast popped; Bojack released a mournful howl.

Allen's backpack, a standard for all explorers, became his executioner. Like a rubber band drawn too taut, Allen snapped backward with a piercing gasp as a hyped's outstretched hand clasped around his pack and tugged him into the eagerly awaiting crowd. The sight of his visage twisting into sheer terror engraved itself in my conscience forever. I beheld the exact moment when

Allen's weak hope morphed into a fearful understanding of the nightmarish end waiting to confront him. It was as though all the pain yet inflicted and all the horror yet experienced flashed through his mind and transformed his face in a split second. As the herd swarmed about their victim, Bojack's tormented howl shifted to an enraged roar.

The roar persisted through the duration of our gunfire. Shell after shell escaped the bolt-action chambers of our rifles, and body after body of the crazed hyped dropped lifelessly to the ground. But it was still not enough. I entertained the notion that Bojack's fury was for us both, for I retained the calm reserve needed to efficiently stop the hearts of the assailants in the distance. On the other hand, Bojack's rage darkened his telescopic sight and he failed to definitively kill many of his intended targets. Truly, it mattered little. The likelihood that Allen still breathed amid the flailing limbs of the psychotic afflicted was virtually nonexistent.

Crelyos neared the scene, and many of the hyped turned to face him with morbid roars. As though anticipating further entertainment, their bloodstained, half-naked bodies tensed expectantly and propelled them forward to meet the man brave enough to dance to their macabre steps. I subconsciously slowed time between my shots to analyze Crelyos' fighting style, about which I knew nothing.

As the first hyped reached the blond mercenary, he rabidly threw his fist in an attempt to connect with

Crelyos' jaw. Unfortunately for him, Crelyos caught his wrist in his left hand with the subtle grace of a bear. The mercenary twisted and drew the afflicted over his shoulder in what started as a standard judo toss. As the hyped inverted during the final portion of the throw, about the time his legs sailed overhead, Crelyos punched his open right palm against the hyped's pectoral. What happened next widened my eyes.

The flesh, sinew, and bone unraveled from the impact. A fissure divided the hyped's chest and shoulder with a deep reverberation accompanied by the hyped's grotesque roar. At the point Crelyos was supposed to release his assailant to complete the judo toss, he clutched the hyped's wrist tighter. In the end, the afflicted sailed through the air with a crater punched into his pectoral; he left behind both a trail of spewing blood and the detached arm flopping about in Crelyos' grip. Crelyos' ability obviously stemmed from a nanite, but my brain reeled with questions as to its origins and the true breadth of its capabilities.

With uncanny awareness, Crelyos instinctively ducked with the momentum gained from his throw. A second attack whizzed over the back of his head from another of the hyped attempting to capitalize on Crelyos' exposed backside, but as Crelyos moved with the fluid tempo of a seasoned martial artist, I realized Crelyos was not dancing to the hyped's macabre steps after all; they were dancing to his.

Crelyos, still crouched, spun toward the hyped and

quickly shot upright. He wielded the arm of the first unfortunate hyped like a deadly mace and brought it to bear in an uppercut against the second's chin. The brute's painful cry reached my ears, not surprising, since the force of the blow lifted him into the air almost an entire foot. His head arched back with such ferocity that I was almost certain a small nudge would have torn it clean from his shoulders.

Crelyos followed the afflicted into the air; he jumped high enough to clutch the hyped's face in his right hand. With gravity as his ally, Crelyos slammed the back of the hyped's head into the ground, and his head exploded in time with that same deep reverberation that I attributed to a nanite. Without wasting time, Crelyos hurled the arm he used as a mace from his left hand toward the legs of a third assailant scrambling to reach the brawl. The severed limb collided with the hyped's legs and tripped him; he sprawled face first onto the cracked earth.

The last two hyped not tearing Allen's body limb from limb trampled over their tripped comrade in their mad dash to Crelyos. The mercenary happily reciprocated their dash in order to meet them halfway. When the two sides drew near, however, the mercenary slammed his feet into the ground and jumped skyward in a mighty leap over the heads of the two confused afflicted to the one he tripped behind them.

The force of his drop accentuated his punch, and Crelyos hammered his right fist into the hyped's skull. My curiosity piqued again. The force of the blow, even when factoring in a basic strength augment, would have no doubt crushed the skull of the unsuspecting hyped, but from the tissue to the brain matter itself, the man's entire head exploded as though disintegrated from the impact. Crelyos' blows were generating far too much power even for the likes of him.

Slowly, Crelyos stood erect to face the two remaining, and briefly confused, hyped. The crimson blood of his fallen opponents dripped from his clenched knuckles and camouflaged attire, and his eyes gleamed with an ominous desire to exterminate what remained of the afflicted herd. By the time he stood completely erect, however, one of the two hyped gripped a boulder that had been driven into the earth as a result of Oswald's terraforming orders and lifted it overhead. Its diameter easily extended more than twenty feet, and given its density and consistency, I estimated its weight at over two tons. Even if Crelyos' nanites provided enough strength to shatter a boulder that size heaved at him, he would not be able to do so without significant injury.

Crelyos sighed, and I could see his head shaking in apparent disapproval. With a single swift motion, Crelyos' tugged his pistol from its holster with his blood-soaked left hand; in the sweeping motion of its draw, Crelyos fired a single round straight through the head of the boulder's wielder. With a grunt and a twitch, the man collapsed, and gravity reclaimed the giant rock. Unfortunately for the second hyped, he stood far too close to the daring strongman to escape the boulder's wrath. When it fell, it crushed them both.

The two hyped still assaulting Allen's motionless body turned and leapt toward Crelyos. Crelyos braced for the impact of their assault, only to watch as the two hyped suddenly vaulted backward. The backs of their heads exploded in a rain of scarlet as they bounced along the earth and came to rest several feet away. The tips of Bojack's rifle and my rifle synchronously emitted wisps of smoke.

We bore responsibility for the intervention and consequential death of the two speedsters. Normally such a feat would have elicited a grin, but the lack of color in Bojack's face coupled with his crippling emotional pain stayed any such expression. After a brief moment of shock, Bojack rushed down the metal rung ladder to the street below where the majority of the town gathered with dreaded anticipation. I followed.

Allen's wife and daughter pushed to the front of the crowd. Tears welled up in their eyes as they watched Crelyos' shadowy figure lumber back to town with an equally shadowy lump he carried in his arms. The doctor's persistent attempts to quell the fear and alarm of his city understandably failed, and after what felt like hours, the silhouette of the blond mercenary stood in the shadow of the city's walls. A hush fell over the crowd as Allen's wife and daughter inched forward, unable to discern the condition of their beloved with the scant light.

Fate and the Reaper, who had been watching all along, enacted the curtain call. Several streaks of lightning scorched the earth nearby and cast an eerie flash of illumination over Crelyos and his burden. In the former soldier's arms a mutilated pile of disgusting pieces resembling Allen haphazardly dangled about in the chilling wind.

What remained of his face, contorted in horror and broken into oozing chunks, conjured hushed gasps from the crowd of onlookers. Gnarled limbs and shredded flesh completed the painting, and the shades of red splattered across them covered Crelyos in random patterns. The mercenary cast a somber look of reverence, apology, and empathy toward the wife and daughter whose eyes widened like electrocapacitor plates and whose bodies shook with a stormy combination of shock and grief. Bojack was already sobbing.

"Ihlia... you take care of watch tonight," Oswald's voice dropped to a compassionate lull; his hand found a home on my shoulder as if to inform me he was counting on me.

Allen's wife and child sank to their knees in front of Crelyos and began gasping and dry heaving as though building up to an anguished release. As their torment peaked and finally broke the silence with a blood-curdling howl, fate saw fit to accompany their agonizing release with vibrating thunder. The two sounds mingling together in the frigid night echoed like the thud of a falling curtain. At the same time, the bottom of the sky opened and a sheet of biting rain clamorously hammered the earth.

It sounded like the Reaper's applause.

File 07: First Departure

Doctor Oswald's obsessive concern over my unique condition raced through my mind as I stood atop the town's highest obelisk overseeing the wastes. My fingers softly caressed the pair of scars criss-crossing my skull just beneath my hair. Considering a scar's location and shape represented a particular surgeon's brand or mark on their patients, the twin scars overlapping one another on my own scalp reminded me of better days.

The first scar, which I received as a small child in a normal world, would later be used by Donovan, the man that wrangled my heartstrings. After his vicious murder, his dearest friend and my constant guardian, Doctor Oswald, crafted a new scar across the existing one in honor of his memory. Despite the underlying masochistic tones, I found the gesture to be most endearing of the old codger.

The frozen sting of night gradually shifted to a more bearable cold as though I stepped out of a freezer and into a refrigerator. The rain shower ceased, and the gluttonous black sky peppered with grumbling fallout clouds brightened ever so slightly with the apparent rise of the sun on the horizon. A chilling breeze carried the scent of the dusty wastes into my face like an ethereal tumbleweed rolling up my nose as I finished the last few moments of my watch. It was quite possibly my last act as a sentinel of Junction City, for no guarantee existed that I would return at my journey's end or return at all for that matter.

“Oy, Ihlia. I'll take over; you still need to muster up some supplies before your big adventure, don'tcha?” I looked down to see the source of the voice, Bojack, offering me his classic mischievous grin.

“I suppose. You work too much, though.” I shifted to the side to make room for his bulky figure at the top of the perch. When he finally heaved himself up the ladder, Bojack slumped over the guard rail with either arm hanging over its edge. When his jaw stretched wide for a droll yawn, he reminded me of an oversized, lazy feline. I did not even try to suppress my teasing smirk.

“After what we saw last night, sleep is a bit difficult for yours truly and work helps take my mind off it. Allen was such a good man.” The stoic manner in which Bojack spoke of the previous night's unfortunate victim may have taken others aback, but I knew it was merely a front to cope with his terrible heartache. While the stubborn man would no doubt assure any inquirer that the puffy red swelling around his eyes was sleep deprivation, the chance that they did not represent a night full of uncontrollable grieving was slim to none.

“He was a good man, but you heard Oswald... his family will be taken care of. He can rest easy now, Bojack.” I was terrible at consolation. With my own views of life distorted through a stained glass window of morbid sarcasm, I actually considered Allen a supremely fortunate individual.

After all, the man endured vicious fear and bodily harm for the sake of providing his wife and daughter with a life full of as many comforts as could be afforded. In lieu of his death, Oswald personally guaranteed the prosperity of his family, and he no longer had to feel any form of fear or pain to achieve it. In my earnest opinion, he was...

"You were just thinking he's better off, weren't you?" Bojack simultaneously interrupted and finished my silent soliloquy. Bojack was not telepathic, he simply knew me too well. I snapped my head in his direction with a look comprised of awkward shock and frustration.

"I absolutely hate it when you do that, you know." My words escaped me with a rush of my breath fogged by the cold morning air. Bojack erupted into laughter; he slapped the rails and grabbed his jiggling gut. I sighed, shook my head, and began climbing down the ladder. As I reached the median of my climb, I noticed that the laughter above me abruptly stopped. When I glanced up, Bojack's husk seemed wrought with quivers as the large man wept alone in silence. After a second of hesitation, I finished my descent.

No sooner had my feet found the earth than I spun to behold Crelyos begrudgingly dragging himself down the street toward the gate. His camouflaged pants and green tank top were accentuated by a pair of black combat boots, yet the aura of discipline which his ensemble was supposed to radiate seemed contradicted by his slouched posture and lackadaisical gait. Obviously failing to properly console Bojack, I decided to try again at social exercises with Crelyos.

"Hey, Crelyos... you know what happened last night was no one's fault, right?" I crossed my arms beneath the faint swell of my chest as he drew near. He locked gazes with mine; a mixture of pain and anger saturated his expression.

"Shut up, it's way too early for bullshit, Ihlia." He shoved his hands deep into his pants pockets. I nodded sullenly; his implied accusation smashed the proverbial nail on the head. Aside from my burning hatred for Bradich which fueled my desire to live no matter the cost, I felt little else toward other humans.

Intellectually, I understood the grief Allen's untimely end inflicted upon his loved ones. Without the emotional conviction to support that understanding, however, any comforting words I might otherwise offer were as Crelyos pointed out: bullshit. Once more external stimuli interrupted my thoughts as the crisp ring of two bottles smacking together in Crelyos' hands drew me from my reflection.

"It's not too early to drink, though?" I inquired and quirked a brow at him; a grin stretched across the corners of my lips. Grasping the offered bottle of sludge in a slender but calloused hand, I tapped the bottom of my bottle against his own and knocked back a solid chug. I wanted to believe I did it to honor Allen's memory, but I probably just wanted to take the edge off a night of constant vigilance.

"Damn straight. It's never too early to drink," Crelyos replied bluntly and knocked back his entire bottle in a few gulps. I half expected the gunk to be bubbling up his gullet when he finished.

"So are we ready to go yet? This place is startin' to piss me off." I could tell the impatience in his voice stemmed from his somber recollection of the previous night's events. Adjusting my rifle's strap against the center of my chest, I shook my head and began walking toward Oswald's bastion.

"Not yet, I still need to get a few touch-ups done on my augments. I won't be back in Junction City for a while, and I don't trust anyone but the doc to handle my brain." I looked back at his figure standing stalwart in the dim gray light just in front of the town's large gate.

"Fine, I'll wait here. I'm as ready as I'm gonna to be. Try to hurry the hell up though." He lifted a hand, waving me away with mock annoyance.

The trek to Oswald's mansion seemed longer than usual. His ardent protests to my departure the previous night resounded like a chorus in my thoughts. I recognized a sunken melancholy tickling the pit of my stomach at the thought of never seeing the old codger again. Somewhere along my journey to reacquaint myself with complex emotions, a part of me had grown attached to Doctor Oswald and his zany, controlling habits like one grows attached to a crazy, overbearing uncle with a seemingly infinite number of interesting stories. As a sad smile haunted the contours of my face, the sight of the doctor's extravagant combination of mansion and laboratory curtained by the early morning fog coaxed me from my trip down memory lane. It was almost time.

"Hey Doc, I need a last minute checkup before I leave. And don't say anything about it, either. Let's make this quick and painless. Literally and figuratively, if you don't mind." My tumultuous declaration as I all but kicked in his front door was met with a frantic gesture of dismissal from Oswald. He retorted mid-stride as he weaved from room to room in his complex seemingly collecting supplies.

"Quiet, that's irrelevant now. Sit down somewhere and wait." Following in hot pursuit of the doctor, his assistant Minette scolded him with desperate fervor.

"Doctor Oswald you can't be serious! I'm not ready to take this place over, that's a huge responsibility! If you leave, who will perform the surgeries? You can't possibly be suggesting that I cut open these people's heads by myself!" Her tiny fingers clutched the back of Oswald's bleached coat. Unfortunately for Minette, her diminutive stature compounded by Oswald's stubborn refusal to alter his course resulted in her adorably tiny feet sliding across the ground. She hopelessly tried pulling him from his endeavors only to be dragged along like a supple doll.

“Doc? What's she talking about?” Following his previous command, I parked my derriere in the contours of one of his quilted chairs and watched the satirical display.

Oswald abruptly halted his footsteps and whirled about to face me. Like a rocket, Minette was launched with a cute squeak through the air and into a small table fully configured with a clay vase and cloth covering. The resulting cracks and crunches of furniture shattering behind the doctor failed to so much as twitch his brow. In the back of the room at the crash site, Minette's crooning, “oooowww...” sounded like a distance echo.

“First, after extensive calculation I determined I only possess a two point four-eight percent chance of convincing you that this endeavor is a terrible idea.” He lifted his index finger to support the first item in his apparent list.

“Well, I'd put them at less than that, but that doesn't mean...” I knew what was coming as soon as I felt the sharp spike of his voice purposely slice mine out of the air.

“Second, given your one of a kind implant that allows you to cognitively slow the perception of time coupled with having the highest recorded number of nanite implants without suffering from hyperaugmentation, the scientific ramifications of halting my research only to resume it at a time designated by my specimen, that is you, is preposterously disagreeable.” No sooner did he lift his second finger than Minette inched her frail frame toward Oswald's back crawling on hands and knees. She curled her small hand around the cuff of his pants leg and squeezed a groan from her throat.

“Uugh...Doctor...” Her spectacles hung bent and battered from one ear. The curtain of her wavy scarlet hair, once a beautiful frame to a delicately freckled face, now housed dusty bits of broken antique. She peered up at Oswald only to be silenced by his incessant rant.

“Third, Minette is well trained and ready to succeed me as a nanite surgeon herself. Furthermore, she is well aware of my governing policies and standards. As long as Bojack is around to enforce what she says, this excursion will prove a valuable training exercise for my dear assistant until we retu— Good Lord, Minette, what are you doing crawling around on the ground? Here I am praising you, and you're acting a damned fool. Get up, get up. My word, you're completely disheveled. Go clean yourself up immediately!” Minette sighed helplessly as she followed Oswald's pointing finger to the lavatory to wash up, but she moved her mouth and twitched her head to and fro, mocking his every word as she obeyed.

Oswald cleared his throat and returned his attention to me as though embarrassed that his train of thought was so easily derailed. Little did he realize how extraordinary the stimulus required to even alter the train's motion a tiny interval, let alone derail it. It was admirable and unfathomably pitiable at the same time. I chortled softly as I stood from my assigned seat and approached the doctor, placing my right hand gently upon his left shoulder

"Oswald, I appreciate the sentiment, really. But the town needs you, you don't have to put everything on hold just to go gallivanting off with me on a wild..." He cut my words short when he hugged both his arms around my shoulders and squeezed tightly.

"Besides, Ihlia. Donovan would never forgive me if I let you do this by yourself. So I'll hear no more of it." His words sent a rush of tingles along the vertebrae in my spine like a crashing wave that ultimately settled into a cozy warmth in the pit of my stomach. I sighed softly and gave his shiny bald head a few soft pats.

"All right, all right. You know what the D-word does to me." I shook my head and sauntered over to the restroom where Minette busily wiped the smudges from her face with a synthetic cloth towel.

"Before you say anything, I'll be all right. If the doctor really has that much faith in me, how can I turn down his challenge?" Minette grinned. Anytime she heard the word "training" her disposition immediately changed. It was a trait she possessed since Oswald and I met her nine years ago.

"Just make sure you kill that bastard and come home, ok?" She laced her words with a faint grunt as she bent the metal frames of her glasses back into their proper position and tucked them neatly against the bridge of her nose with an airy giggle.

"Oh believe me, I will. I'll make him pay for what he's done to all of us." I offered her a nod before turning back toward Oswald, "So, if all this sappy go lucky mushy stuff is done, you ready to head to Texas?" Both my hands found rest on the peaks of my sparingly curved hips. Like he just finished a magic parlor trick, Doctor Oswald stood impatiently tapping his foot with a large rolling cart in tow behind him. He lifted a single brown brow sarcastically.

"Ready? I'm waiting for you my dear, you're wasting incomprehensible amounts of time with your dreary gossip. Get the lead out, let's go!" Without so much as waiting, Oswald stormed out the door of his mansion and briskly began his trek toward the city gate. I walked to the doorway and paused for a moment; Minette arrived at my side with tears in her eyes and a shout on her lips.

"Goodbye Doctor! Take care of Ihlia! And come back alive, ok?!" She waved her hand frantically in an attempt to compensate for her amusingly stunted height. Just as I prepared to take my leave, I felt a faint tug against the back of my black leather trench coat and her quiet words filled me with that odd warm feeling once again, "Ihlia... take care of each other okay? You two are all I have. Come back safe."

"I will, Minette. I just hope the place isn't burned down when we get back!" I laughed under my breath and trotted after the old codger while trying to ignore the frantic list Minette conjured, without pause enough to even breathe, entailing the reasons she would excel at her duty and not burn down the town.

Back at Junction City's main gate, Crelyos leaned against the ladder leading up to Bojack's nest with an indignant scowl plastered across his face. By the time we arrived at the gate, the hustle and bustle of the late morning market exchange was well underway. Allen's residence remained understandably dark as his wife and daughter grieved the loss of their male provider. As always, the community proved its bond, for Junction City's townsmen and women periodically dipped into the abode to share the pain of their fellow citizens and assist them whenever necessary. The ties stronger than blood were enough to shatter the walls of the rockiest heart. Except Crelyos', he did not seem impressed at all.

"I thought you were goin' for an augment touch up, not an organ transplant. Do you have any idea how long I've—Oh you have to be freakin' kiddin' me. Why does Doctor Fancypants look like he's ready to come with us and completely ruin my already bad day?" Crelyos gestured to the doctor garbed in his flowing white lab coat, his bald head gleaming in the dim afternoon overcast, and his rusty cart full of supplies squeaking behind him with his every step.

"My name is Doctor Oswald. Oswald, not Fancypants. And of course I'm going with you. You didn't think I would leave our town's number one mercenary in your vastly incapable, drunken hands did you?" Oswald waltzed right through Crelyos' growing cloud of rage and began snapping his fingers at the two door guards as though they should respond and open the gate without so much as a word.

"That bald son of a bitch... Who the hell does he think he is?" Crelyos' clenched fists quivered in the wake of his fury. I shook my head and nonchalantly followed after the old man while offering Crelyos a short quip.

"He's the guy that pays us." The words forced a sigh from Crelyos and cooled his boiling wrath to a few simmering grumbles. The few words I caught mentioned the fact that the last time the world even used currency was over ten years ago; he continued grumbling even as he followed us into the blood stained filth of the wastes.

"Bojack, I trust you'll support Minette in my absence. Did you procure the item I requested? What is its location?" Doctor Oswald stopped just outside the gate. Turning, and with one hand cupped against his mouth, the good doctor yelled up to the muscularly rotund sentinel at the top of Junction City's sniper roost. With his lion-like mane wildly whipping about his face from the frigid gusts at the top of the perch, Bojack waved his mighty arm in simultaneous greeting, affirmation, and farewell.

"I will, boss! You three take care of yourselves out there! And yeah, the boys are bringing it around now!" As if on cue, the radical roar of an engine tore through the air. From the side of the rounded fortification, a four-person dune buggy with a hitched trailer churned the smoky dust from the ground as it drifted across the wastes. The sound of the jostling trailer blended together with the hoots and hollers of the juvenile driver and his even more juvenile co-driver.

As the dune buggy slid to a halt a few feet in front of us, I gave it a quick inspection. Four giant tires framed a smaller carriage to offer stability and maneuverability. In the wastes, sinkholes and loose sand pits were common threats to the unsuspecting traveler, but the design of the dune buggy offered safety from otherwise grim traps of what remained of nature's wrath. The engine, exposed at the back of the machine for likely no other reason than not wasting precious steel unnecessarily, vibrated and hummed as it consumed the quantity of sludge offered up to it in exchange for its tireless work.

A cage of padded rails framed the four close knit seats. The rails provided hand-holds and lean-posts when a passenger needed to stand at dangerous speeds, and the trying times provided a variety of reasons to stand in a moving vehicle, the first and foremost of which involved returning automatic weapon fire to pursuing bandits. During my quick inspection, in which everything appeared operational, Doctor Oswald stared with brewing contempt at Bojack for allowing a couple of teenagers the pleasure of reckless driving.

“What? Come on Doc, they insisted. Besides, what harm could they cause?” As Bojack defensively pleaded his case, the two boys leapt from the driver and passenger seat with a clasping high-five and a few more whoops before scurrying off to their duties.

"We will discuss this in adequate detail upon my return, Bojack." The Doctor began offloading his equipment, carefully organizing it in the various compartments and shelves that littered the attached trailer's interior.

"What the hell are you bringin' anyway, Fancypants? This isn't some vacation, you know." With his hands tucked away in his pockets, Crelyos peered over Oswald's shoulder to watch him organize his vast array of what Crelyos undoubtedly considered useless garbage.

"Ah, you wish to know my boy? So you do have a mind of observation and inquiry! Understandably so, even a Neanderthal would be curious as to the nature of such fascinating equipment!" The doctor began gesturing to each compartment, and with each pause over a particular tool or gadget he issued an intricate speech as though he prepared a thesis on his entire array of luggage several weeks prior.

His gear consisted of basics such as food, water, medical essentials, tanks of sludge to keep the dune buggy running, and ammunition. Ammunition that, in particular, took the form of ample numbers of his custom high caliber rifle rounds I used in my father's modified, bolt-action rifle. Oswald spent especially winded speeches explaining every nuance of his holocom systems and portable nanite surgery station, both of which he neatly tucked away in the trailer.

While having his holocom and nanite surgery kit would no doubt prove invaluable, his true motive likely involved slicing my head open for observation and postulation at a whim. Lastly, Oswald packed the necessary equipment to create fire and build shelter. In all honesty, it was quite an admirable spread considering the limited time I afforded him for preparation.

"Ugh, it's way past lunch time after listenin' to all that. So sorry I asked," Crelyos droned away as he heaved a satchel, his only luggage, into the trailer. Without skipping a beat, the former soldier unzipped the top and reached within to retrieve none other than a bottle of sludge.

"Hell yeah, lunch time indeed!" Using his right hand, Crelyos gripped and plucked off the cap to a fresh bottle of sludge before inhaling it with the same velocity as the bottle he and I shared a few hours prior.

"I hate to ask, Crelyos," I said as I placed a hand against my forehead to feign disappointment, "but that entire bag isn't filled with sludge, is it?" My hand slid down to cover my entire face, but I left a space between my index and middle finger in the vicinity of my eye just so I could see his expression when he responded.

"Of course it is. Only the essentials here, Ihlia." The robust laughter that shook his chest following his statement coaxed a sigh from my bosom.

"Well, on the bright side, in the event of unforeseeable

circumstances, we have a backup fuel supply. Were I a betting man, and I'd bet you I'm not, I'd wager the entire potency of fuel in those bottles rivals that of at least half a tank of pure fuel-sludge," Oswald said and pushed his glasses up the bridge of his nose.

As Crelyos continued laughing and drinking and the doctor rattled off the statistics behind our simultaneous alcohol indulgence and fuel security, I hopped into the rear seat of the dune buggy and swung my rifle around to my anterior, clutching it in a firm hug against my chest.

If left unchecked, those colorful characters could ramble on and cut up for hours. Finally seated for longer than a few moments, and without my mind riddled with overbearing thoughts, I realized it had been two days since I last slept. The heaviness of my eyelids soon bested me, and I drifted off into peaceful slumber to the sound of the obnoxious soldier and babbling doctor.

File 08: Entering Raze Haven

The breeze planting a near-polar kiss upon my cheeks stirred me from my serene repose. I groaned softly and raised my body into an upright position. Apparently during the course of my rest I had flopped over into the rear seats in a fetal position with an iron clasp on my rifle. I smiled when I noticed the pristine white lab coat draped over my waist like a blanket. The smile quickly faded when I scanned the area to gain my bearings. The foreign environment stiffened my shoulders with anxious anticipation. The dune buggy had stopped in, what seemed to be, the middle of nowhere.

Had we been caught by bandits? Hyped? One of my hands instinctively encroached on the trigger guard of my rifle, and I buzzed my hearing augment to life. At peak working condition, the implant allowed me to detect even faint whispers from a distance of nearly a quarter of a mile, and if targets remained in my proximity, it allowed me to discern their general emotional state from their rate of their heartbeats with relative ease. As my sensitive ears tingled from a mere breeze whistling by, I detected the quiet voices of Oswald and Crelyos.

Gathering my belongings and slinging the doctor's lab coat over my left shoulder, I trudged up the hill in the direction I heard their conversation. As I rounded the hilltop, I noticed both of them lying flat on their abdomens looking off into the distance; Crelyos possessed a pair of binoculars with more attachments and moving parts than an antique Swiss Army Knife. I dug my elbows into the crusted sand and deactivated my audial enhancement. While that soft vibration finished returning a portion of my cortical folds to a more passive state, another nanite whirred to life as I activated my sight augment which easily surpassed the technological capabilities of goggles and binoculars, even those created by Oswald.

"So, what are we looking at boys?" I whispered and zoomed my vision in on the area of their attention; I was surprised to find the semblance of a city a few miles ahead. The architecture looked vastly different than Junction City's, and I found myself marveling at the amount of effort which must have been needed to realize such an exotic design.

The foundation of the city consisted of several enormous cement pillars shoved into the earth. The ground into which the pillars sank churned and shifted notably; unlike the stiff, cracked earth stretching for miles throughout the wastes, the sand directly below the city, particularly where the pillars stood, was soft. In fact, it was almost liquid.

With the support of those massive cement pillars, the entire city sat atop a deadly quicksand trap. The most peculiar thing plaguing me about the pillars, however, was their elaborate design. The manpower and machination required to ensure they stood solid within that sea of shifting sand must have been vast, but the risk to one's life to venture out and engrave superficial art up and down the entire length of each stone slab made the endeavor seem utterly ridiculous. After rising several hundred feet, the pillars connected to the base of what appeared to be the mighty city; it looked like a giant metal clam.

Two plates rested atop one another connected by more, albeit far shorter, elaborately designed stone pillars decorated with pretentious artistic carvings. The plates themselves possessed lips of metal designed to shield the middle section of the city from the freezing winds and rain. The top plate's lip curved downward while the lower plate's edge folded toward the sky. The remaining thin slit in the middle offered easy observation of the world outside the city, and I distinctly made out several guards with binoculars patrolling the perimeter.

The guards, as near as I could tell, were raggedly dressed cutthroats geared to the teeth with various weaponry both melee and ranged. Their presence certainly explained the cautiously prone position of my two comrades. Each man and woman I saw marching back and forth bore a striking mark just underneath their right eye. It looked like an old fashioned form of ink tattooing. The shape the mark took was quite distinct: a flame.

"How long was I out for?" I whispered. Even I disregarded my previous question, but I had apparently slept through the transition that normally occurred between morning and afternoon. It was already well into the evening. I wondered if I slept the entire day away.

"Too long, and you snore so damn loud," Crelyos hissed back while mentally taking note of the number of patrols. It looked like he was already attempting to discern a weakness in their pattern. Not surprising.

"Approximately ten hours and thirty-three minutes, my dear," Oswald waited for Crelyos' immature jab to offer a real answer, all the while shaking his head at the former soldier's juvenile behavior.

"Approximately?" The only manner in which Oswald might have further specified was to inform me of the number of seconds, milliseconds, and nanoseconds of my repose. I chuckled softly before returning my attention to Crelyos, "so we're in Texas then?" With the enhanced speed of the dune buggies, a straight shot across the wastes from old Florida to Texas should have taken no more than nine hours. Ten and a half would have put us well into the heart of the former state.

"Well, my dear, funny you should mention... We aren't exactly in Texas at the moment," Oswald fumbled with his words as he attempted to explain the situation. For a man usually so precise, his stuttering succeeded in eliciting a surprised blink from me.

"What Senior Fancypants is tryin' to say is that he drives really slow and got lost because he wouldn't listen to me. I eventually got us back on track, but... we're still only just now reachin' the Texan border," Crelyos muttered with a shrug.

"Oh, of all the nerve. You were the one who kept attempting to force me to stop at every shady microbial speck of a town to restock your sludge supply, which I'll have you know you completely consumed within the first hour of a journey you knew would take ten! Anytime you gave me directions, my alcoholic friend, it was to another pub or tavern in the middle of nowhere! And furthermore!" Oswald's voice spiked sharply as the heat of his conversation with Crelyos reached peak aggravation. Crelyos lifted his hand and clamped it across Oswald's mouth.

"Shh, quiet Fancypants. You ever stop to think that maybe one of those thugs has a hearin' implant like our girly here?" He tipped his head in my direction before slowly removing his grip on Oswald's jaw; while Oswald gagged and caught his breath, Crelyos continued, "Regardless, we've hit the jackpot. Although it's strange..." He trailed off in thought.

"What is it, Crelyos? You came through this way on your way to Junction City, right? What's the deal?" I kept my voice low and looked over at Crelyos who scratched the stubble that gave his chin a sandpaper texture and sound.

"This is Loftsborough. At least that's what the locals call it. They built it to protect themselves from the hyped and bandits. Considerin' it's on quicksand... it's fairly difficult to assault. You see that bridge there?" Crelyos lifted a hand and gestured to a stone platform on ground level that extended from the firm sand, like that on which we lay prone, out into the sea of quicksand. The makeshift bridge ended in a bulbous metal platform situated between two of the stone columns, and a series of electrical wires snaked up the columns like vines.

"If you want into Loftsborough, you cross that bridge and basically ring the bell. If they like you, they press a button and an elevator comes down to pick you up. If they don't give two shits about you, they send you back on your way. If they hate your stinkin' guts, they push another button and that platform goes bye-bye, and you learn what it feels like to drown in sand," Crelyos explained.

"So... what's so strange about that? Seems fairly efficient," I quirked a brow. Crelyos shook his head and responded.

"What's strange are those brigands. First of all, I know the surgeon of Loftsborough, he's an old friend of mine, and he would never allow the mayor to hire help like that. That aside, those flame tattoos are the mark of Raze. Last I checked, his territory was deep in the heartland of old Texas. He shouldn't even have influence this far out," Crelyos gestured toward the cutthroats patrolling the city.

"Mayor? I thought a nanite surgeon was in charge of a city?" I nodded to my only real basis for comparison, Oswald.

"Normally, yes. But not everyone likes to lead. The surgeon of this city, Eugene, appointed a mayor to take care of that stuff. I forget the mayor's name, though. Anyway, the problem is all those thugs," Crelyos mused.

"So Raze took Loftsborough?" I asked.

"Seems like it," Crelyos responded.

"How?" I was respectfully amazed. As a former Bald Eagle, I had been part of several city sieges and invasions with small numbers, but this job was truly masterful. Even in his prime, Bradich would have likely refused a mission as dangerous and costly as assaulting a town like Loftsborough.

"Hmm, likely a coup or inside job. That, or Raze snuck someone in like a Trojan Horse. While it's hard to assault, once you have someone in who can control the lift, takin' the place over isn't that difficult since Loftsborough doesn't have very many mercs," Crelyos replied.

"So you think Raze is in there?" Like a switch being flicked in my mind, my interest moved from passive to aggressive.

"Hard to say. The place is artistic enough to suit his tastes, but I feel like it's more his style to pull the strings from somewhere farther away. Either way, Loftsborough is where we need to be for answers. I wanna see that friend of mine, Eugene, anyway. The question is how we get in..." Crelyos scratched the top of his scalp, perplexed.

“Easy enough,” I said as I stood and dusted the sand from my flowing tresses and leathery attire. I offered Crelyos a playful wink and patted the stock of my trusty rifle, “we say please.”

“Hah, I like the way you think, girly.” He stood with me and slammed his left fist into his right palm. The dust clinging to his tank top and streaking his blond hair puffed away from his body from the mere impact his fist created against his open hand.

“I... will stay back and guard the buggy. Can't have any hyped or bandits scurrying off with our precious cargo! Especially my computers. Perish the thought!” Oswald clamored to his feet and patted himself down.

“But you two be careful and don't destroy the place. Especially you, drunkard.” He offered a firm finger waggle to Crelyos, who simply rolled his eyes in response.

“Ready, Crelyos?” I chuckled softly and began the long walk down the hill toward Loftsborough. With my vision nanite still active, I watched as several guards with similar enhancements to their eyesight or binoculars took notice of my newly exposed figure. My slender hand reached up with unfettered determination and gripped the thinnest part of my rifle's stock just in case they decided to open fire. Crelyos enacted a few more dust shaking pounds of his fist against his open palm while following within close proximity.

“Oh hell yes I'm ready...” He trailed off with a smirk.

—

“I can't believe you were freakin' serious about the please thing. This is such bullshit.” Crelyos stood atop the precarious platform hovering dangerously above the hungry desert sands with his arms crossed and a scowl on his face.

I stood next to him in front of what looked like a giant conch shell. Its surface gleamed and glittered like a pearl; the spiral contours connected to a small device that looked like a metal speaker leading to a bundle of electrical wires. The wires snaked up one of the stone pillars like a series of veins. The larger opening of the shell faced the two of us as a gaping maw. From the arrangement of holes in the attached metal box, a scratchy distorted voice issued forth in droll monotone.

“Welcome to Raze Haven. State your name and business.” I blinked a few times before looking over to Crelyos. “Raze Haven?” I thought to myself. Crelyos seemed equally bewildered, and in unison we offered one another a confused shrug.

“Ihlia and Crelyos. We're tired and want a place to stay,” I bluntly stated into the gaping conch shell.

"Sorry, no visitors. If you have no business for *Duc* Raze, get lost or get dumped." The monotony of the voice persisted despite the mortal threat scratching through the makeshift speaker system.

"What my companion meant to say is that we want a place to work. Duke Raze still takes on talent, right?" Crelyos interjected with a tone of familiarity and knowledge about Raze previously unbeknownst to me.

"*Duc*. It's *Duc*, with the accent. If he heard you pronounce it Duke he'd have you barbecued. Geez, new people. Look, fine, I don't care, but you better be able to pull your weight around here. *Duc* Raze does not tolerate loafers, as many of the city folk will inform you. We'll send someone down to check you out. Remember, any funny business and I push this little button." The last tidbit carried an inflection of concern to which I mischievously grinned.

The sound of the electrical wires jolting to life caused loud mechanical creaking several hundred feet above our heads. Assumedly, it was the elevator descending from the city. However, the sparking electric bolts hopping between pillars due to faulty wiring made the event seem far more ominous. I nudged Crelyos' ribs with my elbow as the mechanical whine of the elevator drew nearer to our location.

"So that's it? It's that easy? We just make up some impulsive story about wanting to work for Raze and they let us in the city?" I quirked a brow in his direction in response to the grin tugging at one corner of his mouth.

"Yeah, kinda. Raze is... different. He likes pretty things or somethin' stupid like that. And his boys are usually pretty dumb. When you meet him, you'll get it. You wouldn't work for that limp dick for longer than a second if you had any cells left in your noggin'." Crelyos knew much more about Raze than I thought. Originally, I had no intention of pressing the issue when Crelyos changed his mind back in Junction City at the mention of Raze's name, but the more I listened the more I wondered about the true nature of his relationship with the crime lord.

The elevator hissed to a stop just in front of the platform. The man that stepped out stood at an unintimidating five feet nine inches, only an inch taller than me and definitively dwarfed by Crelyos' imposing stature. He concealed his hair, or lack thereof, beneath a ragged, dusty bandana wrapped loosely around his scalp. The cloth ended just above a pair of stale blue eyes. Bits of stubble and abundant grit partially covered the flame tattoo marring the skin beneath his right eye.

While his lean figure lacked perfect posture, he did not strike me as slouched with particularly poor posture, either. In his right hand, the man carried a small, rusty metal box with a giant red button elevated in the center. At the top of the box, a radio antenna extended a good six inches into the air. The man's thumb rested cautiously on that red button.

"All right, you two. Show me your weapons. It's not

like we don't got enough manpower, and we understand that in this day and age not having a gun is pretty dumb, but I gotta make sure you don't have anything out of the ordinary. So let's go, show me the goods." I recognized his voice. After stripping away the scratchy electronic droning and adding a touch of emotional concern to color the previous monotony, I realized the voice belonged to the same individual operating the speaker system. As I presented my various weapons for inspection, I tilted my head to one side and posed an inquiry.

"So... are you the only sentry operating the elevator?" I squinted hard. The man looked up at me from his tedious inspection and nodded.

"That's right," he replied matter-of-factly.

"So... how are you gonna drop us into the quicksand if we decide to pack your shit in?" Crelyos replied in my place. His thought process flowed in tandem with my own. We exchanged peripheral glances as the man under the fire of scrutiny slowly held up the box with the red button.

"Well, I'd just press this button right here. And Kerplop." A satisfied smile pulled apart his lips to reveal rows of black and yellow teeth stained by years of a neglectful bandit lifestyle.

"So... you know how to swim in quicksand? You're standing on the platform too, after all." I pointed a finger at his feet planted securely on the giant metal trap which the three of us shared. The man looked down, then back up to the two of us. The color washed away from his face, and his cheek twitched sporadically when he realized that he shared our fate.

"Y-you don't get to ask the questions here! All right, shut your traps! Your stuff checks out, so up we go. In the elevator now, hurry it up. Talk to Mayor Trumark when you get to the city!" The man seemed frantic to get us into the contraption, and I noted with ardent amusement that his thumb no longer hovered anywhere near the red button. Crelyos was right: Raze's boys were dumb.

At first, Crelyos and I entered the elevator in silence. We came to rest side-by-side behind Raze's nervous goon and exchanged a quick glance. As the doors to the elevator slid shut, we both released a delayed laugh at the apparent idiocy of the no-name's flawed logic.

When the doors finally slid open at the pinnacle of the ascent, the two of us still chuckled softly beneath our breaths. The disheartened minion offered us a dismissive wave as he returned to his post with a face reddened with embarrassment. Crelyos and I offered him a sympathetic nod and journeyed toward the distant glow of the city.

From the elevator station, a single concrete street stretched across the metallic surface of Loftsborough's lower plate. Though no vehicles traversed the paved road, exquisite lights decorated its edges in perfect intervals clearly designed to maximize aesthetics. The resulting impairment to practicality, however, struck me as an irresponsible waste of precious resources. Crelyos seemed unaffected. As we exited the corridor entrapping the station itself, the city that opened up before my eyes temporarily took me aback. First and foremost, the entire city shone with the ferocity of the sun itself.

The first and most notable feature of the city was the lower plate's ceiling or, depending on one's perspective, the upper plate's underside. The ceiling concaved upward to form a giant dome surrounding the whole lower level, and the various metal plates melded together shimmered with a vibrant display of colors which I had not seen in ten years. The gray of the world sang to life as a portrait of the sky before the fallout cloud gleamed overhead like a giant mural.

Though the white puffy clouds which dotted the ceiling were stationary and the blue expanse possessed no singing birds or gentle breeze, the illusion of a beautiful afternoon sky almost evoked a tear of reminiscence from the corner of my eye. Of course, that tear never fell; not a single tear had fallen from my eyes in the ten year span following the tragedy in Cairo.

To top it off, the exact center of this enormous painting framed a bright orange light embedded in the plate itself. The emitted light imitated the majesty of sunlight with nostalgic precision. I even thought I felt the tender warmth of a spring day penetrating me to my bones. As an awe-inspired sigh wriggled from between my sparsely parted lips and misted with the crisp chill that blanketed the world, I realized that the clever illusion was still merely an illusion.

Crelyos nudged me in order to snap me back to reality. The fact that he showed no signs of astonishment almost surprised me as much as the innovative environment itself. Once I returned my attention to the city's entirety, I noted even more intriguing designs allocated to the homes themselves. The breadth of architectural difference between the homes in Loftsborough and those of Junction City was as wide as the Everest Crater formed after the world's tallest mountain was obliterated during the Global Conflict.

In Loftsborough, it seemed as though no one fretted over the inefficient use of space when constructing the dwellings. Instead, random assortments of shapes and dimensions varying from abode to abode inspired a sense of questionable abstract artistry. The person responsible for the house designs possessed extremely eccentric tastes.

“Crelyos, you don't seem all that... surprised.” After finishing my slow surveillance, I focused my attention on the former soldier.

“Eh, been here before. The houses are weird now, but the ceilin's always been like that. Kinda like throwin' a nice suit on a pile of shit, though. Might look prettier, but it's still just a pile of shit.” He spoke haughtily as though his words dripped with the wisdom of an elder.

“So... where is this Mayor Trumark?” I placed a single finger on my chin and began looking around. It struck me, then, that the streets were all empty. Aside from the occasional guard patrolling about with a firearm or sword, the streets were devoid of life, and the homes seemed tightly locked from the inside.

“Probably in that tall buildin' back there, but this place was a lot more lively when I was last here. I don't like it.” Crelyos scratched his stubble and walked toward the aforementioned building. I followed while offering sidelong glances to Raze's scrutinous minions. On the way to the mayor's alleged abode, we passed through the city's center square. In Junction City, the late evening would signify the end to a busy day of barter and trade. Mothers and fathers would be packing their supplies and gathering up any wayward children before heading home to begin the evening meal preparation.

The only thing greeting us in Loftsborough's town square was the whistling wind as it filtered through the slit between the two giant plates and a horrifying ornament that decorated the very center of town. The decoration apparently provided enough novelty to give Crelyos pause. Submerged in the metal ground through what appeared to be brute force, a giant stone stake rose up almost twenty feet. Upon closer inspection, the twisted, gnarled metal plate at the stake's base indicated that something superheated the metal to a temperature soft enough to penetrate with the stone itself. The scorch marks wrapping around the stone like a charcoal design further affirmed that theory.

At the apex of the pillar, tied to the stone with razor wire, a skeletal corpse sat affixed like a morbid hood ornament. The bones were nearly bleached save for numerous deep black scorch marks. The char-grilled jaw hung open in what I imagined was a final expression of gruesome torture and gripping fear.

"They were... burned? The entire stone looks flambeau'd. Even the metal was melted. What kind of fire could have done this?" I inquired as we passed the human scarecrow. With his experience with the town, surely Crelyos possessed some idea regarding the origins of the atrocity.

"Raze. He has a very unique nanite ability. Pyrokinesis, he calls it. Flame manipulation. It's pretty badass, not gonna lie," Crelyos shrugged as we approached our final destination, the large dome establishment supposedly housing Mayor Trumark.

On either side of the sliding metal portals indicating the building's front entrance, two minions clearly belonging to Raze's gang stood attentively guarding the doors. I walked ahead of Crelyos and rapped my knuckles against the metal; after a short delay, a raspy voice echoed from the other side, "Ohoho? We have visitors? How rare, how rare. Please, do come in young ones."

I shot Crelyos a quizzical glance, and he responded by lifting his hands seemingly just as confused as I. After a deep breath, I placed either of my hands into the fold on the edge of the door and tugged. I expected to hear the squeak of old metal grinding against itself as the door slid open, but surprisingly, the door swished open with a soundless ease that nearly sent me reeling from applying unnecessary force. I stepped inside with the heavy thud of Crelyos' boots following close behind.

The interior of the mayor's residence seemed rather plain when compared to the gaudy design of the city. Without decorations or ornaments, the home possessed only basic stone and metallic furniture. With the considerable space of the living area, the lack of decorum made the domicile seem empty and cold; it was a stark contrast from the display we witnessed outdoors. As we approached the main room serving as the mayor's audience chamber, we beheld a tiny old man.

The likeness Mayor Trumark bore to stereotypical little old men struck me as rather amusing. He sat on the floor on a mat facing an extremely short table. His head's wrinkles possessed wrinkles, with brown, rusting age spots crinkled up amidst the various folds that lined his bald scalp. A pair of overgrown bushy eyebrows concealed a droopy brow line that weighed heavily upon the old man's face. The sheer weight of the skin forced his eyes shut in a typical old man's squint.

Just below his sagging, bulbous nose, a long fuzzy mustache completely covered his lips and dipped deep below his chin ending in a wispy dangle. The only way to indicate when the elderly man spoke was the faint wiggle of that mustache as it rose and fell above his hidden lips with each spoken word.

“So, what brings you to our fair city, young ones?” The old man exhaled a puff of cold mist. His manner of speech was slow and methodic, almost like some kind of robot.

“Why is the place called Raze Haven?” I inquired, curious as to the events that led to Loftsborough's capture. The old man paused for a moment. With great difficulty, he lifted a brow enough to show us a foggy green eye. I felt for all the world as though the old man was sizing us up to determine our motives.

“Yes... we used to be Loftsborough, then about a year ago Raze's men got in when one of our sentries turned traitor. Once inside, it was an easy enough task to take the town over. Next thing you know, he says the town is ugly, changes its name to Raze Haven, and sends out our young men to engrave random rubbish on the stone pillars. We lost a good few men like that. The houses were all reconstructed to suit his artistic taste as well. It's horrifying, but at least we're alive, I suppose.” The old man's face betrayed his sadness.

“I don't understand why he wants a piece of junk in the middle of the desert. Place is pretty enough, don't get me wrong, but why does he want it?” Crelyos proposed the question, and the old man nodded in agreement.

“Good question. *Duc* Raze immediately put our men to work and told our women to stay indoors. The line of work he has our men doing is dangerous to say the very least. But at least he's making good on his word. As long as my citizens bring him a fresh supply of captured hyped, he provides us with the means to survive." Another exhaled cloud of mist followed Mayor Trumark's words.

"Hyped? What does he want with hyped? It's hard enough to kill them how does one even go about capturing them alive?" While learning that Raze forced the town to undertake such dangerous tasks just to live surprised me, my piqued curiosity as to the purpose behind capturing hyped far outweighed my shock. What would a crime lord want with the afflicted?

"I'm afraid I don't right know, missy. Raze's orders, we just obey. Those that don't or fail get sent to the top plate as punishment. Surviving there is almost impossible." The old man's eyes rose to the ceiling as though he looked through the roof to the top plate itself. The heaviness in his heart at the thought of his suffering townsfolk further creased his wrinkled face.

"So he waltzes in, arts the place all up, puts everyone to work doin' the same thing, punishes useless or weak people by sendin' them to the barren frozen plate above this one, and shuts all the women and children in the houses? Sounds solid I guess, still don't really know the point though. It seems way too troublesome for a limp dick like him. Someone's gotta be pullin' the strings," Crelyos retorted, looking to the old man for his thoughts.

"Hm, I have no idea. Why don't you ask him yourself? His mansion is about a mile from the city off in a mountain stronghold which he made us build for him." The old man shook like a quaking buggy engine when he stood. The popping of his bones echoed like a tap dancer having a seizure as he hobbled to a curtain at the back of his house.

With a slow, purposeful sweep of his decrepit wrist, he drew the curtain back to reveal a window. Crelyos and I walked over, peering out into the distance. An exotic mansion sat embedded in the distant mountain top. It looked eerily similar to Doctor Oswald's manor back in Junction City, only several times more garish.

"Sir, may I ask why you're sharing all this with us? You didn't ask anything about us, and we only convinced Raze's men that we were looking for work. They likely intended to have us searching for those hyped as well," I asked as I knelt down in front of him.

"Come now, dear. You don't suspect me to be as stupid as his cronies. I knew from the minute you both walked in you weren't from around here and you weren't helpless. If you're here to put a stop to Raze's nefarious hold over my city and its folk, you have my support." The old man chuckled softly, at least I thought it was a chuckle as the sound of stale air wheezing into the night in set intervals from his crinkled lungs was either laughter or he was about to collapse.

"Oh we'll stop him. And while we're at it, we'll make him pay reparations for what he's done to all of you." I assured the old man, who waggled his finger at me slowly with a look of genuine concern molded into his aged face.

“Be careful young lady. Our surgeon, Eugene, had similar notions. Unfortunately things did not go so well for him. Raze doesn't tolerate resistance or rebellion. Poor Eugene...” Mayor Trumark trailed off in sad recollection.

“Eugene?! What did the bastard do to Eugene? Is there anything I can do to save him? He's an old friend of mine!” Crelyos clenched his right fist and placed his left hand on the old man's shoulder, rattling him far more violently than a man in his state should have been shaken. After a few seconds, Trumark placed a crinkled hand tenderly upon Crelyos', and the old man lifted that same single brow just enough to expose a tear-filled, vacant green eye that resembled something like a cross between seaweed and algae.

“What, you didn't recognize him in the city square?”

File 09: Analytical Fighter

“Did you know him long?” I stood behind Crelyos in the town square while he gazed up at the charred skeleton of his late companion. The chilly breeze whistling through the slit between plates feathered back my hair and whipped about the pieces of my outfit loose enough to billow. The only parts of Crelyos that moved in the wind were the lining of his olive tank-top, the tips of his messily spiked hair, and the heaving, infuriated swell and deflation of his muscular chest.

“Not really. He did a little work on me, and we had a few drinks. But it was long enough. Good surgeon, nice fella. Didn't deserve to end up like this.” Crelyos grunted his words through his grinding teeth. His feelings bled from him like an open wound, but the frightening part to me was that the emotions he exhibited, rather than grief and pain, were fury and rage.

“I see, well I hate to interrupt your moment, but I'm not sure how much longer our audience is going to remain patient,” I laced my words with cold sarcasm. Surrounding us and the unfortunate body of Doctor Eugene, most of the guards stationed in Loftsborough from Raze's outfit stood with spears, blades, and firearm muzzles aimed angrily in our direction. Why did they seem so angry? They had caught Crelyos with his hand in the cookie jar, so to speak. A random minion with a semi-disintegrated chest cavity spurting blood and suffering from postmortem spasms was the cookie jar. Crelyos' right hand was, well, the hand.

Shortly after Mayor Trumark informed the former soldier of his old drinking buddy's fate, Crelyos' rage exploded into an unstoppable frenzy. With an animalistic scream of vengeance, Crelyos rushed from Trumark's abode and turned his unbridled feelings on the two guards standing watch outside the door. The man to the right of the entrance heard Crelyos' shout and poked his head around the corner at entirely the wrong time.

The phrase "curiosity killed the cat" took on far too literal a meaning when Crelyos smashed his right fist into the thug's face. The resulting reverberation from Crelyos' mysterious implant saturated the area with a gratuitous amount of liquid as chunks of cranium and brain matter exploded into the freezing wind. The guard's body careened through the air several feet before skidding to a halt in a pool of his own vitae.

Because the first guard's blood misted in such random directions, Crelyos emerged from the doorway with a mosaic of the crimson fluid painting his entire right arm and blotching the right side of his face and chest. The darkness surrounding him added to the dreadful aura he exuded, and as he hissed a cold, foggy exhale through the slender space between his lips, his gaze turned slowly to the remaining guard on the left.

From my position pursuing the behemoth of a warrior, I

was unable to behold the expression of the remaining sentry. I imagined a gawking, trembling face frozen in horror at the sight of Crelyos, the demonic personification of rage. While I failed to witness the sight of Raze's minion ruining a perfectly good pair of pants, I certainly heard the quivering whimpers building up to a deafening cry of desperation when Crelyos drew his right hand back and plunged it mercilessly into the man's chest.

The squish of flesh and crunch of bone, along with grotesque gurgling sounds, replaced the guard's pathetic cry. When Crelyos next spun around, his fist was lodged within the partially disintegrated rib cage of the goon. The deceased's involuntary twitches made me cringe even as the fuming blond beast trudged to the center of the town square to pay his final respects to Doctor Eugene. Consequently, that was where our trouble began when the rest of Raze's minions, having heard the final cries of their comrades, rushed to investigate the situation. Apparently, they were not pleased with their discovery.

"Well, the assholes came here for a show. So... let's give 'em a show." Crelyos growled. I responded with a furtive grin.

My Cognitive Accelerator stopped time's machinations while I quickly assessed our situation and the course of action necessary to overcome it. I counted a total of ten enemies in front of us and within the scope of my peripheral vision. Though I was unable to see directly behind me, my enhanced auditory sense detected the heartbeats of three more at our rear. The grimy gentlemen sported an assortment of red and white rags they undoubtedly considered fashionable clothing.

Though some wore face masks or scarves to conceal portions of their displeasing countenances, the flame tattoo nestled beneath their right eyes remained unanimously exposed. Of the thirteen assailants, one to our right flank and one in front and slightly to the right of Crelyos belonged to the female gender. The woman ahead of Crelyos wielded a double barrel shotgun which, much to our advantage, was far too large for her petite frame. The other young lady carried a pair of short swords similar in length and design to the long daggers nestled within my sheathes.

Aside from the tiny girl's shotgun, I noted three other firearms among the pack of brigands. Next to the shotgun lass, and directly in front of Crelyos, a man with beady eyes and an angry expression held a fully automatic Uzi. To my right, a gargantuan, muscular brute held a six-shot revolver far too small for his enormous hand; he gripped it so tightly that I envisioned the steel grip molding to his clutches like a crushed aluminum can. Finally, a slouched thug with a shaved head and a torn bandana wrapped around his mouth clutched an assault rifle. His firing stance and grip on the weapon screamed "novice."

As though on cue from Crelyos' reckless comment, the expressions of our assailants began sluggishly morphing from intent gazes of a high stakes stand-off to snarling war cries of snapped tension. The hasty lot intended to make the first move and clean house before we had the chance to even properly greet them. I felt a prickling sense of anticipation well up within my chest. My nerves remained steadfastly calm in the wake of that sensation; rather, the cold weight pressing heavily atop my heart served only to heighten my awareness of the stakes and to remind me of the consequences for underestimating death's impartial affection. I knew what needed to be done.

Though the speed at which I perceived time lent me the sensation of moving while completely submerged in water, I sliced my hands through the air like the fangs of a predator through a jugular. I criss-crossed my right and left arms at the elbows; my right hand found the dagger's hilt sheathed on my left hip, and my left hand crossed over my right arm to the dagger's hilt sheathed on my right hip.

The expressions of our opponents finished transforming, and their jaws hung open ready to conjure forth a mighty shout. I ripped my arms wide across my chest as though ready to return death's cruel embrace. The action also loosed my lengthy daggers from their respective restraints, and with the momentum gained from the vicious whip of my shoulders fortified by my Supersoldier nanite, the silver instruments of death shot like bullets from the tips of my fingers and turned pommel over blade toward their respective marks.

In perfect synchronization with the swishing blades sailing through the air, I shot my right hand up to the stock of the rifle loosely slung across my back. I used the feminine curve of my right shoulder as leverage and yanked the stock down; the barrel of the rifle flipped up and over the hill formed by my collar bone and descended into my waiting left hand. By the time the business end of my rifle settled onto my target, the shotgun toting damsel to Crelyos' right, our enemies with firearms started applying pressure to their triggers, and those carrying more up close and personal tools of life-rending began drawing back their chosen weapons in time with their battle charge.

I took a second, in my time's perspective, to aim at the unfortunate female. My naturally sharp reflexes, the Supersoldier nanite stimulating my every muscle fiber, and the speed and agility training I received in Bradich's mercenary unit propelled my physical and mental quickness into a league all its own. While it was true that my own motions, within the prison of my Cognitive Accelerator, felt to me as though I moved through some sticky gelatinous substance, the minions' movements were as slugs straining to creep across a blade of grass. To my enemies, I may as well have been lightning incarnate.

I squeezed the trigger at the lowest valley of my foggy exhale. The resounding crack exploded like a bolt of lightning tearing asunder a thundering cloud. A symphony of sounds flooded the air in unison with enough force to tear the concentration fueling my Cognitive Accelerator. Mixed with the battle shouts of Raze's guards, the satisfying squelch of my blades traveled across the battlefield when the daggers found new sheathes within the mouths of their targets.

I had refrained from aiming for the thugs' hearts or lungs since such blows would not have guaranteed a secure kill. The threat of Panacea keeping them alive posed too great a risk to chance aiming for their torsos. However, with their maws agape to join their comrades in a vicious shout, they ignorantly removed the only barricade which may have skewed an attack to their medulla oblongata: their teeth.

When Raze's minions parted their enamel defenses, they may as well have painted proverbial reticules on the backs of their throats. Though the target allowed for no margin of error, my confidence in my aim applied to all things, including tossing the long daggers with which Bradich ceaselessly trained me during my days as a Bald Eagle. Ironic, since I intended to use that training to end him. But thanks to that training, my daggers became talons used to snatch the life from my targets without fail, and as a result, the two gurgling and sputtering men were dead before they hit the ground.

Almost simultaneously, the head of the woman brandishing the shotgun burst like an exploding melon as Oswald's custom, high caliber rifle round collided with the lady's skull. When attempting to head butt a bullet, the exchange was brief but relatively messy. Given her diminutive stature and the effort she expended to even hold the weapon erect, I determined that the danger she posed was less eminent than her male counterparts if only by a microsecond. Such a small nuance determined the order in which I exterminated the ranged combatants.

The only remaining thug in possession of a firearm stood directly in front of Crelyos. I only hoped my blonde comrade would follow my lead and control his rage long enough to dispose of the immediate threat before succumbing to his rampage. I possessed little time to process that thought, however, as the cacophony of noises that tore me from the advantages of my Cognitive Accelerator meant our enemies moved swiftly once again. I knew that because the twin blades of one of the remaining females flashed in a blinding arch straight toward my face.

The recoil of my single shot along with my own decision to lift the rifle skyward granted me an advantage; I allowed momentum to do its work and pulled my rifle in front of my face. Her swords collided with its steel underbelly. The metal clang of steel against steel sent vibrations along my palms. I shoved her blades away and leapt straight up in the air, for my peripherals caught sight of one of the men to the left thrusting a sharpened metal spike, shaped to resemble a spear, toward my knees. The leap allowed me to avoid the low blow, and I heard the dull thud of the steel spear colliding with the iron ground.

As the thug failed to embed the spear's tip into the metal ground as someone with a Supersoldier nanite like Crelyos certainly would have, I quickly noted the man wielding it lacked any form of strength augmentation. While still hanging in the air, I twisted my hips and spun, bringing the backside of my right heel to bear against the side of the assailing woman's head. The force behind my leaping spin kick, empowered by my Supersolider implant, shattered her skull and snapped her neck with a loud crunch. She flew through the air several yards before slamming into the hard ground and bouncing twice. Her lifeless corpse rolled to a contorted heap, and her blades careened off in two different directions.

I followed through with the kick, and as I descended I slammed a single foot onto the man's spear, pinning it to the ground. Without any form of strength augmentation, its wielder unsuccessfully struggled to wrestle it from beneath my foot. While he pulled and grunted in vain, I calmly tugged back the bolt-action chamber of my rifle to eject the shell and load another shot. I watched him with a morbid smile, admiring his persistence even as I prepared to blow his head off his shoulders.

The sound of gunfire somewhere to the right drew my attention. The red sparks flying from the tip of an Uzi lit up the night and blended into the bright glow cast by Loftsborough's imitation sun. Crelyos dashed headlong into the hail of gunfire, and he roared a sound resembling a cross between maniacal laughter and a furious howl. The hot lead spitting from the tip of the Uzi thudded into soft flesh with such tenacity that the squishes satisfied the beady eyed thug, his high pitched guffaws drenched with sadistic insanity testified to that fact.

Unfortunately, in his intoxicated madness, the fool failed to realize the vast majority of his volley penetrated the wrong flesh. Crelyos kept his right hand embedded in the gaping chest cavity of the guard he arbitrarily slaughtered at Trumark's abode, and he used the cadaver as a giant shield to protect his vitals. With that trusty shield, he charged toward the crazed gunman with the invariable stubbornness of a bull. I was uncertain whether Crelyos predicted he would need a shield with the foresight of a tactical genius and thus had held fast to the limp, mutilated body or if the corpse's presence merely slipped his mind until that moment. Either way, if time had allowed me the luxury, I might have marveled at Crelyos' cruel ingenuity, but I possessed my own plethora of problems.

The theater of emotions on the face of the man struggling to free his metal spear from the underside of my foot intensified with each transpiring second. At first, the expression resembled frustration laced with the determination to prove his manhood. Phrases such as, "You're so dead, bitch," and "Just you wait," dappled his strenuous grunts as he tugged and twisted the metallic bar in vain. As the resounding clicks of my rifle returning to a readied state drifted through the air, however, the tight wrinkles of aggravation warped into sagging lines of fear, and beads of perspiration soon complimented his horror. By the time the emotional transition ran its course, it was far too late for him.

I nonchalantly shouldered the weapon with the barrel situated mere inches from the thug's face. As I curled my finger around my trigger, I could not discern, for the life of me, why he refused to simply relinquish his hold on the metal bar and take cover. By the time the realization of impending doom dawned on the ignorant sap, his body shivered with notable discomposure. My smile widened.

However, the smile vanished when I caught a gleam from the corner of my eye. I drew my rifle flat to my chest and ensured its metallic underbelly faced upward when I arched my back. And I did arch my back. In fact, the velocity with which I curved into a gymnast's backbend may have snapped a weaker person's spine. The reason for my evasive maneuver passed overhead in a broad horizontal sweep.

A giant steel blade swung within inches of my hips and threatened to shave the flesh from my torso like a razor peeling the skin off an orange. Thankfully, the silver edge of the makeshift great sword collided with the metal underside of my rifle; the improvised parry forced the slashing motion upward along the length of the firearm and away from my midsection and breasts during the apex of my backbend. The screeching grind of steel against iron birthed a myriad of sparks, and I used the momentum of the exchange to turn a back flip. I planted the soles of my feet firmly against the ground to regain balance and lifted my gaze to my new assailant. I cautiously repositioned my rifle across my back.

The man was a giant over seven feet tall. I surmised that he was one of the thugs standing behind us during my initial evaluation. Several thin strips of wooly black hair stood in disarray atop an otherwise bald head riddled with scars. A white mask constructed of a material resembling clay veiled his face; various cracks snaked across its surface along with blotches of blood stains and dirt. The concealing ceramic encompassed his whole face save a large opening revealing his right eye, the flame-branded cheek below it, and the right half of his thick mouth. His every exhale forced a gush of white mist from the exposed half of his lips like an arctic gale.

His black skin, dead and ashen from lack of exposure to the sun, stood in stark contrast to the paler complexions of his comrades. Oversized muscles popped from his upper body beneath a pair of straps that looped around his shoulders and attached to a pair of thick overalls tucked into enormous combat boots. More scars littered much of his exposed figure; I briefly shuddered in apprehension.

Neither his overwhelming stature nor the tight draw of his flesh around bulging muscles bore responsibility for my shiver, nor could the gargantuan steel great sword, fashioned by shaving an edge onto a large metal plate and attaching a hilt to it, boast of conjuring my apprehensive quake. It was his lone, exposed eye that caused my momentary sense of dread. Unlike the vacant crazed eyes belonging to the majority of Raze's henchmen, the large dark man's gaze was a dictionary of murderous intentions and brutal warmongering. He was different. He was a warrior.

"Joachim, man, yer a lifesaver! That bitch was totally about to shoot me in the face!" The skittish thug who lost his iron spear to my powerful stomp stepped forward and placed his hand on the dark giant's shoulder blade.

Joachim's eye shot down toward the man's relieved clasp with passive annoyance. My eyes widened as the great sword resembling a colossal butcher knife moved so quickly it seemed like a silver flash in the night. It passed through the twitchy goon's figure with a distinct crunch laced with the squish of splitting flesh. The smaller thug's face quivered in an interim state between horror and pain. After a few seconds, the grotesque sound of the man's body splitting apart heralded his descent to the ground in two separate pieces. A few coughs and sputters escaped the man's throat as he furiously swiped and clawed at his own entrails attempting to stuff them into the gaping cavity created by his bisection.

His death would be slow and painful. Panacea would attempt to stitch the flesh together and expedite the cellular regeneration present in all human beings. Unfortunately, the miracle nanite possessed limits. Being totally split in two pieces definitely qualified as one of them. I felt a flame of passion smolder within my chest. It mattered not that I intended to personally end the weaker thug's life anyway or that Joachim instilled fear in me, my indignant abhorrence toward betrayal flared like a raging fire, and I focused my ire upon the overgrown brute. I was now resolved to kill him or die trying.

File 10: Joachim Izrahi

"Annoying pest," Joachim wielded his giant weapon using only his right hand, and he swung it with the speed and accuracy of a fly swatter. Even the tone with which he dismissed his late companion suggested Joachim believed he had merely squashed an annoying bug buzzing about his ear. I furrowed my brows and grimaced, but the anger I rarely felt armed me with an acute sense of awareness that penetrated my surroundings like an arrow through a bull's-eye. The two other men, who I assumed stood at Joachim's right and left during the initial confrontation, seized the opportunity presented by Joachim's display to flank me.

To my right, a crazed maniac bore down on me with a metal spear similar in design to the betrayed man's pole; when I noticed him, he was airborne and attempting to use gravity to increase the force of his attack. To my left, a man with cold calculating eyes brandished a blade with swift precision. I never broke my direct stare with Joachim; the sensation of his single, demonic eye bearing down on me fueled my actions. I aimed to prove to him I was a fearful opponent. Though he possessed every opportunity to rush to the aid of his comrades, he stood like a motionless bulwark in the darkness and observed with intense scrutiny.

The man on the left aimed his sword for the base of my

neck with a horizontal stroke. Synchronously, his partner haphazardly thrusted his metal spear toward my ribs. I maintained my stance until the final instant before activating my Supersoldier nanite. I quickly hopped back toward the swordsman as though rushing to my demise, but to his dismay I bolted my left elbow skyward and rammed it into the underside of his wrist. The blow halted his strike altogether. Without a weapon of my own, countering the edged steel in such a fashion possessed significant risk, but it was far more agreeable than the alternative.

A roaring pain ripped through my torso as the metallic spear grazed the front of my chest. The bandit successfully tore another gash in my already shredded attire and peeled away a significant amount of my flesh. The decision to move just enough to avoid impalement allowed me to quickly send my right hand through the air and grip the metal pole as it traveled the full width of my midsection. Using the momentum created by the psychotic attacker's descent, I redirected the spear. The laws of physics prevented the airborne thug from changing his course until his feet touched the ground, so his new target became one designated by my hand. I chose the gut of the sword bearer.

The sickening squelch of the spear penetrating the left bandit's abdomen joined his tortured cry. The shock of his agony zeroed his attention to the point where the metal pole skewered him; he uncurled his fingers from the hilt of his weapon, and it began a careless plummet toward the ground. I activated my Cognitive Accelerator. I spun on my heel; I detached my right hand from the silvery spear and slid it through the air toward the falling blade. As I gracefully placed my palm against the sword's handle, I plucked it out from air with relative ease. It weighed significantly more than my daggers, but circumstances facilitated a quick adaptation to my new weapon.

My perception jolted to normal. I finished my twirl and unleashed my wrath upon the spear maniac. I lifted the sword diagonally toward the him during the final second of his descent just as his feet contacted the ground. His contorted expression of mortification complimented the sing of the blade's edge as it tore through his arms with enough force to bisect them at the elbow. His screams and groans mingled with the spew of his life force. He staggered back, and I followed through in pursuit. My limbs pummeled the brigand in a series of blinding strikes designed to inflict pain to the soft, sensitive locations on his body. The desired result was his continued staggering retreat; the desired result was accomplished.

After traveling a sufficient distance, I ended my flurry of blows with a vicious thrust kick to the pitiable thug's knee cap. The bone's crack echoed loudly, and he dropped to one knee with a dull thud. With the thug in such a position, a simple horizontal sweep of the blade across my waist separated his head from his shoulders with ease. A spurting fountain of his crimson vitality splattered across my face and leathery garb, but I paid it no heed. Instead, I slowly turned to my other target.

The calculating thug heaved and gagged as blood wormed its way up his throat from the pit of his stomach. His blood drenched hands grasped the metal pole and worked to free his midsection of impalement. Still covered in his partner's blood, I spun with the force of a whirlwind and brought the bottom of my heel to bear against the tip of the spear. The magnitude of the spin kick drove the spike through the goon's entire body and ejected it from his back accompanied by a morbid symphony of torn organs, a shattered spinal column, and tortured screams.

As the brigand fell backward onto the ground and writhed in pain, I calmly stepped forward and drove the tip of my new sword through his throat with the nonchalance of an executioner. After twisting the weapon, I lifted my scarlet painted face to Joachim; the exposed right side of his mouth stretched upward in a disgustingly pleased smile.

"I understand," Joachim's voice sounded similar to the deep guttural growl of a feral predator. It rumbled from the pit of his chest like rolling thunder. The large man slammed the tip of his blade into the iron floor; the resulting dent testified to his overwhelming strength, and I questioned how many augments he possessed. For several moments we stared at one another, but while I attempted to evaluate his capabilities, his gaze was devoid of any emotion save the desire to fight. The weight of that monstrous stare was a ten ton boulder pressing against my shoulders. I needed to pull myself together, and I needed to do so quickly.

"I understand..." Joachim repeated, "you decided the more dangerous of the two was the pest wielding the sword. His calmness and careful aim posed more of a threat than the reckless attack of the insect using the spear, but you also calculated that meant he would react more to pain. You focused your efforts on completely negating his attack while making it hard for him to dodge the redirected spear by waiting until the last possible moment at the expense of your own well-being. 'It will be okay, Panacea will heal the wound quickly,' you must have thought! Haha! Glorious!"

Joachim lifted his free left hand and gripped the mask covering his face as he released a boisterous laugh into the night sky, "and it only gets better from there!"

"Since he reacted normally to pain, you chose to stab his gut! Having your stomach pierced by a bullet or spear is likely the most painful thing you can encounter," Joachim brushed his fingers against the scars decorating his stomach, "it was only natural that a man with his senses about him would double over in pain and drop whatever he was holding. Like the sword. And you wasted no time taking advantage of that. It's almost too cruel for words."

Joachim laughed again, "Once you plucked it from the air, you moved pretty quick to cut off both arms of the man holding the spear just to keep him from pulling it out of his partner. This served to 'disarm' your opponent and forced the man formerly holding the sword to contend with his own wound, effectively turning the fight into two one-on-one bouts in which you clearly possessed the advantage. Genius." Joachim lifted his hand and flicked his thumb skyward to display his approval.

"The rest of the fight goes without saying. Killing them at that point was more an act of mercy than violence. Stranger!" Joachim pointed at me, "I've waited for a fighter like you for years! Day in and day out we guard this useless town to avoid Raze's wrath. Where's the fun? Where's the challenge?!"

Joachim drooled as he spoke; the pupil in his bloodshot eye dilated, and he cried aloud, "My blood is boiling just thinking about it! Defeating you will be the greatest honor!"

"Honor?" I venomously spat. I ripped the sword from its hearth in my former opponent; it squished from his flesh with a sickening crunch. I sauntered a few paces to the right and knelt down. At my feet, the man with enormous muscles wielding a revolver lay motionless with my long dagger embedded in his brain stem. After grabbing his blood-stained, rusty revolver and sliding it into my pants' waistline, I plucked the elongated dirk from the back of his throat and gripped it firmly in my left hand. I fell into a combat stance.

"There is no honor or battle for a traitor that slays his own comrades. No, I'm not going to fight you," I tipped my head down; my bangs veiled my face in a darkness resembling the hatred seeping into my chest. "I'm going to slaughter you!" I growled.

"Oh? How disappointing," Joachim sighed, "I thought perhaps we were more compatible. Hmph. Very well then, stranger. But you should know the name of your killer before you die." The warrior lifted his enormous blade with one hand and with his free hand gestured to himself, "My name is Joachim Israhi; take it with you to your grave!"

Like a locomotive, the man charged. The thunder of his footsteps drowned the distant quakes caused by Crelyos as he fought the remaining thugs several yards away. As long as I heard such robust noises emitting from my ally's vicinity, I would not worry. Given Crelyos' fighting style, it would be silence that concerned me most.

As Joachim approached, he coiled his legs and took to the air in a mighty leap. His great sword dragged behind him, and he prepared to bring it down in a forceful overhead strike powered by gravitational force. Did none of the thugs understand that leaping so dramatically into the air forced one into a predestined trajectory unalterable once one left the ground? I kicked my Cognitive Accelerator into high gear; as time slowed around me I danced with languid movements to Joachim's right. From that position, even if he suddenly changed the trajectory of his blade, the resulting impact would be significantly weaker since he would be swinging away from his body.

In slow motion, I prepared the twin blades for a deadly strike. My feet dug into the artificial ground and propelled me upward along Joachim's right side, but as I steeled my resolve to thrust the tips of each weapon through the warrior's skull, my eyes twitched. I beheld the man's right hand, empty, snaking through the gelatinous air toward my head. His right eye, which should have been focused on my previous position, locked onto my airborne figure. I incorrectly deduced that with Joachim's large stature, his movements would be sluggish compared to my own. I underestimated him.

His palm encompassed my face like a man gripping a tennis ball. Plucked from the air like a fly, I winced from the initial pain of Joachim's grip. My eyes raced to the vicinity in which his blade should have been free-falling since he released it from the grasp of his right hand. Indeed, with my enhanced perception it seemed to flutter downward with gentle abandon, but as it neared the synthetic ground Joachim's left hand swept through the sky and coiled around the hilt.

Ambidexterity? No, his clumsy grip turned the blade the wrong way. The simultaneous actions of Joachim's left foot touching the ground and his left hand powering the length of the blade toward my lithe figure left me no time to defend. I returned my gaze toward the hulking human and swiped my sword toward Joachim's exposed eye just as the blunt side of his makeshift giant cleaver dug into my ribs with a resonating crunch.

The searing pain spread like a wildfire from the point of impact up and down the entire length of my body. My eyes widened in bloodshot twitches, and my body began folding awkwardly to the left as the force of the blow bent me in half like someone folding a towel over a towel rack. My lips parted and unleashed a fervent scream that heightened in pitch and volume with each crack of my splintering ribs. The pain, coupled with my own shriek, snapped me from my accelerated state, and I catapulted through the air like a stone released from a sling. But as I whistled through the air, I kept a single eye opened to deduce whether or not my desperate attack connected.

Joachim cried out in pain as well and gripped his face to cover the gash splitting his exposed eye. While a small trail of blood trickled out the corner of my mouth, a steady gush poured from the dark warrior's face. I felt relieved, at least until my body smashed into one of the large stone pillars separating Loftsborough's lower plate and upper plate. The impact shattered my shoulder blades and the cracked stone itself with a heavy thud; I ended the transaction in a broken heap among a few dislodged stones and gasped for air.

"Graaagh! You whore! I know what you're doing! You think this wound will buy you some time to heal up! I'll see to it that doesn't happen... arrgh!" Joachim furiously rubbed at his eye as though the contact would expedite the process of Panacea stitching his ocular back together. Though my own healing augment ardently worked to piece my bones together and seal the holes in my punctured lungs, I cursed its sluggish pace. I thought intently on the events that transpired as I struggled to return to combat-ready status.

Joachim was not ambidextrous, for the clumsy manner with which he wielded the great sword in his left hand prevented him from exacting a fatal blow. So why make the switch? Did he predict my actions or somehow figure them out during the course of his descent? I was skeptical; even assuming his mind processed information at a rate superior to my own, I certainly would have detected the change in his course and counter-attacked his counter-attack. The exchange would surely have continued until one of us committed a folly, and there the fight would have ended. No, his actions bore no semblance of reasoning or preparation. It was almost as though...

"Play time's over, stranger! Raaagh!" With blood still streaking down the right side of his face and his eye shut tight, Joachim charged in my direction once again.

My intuition perked for two reasons. First, Joachim's charge carried him in a straight line toward me with immaculate precision. By the time I was flung from the blunt edge of his sword, he was already suffering from temporary blindness, therefore he should not have been able to pinpoint my exact location based off the vague knowledge he possessed regarding my trajectory.

Second, during his intimidating bull rush Joachim trampled over the corpses of his alleged allies; his foot's connection with the fallen bodies caused him to stumble if only a bit. How was it he possessed perfect precision in regards to my position but remained oblivious to the locations of his deceased comrades?

By the time he arrived, Panacea barely repaired my

body enough for me to move. His momentum, accompanied by his feral growls, fueled his strength as he brutally thrust the length of his great sword toward my body. I rolled to the left with grace obtained through years of training and barely avoided impalement. I noted that if his thrust connected, it would have precisely pierced my heart. The thwack of the man's steel against the ground and debris reverberated the air behind me.

I seized the opportunity and rolled back planting both hands flat against the ground; the buzz of my Supersoldier augment rattled my temples as I used my enhanced muscle power and shot to my feet with a quick handspring akin to an ancient ninja technique. The action sent electrical twangs of pain coursing down my still-healing ribs. I grunted and prepared my next move; there was no time to feel pain.

Surging forward, I drove both arms down in a diagonal criss-cross slash against his chest. The flesh starting at the base of either of his pectorals split apart with a satisfactory squelch that ripped down to the diaphragm where the wounds crossed paths before finishing their merciless exit a few inches above his wide hips. He howled in pain and jerked his blade from the chunks of stone in preparation to strike.

My eyes flashed, and with enhanced strength coursing through each of my legs, I sent a herculean spin kick into the underside of the giant's left forearm. The concussive force sent his hand, and the blade encased by it, flailing far to the side. As I brought my leg down, I used the momentum to drag my body into a spin and put my daggers to work. Applying centrifugal power to my attacks, I tore two horizontal wounds across the breadth of his middle with both blades. Before Joachim could stabilize his left arm to prepare another swing of his cleaver, I coiled as much power into my left leg as I could muster and brought it in a wide, powerful roundhouse toward the blinded giant's right temple.

With his eye still clamped shut and healing from the previous gash, I intended to end the fight by rendering the man unconscious and executing him during his stupor. To my astonishment, his bulky hand shot up like a rocket and encompassed the circumference of my ankle before the kick could connect. How was that possible? My eyes widened as he stepped back and yanked my body off the ground with that single hand. Up and over the top of his head, he swung me in an enormous semi-circle; he twisted to maximize the velocity of my descent and slammed my body into the ground.

The iron floor groaned beneath the force of impact, and as the bones in my shoulders and back crunched, I opened my eyes and looked up from the small crater of bent metal in which I rested. My gaze locked onto Joachim; the enormous man wasted no time bringing his cleaver down with the titanic power of a falling anvil. I twisted my body to spin from the blade's projected path, but was stunned to find my range of motion limited. A glance down revealed my ankle still entombed in the vice clamp of his hand.

I grunted and snapped to an upright seated position while criss-crossing my blades above my head and aligning my spine to prevent injury. Though Panacea worked tirelessly to stitch my broken bones together, I knew the impact would devastate my battered shoulders, so I steeled myself for the inevitable pain like a child preparing for a vaccination.

The clash of steel against steel sent a small shockwave along the ground when the great sword slammed into the wedge created by my blades. My shoulders and collar bone immediately popped in rapid succession. Normally, I would never attempt to directly compete with someone of Joachim's stature in a contest of strength. Even with my Supersoldier augment, the sheer volume of his muscle mass overwhelmed me to the point that I cried out in hopes my adrenaline would respond and offer me the small amount of power I needed to merely survive the exchange.

Oddly enough, I learned in that moment Joachim did not possess a strength enhancement. If he had, the contest would have ended far more quickly; how lucky for me. My arms quivered with the strain of trying to keep his blade at bay; as I gazed up at the dark warrior, his right eye snapped open.

"I see you..." He chuckled and drew the blade back in preparation for another strike. He knew, as I did, that a direct assault would eventually break every bone in my body. Why cleave me into pieces if he could just bludgeon me into dust? I gritted my teeth and lurched forward the moment I felt relief from the suffocating weight of his cleaver. I plunged both of my blades down into his large forearm; in particular, the one belonging to the hand keeping my ankle prisoner. Strangely, even with the return of his eyesight he made no attempt to deflect the blow. He growled in agony when my sword and dagger squished into his flesh.

"You bitch!" He shouted and instinctively flung my body to his right with enough force to send me rocketing through the air as though he had just thrown a softball. As I cut through the sky, I beamed the sword I borrowed from my former opponent at Joachim's face with the velocity of an arrow loosed from a bow. Despite the constant pain distracting me, I forced my Cognitive Accelerator to activate if only for an instant: the moment the blade should have penetrated the warrior's skull.

His free hand, wounded from my previous attack, drifted up in the sluggish manner with which I perceived the world. Thick fingers wrapped around the blade's edge just before it could impale his forehead, and a few streaks of blood splashed from the slice the weapon made against his palm as punishment for grabbing the wrong end. Interestingly, several seconds in my slow motion world passed after his daring catch before his right eye slid over in its socket to actually behold his own action.

A grin spread across my lips. I deactivated my Cognitive Accelerator and turned a flip in midair; as a result, my feet touched the ground with feline grace, and I retained my balance as the throw's remaining force acted upon my body and slid it back several feet across the ground.

"I understand..." I spoke cryptically and glanced down. Joachim's throw succeeded in distancing the two of us, and it came with the added perk of launching me across the battlefield to the slouched thug wearing my other long dagger in his throat like a deranged piercing. I reached down and gripped the hilt of my familiar weapon, and when I tugged it from its fleshy sheath I twirled it nonchalantly in my hand. I returned my gaze to the stout warrior. Joachim smiled and tossed the sword he plucked from the sky aside like a used toothpick.

"Oh? I think you're bluffing," Joachim growled.

His guttural sounds resembled a ferocious excitement instead of an annoyed frustration. I quirked a brow and stopped twirling my long dagger; as I gripped the handle properly, I could not help but relinquish a sigh of relief. Nothing compared to the comfort I felt wielding my own weapons. I trained for years to turn them into machines of efficient death dealing, after all. I dropped into my combat stance and steadied my nerves before hissing with a misty breath, "Why don't you find out?"

Joachim rushed at me with a roar of anticipation. I reciprocated his gesture and dashed with a pregnant silence across the iron ground. I kept low, cutting through the whipping night wind with predatory agility. Before the world turned to ash and exterminated earth's animals, a spectator may have easily confused our confrontational charge to be a lumbering bear and swift panther engaged in mortal combat. Joachim still held the cleaver fast in his left hand, and swung it when he reached a distance that his professional fighting experience suggested would be most effective.

By taking an infinitesimal half-step just before the blade crashed into the ground, I avoided having my chest opened like a stuffed animal with a split seam. The quickness with which I prided myself took control, and my feathery footsteps tapped against the broad edge of his blade as I ran along the blunted edge. His shot his right hand across his chest in an attempt to pluck me from the air in a similar manner as he did the first time.

I grinned and leapt toward his left when I reached the handle of his great sword to avoid the grapple. For a moment it seemed as though I attempted to disengage completely, and during that moment Joachim switched his grip. Releasing the blade with his left hand, he curled his right fingers around the cleaver's hilt. His sent his left hand through the air to the position in which he predicted I would descend; he intended to snatch me up before I had the chance to put my agility to work.

"You think you can just zip around like a gnat and poke and prod at me to wear me down?! Not happening! Haha!" His words cut through the night sky like a signaling pistol shot for me to act.

I twitched in my moment of prescience and plunged the blade in my right hand into his left bicep; keeping a firm hold against the hilt I used the long dagger as a pivot to swing my body up and around Joachim's colossal frame. Like a gymnast on the parallel bars, I vaulted onto his left shoulder and left the long dagger shoved within his massive arm.

With one foot on his collar bone and the other braced against the dagger protruding from his bicep, I quickly fished the revolver from my waistline with my newly freed hand and took aim at the open portion of his mask where his right eye glared at me. I depressed the trigger and braced my injured shoulder for the recoil; the gun spit its spiraling cone of lead from a cloud of fire. In time with the cacophonous crack, Joachim moved. At the last possible second, the dark warrior's head swerved to the left and the bullet skimmed passed his cheek.

"Hah, what, point blank was your answer? I'm disa—" Crunch. The sound of Joachim's spine separating at the base of his neck near the brain stem ceased his haughty ramblings and widened his eyes. My left hand held fast to the pommel of my long dagger which I buried to the hilt in Joachim's neck. He began twitching and sputtering, trying in vain to move his body. With his nerves cut and his spinal cord severed, Joachim could only shiver, gasp, think... and listen.

"I understand," I repeated as his body swayed in the wind, "You have no spirals in your eyes, so it's safe to assume you possess three implants. Panacea is a given for all mortals living in this world. So that's one. You praised me for my analytical prowess only to tell me it would not work on you. That was your first mistake. My tactics only failed because of how you fight; you left me with no way to analyze your thoughts because you didn't think. Your entire fighting style revolved around instinctual reflexes that must be enhanced by a nanite."

"It's easy to over think the actions of a person if they're only operating on base levels, so when you reacted to attacks and your body betrayed no signs of your attacks or defenses, it simply left me to assume you were just that quick. But that wasn't the case, was it? Your second implant is one that augments your reflexes. Yet you did nothing to dodge attacks on your body or the one I drove into your forearm. Your inconsistency was your second mistake." I twisted the dagger; the action released a satisfied crack that caused Joachim's eyes to roll into the back of his head as blood sprayed from the gruesome wound.

"Your reflexes activated only in the proximity of your head. Their superhuman quality screamed 'nanite,' but the masterful manner in which they prioritized your most vital spot, your brain, spoke volumes of your experience as a fighter and suggested that the nanite is implanted in your frontal lobe. Interesting choice for an involuntary effect like your reflexes. As long as one did not approach your face or head, you were just a normal fighter, albeit a damn good one. But the nature of reflexes in the human body is the sharp reaction to stimuli from a sensory organ. In your case, your third mistake was this mask." I reached forward with the barrel of the revolver and tapped the mask on the area covering Joachim's left eye.

"Your mask hinders your eyesight. I assume it's either an injury to your left eye, or some other form of defect that renders your sight on that side useless. Because of this, as a seasoned fighter, you decided your last implant would not be enhanced vision as many fighters use. Instead you chose to enhance your hearing. By linking your hearing to your reflexes, your body responds with inhuman speed to anything perceived by these ears of yours. And since your ears operate at a superhuman level, the synergy between the two implants makes you almost invincible. If you at least pretended your left eye wasn't useless by not wearing a mask, it might have taken me longer to deduce that you used hearing instead of vision."

I shook my head, "Instead, it was easy to discern that you caught my sword with your hand long before you actually saw it after you threw me. This is because the sword's path disrupted the air, as did my kick earlier when you could not see at all and still managed to catch it, and when you charged straight at me but did not avoid your comrades on the ground. That's because you heard my heartbeat but didn't hear theirs since they no longer have one. Am I right? Ah, you can't answer. Then, I'll continue."

The dramatic manner in which his body remained standing reached a climactic finale, and as the breeze fluttered through my long black tresses, I remained atop the massive being as he descended slowly, in my mind's eye, toward the ground.

"Your pride was your final mistake. You did nothing to

hide these things during our fight, likely because you assumed I experienced the world the same way everyone else does. There's no way normal or even enhanced vision can detect the details I did. I have my own secrets... but they don't mean anything to you now, I guess." His body thundered against the ground like a felled tree. He continued to sputter and twitch as he struggled to grip the true extent of his situation; he was going to die.

"But how... did you... defeat... that?" He managed to choke out words.

"Simple," I shrugged, "you were too sensitive. When your senses are amped too high, controlling them becomes difficult. If you have sensitive touch, then pain is just as enhanced as pleasure. If you have sensitive hearing... loud noises are just as enhanced as quiet ones. You reacted to the sound of the gunshot, as your nanites were programmed to do. It was the loudest stimuli, and because it was so loud it overloaded your auditory senses and made it impossible to detect the disturbance in the air when I stabbed you at the same time."

"Kind of like coughing at the same time someone claps. You don't really hear the cough, just the clap. Because there was no stimuli to react to, your reflex nanite didn't activate when I drove this dagger into your neck. Think of it like your Achilles' heel." I stood erect over his fallen form and slowly removed the rifle from its strap against my back.

"Amazing... I couldn't have... asked for... a better

opponent... Please, Tell me your name... before I die. I want to take it with me... " Joachim's eyes were fading fast. I sighed softly and pressed the tip of my rifle against the center of his mask.

"Sorry. Where you're going, names don't exist, traitor." I squeezed the trigger.

File 11: Leaving Loftsborough

I desired more power. As I stood over the spreading red pool of Joachim's former cranium, I grimaced. I grimaced because the snap, crackle, and pop of my bones finishing their rapid regeneration sent zaps of pain surging through my body. I grimaced because the battle with Joachim took far too long and exacted too severe a toll on my health. I grimaced because if Bradich had fought Joachim, the fight would have ended before the traitor had the chance to speak a word.

I grimaced at the thought of my own weakness; I felt an unbridled rage at my hypocritical drive to chase Bradich without the knowledge that I possessed enough power to extinguish his treacherous life. As I discarded the revolver I used to fool Joachim's sensitive hearing, I retrieved my possessions. I loaded another shot in my rifle and slung it across my back before gripping my long daggers and returning them to their sheaths. Suddenly, I felt a jolt of pain course through my entire body induced by a crushing slap planted between my shoulder blades. It was Crelyos.

“Hey, good job. Not sure why you got this pissed mist all around you.” Blood covered the former soldier from the tips of his blond hair to the toes of his combat boots. As I stared at him, he drew his lips into a lopsided smile. How was it Crelyos went from a storm of rage and anguish one moment to a happy-go-lucky child the next? On the other hand, I started the fight feeling exhilarated and ended with an overwhelming despair. The irony coaxed a brief, empty grin from one corner of my mouth.

I looked beyond Crelyos to the area where he fought Raze's remaining goons while I dealt with Joachim. The iron floor appeared as though someone repeatedly slammed a wrecking ball on it with careless abandon. Disintegrated holes of various sizes, ranging from that of a human body to a huge sinkhole, peppered the imaginary arena as craters peppered the moon's surface. Nestled in the craters' lowest points, crimson smudges indicated that Crelyos' unique ability made short work of the offending assailants. Though Joachim kept me too busy to watch Crelyos' confrontation, I imagined the battle ended fairly quickly given his overwhelming combat prowess.

As Panacea finished mending my injuries, I arched my back and stretched; the sound of my healed bones creaking and popping joined my satisfied sigh. I gave my arms a few rotations for good measure and returned my gaze to Crelyos. I examined his wounds; though blood covered his entire body, most of it belonged to his opponents. The liquid trails that stemmed from injuries he might have sustained had long since healed. I quirked a brow at him.

"Just how long were you watching, anyway?" I crossed my arms beneath my modest chest and cocked a hip to the side; I purposely attempted a nagging housewife pose.

“Long enough, girly. I'd say about the time you got that rip in your shirt,” Crelyos gestured to the scrape the maniacal spearman made down the center of my chest. The exposed flesh was a bit scandalous, but I merely glanced down at it with an apathetic stare.

“So basically the entire fight with tall, dark, and handsome,” I sighed and shook my head.

“Pretty much. Once I got rid of mister Uzi, the rest of their gang was a joke. You seemed fairly involved with the black guy though, so I decided to let it play out. Don't worry, I'd have saved you if I thought you really needed it.” Crelyos placed both his hands on his waist, widened his stance to that of a cocky brat, and bellowed a boisterous laugh into the night sky. I rolled my eyes and stepped passed him; my languishing gait carried me toward the town's exit, but a hoarse, dusty cry of shock stopped me in my tracks.

“Wh-wh-what have you done?! My town! There's blood everywhere! And holes, and... oh my goodness, what is that?! Youngsters these days!” Mayor Trumark appeared out of nowhere; the wrinkled codger gripped his face and wriggled in place with the speed of a sloth. In my opinion, even a sloth's moved far too fast a pace for an old timer in his condition, but the surprise of Loftsborough's new decorations may have warranted such a reaction. The womenfolk of the city poked their heads from the windows and doors of the various houses, and an overall sense of conflicting horror and joy washed over Loftsborough as Crelyos and I trudged toward the exit.

"You sure you don't wanna stick around for a bit? We're kinda heroes. They might even treat us to drinks and those women could become our fans. Well, my fans anyway. You can have a couple if you swing that way, I guess. Man, I could go for some sludge right about now." Crelyos stuck close to my right as we passed through the giant arch leading to the elevator station. I ignored his mindless gibberish with the exception of a single statement.

"Heroes, huh?" I laughed softly as we approached the shack housing the dim witted elevator operator. "I wonder how many heroes in history books are considered such from a coincidence like that one," I mused and glanced over at the large man. My cryptic statement was enough to garner his attention.

"What do you mean, 'coincidence?' The town can rest easy from Joachim and his thugs, and we're marchin' on our way to take care of Raze and his gang so the menfolk can go back to livin' normal lives and providin' for their families. That sounds pretty heroic to me," Crelyos snorted.

"I'm after Bradich. None of that other stuff matters. If there was an easier, more direct way to get the information I wanted without wasting time fighting idiots, I'd have left this town to rot. If they're so weak that they can't fend for themselves, then they deserve that fate. It's none of my concern." I felt flustered, and blood rushed to my cheeks. Was I experiencing frustration? I buried the thought the moment it arose. The cold mist of my breaths contrasted with the fire in my face. A loud smack interrupted my thoughts; Crelyos slammed his hand between my shoulder blades again. His robust laughter accompanied the playful assault.

"Aw, that's cute. You know I've thought this for a while now, but you're not very good about bein' honest with yourself. You told the mayor you'd make Raze pay for what he did, but now you're talkin' stupid about weak people deservin' their fate. Haha, I think you're really just mad that Joachim smacked your ass around like he did. Made you feel weak, yourself, eh?" Crelyos' words cut me like a razor.

I instinctively wanted to slam my fist into the underside of his chin, but despite his crude manner of speech, Crelyos spoke the truth. My callous attitude amounted to little more than lashing out at an invisible scapegoat. For some reason, the incident in Cairo altered my grasp on emotions considerably. Since Bradich's betrayal in Egypt, I understood emotions and often felt brief moods of anger, joy, amusement and sorrow, but the feelings did not match what I remembered before the incident.

I understood when a happy occurrence transpired that I felt joy, but the joy I felt differed vastly from the joy I felt during the days prior to Donovan's death. It was as though I experienced the joy in my head rather than my heart. Oswald claimed that the entire ordeal coupled with the physical injury to my head simply left a traumatic scar. According to the good doctor, my mind chose emotional dissociation as its defense mechanism to cope with Donovan's death and Bradich's treachery. I liked logic better, anyway. Cold, hard logic.

I calmly opened the door to the elevator shack. The same daft punk that allowed us entry sat leaning backward atop a metal stool. The unwary sentry had rocked the stool back on two legs and plastered his back against the nearby wall. With his legs propped atop the only table in the room and his hands clasped atop his chest, the thug snored softly and failed to wake even after our entrance. I sighed annoyedly and shoved his legs off the table. The gentle snores cracked into abrupt snorts and confused, broken questions which made little sense such as, “Wha- who goes where? I mean there?”

“It's us. We want to leave. Let us down,” I offered the man my best impression of an impatient glare.

“You woke me up for that? Just use the stupid thing over there.” The goon gestured to the metal box with the giant red button. Just beneath it, two smaller buttons embossed the box's surface: one with a green arrow pointing up and one with a blue arrow pointing down. The man began sinking into his position of slumber but suddenly bolted upright. He stared at Crelyos and I with his mouth agape, “What in the world! You guys are covered in blood! What happened in there?!”

“Oh, uh, we killed all the guards.” Crelyos blurted out without a second thought.

"You did what?! Hey now, y-you stay away from me!" The man scurried into the corner like a frightened rodent.

"Calm down. I'm already filthy. I'd rather not add your blood to my clothes. Just keep quiet and keep doing your job, and you won't get killed." I snatched up the device in question and turned to take my leave.

"Hah, yeah right! As soon as you leave I'll be sending a message straight to *Duc* Raze! You won't get away with this, mark my words!" The thug seemed genuinely pleased with his threat. Crelyos and I stopped dead in our tracks and exchanged a glance. After a few seconds the thug's smug demeanor melted and he lifted a hand to cover his mouth, "Uh-oh..." was the last thing he would ever speak.

We left the sentry's body to be disposed of by the townsfolk. We stood in silence during the elevator's descent, bearing with the screeches of rusty metal caused by years of neglect. The remaining journey to our rendezvous point transpired uneventfully. Oswald was there when we arrived; the doctor busied himself with his portable tools creating nanites which, later, he would undoubtedly insist on surgically implanting in my brain.

Crelyos gestured to the doctor while offering me a bemuddled stare as though to say, "Look at 'im! I could punch his lights out and he'd never know! Guard the buggy my ass!"

I shook my head. I desired nothing more than to agree

with Crelyos and rile the old codger up by scaring the long-forgotten daylights out of him, but I knew the man's astute awareness better than anyone. As Crelyos began creeping toward the doctor's back with his hands poised to grip Oswald's shoulders, I grinned with the knowledge of the events about to transpire. Oswald did not disappoint. Without interrupting his work for even a moment, the doctor's voice bubbled up with a disinterested inquiry.

"Back already, you two? I assume all went well." Oswald's words halted Crelyos' advance, and the former soldier relaxed in a disappointed slump when he realized he would be unable to startle the keen scientist. Meanwhile, I decided it was time for a new shirt. I moved to the trailer hitched to the back of our buggy and rummaged through the pitch black compartments. I activated my night vision nanite. My dim eyes lit up with an iridescent jade, and as I searched for one of my synthetic black tops identical to the shredded cloth adorning my midriff, I recalled the last time I needed to activate my night vision implant: my fight with Al.

The circles of Dusk Territory revered Al's information network as peerless. The contact to which he referred me was someone Crelyos knew and someone that collected hyped. Al also claimed this man would know about Bradich. As I changed out of the shredded piece of cloth and used the parts of it untouched by bloodstains to wipe down my face and arms, I began piecing together the various information.

Why would Raze suddenly change his territory and begin collecting hyped? It must have been connected to Bradich. Perhaps Bradich was forcing Raze to collect hyped for him in exchange for the new territory? I no longer posed the question of what Raze wanted with the hyped; what did Bradich want with them? I tossed the old shirt onto the floor, tugged the new one over my head, deactivated my night vision implant, and hopped out the trailer. I emerged to Crelyos recounting our encounter in Loftsborough to Oswald.

"...And that's when we had to kill everyone." Crelyos finished the story with the same tone often used to express "and they lived happily ever after, the end." The doctor, apparently taken aback by Crelyos' matter-of-fact retelling of the events, threw up a hand to silence the former soldier.

"Wait, why did you have to kill everyone? You could have simply obtained the location of Raze's fortress and returned. If we eliminate Raze, I calculate the remaining bandits will disperse without qualm." Oswald placed a finger against his chin, no doubt mulling over the variables in his calculation.

"Doc, what reason would Bradich have to collect hyped?" I stepped forward with my inquiry, hoping to derail his mathematical equation.

"Well, we had to because Raze torched my friend with his pyro powers, so I got pissed and killed a couple and the rest decided they wanted to die too," Crelyos interjected with his own response. The clamorous conversation resulting from our simultaneous uproar forced Oswald to hold either hand up in our directions to cease us from rambling.

"A moment, please. Crelyos, pyrokinesis, which you adorably refer to as 'pyro powers,' doesn't exist. The very concept is preposterous. As a scientist closely following the development of radical superhuman abilities obtained through brain augmentation, I assure you the idea of manipulating an obscure energy source such as fire simply does not, nay, cannot exist. Perhaps he conceals a flamethrower of some kind and uses legerdemain to utilize it without the knowledge of his peers?" Oswald's voice trailed off; he went on a tangent as he used the hand previously lifted before Crelyos to ponderously rub his chin.

"What? That's bullshit, I've seen him do it. He waves his arms around like some sorta fairy and then—" Oswald cut Crelyos' protest short when he snapped his voice in signature fashion to address my inquiry.

"As for your question, Ihlia. I cannot begin to fathom the implications of collecting test subjects as unstable as the hyped. First of all, even if one were to consider using them for scientific advancements, they possess no control group. Each hyped is different, each symptom unique. Even if you gathered every hyperaugmented individual in the world, only a handful would possess similar enough characteristics to serve as a control group. If he's not utilizing them as test subjects, then I see absolutely no reason for involving oneself with the beasts." The doctor's last words possessed no hatred; in fact, the most fearful part of his description of the hyperaugmented was the apathetic manner in which he stated the word "beasts."

"Oy, I'm not entirely sure what yer saying, Fancypants, but if yer callin' me a liar then you and I need to have a chat. Over there. With our fists." Crelyos gestured off into the distance as though he wished to spare me the sight of Oswald being beaten like a school kid for his lunch money.

"Eh? I'm afraid these dusty old ears are unable to discern your words from your stupidity. Speak louder, dear boy— on second thought, speak quieter— tertiary thought, stop speaking. I'm afraid I can't piece together the formula that would explain your survival in this world for as long as you have. You're truly a marvel of science," Oswald chuckled.

"See here, drunkard, I'm not calling you a liar, I'm saying there's a trick to it. There has to be. I've only ever encountered one thing in this world that defies science, and pyrokinesis is not that thing." Oswald's jabs, as always, struck at the intellect or lack thereof, and though Crelyos' head was thicker than the plates of Loftsborough, I considered him fairly intelligent albeit in a simple, concise manner. As Crelyos' rage darkened his face several shades of crimson, I stepped between the two men and placed a hand against each of their chests.

“Boys, we still have a long way to drive. Shake your dicks off, pack your stuff, and let's get moving.” I offered each of them an “I'm serious” glare.

They jerked their heads away from one another. Crelyos spat, shoved his hands in his pockets and made his way to the passenger seat of the buggy; Oswald used his middle finger to press the bridge of his glasses up his nose, muttered under his breath, and took the driver's seat. I slid into the rear seats and folded my arms. After a few moments of awkward silence, we were zipping across the sands in the direction of Raze's fortress.

File 12: Crelyos's Past

"Crelyos... I've been meaning to ask you a couple of things," I raised my voice to overpower the popping engine as it guzzled the fresh batch of sludge dumped into its fuel receptor.

"Shoot, girly," Crelyos called back.

"How do you know Raze?" I leaned forward to listen better. I would have activated my auditory augment, but with the sputtering engine behind us, the crackling swoosh of the sand being ground beneath the giant tires, and the sharp whistle of icy wind whipping across my face, I decided against enduring an unnecessary, and ultimately unprofitable, headache.

"Eh, he was an old war buddy. When you and I got drunk, you spilled the beans about that merc faction you were part of. The ball-less eagles or something, right? Well Raze and I were in the military during that time. Back then though, we called him Smiles because he was always so damn optimistic. Army dogs, the three of us, and we were damn good at it." Crelyos tipped his head back and tossed out a few chuckles mostly swallowed by the rushing air.

"That's Bald Eagles," I retorted, "and three? You, Raze, and someone else?" I noticed his countenance shift from mild amusement to deeply depression.

"Aye, Sarge. He was our squad leader. But the three of us were kind of a squad within our squad. We were always the point men, the grunts, the first guys into a buildin' and the last ones out of it. Smiles was a good shot and a good fighter. In fact, when it came to knife fightin' he had no equal in our squad, and we were the best of the best. I was the muscle behind the outfit. Even though I couldn't best Smiles with a blade, when it came to hand-to-hand combat everyone was putty in my hands."

"I was a good shot; not phenomenal but my reflexes were quick and I showed no hesitation in my actions. I dunno why, maybe I got tossed into the air, hit the ceilin', dropped to the floor, and rolled out the window too many times as a youngin', but I understood somewhere that thinkin' meant dying. And I wasn't about to die." Crelyos leaned back in the seat and stared up at the growling clouds blanketing the cold night sky.

"Sarge? He was in a league of his own, though. The man was a tactical genius. He knew how to use every one of us to our fullest potential. And that was just a bonus; Sarge was a better shot than Smiles and I, could give me a run for my money in hand-to-hand combat, and go toe-to-toe with Smiles in melee weapon combat. His future in the military was brighter than the stars we don't see anymore," Crelyos smiled with unadulterated admiration.

But his countenance soon darkened, "Funny thing about Sarge, though; he told me over sludge several times how much he hated the military. I've never seen hatred like that for somethin' someone chose to do. It's like sayin' you hate sludge while you chug a barrel o' the stuff." Crelyos lifted a finger as though his observation was nothing short of genius.

"But Sarge is another story for another day." Crelyos curled and uncurled the fingers in his right hand, staring at them with a forlorn reminiscence and a vacant smile. Despite my powerful curiosity, I decided not to press the issue regarding Crelyos' squad leader. As the former soldier mentioned, it was another story for another day.

"The three of us got special orders for experimental augmentation. Some higher up jargon for makin' us guinea pigs. After the surgery, we were assigned to a special, three man team. Our debut mission involved infiltratin' a French encampment situated on a key supply line. As you're probably aware, there were no greater warriors than the French. They had the best nanites and the toughest troops. To assault one of their bases with just three individuals was suicide. The higher ups wanted to see how their prototype nanites operated," Crelyos sighed.

"Our experimental nanites were a top secret project that came from the research of a really famous scientist at the time. A guy that believed strongly in the nanites havin' personalities of their own. Doctor Lesfort, I think his name was. Actually, I think it might have been that Donovan guy you told me about when we got drunk together that one time, girly." Crelyos peered back to ascertain my reaction.

I offered him a blank stare. Though a twitch of emotion did contort the corner of my mouth at the mention of Donovan, the fact remained that Donovan led the field in experimental nanite technology based on his personality theories. For the military to make use of his knowledge failed to instill surprise; in fact, only Crelyos' referring to Donovan as "Doctor Lesfort" pinched any of my dormant emotions at all. As brothers, Donovan and Bradich shared the Lesfort surname, but any connection made between the two of them, family or not, churned the bitterness in the pit of my stomach.

"Apparently, the nanites were supposed to manifest unique abilities dependin' on what the AI programmin' felt would assist the user the most. We thought the mission was to see what kind of cool powers would manifest. Instead, it was a test to see if they would manifest at all. The infiltration was a disaster. When the combat finally heated up, only my nanite showed results. And let's just say they weren't optimum. Sarge and Smiles displayed no enhancements, and ultimately the mission failed." Crelyos stared at his right arm again.

"I've been meaning to inquire, dear boy, but what exactly is the secret behind your nanite? Since you won't allow me to operate on you and discern the cause behind your ability myself, perhaps you could at least alleviate my curiosity with a brief exposition?" Oswald interrupted.

"Vibratory Disintegration. That's how it was classified when we got back to base. The nanites respond to my will and store insane amounts of energy. Each nanite can hold thousands of times its size in energy, and there are hundreds of thousands of nanites that dock at that implant's particular hub. When directed to a certain part of my body, the nanites gather near the surface of my skin and, utilizin' impact, unleash the stored energy in the form of vibration waves."

"The waves're immensely powerful, but they're also sharp enough to penetrate and shake apart just about any substance down to its atom level. The stronger the impact used as a catalyst, the more intense the effect. In stupid terms, the harder I punch the bigger the crater. That's about the extent of what they figured out at the labs; the war and world ended before any further tests could be run." Crelyos ended his synopsis by dramatically clenching his right fist. Oswald's eyes widened; his scientific mind no doubt reeled with the concept of such an incredible implant. Even I understood the advanced nature of it.

"But that would mean..." Oswald's trailed off when I interjected to prevent him from nonsensically rambling.

"So, you used your new power to save the day and pull your comrades out of danger like some kind of hero?" I smirked and slapped my palm against Crelyos' left shoulder. He turned to me with a dopey smile and shook his head.

“Not even. They're the ones that saved me,” Crelyos erupted into laughter; however the echo of his voice cracked with a sense of nostalgia uncharacteristic of the blond mercenary. Though unable to place the feeling sinking into the pit of my chest, I subconsciously understood that Crelyos sat on the verge of tears.

“Ah, some things happened after that, and the project was ultimately called a failure since it only had a one-third success rate. Before the three of us could return to our squad, though, we received word that the war was endin' and our services would no longer be needed.”

“The rest is history, if you know what I'm sayin'. The Titan Crisis happened, and the three of us found ourselves wanderin' around when most other former military men went to work as guards for Dawn Territory, or became thugs in gangs roamin' around Dusk Territory,” Crelyos shrugged.

“We eventually went our separate ways. I wandered about for a while, and then ran into Smiles back when he was in the heart of Texas. I ran around with his gang for a bit just out of a sense of camaraderie. Apparently his nanite was just a late bloomer though, because his special nanite is what turned into his pyro powers.”

“He changed his name to Raze and has been ever since. Man, is he weird now though. That mission changed him, I know it did. Or maybe he just went crazy when his implant's power manifested...” Crelyos scratched the back of his head, “Anyway, that's the extent of my knowledge. I don't know what he has to do with Bradich or why he's collectin' hyped."

By the time Crelyos finished his story, the environment had vastly changed from the desert surrounding Loftsborough. Jagged cliffs rose from the cracked earth on either side of our vehicle. The sharp stones reached toward the darkened sky like fangs jutting from the bottom jaw of an under bite. One atop the other, the rock formations layered as an impassable barricade funneling our path toward Raze's fortress.

The wind screamed through the rocks as the air drew tight through the jagged spaces resembling pursed lips. In the distance, the incandescent dance of torchlight shaped the stony perimeter of Raze's enormous fortress. Like a tumor sticking out of the mountainous landscape, the giant bastion seemed like something straight from the ancient medieval era.

"Oswald, find a side path somewhere. We need to scout the—." I tapped the old man on the shoulder. As though he read my mind, Oswald interrupted my command and veered to the right the moment a path presented itself. The crusty grind of rubber tires against the decrepit soil flung loose bits of dust into the air when we abruptly stopped. Crelyos and I hopped from the buggy and marched up the top of one of the many steep slopes forming the teeth of the cliffs. A sharp whisper behind us stopped our advance.

"Now, now, don't think you can wander off and leave

me behind. I'll just tuck the buggy and trailer over here behind these rocks... Yes, yes I believe that's adequate." Oswald drove the dune buggy behind a larger spiked ridge and joined us atop the pointed slope. The soft clap of his hands as he dusted his palms echoed alongside his voice.

"I shall ascertain the nature of this trickster's power and prove that science trumps fantasy. After hearing your story, Crelyos, I can only imagine that your gullible nature obscured your reason and kept you from the truth. Vibratory Disintegration is one thing. While a bit farfetched, it is feasibly sound based on the description you offered. Pyrokinesis, however? Absurd. Ridiculous. Utterly impossible." Oswald shoved his hands into his lab coat's pockets and vigorously shook his head at the thought of what he believed to be outlandish mysticism.

"Whatever, Fancypants. You'll see," Crelyos responded.

Under normal circumstances, my annoyed command for them to both shut up would have sliced into their argument with merciless precision. Instead, I ignored them. My feet carried me to the peak of the jagged ridge on which we traveled. With a bird's eye view, I noted the road formed the valley separating the two towering cliffs. Before the Titan Crisis, one of Texas' many rivers, canals, or rivulets likely filled the barren valley and formed the state's natural borders. I marveled at the severity of geological changes scarring the world after ten years; whether the waters dried leaving the soil parched and barren or the rivers were redirected along another path, the former river became a highway to traverse the wastelands framed by jagged cliffs created by cleaving winds and acid rain.

The incessant thunder rumbling overhead set a dismal mood. I tucked loose strands of my hair behind my ear and activated my vision nanite. I stared the fifty-three hundred feet down the winding, makeshift highway to the looming fortress. The flickering torches illuminated several guards patrolling the stone walls of Raze's base; their garb and demeanor nearly matched the goons who infected Loftsborough. Many of them sported high powered rifles; given the sandy blacks and grays forming camouflaged patterns across the stocks and bodies of the firearms, I deduced that they were military grade.

Considering Crelyos' story, it seemed sensible to assume that Raze provided the wall's sentries with their firearms, and I surmised that most of the thugs in his bastion possessed military grade weapons as well. The few guards atop the wall without snipers toted submachine guns or assault rifles; only the two sentries overseeing the double door kept simple edged weapons of moderate length sheathed at their hips.

The door itself stood a monstrous thirty feet tall; its dull rusty iron formed a distinct contrast with the stone outcrops surrounding the fortress. An impressive overhang stretched above the hollowed out portion of the base containing the giant gateway. Raze's goons vigilantly guarded the iron portal while taking shelter from the elements beneath the overhang. A small pad with several numbered buttons was embedded in the left half of the giant door, but I noted that, if necessary, scaling the rigid walls remained a possible means of entry.

I stepped down off my perch and stared at Oswald and Crelyos, still bickering over the validity of pyrokinesis. Stepping between them, I raised either hand to their lips to hush them and explain Raze's security situation.

“Sounds about standard,” Crelyos nodded, “It's not much heavier or lighter than when I ran with them. So what, you wanna sneak in or bust our way through?”

“I believe utilizing stealth would be a most effective measure in this scenario,” Oswald nodded.

“I agree, we'll give that a shot. We need to wait, though.” I repositioned myself near the top of the ridge I formerly used to scout Raze's abode. Crelyos offered me a blank stare several feet below my perch.

“What? Wait for what? Aw man, I can't stand sittin' still without something to drink. I knew I should have brought another bag of sludge bottles,” Crelyos pouted and plopped to the ground.

Two hours passed, two hours full of Crelyos' impatient grumbles and squirms. Oswald had long since retreated to the buggy concealed behind a rocky ledge to resume his nanite creation, and I maintained a keen watch on the cracked road feeding into Raze's encampment. Finally, after the two long hours, my target appeared kicking dust up from large tires as it zoomed along the highway. A buggy similar in design to our dune buggy growled and shot toward the fortress with a caged trailer in tow. Though every buggy differed slightly in its hodgepodge mechanical design, the main difference resided in the color scheme. A flamboyant crimson and salmon pattern stretched across the buggy racing toward Raze's bastion.

I focused on the barred trailer, wondering what kind of cargo the buggy pulled. When a gnarled, pale hand shot from the trailer's confines accompanied by a vicious screech, I knew. They were pulling hyped. The howls of the hyperaugmented echoed through the valley from the trailer's barred confines. My enhanced telescopic gaze fixated on the double iron doors as the buggy skidded to a halt.

After one of the guards sauntered up, leaned toward the driver, and exchanged a few words, he offered the number pad's guardian a signal. I paid close attention to the order in which the guard pressed the numbers: "1337, followed by pound," I noted. As I descended from my perch, the pretentious vehicle coasted through the giant door after its sentries tugged the gate open with moderate effort.

"All right, gents, we're set." I gestured to the fortress. Crelyos leapt up and popped his knuckles. Oswald lingered a few moments with his nanites, sighed, then stood and offered me a resolved nod.

File 13: Raze's Fortress

We slowly crept along the jagged valley the remaining mile to Raze's stronghold. Though Crelyos protested waiting idly for me to discern the door's code, his military training placed him right at home in the field of subtle infiltration. His gait's silence rivaled my own as we stalked from one stone protrusion to the next, and we would have remained as undetectable as phantoms if not for the soft click and clack of Oswald's shoes. In fairness, the good doctor attempted to remain covert, but his lack of any formal training left much to be desired in the art of stealth.

Thankfully, the jagged outcrops of rock provided adequate concealment to deter the visual acuity of our enemies. To prevent audio detection, I lifted my fist when we approached within fifty yards of the iron gate. I gestured to Oswald and pointed at the ground; he nodded. I gestured to Crelyos, lifted a thumb toward the two guards in front of the iron door, then ominously dragged that thumb across my throat; he grinned.

I prowled low through the darkness like a feral stalker. A studious glance at the fortress walls informed me which thugs used telescopic sights on their rifles and likely did not possess visual enhancements, and which of the bandits utilized only iron sights. Those using rifles with only iron sights possessed an increased chance of a vision augment, which would certainly place a damper on our stealth operation. As such, I took mental note and avoided their line of sight. My trajectory carried me to the walls surrounding the castle a few yards to the left of the cove housing the iron door. The indention likely served as a roof to shelter the guards from the elements. The thought struck me that it was an awfully kind gesture for a crime lord to implement.

I gripped the bumpy protrusions poking from the hewn wall. With my petite figure and enhanced muscles, scaling the rocky surface was no more difficult than strolling down a street. As I crawled along the vertical surface like a black widow, my motions carried me up and across the wall; I stopped just above the indent leading to the iron door. I flattened my body horizontally across the stones before digging my fingers and feet into the bumpy protuberances. Below, I overheard the guards' casual conversation.

“Man, I'm so bored. Jet, let's get a drink after this. Then maybe we can hitch a ride down to Raze's Haven; oh man, I bet the girls there are in their prime! We'll just snag us a few and have our way with them!” The sound of the chattering sentinel's playful punch was closely followed by its recipient's sigh.

“Biggs, we go through this every night. Every night it's the same thing, ‘let's go pick up chicks man’ blah blah. But just like last night and the night before, we're gonna get done and you're gonna drink until you pass out, and I'm the one that's gonna to have to carry you to the barracks. I don't understand why you have to be 'that guy,'" the man allegedly called Jet responded in a monotonous, annoyed tone.

"Aw, seriously? You gotta call me 'that guy'? That's fucked, man, really fucked, I can't believe..." Their conversation continued. At that point the exchanged words were irrelevant considering I fully prepared to spice up their night. I would ensure I was all the "chick" they could handle. I held my position and awaited Crelyos' move.

Crelyos had followed close at my heel until I began scaling the wall. At that point, the hulking mercenary slithered against the wall toward the cove like a serpent. When he stood poised at the edge of the overhang and I hung securely above, we initiated our attack. Crelyos rounded the corner, stepping from the shadows directly behind Jet and into the view of the chattering Biggs; the thug's eyes popped in his skull and he gripped his blade tightly.

His surprised countenance drew the scrutiny of his comrade, but before Biggs' lips parted to issue the sharp warning that would have no doubt closely resembled "Jet look out behind you," I gracefully dropped from the overhang. My body twisted and my knees parted as I slammed into a knelt position atop Biggs' shoulders. I wedged his opened mouth and shocked facade snug between my thighs facing my hips. I briefly wondered if the sight of my tightly drawn leather pants contouring to my figure provided a pleasing final sight, or if the inky black which suddenly descended upon him induced a nightmarish finale to his life.

My sudden drop surprised Jet, who gripped his sword in response to his comrade's unfortunate plight. His mouth dropped open, no doubt to elicit a protest, until Crelyos' massive palm clamped over his lips. My blonde comrade's free hand tightened around Jet's shoulder for leverage and he twisted the poor man's head so hard I cringed when the rapid series of neck-cracks reached my ears. At the same time, I twisted my hips with an alluring brutality that conjured similar crunches from my target's vertebrae. As the base of their necks simultaneously snapped and their limp bodies collapsed to the ground, I approached the keypad on the colossal iron door.

“1337, pound,” I muttered in time with my button mashes. As the small strip above the numbers flickered green, a series of sparks sprayed from the panel in conjunction with a solid thunk. I assumed the sound represented the mechanical lock disengaging. Crelyos reached forward and gripped the door's handle with his left hand. The minor augment responsible for enhancing his muscles offered him little assistance, but the natural swell of bulging muscles he acquired through rigorous training provided all the force necessary. He pulled the door ajar with a haunting creak until a large enough gap formed to allow our company passage. Crelyos and I exchanged nods before separating.

Crelyos slid into the fortress, and I poked my petite frame from the overhang to wave Oswald over. The doctor was no fool; given his inability to move quietly, his path mimicked ours with precise steps. The old man's memory served him well, but his footwork betrayed him. During the final stretch toward the iron door, Oswald tripped and the loud clacking of stones falling in disheveled clumps around his fallen frame forced me into impetuous action. The chance the thugs patrolling the walls above us were not privy to the blatant ruckus caused by our lovably clumsy doctor was nonexistent.

I hastily dove from beneath the overhang and twisted my outstretched body to face the fifty feet of walled rock that stretched overhead. At the same time, I ripped my long daggers from their sheaths. I stared intently toward the top of the wall and activated my Cognitive Accelerator. Years of experience and proper learning from the best fighters in our mercenary squad helped me distinguish the order in which I should kill my foes. As I prepared to single out the rifle toting scum with enhanced perception, I found that only a single target stood atop the wall. In my mind's perspective, I slowly drew back my arm and prepared to toss the deadly dagger at... Crelyos? I deactivated my accelerator before my shoulders slammed into the ground with a painful thud.

“What are you two doin'? Stop playin' around and get in here,” he hissed and tossed two corpses, clutched in his left and right hands, to the ground. I quickly rose, brushed the pebbles away from my clothes, re-sheathed my long daggers, and offered my hand to Oswald. The doctor accepted the assistance while readjusting his glasses which had sloped to one side of his face during his nasty spill.

“Yes, quite,” Oswald stated simply. I rolled my eyes and we returned to the slim crack in the mighty iron doors.

At such times I pondered the true depth of Crelyos' tactical mind. While certainly possible, the chance that our brawny ally blindly annihilated guard after guard before unintentionally ending his rampage on the wall at the precise moment we needed him closely approached the “no fucking way” end of my rationale spectrum. Crelyos far more likely followed his chosen course based on quick strategic insight. He knew Oswald lacked our stealth capabilities, and he instinctively adapted his attack pattern in order to compensate for that weakness. Just how much of a tactician's mind was Crelyos hiding behind his gruff facade?

The moment I crossed the threshold into Raze's fortress, an overpowering stench threatened to knock me flat on the ground. I instinctively slapped my hand over my nose. It was sludge. The odor of the synthetic, high powered fuel permeated the air of the entire compound like a thick miasma. I quickly staggered to a nearby wall cloaked in shadow. I needed to conceal myself while I gagged back the urge to vomit. Oswald failed to choke it back, much to the waste of any food he ingested over the course of the day. After a few seconds, our noses adjusted to the potent smell and we began breathing.

Crelyos leapt from his position atop the wall; he

obviously finished eliminating the poor saps unlucky enough to be stationed on guard that night. By coiling his legs as he landed to absorb his momentum and placing his palm against the ground to soften the thud, his bulky frame created virtually zero disturbance when he impacted. I was surprised, half by the silent landing and half by the giant dopey grin plastered on his face.

"Do you not smell that atrocious fetor? How in the world are you capable of standing, let alone pouncing around like a —" Doctor Oswald whispered through the cup of his hand covering both mouth and nostrils. Crelyos immediately interrupted the good doctor.

"Mmm... What is that? Makes me thirsty." Crelyos inhaled deeply, filling his lungs with the odor saturating the fortress. I shook my head and held my hand up to signal silence.

I examined the top of the wall peppered with open flame torches and twitched my brow, annoyed at Raze's obvious recklessness. Either the man possessed extraordinary luck or the brain of a mathematical genius. The flames flickered and danced just outside the range of the sludge's explosive fumes. I shifted my gaze to the compound's interior to seek out the sludge's source. I expected to find massive fuel reservoirs or open containers overflowing with the inky liquid, but no, the powerful odor wafted from two enormous hangars situated on either side of the compound.

From the safety of the shadows, I further noted that the

scarce light fixtures dotting the inside of Raze's compound possessed a luminescent quality as opposed to the torchlight lining the tops of the walls. Rather than illumination through heated lamps or fire, the bulbs used gas vapors similar to florescent lights. I thought florescent technology vanished after the Titan Crisis, but it would have certainly solved the safety problem of irresponsibly storing such large quantities of fuel in a single place.

Besides the two hangars storing an incalculable amount of sludge and the archaic stone wall, a surprisingly militaristic organization dominated the compound's layout. The lights, though scarce, maximized the compound's illuminated surface area through carefully selected placement. Two sets of barracks lined the far back corners in perfect array, combining a seamless blend of aesthetics and efficient space management. With a quick estimate, I figured at least fifty men would be able to lodge comfortably within their confines.

Toward the front corner of the compound, a large warehouse shrouded in darkness towered over the hangars which stored fuel and coupled as our shadowy hideaway. I cautiously slid up the building's metallic surface and peered into one of the windows. Dune buggies lined the warehouse's interior along with several empty spaces where dune buggies would no doubt park once they returned from their forays.

In the opposite corner of the compound roughly fifty yards from our location, another large warehouse stood against the perimeter wall. As I focused on it, three men emerged from its confines and slid the enormous door shut behind them. After locking it down with a large iron pad lock, they began conversing and walking toward a long rectangular building positioned in the center of the massive courtyard. I activated my auditory enhancing nanite to eavesdrop on their conversation.

"That oughta hold 'em just fine until *Duc* Raze comes to get 'em. Let's rustle up some grub. I hear the cook's figured out a new way to fry up some of that starch," One of the men laughed.

"Say, what do you suppose the *Duc* does with all those hyped anyway? They're here one minute, then gone the next." Another of the men looked back toward the locked warehouse. With my enhanced hearing, I detected the muffled sounds of guttural howls and enraged grunts. They undoubtedly belonged to the harvest of hyped I witnessed earlier when I acquired the passcode to enter Raze's domain. The feral sounds emanated from the padlocked warehouse. "What a fancy prison..." I thought.

"Who cares... if all we have to look forward to is Chef's starchy gruel I'd rather just head to bed." The third thug yawned and rubbed the back of his neck. His two comrades laughed.

The crunching of gravel beneath boots reached my ears. The sound was close, so I instinctively whipped my hand to the side and forced Crelyos and Oswald flat against the vehicle warehouse. Within a few seconds a man emerged from around the corner. The manner in which he rotated his shoulders suggested he drove the vehicle and ached from a long day of holding up his arms. As he closed the distance between himself and his three friends, he called out to them.

"Hey you three, heading to the chow hall so soon?" The man's words were laced with a grunted chuckle.

"Yeah, come join us," One of the three cried out and gestured toward the building in the center with his thumb.

"You know we have to relieve the guard for the next few hours." The man a few yards from us crossed his arms and shook his head. His three companions groaned and gripped their foreheads.

"*Duc* Raze is working us like slaves! Come on! We're hungry!" They grumbled.

"I know, but you know we're spread thin right now with all the hyped hunting parties. Those guards haven't been able to eat either. We'll get our turn. Teamwork, gents, teamwork! Haha! By the way, how many of the Raze Haven menfolk raiders came back?" The man attempted to change subjects; he was likely trying to take the men's minds off food.

"Ugh, you had to remind me," One of the three distant bandits exclaimed as they all began walking toward the wall, "I've gotta babysit one of those groups tomorrow. Such bullshit."

As the men neared the staircase leading to the top of the wall, I exchanged a glance with Crelyos. He nodded, and we rushed across the dusty earth in the direction of the group. Our footfalls were like the hushed sound of fingernails drumming atop paper mache. By the time the three men sauntering in our direction noticed our approach, we reached the man with his back to us.

A commotion atop the wall itself halted the alarmed eruption of their voices. From the corner of my eye, I noted three guards at the wall's apex gathering together. Two of them seemed to be pointing down the other side of the wall where Crelyos had dropped the corpses of his previous victims; one rushed to the edge facing us and cried aloud, "Quick, sound the alarm! We have intruders! The other guards up here were killed!"

"Everything just got a lot more complicated," I thought as I closed in on my target.

File 14: The Duke of Flame

Apparently, the patrols rotated wide enough that even sentries from the other side of the wall eventually circled around to the side with the iron door. Frustrated, I continued to the men Crelyos and I marked as our prey. When I reached my particular target, I clenched my teeth and drove my foot into the back of the unsuspecting man's leg in perfect timing with the call to sound the alarm. His body gave from the force of my blow, and he dropped to a knee. I used momentum to propel myself over his surprised figure and toward his three friends. I tore my twin daggers free of their sheaths and twisted them so the blades faced down during my descent. As the three men struggled to free their firearms, the two closest to one another and in my direct path met a quick end. I shoved either blade down through the tops of their heads, simultaneously freeing both men from their mortal coil and cushioning the impact of my fall.

Behind me, as soon as the man serving as my catapult dropped to a knee with a “Hey, what the—” Crelyos arrived and gripped the back of his head in his right hand. The sound of Crelyos' nanite became clear to me then, the crackle of vibration building up through his right arm tickled my heightened audio senses. He slammed the man's face into the dirt, and the exchange of force transferred the millions of units of stored vibration through Crelyos' palm and into the bandit's cranium. The explosive thud marked the discharge, and the spray of the man's brains and blood became the finished product. Though it still seemed rather mystical to me, understanding what transpired for the first time birthed a powerful sense of respect for Crelyos' capabilities.

The man on the wall gasped and gestured for his two allies to rush over while he synchronously aimed his rifle in my direction. The last man alive on the ground finished drawing his submachine gun with shaky hands and trained it on my body. I resolved myself to endure the pain of his hail of bullets and retrieved my daggers from the heads of his friends. “You monster!” he screamed.

The sound likely would have marked the moment his finger squeezed the trigger, but though I steeled myself to accept the pain of his revenge, I found myself pleasantly disappointed when a flying, headless corpse rammed into his body. As he toppled to the ground with a distinct “oof,” I glanced over to see Crelyos poised as though he had lobbed a beach ball. I wasted no time in plunging my dagger through the fallen man's skull, “Sorry, you're out,” I whispered as I twisted the dagger and yanked it free.

“Crelyos, the wall!” I called out. The man brandishing a rifle finished taking careful aim at my forehead. I harbored few qualms with preparing myself for a hail of nine millimeter rounds to the body, but a high-powered round to the forehead was a headache for which there was no ointment.

"On it!" Crelyos called back and rushed toward the fortification's perimeter. I followed in hot pursuit; I flipped both daggers around in my palm so the blades faced skyward. Just as the first man prepared to depress the trigger, one of his friends reached up and gripped his rifle.

"Hey, you know we can't fire that into the base! *Duc* Raze's orders! It could ignite his sludge!" The first man jerked his firearm away and took aim once again.

"The others almost lit this place up with submachine gun fire! It'll be fine!" He growled at his cautious ally.

"Yeah, but they didn't! They got iced, and it's a good thing, too! They could have blown us to hell!" His ally retorted.

"We don't have time for that! We have to alert the base anyway!" He shouted at his comrade.

"Then fire it into the air, stupid!" The "duh," look that crossed the man's face as he shouted was priceless. Unfortunately for them, their hesitation would prove a fatal mistake.

After reaching the wall, Crelyos leapt as high as he could and attached his enormous hands to its jagged surface. As he hung, he twisted his head and shouted back in my direction, "Ihlia! Alley-oop!"

I understood even without his ancient terminology. The moment he drove his hands into the rock and the crumble of dislodged stones assured me of his secure grip, I activated my Supersoldier nanite and used my strengthened legs to launch up the side of the wall. The power of my propulsion granted me enough height to plant my feet onto his shoulders. With a second spurt of power, I leapt the remaining twenty feet needed to clear the top of the wall.

The brief second my face hovered mere inches from the enemy sniper's, I beheld in great detail the horrified lines of despair running like veins across his skin. After that second passed, however, I sailed over the top of his head and swiftly curled my body into a ball. I turned a front flip above him, and as my legs circled around, I flexed my ankles and drilled the heels of my boots into the center of his spine. Using him as a platform, I launched toward his two surprised allies like a rocket; unfortunately, a platform is generally far sturdier than a human body.

For every action, physics demanded an equal and opposite reaction. As I vaulted forward, the unfortunate man serving as my springboard cried out and toppled over the side of the wall. I passed between the two remaining guards and drew my arms across them in a blinding flash. The sing of steel as it cut through their throats left the two men gurgling. Try as they might using both hands, they were unable to stop the geyser of crimson life force spurting from their necks. To ensure their demise and end their suffering, I spun both blades around to face behind me and swung my arms back. The blades sunk into their brain stems with little resistance.

The shouts of the man who fell from the wall were stopped shortly after; I assumed Crelyos leapt from the wall to meet the flailing man midair. The former soldier's hand likely encompassed the thug's entire face, and as Crelyos descended he probably activated his nanite. The impact with the ground would be unfortunate for Raze's minion, for as Crelyos previously noted, the harder the impact, the stronger the vibrations transferred. The dull thunk that resulted from the strong chance that he drove the man's face into the ground ceased any further noise. I gingerly hopped from the wall myself and landed with the same grace Crelyos displayed the first time he landed; though given my small stature and light body, I was far quieter.

"Oh shit... oh damn, oh man. Intruders, what do I do? That's right, push this button... the alarm, yep." Crelyos and I looked over to see a frantic bandit inching toward a giant red button near the vehicle hangar. I gritted my teeth; just when we succeeded in salvaging our stealth operation? That guy. No matter how far into the future mankind progressed, "that guy" would forever remain a cause for ire.

The man's finger quivered, but right before it reached the button, the soft sound of metal piercing flesh stopped him dead in his tracks. My brows relaxed, and I offered a few surprised blinks to the man; his tongue lolled from his mouth, and he muttered a few lines of drunken gibberish before collapsing to the ground. Oswald was left standing behind him holding an empty syringe.

"By Jove, it actually worked," Oswald crossed his arms quizzically and stared at the needle between his fingers. Crelyos notably cringed.

The doctor continued, "I was saving this for our impertinent blond comrade if we ever needed to render him unconscious. It's an experimental serum designed to induce sleep and shut down Panacea more efficiently than current formulas. I've been working on a new formula designed to bypass, or trick, the activation programming of the nanite's AI more quickly to allow surgeons like myself to begin operating much sooner than current nanite anesthetics allow. Didn't expect such smashing results on a first attempt, though. Astonishing." Oswald's self-satisfied smile was almost creepy.

"Fancypants, shh. Honestly." Crelyos began rubbing his arms as though the cold weather cut through his skin. I knew better. Crelyos despised needles and anything related to them. With Panacea, most vaccinations were a thing of the past, so even as a military man he had rarely experienced the bite of a needle. I wondered if needles and other pointy objects remained part of the reason Crelyos refused to allow Oswald operational privileges on him.

After terminating the unconscious "that guy," our group decided that swiftness was key. We held no knowledge as to the guard rotation schedule or the next time a hyped raiding party was due to return. Subtlety and haste would prove our closest allies, but as we rounded the corner and started across the main courtyard, the sight before us gave me pause. Behind the large rectangular chow hall, an ostentatious building similar in design to the houses in Loftsborough towered like a mansion over the other structures in the fortress. I understood what Mayor Trumark meant when he claimed Raze revised their entire architecture. The inspiration for the strange abodes in Loftsborough was clearly that giant attempt at "artistecture."

"Yep, that's his house. He calls it his chateau." Crelyos seemed completely unaffected by its appearance.

If the combination of blocked corners, random unnecessary arches, and asymmetrical spires jutting from random areas of the roof were not enough to conjure a gag reflex, then the color scheme would assuredly do the trick. Blinding white swirls colored the foundation of the house just below the first floor windows. The yellow columns supporting the roof matched the rest of the first level up to the second story windows. Above that, gaudy florescent red paints that I thought no longer existed splattered the remaining height of Raze's dwelling; the entire pallete looked like the crime lord had offered a paint bucket to a toddler. The most sickening part was that, despite the horrible presentation, I was able to discern that Raze wanted to portray his house as a roaring fire.

"Let's just get this over with..." I placed a hand on my

forehead, and our group returned to its stealthy infiltration. We passed the chow hall with relative ease, and as the general population of Raze's gang either slept, ate, or died, slipping into his chateau proved as easy as opening the door and sauntering inside. The smell of sludge diminished considerably, but a mix of lingering grime and a synthetic concoction resembling old world perfume replaced it. I honestly felt, for a moment, that the odor outside seemed more inviting. The interior of Raze's sanctuary differed little from its exterior. With the flamboyant colors and pseudo-artistic patterns decorating the walls, I understood why Crelyos claimed the man suffered from madness.

"Hm, I don't like it. Way too easy to get in; last time I was here he had the place crawlin' with guards." Crelyos scratched his chin as we continued inside.

The main hall in which we stood consisted of an enormous open floor; it reminded me of an ancient ballroom dancing hall like the ones in antique Victorian mansions showed to us in historical films. Situated above the expansive floor, a second story accessed by ornate, curved staircases on opposite ends of the room loomed overhead. A long, polished steel table stretched across the balcony; atop its surface sat several stone bowls of salvaged nonperishable rare foods, and in the center of the table, a large container sat with an open lid. The faint smell of sludge seeped from it.

Toward the back of the elevated balcony, several monitors lined the wall displaying every nook and cranny of the compound which we just invaded. I even noted the corpses of several men lying dead on the screens. Surveillance systems? Oh no, that meant that our surprise attack was actually...

The sound of methodic applause interrupted my thoughts. A man seemed to float from his seat at the end of the table toward the rail designed to prevent an individual from a nasty fall off the balcony. When he stood, he slid slender fingers around a fine steel chalice embroidered with dirty but nevertheless impressive gemstones. As his free hand came to rest against the rail, his form was illuminated in all its androgynous glory. Long tresses of blond hair more silken than my own flowed about his shoulders. His bangs, parted to one side to dramatically cover one of his crystal blue eyes, defied gravity as they bounced with his every breath.

He donned a white suit with a red shirt beneath, and bright scarlet frills framed his entire ensemble. Frills jutted from his collar; frills jutted from his wrist and ankle cuffs; frills even jutted from his leather belt. Attached to the fancy belt, a strap holding a rapier sat in perfectly poised position against his hip. His black shoes shined like obsidian and even possessed a makeshift buckle and strap.

“Felicitations, mon ami! I knew zat your head was more zhen just a place to hold zat pretty face, oui?” His voice made me cringe. In fact, every time a morbidly forced 'z' replaced one of his 'th' sounds, I died a little inside. The accent was not merely fake; it was abysmally fake. I shook my head and stepped forward.

"Raze, I take it? You were watching us?" I gestured to the monitors. "It's impressive that you have surveillance equipment that still works. But why didn't you sound an alarm or prepare for our arrival or something? What's your angle?" I folded my arms at my midriff and waited.

"Eh, Crelyoz? Who iz zis little wench who darez to speak out of line? Sacrebleu, zee nerve of intruderz in zis day and age. It iz enough to drive a man abzolutely crazy." The man flipped his hair, a motion he accompanied with an indignant hand gesture and slow sip from his silver goblet. I clenched my jaw and tried to remain patient.

"Uh. You got cameras, Raze. Why didn't you try to stop us if you knew we were comin'?" Crelyos repeated my question with an arched brow.

"Ah, zat iz a most intelligent queztion, mon ami. I alwayz knew you were zharp as a tack, haha!" Raze pressed his fingertips to his lips before extending his hand toward Crelyos. To my surprise, the former soldier leapt aside as though seriously attempting to dodge some unseen projectile. My patience grew thinner by the minute. Raze continued.

"Oh, my. Where are my mannerz? You are zee one zey call Doctor Ozwald, oui? Bienvenue to my humble chateau!" Raze bowed then opened his arms to gesture to the entirety of his mansion, "as for your queztion, mon ami, the answer iz zimple. I dezired entertainment. You provided it for moi. It becomez so boring around here, you zee." Raze tossed a wink toward the two men.

"Enough. I want information, and I want it now," I reached for my rifle, spun it over the top of my slender shoulder, and took aim at our alleged host. "How do I find Bradich, and why are you collecting hyped?" I growled.

"Hm, mon ami... I believe zat your dog iz barking. I do not zpeak canine, but I can surmize from zee rifle zat zhe planz to fire if you do not rub her belly or somezing. I would warn her of zee dangerz of firearmz in my prezence if you wish for her armz to remain intact, Crelyoz." Raze seemed completely undisturbed by the business end of my rifle. Crelyos placed a hand on my shoulder as if to say, "calm down, girly."

"Raze, we need info. Why are you collectin' hyped for Bradich? How do we get to Bradich? That's the whole reason we're here. So just go ahead and let us know and we can put this messy business behind us," Crelyos stepped forward.

"Zo allow me to get zis straight. You break into my fortrezz, kill mozt of my guardz, zneak into my chateau, and zhen expect me to offer you information?" Raze placed one of his elongated fingernails between his teeth and scrunched up his face, "I knew I liked you for a reazon, mon ami. You are just zo brazen and demanding. Zuch fine qualitiez in a man." Raze turned and leaned his rear against the rails.

"Unfortunately, I cannot give you zee anzwers you zeek. You zee, I do not know where Bradich iz, though I am aware zat I am ultimately working for zat ravizhing man. You are miztaken on one point. I am not collecting hyped directly for Bradich. I am collecting zhem for Sarge." Raze turned his face just enough to ascertain what manner of response he invoked in Crelyos.

He was not disappointed; Crelyos' face contorted with a combination of curiosity, shock, and rage. His lips parted, and he shouted up toward his old military friend, "Sarge is workin' with Bradich, too? What the hell, where is he? How can I find him?"

"Non, non, non," Raze said synchronously with three wags of his finger, "zat iz all zee information you shall get from me. Unlezz, of courze, you can provide me wiz even more entertainment, haha!" As if by command, every door in the room burst open and a flood of guards dashed in to surround us. I twisted my head in observation. They outnumbered us by quite a radical ratio, especially taking into account Oswald's poor combat capabilities. I shouldered my rifle and sighed.

"I guess it's just going to be one of those nights..."

File 15: Ballroom Blitz

"I believe this may be too obvious an observation, dear compatriots, but it would appear that we've been surrounded." Oswald's ability to remain calm in situations others would consider dire resonated through his voice during his tasteless quip.

"Ya think? Man, you're the dumbest smart guy I ever met." Crelyos' battle stance failed to waver even as he served the doctor blatant sarcasm.

I held fast to my rifle and glared at Raze, the grand orchestrator standing above his deranged symphony. The assortment of bandits encasing us in a circle of death displayed all the same fashions and attitudes of their fallen allies: pretentious red and white clothing, ugly gritty faces contorted with the anticipation of slaughtering us, and that damned flame tattoo permanently marring their right cheeks.

For some unexplainable reason, after actually meeting the haughty crime lord, the tattoo started annoying the living hell out of me. I parted my lips to speak, but I was interrupted when a scrawny thug stepped forward and reverently lowered to one knee. A red scarf concealed the lower portion of his face, and a head full of messy, haphazard dread locks hung low. He likely took a knee to show Raze some kind of due respect. I rolled my eyes.

"M-my lord, I a-apologize for my blunder. To think these l-low level m-miscreants were able to bypass s-security, I take f-full responsibility!" Obviously in charge of security or some high ranking officer in their pretend caste, the shivering thug clenched his eyes shut and delivered his profuse apology. I would have pegged him as suffering from a speech impediment if not for his apparent apprehension. He slapped both hands together in front of his head in a pathetic begging motion, "P-please forgive me, Duke Raze!"

My eyes traveled to and fro between the remorseful minion and his apathetic master. Each word aimed at degrading us that reached Raze's ears pulled the corner of his lips into a wider smile. Just before the bandit's final appeal, I noticed Raze lift his hand dismissively as though preparing to, in his boundless grace and mercy, forgive the insignificant human of his egregious transgression.

Suddenly, however, his countenance morphed. The slow building Cheshire cat grin sank like an iron weight into a callous frown. Raze's exposed crystal blue eye, once the picture of merciful salvation, darkened with the vehemence of the perpetually black sky. Raze lifted his hands before his body and began swirling them about one another ceremonially. The movements resembled the theatrical motions used by magicians to capture the attention of their audience. The bandit reacted immediately.

"No! Your eminence! Your grace! Please have mercy, I

beg you! I don't want to die! Please!" The man was on the verge of tears. His companions all murmured amongst themselves, phrases ranging between "By the stars we no longer see, not Mortimor," and "He done fucked up!" stirred the suspenseful atmosphere. I returned my gaze to Raze, and for the first time since our encounter, the amazement he instilled in me stemmed from wonder rather than disappointment.

"It iz *Duc*! You impertinent zwine!" Raze ended the extravagant motions of his hands and snapped his fingers. The instant sound of roaring flames elicited a tortured scream from the apologetic minion. In the very moment Raze snapped his fingers, the man spontaneously combusted. Flames twisted around his body from head to toe and wasted no time consuming hair, clothing, and flesh.

The man's coat of fire took less than a minute to reduce him to a hissing pile of charcoal. During the course of the unpleasant bonfire, I noted another extraordinary quality of Raze's flame: It grew over the duration of that minute. Rather than die down as less of the man's body was left to burn, the flames intensified like someone tossed fresh heaps of wood atop him. For the first time in a long time, my jaw dropped a little. The entire room observed absolute silence following the grim execution. After a few moments, a robust voice awkwardly cut through the air.

"I told you, Fancypants! I told you he has pyro powers!" Crelyos roared and began frantically pointing at the unfortunate victim's charred remains. I glanced to Oswald; even his jaw had dropped. Crelyos' voice snapped him from his stupor, however, and the doctor lifted a finger to push his glasses up the bridge of his nose.

"Yes, ahem, well. Clearly there is a logical explanation for this occurrence. And it's pyrokinesis, you buffoon." The gleam off the doctor's glasses hid his eyes. I suspected that beneath the reflective light, those eyes darted left and right as he scrambled to provide a satisfactory reason for Raze's encroachment on his concepts of reality.

"Whatever, it's 'I was right, you were wrong.' That's what it is," Crelyos puffed out his chest. I steeled my resolve and turned my attention back toward the man with the unique ability to conjure flames from the air. As I clenched my teeth, I realized that if we were unable to end the man quickly, all the efforts of our infiltration would go up in smoke. Literally. Of course, considering the familiar hatred that stirred in the pit of my chest, I had another reason for wanting to end him without delay.

'Are you going to argue all zee night long? Zer' iz no reazon to fight, monzieurs, zer' is quite enough of me to go—" Raze's eyes widened. With the swiftness in which I excelled, I raised my rifle into a firing position. I trained the iron sights on Raze's forehead and depressed the trigger without hesitation. No sooner had the cacophonous crack echoed throughout the ballroom, than something felt horribly awry in my right arm. The sound of smashing glass followed by buzzing electricity drifted down from the balcony; the bullet found its new home in one of the monitors against the back wall.

Raze had swerved his head to the left with enough regal grace that the bullet merely passed by his cheek. Several strands of blond hair fluttered down from the balcony, and after a few seconds passed, a thin strip of blood seeped from a small gash along the side of his face. I only grazed him, and based on the wrathful glare that emanated from his eyes, it pissed him off. But I was sure it was nothing compared to the disgust swelling in the pit of my stomach after watching him kill one of his own.

"Treacherous snake..." I mumbled.

"Enough of zis. Kill zem." Raze dismissively waved his hand as though he merely gave an order to take out the trash. In his mind, that was probably exactly what he did..

I slung my rifle into place against my back and tugged my long daggers free. My body instinctively inched toward the doctor; I regretted allowing him to accompany us. Protecting myself and Oswald at the same time would prove nigh impossible. A grim smile found its way to my lips when I attempted to recall the last time I felt so alive due to almost certain death. I swiveled my head and offered the old codger a glance from the corner of my eye.

"So, Doc, what are our odds?" The thugs roared their

approval of Raze's orders. Their thunderous clamor rattled the walls as they began their brutal charge. My mind drowned the blustering cries into a sound that resembled distant waves crashing against the shore. The advancing bandits blurred as I focused my gaze solely on the good doctor whose glasses still reflected too much light to reveal his eyes. He grinned up at me.

“Do you want our chances of victory or our ETD?” He asked. The silence hung in the air like a cracked glass table. Our conversation was as a thumb tack descending in slow motion toward it.

“ETD?” I inquired with a soft chuckle.

“Estimated time of death.” He tilted his head up toward me, revealing his eyes. They radiated confidence.

‘Oh, perfect.” The words that escaped my lips were the tack's collision against the glass table. They became the catalyst, refocusing the image of the bandits and transforming their cries from a distant wave to a deafening tsunami. The time for talking and thinking passed; our options were to die or fight and still, probably, die. I preferred the second option sans the death, but beggars could not be choosers.

The first thug approached; his right fist, buried in a heavy steel gauntlet, arched wide overhead aimed toward my slightly uplifted face. Unfortunately, his inexperience betrayed him; his shoulders generated the lion's share of his power, and it threw him off balance. I stepped to the outside of his attack while offering gentle pressure to the back of his armored forearm with my blade. Its twin sank into the side of his neck as he passed by, pausing only briefly when the tip rammed against his spine just beneath his skull. The crunch following the pause sent the crimson-painted tip out the other side of his neck, and he relinquished a brief, choked gasp before his sudden death.

I withdrew both daggers and allowed the oaf to slump to the ground. A prickle at the back of my neck drew my attention; as I spun, I instinctively criss-crossed my blades above my head. An attacker's sword viciously clanged against my impromptu parry. I exerted tremendous effort, enough to push his sword up and away from its dangerous position, and brutally front-kicked his exposed chest. The precise activation of my muscle enhancer strengthened the blow enough to conjure the sound of several cracked ribs and a shattered sternum from his chest. The unfortunate man flew backward into a group of his companions who began trampling over him with little remorse.

I turned to see Oswald shrinking into a corner; at the moment his apparent plan to remain as obscure as possible seemed to be working. The ruffians took far more interest in the blood waiting to be drawn from Crelyos and me. My blond companion seemed right at home in such a brawl. When a goon gripped a dagger in both hands and charged toward Crelyos aiming for his chest, the former soldier dipped to the side at the last second. He lifted his right fist at the same time, and the solid thunk of Crelyos' forceful punch resounded throughout the room. The soft buzz of transferred motion sent a gooey explosion of disintegrated flesh spraying from all directions of the thug's midsection. I returned my attention to my immediate surroundings.

Another combatant drew close for a chance to take my head; his hand gripped a thick metal shaft connected to a wide axe head. His wide, horizontal attack swept the broad wedge toward the base of my neck. Unfortunately for him, the dangerous properties of an axe were mostly illusory. While the entire breadth of the weapon's attack appeared threatening, the bladed edge retained the only substantial threat to one's life. And much like the kick of a man with extraordinarily long legs, revealing its weakness was as simple as darting forward toward the source of the assault.

I immediately closed the gap between us, drove both my blades into the center of the man's chest, and gripped his extended arm in one fell swoop. Using his forward momentum and the enhanced strength in my core, I twisted and hip-tossed the lamenting bandit onto his back in front of me. The pain coursing through the front of his torso from my daggers and the ache racing along the center of his spine from the impact of my throw shattered his concentration and loosened his grip on the axe. I relieved him of it with little effort.

From my crouched position over the felled minion, I activated my Cognitive Accelerator and surveyed the ballroom. The adversaries to my immediate front finally finished trampling across their fallen friend and inched closer with every passing second. With my senses peaked, I detected the thunderous thump of a thug's heartbeat in close proximity at my back, and the heavy hum vibrating the air above him suggested he was rapidly twirling something over his head.

In the distance, Crelyos held a bandit taut and outstretched in a horizontal position; he dedicated one hand to encompassing the thug's face while the other secured his white and crimson pants line. Using the strength in his upper body to drive the bandit down, Crelyos simultaneously drove his knee up into the unfortunate man's back. I winced at the ear shattering bone cracks; the human body was most definitely ill-equipped to bend in such a manner.

While my companion focused on his living rag doll, a few of Raze's men broke from the group charging toward me and, instead, rushed toward Crelyos' back. The man leading their sneaky charge leapt into the air with a metal bat drawn high overhead. I foresaw a most unwanted skull bashing in Crelyos' future. While an axe or hatchet remained quite the unwieldy melee tool, it made an excellent projectile.

The heavy head allowed for an impressive traveling distance when properly tossed, and its sheer mass ensured gratuitous bludgeoning damage even if the bladed wedge failed to connect. The axe I pilfered from the stunned opponent beneath me would serve such a purpose. As the man first began his jump toward my muscular companion, I heaved the axe like a tomahawk at the space in which the man would reach the apex of his jump. The bladed edge embedded itself in his temple as he crossed its trajectory. His body jerked from the air in a manner that reminded me of a leashed dog bounding carelessly across a yard only to find himself yanked back when the leash drew taut.

The bloody crunch and pained cry served their purposes as Crelyos, newly alerted to his rear assailants, spun about to acknowledge their murderous intent. Without missing a beat, the blond mercenary sent his right fist into the nearest bandit's chest; his entire torso disintegrated with a loud squelch. The sudden splattering jarred my awareness to normal levels, and I used the momentum I gained from chucking the axe to spin about and face the threat behind me. My reflexes seized control when I beheld a silver glint whirring down toward my face. Until that moment, the assailant spun a chain above his head like a helicopter, but when I turned to face him he swung it down and cackled delightedly.

The chain was roughly ten feet long with weighted grappling hooks attached to either end. I quickly threw my right arm above my face at an angle; the metallic links jingled as the chain wrapped around my arm several times. An inward hiss escaped my lips when the claws of the grappling hook on one end pierced my forearm. The thug tugged viciously until the loops about my arm clenched tight and the hook's fangs tore into my flesh.

"Hoo-hoo-hah! Looks like I caught a little birdie!" The man's voice sounded like it belonged to a prepubescent punk. It was full of squeaks and cracks.

The two of us stood locked in a test of strength. The chain rattled from the tension applied to each of the links. While the bandit pulled with the weight of his body and an iron grip which he supported by coiling the chain about his knuckles, I suffered with every pound of resistance I offered. The grappling hook squished deeper into my arm until a steady stream of blood trickled along the metal links. I heard the men upon whom I turned my back drawing closer. Through the searing pain, a grin tugged at one corner of my mouth.

"Hm? A birdie? Nonsense. What you caught..." I released the tension I held and lunged forward into his pull. The chain's grip about my arm failed to loosen, but the clanking links in the middle fell slack and caused the bandit to stagger backward with the force of his fervent tugging. I closed the distance between us and rammed my metal-encased arm into his throat. With his own staggering momentum and the brutality of my strike, I harshly slammed the back of his head into the wall behind him. I leaned forward, sealing his wind pipe and pinning him to the wall. I glared up at him through the shadow cast on my face by my black bangs while he gagged and twitched beneath the pressure of my forearm, "... was a snake." I pushed forward hard and crushed his neck into the back of his throat. His body fell limp.

As the chain toter's body slumped to the ground, I turned to see the man whose chest still housed my daggers stumbling to his feet just in front of the group of men charging toward me. With a quick jerk of my right shoulder, I lifted the free end of my new chain and began swinging it above my head. After a brief second, I launched it forward; its remaining length sailed through the air and whipped around the confused thug who had finished wobbling to his feet.

The minion tasted the same searing sensation I experienced as the other grappling hook tore into his pectoral once the slack in the chain finished looping about his throat. After wrapping the links about my hands for grip, I tugged hard. A grotesque cross between a cough and a gag escaped his lips, and the minion staggered into my awaiting arms. I embraced him rigidly, his back to my chest.

"I believe you have something that belongs to me..." I sarcastically cooed. Reaching around him, I gripped the hilts of my long daggers and tore them from their sheaths in his body. He cried out briefly before I plunged them into the sides of his neck to end his suffering. I utilized the last few seconds before the crowd of ruffians reached me to rip the grappling hook from my forearm and discard the chain. It jingled to the ground in a coiled lump. I spun the dagger in my left hand around in a reverse grip. A sigh parted my lips. The men carried an assortment of weapons ranging from swords to spears and from claws to axes. I steeled my nerves and dashed forward to meet their loud advance and unleashed a battle cry of my own.

The flash of steel glinted in my eyes as the sharp clangs

of our colliding weapons sang out in the night. The silvery twangs, evasive swooshes, and grim ripping sounds served as the music in our bloody waltz on Raze's ballroom floor. I drifted from partner to partner, and while some of the men provided a challenging exchange of footwork, none of them were up to the task of taking the lead. More than once, the dizzying pace of the twirling dance was interrupted when a blade pierced my side or sliced a valley in my back, but I choked back my weakness with feral growls and gritted teeth.

Though I likely could have avoided the grievous wounds inflicted on my body by the lashing Dusk inhabitants, I chose instead to prioritize the safety of my head and throat. With the number of combatants brandishing deadly weapons, a single wayward strike to the back of the head or throat meant the end of my goal. It meant the end of my journey to kill Bradich.

Each time the sparks raced down the length of my daggers from their collision with an opposing metallic instrument, their origin was rooted in a parry designed to guard those vital points from my neck to my scalp. Defending from multiple directions required a fair amount of ambidexterity, and the lithe motions of my body handled the stray attacks which my twin daggers failed to deter.

At one point, my assaulters forced me to raise my blades above two sides of my head; I locked my right dagger with a spiked metal bat in front of me while my other kept a curved blade at bay to my left, I possessed little leeway to deflect an overhead strike cutting through the air at the back of my head. As the thug in my face drew his bat from my parry in preparation for a horizontal swipe toward my face, I jerked to my right away from the curved blade and twisted to look upon the man behind me. His hands gripped a long rusty spike crudely curved to resemble a dagger sans a handle. Instead, the spike possessed a flat circular head at the end opposite the tip where the man's hands desperately clutched. It looked like an overgrown steel thumb tack.

He forced it down toward the top of my skull, and I dragged the length of my newly unoccupied left dagger across his eyes in a swift slice. At the same time, I spun my right dagger into a reverse grip and brought it to bear against the horizontal strike of the spiked metal bat previously in front of me. The man with the rusty thorn dropped to his knees. His frantic screams echoed “My eyes! My eyes!” as he clutched his face with one hand and felt around blindly with his other. The man whom I temporarily abandoned, the one wielding the curved blade, seemed offended by my neglect and stepped forward to reclaim his place at my side. It was adorable.

As I parried, swerved, and counter attacked, my breath grew heavy. Panacea worked rapidly to seal my acquired wounds, but the nanites were far from miracles. As each opening sealed, two replaced it. The loss of blood slowly exacted its toll on my stamina, and from the thunderous panting nearby, I gathered Crelyos faced similar fatigue.

I deliberately angled my path of carnage to draw me

closer to my comrade, but after several minutes of fighting, the distance between us still seemed like a canyon. I glanced up at the rails upon which Raze leaned his thin figure; the flamboyant pseudo Frenchman simply stared with a wide, amused smile. I parted my lips to shout something toward him, but a grip around my right shin followed by a sickening thwack elicited only an ear piercing screech from my lips. My eyes widened as a tempest of pain swept through my leg from my ankle to my thigh.

The man whose eyes I shut with a swipe of my blade had spent the duration of his time reaching, searching blindly for something to grab. He had found it: my leg. Once he had secured the grip on my appendage, he plunged his thick metal thistle through the top of my shin.

The flat, circular top dug into my leg, and the slightly curved spike carved a destructive path through flesh and muscle tissue right next to the bone. The crimson point erupted from the back of my calf like a gruesome piercing; as my leg shook from the pain of supporting my weight with such an uncomfortable protrusion, the man's fellow bandits took the opportunity to renew the fervor of their assault. I dropped to my right knee, and as I did I brought one of my daggers into the skull of the muttering idiot that turned my leg into a pincushion.

Why had I not noticed him with all my senses acutely enhanced by neurotech? It dawned on me that I had noticed him, the whole time in fact. The problem was as he writhed about on the floor in pain, I grew accustomed to his harmless presence and ceased acknowledging him as a threat. So sensory enhancing nanites possessed a flaw after all, albeit a user error. Unfortunately, my position of peril warranted little time for internal debate.

To my left and right, a pipe and cleaver raced down toward my lowered cranium from above. I remained on one knee and lifted both daggers to avert the oncoming assault. While my muscles strained against the weapons from my lowered position, a third thug rushed me from the front to capitalize on that very issue. In his hands, a long spear constructed entirely of steel glistened in the chemical lights lining the walls. A sensation of finality wrenched the deepest parts of me as I stared down the length of the pointed rod intended to skewer my face. As I prepared myself for the inevitable blackout, I cursed fate for its cruel machinations, cursed my poor luck for rearing its ugly head, and cursed myself for my utter failure to remain aware of my surroundings.

"Ihlia!" Crelyos' voice broke my dismal resignation. A body, flopping through the air with a mangled figure and fractured bones, slammed into the right flank of the man who threatened my life. With a sharp yelp, the two of them tumbled across the floor into a twisted heap. The soft light illuminating my face changed to darkness when my blond companion soared overhead and cast his shadow upon my two opponents and myself. When he struck the ground directly in front of me, he used the force of gravity to drive his fist into the checkered tile.

The humming vibrations cast tremors across the pristine

floor as it sank into a crater. Bits of stone sprayed into the air and disintegrated before my eyes; the sudden depression sent a powerful shockwave across the ground. From my position on a single knee, I was virtually unaffected, but the two men at my right and left stumbled and cried out "whoa!" as they lost their footing beneath Crelyos' destructive architectural alteration.

Crelyos' ragged breathing failed to impede his efficiency. He launched himself toward the off balance thug on my right; the bandit released a frustrated growl and wildly swiped his cleaver at the former soldier's throat. Crelyos crouched beneath the attack, his legs coiled toward the ground like a pair of springs while his arms tucked near his chests like dormant pistons. When he released the tension an instant later, his figure rocketed skyward. His right fist exploded from the center of his chest toward the underside of his attacker's jaw.

When he activated his vibratory disintegration nanite, pieces of the man's head and face erupted into the air like a decorative fountain. The other thug, the one brandishing a metal pipe, brought it down atop Crelyos' shoulder. A fleshy thunk echoed through the room; for a brief moment, Crelyos merely stood in silence. When he turned, the blond mercenary reached forward and gripped the bandit's face in his right hand. I heard the muffled screams of Raze's minion. He dropped his weapon when the bones in his face started cracking and his skull began collapsing.

"Girly, you need to pull yourself together." Crelyos'

blood-covered figure, tall and broad, stood like a daunting behemoth in the face of our adversaries. Despite his injuries and fatigue, the former soldier pressed on as his training dictated. The dull throb in my shin escalated. I sighed and closed my eyes; for a moment, I pondered activating that nanite. A sickening dread sank into the pit of my stomach at the mere thought of it. I shook my head and forced myself to my feet despite my roaring protest. Beads of sweat raced down my cheeks and forehead even though the cold night air still pierced the mansion walls. My misty breath escaped my lungs in heavy sporadic intervals. I glanced at Crelyos.

"I'd have done so even if you didn't say anything," I responded between pants.

"Good," Crelyos grinned. After he finished crushing the man's skull, he reeled back and hurled the limp corpse in my direction. I stood my ground as the body sailed passed my right shoulder and smashed into an advancing adversary. My enhanced auditory sense detected one more; with a quick twist I drew my impaled leg up and swept it in a wide arch behind me. With an enormous spike jutting from the back of my leg, such kicks became deadly techniques in their own right.

My leg's broad stroke cut through the air like a hungry scythe. Catching a glimpse of the bandit as I turned, I noted his arms were drawn above his head in preparation to bring a metal bat down atop the back of my head. A quick adjustment of my leg's height mid-spin brought the spike sticking from my leg crashing into the side of his neck. The residual crunch resulting from his spine separating at the base of his skull also served to drive the enormous tack part ways back through my shin. I withheld my vocal agony and snapped my leg back to the ground to prepare for the next assault.

When I once again faced Crelyos, the sight of his gargantuan right fist sailing through the air at my face immediately greeted me. Verbal communication was unnecessary. I dropped to my knees and arched my back. Thanks to my innate flexibility, the depth to which I bent caused the spike jutting from my calf to prod at the cheek of my derriere in a most uncomfortable manner. The force of wind trailing behind my companion's fist as he swung his arm in a wide hook just inches above my torso threatened to rip the very clothes from my body.

As it turned out, he aimed his sweeping punch and its disintegration effects at a goon assaulting me from the left. My ears perked at the sound of his exploding midriff and distorted cry that fell on the spectrum somewhere between the realms of shock and torture. As I sprang to my feet like an elastic rubber band drawn too taut, I watched a bandit take advantage of the chaos; he leapt from his position behind Crelyos and attached himself to the hulking former soldier's back. In his raised right hand sat a dagger poised to plunge into the back of Crelyos' neck.

The peril my ally faced did not afford me the luxury of time to think or aim. I immediately loosed the dagger in my right hand; it sailed through the air and plunged into the bandit's right shoulder. The pain it caused temporarily stayed his hand of execution. I shifted my weight to my left foot and drove it into the ground to propel myself up while spinning my remaining dagger into a reverse grip.

I gripped Crelyos' shoulder, extended from the brutal impact of his punch against my attacker, with my right hand and hoisted myself atop his collar bone. The momentum obtained from my Supersoldier enhancement allowed me to support my whole weight on that single hand and turn my legs skyward. As I performed the handspring on top of Crelyos, I brought my thighs to bear against either side of the thug's head. Wrapping both legs around his neck and pivoting until I sat atop the thug's shoulder blades, I clamped my right leg down and drove its new scythe attachment deep into his chest.

After I crossed my legs, I fell backward. The reverse head-scissors takedown peeled the offender off Crelyos' shoulders in a back somersault. To prevent my head from smashing into the ground, I placed my empty right palm flat against the ballroom floor and aided in the criminal's back flip. In the end, I found myself seated atop his shoulders with my legs tucked beneath his prone body. I drove my remaining dagger into the back of his skull, snatched both my killing utensils from his corpse, and rolled to my feet. The pain burning through my right leg gave me pause.

"Ok... that's enough of that." I gripped the flattened head of the spike, exposed after the two impacts of the pointed end into Raze's men, and tugged it out with a painful cry. I shivered notably as the experience left a dull, empty pain throbbing in the gaping chasm in my leg. After leisurely tossing the bloody spike aside, I stood and pressed my back firmly against Crelyos'. He finished obliterating another bandit and leaned back against me as well. I took up a fighting posture.

"Ouch, that hurt," I jested.

"Oh? I'm surprised it didn't tickle," He responded sarcastically.

"Zurprised? I am zee one who iz zurprised, mon ami." Raze's voice washed over the room like a dramatic announcer's. Crelyos and I snapped our attention to the balcony. Raze's hands were already slicing through the air like a languid mirage. When he positioned his hand with fingers prepared to snap, my eyes widened.

"Crelyos, look out!" I dove from my position behind my blond companion. I instinctively slowed my perception at the point my feet left the ground. The heat built up like a raging furnace against my back, and the skin at the back of my neck prickled as though someone pinched and pulled at the hairs nestled on the nape of my neck. At the moment just before the roaring ignition, a strange, almost undetectable scent worked its way into my nostrils. The sensation toyed with my awareness and snapped me from the effects of my Cognitive Accelerator as I collided with the ground. I rolled forward to my knees and looked down to behold the tips of my lengthy obsidian tresses singed and frayed. A quick glance up revealed Crelyos in far worse a condition.

"Crelyos!" I cried out as his entire right arm suffered the wrath of Raze's flame. The orange glow swirled, roared, and danced atop the flesh of my comrade. To my utter astonishment, Crelyos calmly lifted his right arm in front of his face and stared at the sea of crimson consuming his limb. For the first time since we began our journey, I regretted conning him into my selfish endeavor. If it meant permanently marring a drinking buddy, I would rather have taken my chances alone. I was torn from my remorse by Crelyos' nostalgic sigh. My eyes were electrocapacitor plates. Did he feel no pain? His flesh had already melted to the floor, and the fire charred his distorted bones black. I paused. Melted flesh? Black, distorted bones?

Crelyos turned toward Raze and kept his arm extended away from the other flammable portions of his body. When the flame died, it left a surprising sight in its wake. Crelyos' right appendage was one hundred percent cybernetic. From the metallic tips of his fingers to the synthetic tendons and bones embedded in his partially artificial right pectoral, Crelyos' right arm was a whirring black machine lined with glowing blue tubes and rotating discs. I looked down toward the goo on the floor that previously concealed his steel limb. It seemed rubbery and limp; its latex consistency spread out in random disarray and still hissed from the heat of the fire that consumed it.

File 16: Harmonic Resonance

“I did not expect you to dizplay zat power again, mon ami. Not after... it did zat to your arm during our lazt mission. Zough I did beg you to employ it during our time working togezher as thugz, you alwayz refuzed me! Oh how it cauzed my frail heart to ache zo. But to zink it was zis powerful... tres bien, mon ami, tres bien.” Raze pressed his formerly snapped fingers to his lips and blew a kiss in Crelyos' direction.

“Crelyos?” I stood. The gaping wound in my shin was already well on its way to sealing shut thanks to Panacea. I recounted the vast situations in which we found ourselves that forced Crelyos to pummel things, living and nonliving, out of existence. A realization struck me; Crelyos only ever utilized his unique nanite through the medium of his right hand. But while the realization alone stunned me, the fact that I never noticed it before that moment sent me reeling. Crelyos shrugged off my inflective use of his name and continued curling and uncurling the black fingers on his mechanical limb. The various disks and moving parts lining the arm worked in unison with every faint motion of his fingertips.

“Remember when I said the results of my nanite manifestation durin' the French base infiltration weren't optimum? This is what I meant. The first time my nanite activated, it was to punch through a wall inside their main hangar. At that time, none of our nanites manifested anythin' useful, and we were surrounded. I thought things like ‘Is this it? Is this where we die after bein' together for so long? Is this the extent of our power?' Yeah... good times,” Crelyos' lopsided grin slowly faded.

“I decided that, no matter what, I would see us through the situation, even if I had to rip apart the entire base with my bare hands. Ironic, considerin' that's what happened when I drove my right fist into the wall,” Crelyos ran his left fingers along the length of his black cybernetic limb.

“At first everyone was amazed, includin' me. The wall exploded, but rather than send shrapnel or metal pieces sprayin' out the back of the hangar, the tiny fragments just kinda vanished into poofs of glitterin' dust. A second later, however, and I was feelin' awful funny. It started at my knuckles. I'll never forget the pain, it's like time slowed down to a crawl,” he shook his head and frowned.

“A second was a lifetime. Apparently the force of the blow had some kind of backlash, and my arm began crumplin' like a tin can startin' with my hand and movin' down. Several pieces of my arm just broke off and turned to pink ooze. Others sagged and got twisted up as the bones turned to dust. Our amazement changed to horror, ‘specially mine,” Crelyos continued, nostalgically staring at his prosthetic arm.

“Thankfully, so did the French's. They started runnin' as though I was about to explode like some time bomb. It gave Raze and Sarge enough time to drag my ass out of there to the evac point. I was a squealin' pig by then. Terrified, hurtin', and utterly useless." Crelyos offered me a sidelong glance.

"Right before the world ended, as a last ditch effort to salvage their lil experiment, the top dogs hired a team of guys that think just like Fancypants to construct this arm with the most state-of-the-art technology they had available with the army's limited budget. The movin' parts and rotatin' disks are specifically designed to offset the backlash of my augment, and the tubes carry the nanites down to these black knuckles here," Crelyos wiggled his mechanical fingers.

"Still, the size of the object I'm punchin' is taken into account, so is the force I transfer. I was warned that if I try to disintegrate somethin' too big, this arm could be destroyed by the recoil just as easy as my real one. As for that stuff..." Crelyos looked down toward the melted latex-looking material that offered his arm near-identical human texture, "That's just prosthetic skin. But it's real elastic, like rubber. So when the backlash gets transferred along the disks in my arm, it just kinda bounces around and absorbs the shockwave. Well, most of the time, anyway. Useful stuff, I guess."

"So that's why you walk like you're carrying a brick in your right pocket..." My eyes were drawn to the marvel of his prosthetic limb.

The thought that a detail so intricate eluded my attention for so long still captivated my senses. My gaze fluttered to the ring of thugs surrounding us; I noted their feet shuffling back every few moments. Unfortunately, I was unable to discern if it was a result of the intimidation posed by Crelyos' right arm or the thought of Raze arbitrarily igniting one of them. I settled my eyes on my comrade again. Crelyos nodded at my comment.

“It waz... an interezting exzperienze to zay zee least. I zought for sure zat you were, in fact, doomed, Crelyoz. But Sacrebleu, here you are!” Raze daintily clapped his palms together above his head in symbolic applause.

“Harmonic Resonance. It is a vibration all objects in nature possess, and when vibrations approach and match an object's natural resonance, the object suffers such shock that it literally shakes itself apart. The concept's applicability to destruction was first explored by an ancient scientist named Nikola Tesla, who allegedly nearly shook apart an entire neighborhood with a seven inch device. It would appear your nanite is a far more advanced version following similar principles,” Oswald emerged from the shadows beneath one of the spiral stairways. I glanced over at him as he interrupted the faux Frenchman.

“The key difference is the power source and the advanced level of your implant's artificial intelligence. I cannot begin to fathom how advanced that nanite must be. Donovan outdid himself with you, Crelyos. As best I can surmise, your nanite operates in two distinct stages.” Oswald held up a single finger.

“First, it moves faster internally, that is within your thick skulled body, than any nanite I've ever heard of. When your fist directly connects with an object, the initial vibrations sent from your fist resonate with the object in question. The waves are then sent back through your body like an echo. Here is where it gets interesting my boy, so pay attention,” Oswald's eyes lit up with the thought of discovering such technological advances right under his nose. Despite the danger of our situation, and everything else, Oswald was a true scientist at heart.

“The nano perceives the echo sent back and processes the information faster than an electric impulse to derive the object's natural resonance,” Oswald held his second finger up for the next part of his explanation.

“This information is then transferred to a second wave of nanites that store vibrations at the perfect frequency to disintegrate the object. And when I say perfectly, I mean a number that matches the frequency to several million decimal places. That is the only way the vibratory force would be so powerful and accurate as to completely disintegrate an object to its molecular level instantly. It is astounding. No, it's stupendous. It's a work of genius!” Oswald excitedly pressed his finger against the bridge of his spectacles and shoved them up his nose. When next he spoke, his voice lost its tangible excitement and a frown touched his lips.

“However...” He glanced at Crelyos, “Like all amazing things, it is not without its repercussions. The transfer of waves, while precise and purposeful to the processing power of the implant, is erratic and dangerous to its user. The nanite's flaw when it conceived its unique ability was that it failed to consider the frailty of the human body. You mentioned before that the scientists warned you of disintegrating things too large..." Oswald shook his head and paused, as though giving careful thought to his next words.

"I would assume you misunderstood them. It is not size but density which you need to be concerned about when utilizing your ability. The more dense the object, the more recoil from the force when the waves are transferred. While it is unfortunate that such a discovery cost you your arm, I am quite relieved to hear my suspicions were correct." Oswald smiled.

"Your suspicions, Doc?" I arched a brow. He clenched his fist excitedly and shouted at me from his position of relative safety.

"Nanites are not miracles, they're not perfect, and they most certainly are not magic! You can do this, Ihlia! Bring this pompous bastard down a peg or two!" Oswald's shout caused one corner of my lips to tug up into a quirky grin. When the "pompous bastard" in question shot the old codger a poisonous glare, Oswald sank back to his dark retreat under the stairs. I spun my daggers for visual effect and took up a fighting stance.

"Well, then, I guess we should get this party started." I stepped over to Crelyos and placed my back against his once more.

“Hm, quite an informative explanation zat waz, Doctor. However, I am afraid you are quite miztaken. Zee nanite iz not zee miracle, perfection, or zee magic. I am!” Raze worked his hands in their usual fluid motions and extended his fingers in pre-snap position toward his minions. They groaned; their quaking voices rose through the dim light of the ballroom like the slow sound of a siren approaching on a highway.

Raze smirked, “If you do not want to be burned... zen you will fight!” With a snap of his fingers, the thug on the outer ring of the gradually retreating horde burst into a blanket of orange. His cries far outclassed the cries of his companions as he frantically swatted his body and rolled around on the floor. There was no alleviation for him until his motions stopped and he lay as a blackened corpse. I began furiously grinding my teeth. It was the second time he killed one of his own.

All at once the group resumed their savage, bloodthirsty cries and charged at Crelyos and me as though their boss had nonchalantly called out, “Break's over! Get back to work!” I held fast to my daggers in reverse grip and braced for the onslaught as one might have braced for a rolling wave on a beach. I suddenly felt the back of my trench coat firmly entrenched in Crelyos' fleshy left hand. A soft gasp of surprise escaped me when he drew me back with the ease of a pitcher preparing to throw a baseball.

“I'll handle these guys, girly. You take out Blondie.” Crelyos grunted and tossed me up to the balcony. Though unprepared, my feline reflexes activated and I turned a handspring over the guard rail only a few feet from the pompously primped prick. A quick glance from the corner of my eye beheld Crelyos' defiant stance as he unleashed an enraged roar. The ensuing sounds of battle drifted to my ears as though they took place across a vast ocean. I focused my attention on the duke.

"Hmph, he intendz to leave me wiz zee dog? Zat iz most unfortunate. What incroyable mannerz. Very well zhen, if I am to put down zee dog, zo be it." Raze tossed aside his blond tresses of hair and swiftly unsheathed the rapier resting at the side of his frilly pants. Tucking his left hand behind his back, Raze cut a few patterns into the air while maintaining immaculate posture. As I watched, something about his weapon bothered me. It was the blade length; it was far too short for a rapier.

"I'm impressed. In a world of rusty metal cleavers you have quite the exotic weapon. Never seen a rapier quite so wanting for length, though. Run out of fancy metals?" I chirped.

"And to zhink you almozt imprezzed me by recognizing zis weapon az a cut above zee rezt. But zis iz no rapier, wee puppy. Zis iz zee zmall zword." Raze lifted the inconceivably thin blade in front of his face as though showcasing its stunted length. He maintained his stiff pose, keeping his left arm pinned to his back. With his perfect posture and the angle of the blade, the "small sword" almost appeared to vanish in front of his nose.

"Small Sword? Never heard of it," I sank into a battle stance.

"Oui, zee zmall zword. It iz far more zuitable a weapon for tight quarterz. Quarterz such az zee onez in which we find ourselvez, no? But zhere iz little reazon to teach an old dog new trickz. Engarde, puppy!" Raze extended his right foot forward; lowered his center of gravity; and extended his small sword with a flourish. When he finally took his fighting stance, I twitched in shock. As one who specialized in short blade fighting techniques, I recognized his readied position as one similar to my own. Maybe even better.

When Crelyos had recounted on the drive to the fortress that Raze was the best knife fighter he had ever seen, I discarded the information as a lack of experience on the former soldier's behalf. But witnessing Raze's stance for myself, I understood the gravity of what it meant to be the army's best. His aimed his small sword with deadly precision at the area of my neck which would guarantee a piercing straight through to my medulla oblongata. His free hand hovered above his head with a flair I attributed to his exotic tastes.

Despite the professional demeanor with which he stood, however, rapiers possessed a fatal flaw. Their wielders attacked utilizing extraordinarily linear thrusts, and even minuscule redirections from an expert hand rendered them futile. Considering the likeness his small sword bore to the rapier family of weapons, I assumed it was not exempt from the rapier's flaws. I could only hope my assumption would not prove fatally misguided.

I rushed forward and lifted my left dagger. As I neared, Raze lunged forward with an advance typical of those utilizing bladed weapons to fight. As anticipated, the point of the small sword drove toward my throat with fatal accuracy. Following the instinctive rise of my arm, my left dagger shot up and barely tapped the side of his flimsy blade.

A look of confidence washed over my face; I predicted the blade's path would carry it harmlessly to the left of my neck. As I prepared my right dagger to counterattack, a searing pain shot through my throat near my left collar bone. The sound of his blade penetrating my neck forced a gagged cry from my lips. I recoiled back, and his blade slid from the puncture wound it created. But how? I definitely parried the attack. As Panacea worked to seal the wound impeding my breathing with gargled blood, Raze wasted no time in closing the distance between us.

A flurry of thrusts propelled him toward me, and with both daggers I began swatting his wobbling small sword from the air. The concept that Raze drove me back with a single weapon against my dual wielding frustrated me. But worse than that, each parry attempt that I made seemed off if only by fragments of distances. If he aimed his attack for my stomach, I parried with gratuitous space in mind to send the blade whizzing by my body. Instead, it would puncture my side just next to my stomach and leave a thin hole seeping blood. Similar wounds continued peppering the outskirts of my body, always to the left or right of his targets but always connecting with my flesh. The sting was maddening and the accompanied anger I felt toward the dainty man in frilly clothing began clouding my judgment. Even I could feel it, but I was unable to stop it.

As the dance continued, my parries gradually became shorter and less polished. Eventually his attacks struck closer to their original marks, and before long I felt the tip of his blade enter my flesh long before my dagger connected to swat it away. After a few moments of stepping back defensively, my back thudded against the wall. As though he waited for that moment with immaculate patience, Raze drove his slender blade into the center of my chest with unrestrained ardor. I felt my flesh part for the thin sword and heard the dismal click of the blade hammering against the stone wall when its tip burst from my back. I coughed blood.

"Well, iz zat all zee dog haz to offer? Juzt as zee French outclazz every country wiz zhere brazen warriorz, so too are you outclazzed by moi. It iz zee hard reality. All you can do iz face it bravely before I cut out your heart!" With his venomous words, Raze twisted the small sword in my chest; the sudden pain sent a gargled cry racing up my throat. It exploded from my lips with a fresh splatter of crimson life force. I clenched my scarlet stained teeth and narrowed my eyes at him.

"Don't you... know what dogs do... when cornered? They bite..." I growled and rushed forward. My charge buried the blade into my chest at the hilt, but it was enough to startle the pretending Frenchman. I sent my right dagger in a swift arch toward the side of his temple. Just as when I shot him, a strange feeling overtook my hand. The picosecond of awkwardness was all that Raze required to jerk his head backward and avoid the full force of my attack.

My dagger scraped across his pristine forehead and split the flesh like a third eye slit. My left dagger followed suit toward the center of his chest, but the same odd feeling accompanied by a quick twist of his agile body changed my dagger's impact site to a meager impaling of his shoulder. I stepped forward to prevent him from drawing his small sword from my body and continued my onslaught with a gurgled war cry.

His eyes were wide, but his face remained impartial and calculating. As I elevated the tempo of my assault, my blows seemed, even to my own frustrated eyes, more like wild flails and less like the careful, deadly strikes I intended them to be. Thankfully, though the strange feeling in my arms never subsided, the sheer speed with which I executed my attacks seemed to be catching up to him.

Raze's left hand, still dangling with fragile poise above his head, began the familiar fluid movements, and his face contoured to a display of panic. He instantly recognized that I had gained the advantage. The duke swiftly lifted swiftly his foot and drove it into my ribs. With a brutal rock of his hips, he kicked my body off his blade as though peeling a fly off a swatter. I rolled back into a crouched position after releasing a sharp cry of pain from the sting of his small sword's exit.

The same strange smell that permeated the air just before Crelyos' arm burst into flames suddenly assaulted my nostrils. I gazed up at Raze long enough to see his fingers snap; just as the sound echoed, I felt an overwhelming need to move. My body acted instinctively; I dove to the side over the balcony. As I fell, I clamped my palms down on the protective railing. I hung over the side of the balcony awaiting the hissing sound of fiery combustion, but it never occurred.

When I vaulted back up and perched atop the rail itself, I was met with Raze's fingers already prepared to snap. The sound echoed once more, and again the sense of impending doom welled in my chest and motivated my body into a diving roll. But the sudden change in his pattern caught me off guard. Before, the flamboyant duke would wave his hands about in a graceful show before snapping his fingers. But during my dive, he merely executed a quick snap; the brevity of his snap proved effective. Even as I tumbled from my original location, the back of my right shoulder burst into flames, flames that quickly raced across my back and right arm. I howled in pain and rolled across the ground trying to relieve my body of the scorching agony tearing through my flesh. Finally, I wriggled free of the burning trench coat and lifted myself to a single knee.

My right hand hung limp next to the partially gooey coat. Black charcoal holes dotted the right side of my tank top. A raw mix of scarlet and black patches marred the skin exposed along the right side of my body where the leather coat and my flesh melted together like star-crossed lovers. I choked back profane shouts and cradled my right arm with my left hand. Despite the searing pain, I kept a tight grip on my daggers.

"It burnz, no? Zhere iz no zhame in giving up, little canine. Zhere iz no pozzible way zat you could beat me." His eyes radiated a sense of supremacy. Like a king overlooking a suffering subject, the man dared to allow a gleam of pity to twinkle in his ugly pools of azure.

"I think I'm starting to get an idea..." I panted a few more times and stood. A sigh escaped my lips as I struggled to suppress the protests in the right side of my body.

"Iz zat so? Zhen show me, little doggy." Raze swirled his small sword in the air as though completing a choreographed show aimed to impress a court.

I regained my composure as the various wounds in my body squished shut from Panacea's toils. After recalling the pain and nature of the piercings, I realized they blinded me with frustration far more than they actually caused damage. I flipped my left dagger into a reverse grip before dashing headlong at Raze. We engaged in the routine song and dance like a performing duet. My attacks skimmed by his vitals, at which I clearly aimed, or merely grazed portions of his flesh deemed unimportant enough to protect in lieu of those vitals.

With each eluded blow, I felt the odd sensation overcome my hand at a precise point. Likewise, my parries failed to deflect his counter strikes. With every clang of my daggers against his small sword, the sharpened point of his blade slid into my flesh like a homing missile.

Finally, at the height of the exchange when the tempo peaked, I awakened my Cognitive Accelerator. Raze lunged forward and thrust his small sword toward the center of my chest. The blade moved through the air as a needle until the flattened edge of my left dagger, held fast in a reverse grip, sent it on a detour; its trajectory was altered toward the outside of my left shoulder. My right hand thrust its blade to the left of Raze's cheek, though I arched my arm at the start of my thrust to offer the illusion that the attack was aimed to pierce his face.

A smile touched my lips; using my peripherals, I caught his small sword's length wobble around my dagger like a whip. The point threatened to puncture my chest just above my left breast. The odd feeling overcame my right hand, and my dagger tugged involuntarily further to the left of his cheek. Rather than fight it, I contoured my thrust to the flow of the feeling and plunged the tip of my dagger into the palm of his floating left hand. His eyes widened, and the peripherals I used to track his small sword's movements did not disappoint. The wobble of the blade straightened with a jarring vibration. Its length skimmed passed my left shoulder as I originally intended. Raze's cool demeanor melted into a concoction of heated rage, disgusted hatred, and frustrated pain.

"Raaagh! You bitch! Oh, zat zmarts! Ugggh! My hand, my beautiful hand! Sacrebleu, zon of a bitch!" His rage exploded into a series of attacks utterly different from the pretense of a poised gentlemanly duel he displayed until that point. He ripped his bloodied hand away from my dagger, kicked me hard in my chest, and launched several barbaric punches into my torso and face. The pop of my bones from the immense power of his blows surprised me, as until then he displayed no aptitude for physical prowess. Alongside his curses and profane spitting, Raze sprinkled wide slashes and stabs with his beloved small sword into his assault. I protected my head and heart, but the crimson vital force spewing from the multitude of holes littering my frame elicited gasps and cries of pain from my lips.

His finale was an uncouth thrust kick; he hammered his right foot into the center of my sternum and sent me whistling through the air right back to the wall from which I mounted my counterattack only a moment prior. His left hand moved with his trademark fluid grace, though far quicker, and as the smell invaded my nostrils and Raze snapped his fingers, a fiery column exploded to life behind me in the path of my involuntary travel. I hit the ground in the burning pit and rolled through it after it scorched my body and singed my hair. When my back finally slammed into the wall to halt my journey, I coughed up a thick glob of blood.

"Zhere... you zee?" Raze huffed before standing erect. The swiftness with which he regained his composure was astounding. "Zat iz what happenz when a dog bitez itz mazter'z hand. Zee zat you do not forget zis pain. Zis humiliation. Zis torment." As Panacea worked to close the wound in the palm of his hand, the recovery nanites barely began the treatment necessary to seal my numerous wounds.

Raze lifted the hand clutching his small sword and used his fingers to slick back his blond locks of hair which had been disheveled during his outburst. He slowly stepped forward until his body loomed just outside the wall of fire he created. "You underztand now, oui? Zhere iz no weaknezz. Zhere iz no idea zat you can have zat will give you any hope."

I coughed blood again. The pain coursing through my body threatened to rob me of consciousness. Still, I glowered up at the pompous prick through a curtain of singed and bloody raven bangs. "There is," I sputtered with subtle amusement.

"Eh? You are ztill talking zee canine language, I zee. Bark, bark, bark. Your zenses muzt be lozt wiz all zhat blood." Raze shook his head.

"Hah... none of that... matters. I know... how to beat you..." I coughed the words as I press my back to the wall and wriggled up it until I stood upright. I flipped both daggers into a reverse grip and leaned into the best combat stance my current condition allowed me to take.

"That last one was... a nice attack, by the way... it's the only real thing about you... we've seen so far." Despite my harrowing fatigue, the unbearable pain gripping my body, and the impending sense of death lingering over me like a thick shroud, a large smile decorated my bloodied lips.

File 17: Stripping Humanity

"*Real*, you zay? What do you know of real, puppy? I am as real as it getz. It iz becauze I am zo real zat I am unable to forgive zis world for expecting me to be fake. Like a caged tiger or helplezz pet bird. I am real wizhin zee confinez eztablished by zis world. But zat iz only a zmall part of me. Zee wildnezz, zee freedom, zee true me zat exizts wizhin zee cage cannot be underztood zo long as zhose barz confine me. Zo..." Raze furrowed his brows into an expression far more passionate than the cool facade he typically displayed. As he monologued, he seemed entranced by the sight of his wounded palm sealing shut with a quivering suction noise.

Panacea had finished its work on him, but the recovery process was still heavily underway on my own body. Worse, my world gyrated in front of my eyes as the liberal loss of blood I suffered took its toll on my senses. Raze glanced in my direction through the smoldering wall of flames separating us and clenched his fist, "I zought power. Power enough to break zee chainz zat bind me to zee ignorance of zis world. Bradich iz a man who can provide zat power. If working for him will free me from zis cage, zhen it iz a zmall price to pay."

"And if you're wrong? If he doesn't set you free?" I inquired. I needed to buy just a little more time to heal, and Raze simply oozed with the desire to spill his guts to someone.

"Zhen I have no need for zuch a world. I rezolved myself long ago, zat if I could never be free of my bondz, zhen I would burn zis world to zee ground." His eyes flashed; disdain dripped from his words like a toxin.

"Hence the name Raze..." I conjectured. The more severe wounds decorating my body finished closing; I inhaled deeply in an attempt to stabilize my vision. Unfortunately, while the heavy blood loss desisted, the vitality I already lost kept my vision blurred and my head foggy.

"Zat iz correct. Zuch a clever pooch. It iz a zhame zat you are a woman. Ozherwize, we might have underztood one anozher." Raze stepped through the wisps of fire smoldering on the tile floor and stood mere inches in front of me.

"A woman? What does that have to do with it?" I arched a brow at his accusation. I asked the question to bide time, but somewhere in the pit of my stomach, I understood exactly what that had to do with it.

"Everyzhing!" Raze growled and intruded the point of his small sword against the tip of my right breast. I drew a hiss into my throat from the burning ache; my left hand shot across my chest, dagger and all, and gripped the sharpened length of the flimsy sword. A stream of blood trickled down the length of my wrist from my palm as I struggled to keep Raze's torturous maneuver at bay.

“I hate your kind. Ezpecially women like you. Beautiful women who chooze inztead to fight. You could be experienzing romanze. You take for granted zat it iz aczeptable for you to be in love wiz a man. Zat at any time you could put down zese ridiculouz daggerz and find a partner, a man who lovez you and aczepts you for who you are.” The bitterness in Raze's tone seeped through every pore in his body like biohazardous waste.

Synchronously with his words, Raze twisted the small sword's point against my sensitive breast. A sharp cry escaped my lips as my bloodied hand shook; I struggled to force away the intrusive steel. “But moi? Becauze I am a man myzelf, I am ridiculed for preferring zee company of ozher men. ‘Inefficient” zey zay, ‘unproductive’ zey zay, ‘illogical’ zey zay!” With every spat word, Raze shoved the point of the small sword harder against my modest swell. Though he failed to puncture the skin largely thanks to my wounded hand, he succeeded in drawing three sharp grunts of agony from me.

Raze's fury was not unfounded. In historical times, opinions regarding same sex affections split countries in half. As time progressed and open minded generations seized the political helms of the world, it ushered in an age when people regarded the freedom to choose with the same precious protection as the very freedom to live. Unfortunately, the reconciliation of the philosophical and moral ramifications of the issue was short lived. When the Global Conflict erupted, the rate at which human beings died trumped such issues.

Our ability to deal death as a race truly knew no equal; because of that, the desperate encouragement to bring new life into the world superseded all ethical questions regarding controversial topics such as homosexuality and abortion. As a species, in order to survive, we needed babies. Lots of babies.

Thus, a stigma swept the globe against any people unwilling to utilize their genes for breeding purposes. Homosexuals were the obvious first scapegoat. It amused me to think that questions of morality evaporated in the face of necessity. The conservative shouts of "Immoral!", "Sanctity of marriage!", and "How will the children turn out?!" morphed into misappropriated accusations like "Unproductive!", "Extinction of humanity!", and "How will we bear enough children?!" While the enraged fists shook in the direction of the alleged offenders, the community preferring same-sex partnerships were taken aback.

Until the Global Conflict's hefty death toll, those with differing sexual orientations enjoyed a life of protected freedom and tolerance. All of a sudden, without much warning, society thrust them into defensive positions as it dumped its human extinction problem directly atop their shoulders. Their ancient pleas that rang out, "Intolerant!", "Equality of rights!", and "We deserve to love who we want!" resurfaced as aghast cries of "Unfair!", "Protection of freedoms!", and "Don't shove the world's problems on us!"

It was an ageless beast. In ancient times when the world

struggled to find its balance between morality and tolerance, it bore stripes and answered to a name. In the times of abundance and transcendent thought, it slept dormant within the hearts of men. Finally, during the Global Conflict it awoke wearing spots and answering to another name, but it was the same seemingly immortal creature nonetheless. Far worse was the fact that the majority of homosexuals happily offered their sperm and eggs as tools for procreation.

With technology at its apex before the Titan Crisis, utilizing the raw genetics of a person's sperm or egg to “forge” a baby was a small task. Before humanity's fall, tales circulated in the medical community regarding “genetic specialization.” The concept referred to parents picking and choosing which genes, including long dormant or recessive genes, emerged in their offspring. With “build-a-baby” technology, a complete artificial gestation was only a small bridge to cross. But most homosexuals' willingness to happily provide their genetic code for reproduction failed to stop the fanatics from levying accusations against them. No matter our level of enlightenment, crises spurred one of humanity's darkest traits straight to the surface: the need to blame.

Intelligently, I understood the concept of necessity and the world's overwhelming struggle to procreate after its cataclysmic population sink. Intellectually, I felt disgusted by the manner in which those purporting ideas of necessity treated homosexuals like subhumans. Their community became regarded with a tenacious stigma unfounded in facts and driven only by purposeless hatred.

Emotionally, I stopped caring after the Titan Crisis. Even in the grand scheme of our species, we possessed a myriad of more pressing problems. I felt the sexuality of others bore no significant impact on me or my goal to bleed Bradich dry. Many would refer to my apathy as riding the fence. I referred to it as minding my own damn business.

"I... would have probably sympathized with you... a lot better... over a pint of sludge, asshole..." I growled the words between clenched teeth. With Panacea finishing its work on the remainder of my wounds, I pressed my back firmly against the wall, and with the full force I could muster in my position, I shoved my right foot straight up between the duke's legs. His features contorted, and he released a sharp wail several octaves higher than his normal annoying voice.

The shock served its purpose as the force behind his small sword all but vanished, and I knocked it away with my dagger encumbered hand. I reached forward and placed my palms atop his shoulders; with a powerful heave I launched myself up and over the top of his head, and by kicking off the wall at the pinnacle of my leap, I turned a quick flip before landing behind him. During my descent, I buried my hands into the flowing mane of blond that framed Raze's pretty face. I landed back-to-back against the duke with my arms slung over my right shoulder and my fingers entwined in his silken tresses. I used the momentum of my front flip to bend forward, heaving Raze over my back as I activated my Supersoldier nanite.

I purposely aimed for the ornate steel table positioned in front of the security monitors, the same table in front of which Raze stood during our initial infiltration into his mansion. He turned an involuntary flip before smashing atop the lengthy tabletop on his stomach. The large container erected in the center of the table which housed Raze's fine sludge beverage shattered on his chest. His echoing "oomph" coincided with the creak of the table as it bent into a slight arch beneath the force of his impact.

"I do not need your zympathy, dog... agh, I only need you to die." Raze rolled from the table; he planted his feet on the ground and stood erect gasping for breath and clutching his stomach.

"You have it regardless. You pretend to adhere to society's norms for the sake of the world. Pretend to be French to justify losing to them during that operation. And now you pretend to have pyrokinesis to intimidate others. You've led a fake life," I flipped my daggers in my hand to make them more useful in combat and less useful for grabbing shirts and clutching small swords.

"Fake pyrokineziz you zay?" Raze grinned, but his face betrayed his apprehension.

"That's right. You have psychokinesis, not pyrokinesis. I would wager when your talent developed you discovered it wasn't capable of heavy lifting as some of the more renowned psychokinetic implants. It was indeed unique, however." I sighed.

“Ah, yes of course. Finite psychokinesis! Why, what an astute observation my dear!” Oswald's voice yet again emerged from the shadows of his hiding hovel beneath the stairs.

Like clockwork he stepped forward and folded his arms across his chest before continuing, “Instead of gauging its applicability using an amount of weight, Raze's psychokinetic abilities are extraordinarily precise. Remarkable. When human minds transcended their limitations after the creation of thought enhancing nanites, several new forms of energy naturally existing in the world were discovered, one of which involved the interaction and purpose of a sub-atomic particle called the neutrino. Hmm, how to put this in grade school terminology for the intellectually impaired...”

“A neutrino is a particle that possesses mass but is not affected by any force save gravity and weak sub-atomic forces. The mathematics and numbers are long and boring, but suffice to say that without being affected by magnetism or nuclear forces, neutrinos pass through matter virtually unimpeded. It was discovered that our brain is capable of harnessing the dormant force these particles can carry with our thought waves. Once given force when caught by our brain's receptors, neutrinos are imprinted with information generated by our thought waves; they are then projected as a wave. Of course, a transfer of energy with enough force or neutrinos to move objects would fry your brain. Actually...” Oswald tapped his chin and stared up at the ceiling.

“If I'm not mistaken, a few brains were fried for the sake of experimentation with psychokinetic waves. But I digress. After long years of intellectual pursuit, scientists engineered specific nanites to serve as the bridge between our brains and the necessary power storage to convert neutrinos to usable psychic phenomena. The nanites serve as the receptors for the neutrinos, store the information generated by our thoughts, and handle the conversion; the thought is then projected as a wave to influence the desired object,” Oswald carefully explained.

“Typically, the waves are very low in frequency and move objects as a thuggish brute would push a rock or slam a door. It would seem that yours, however, are incredibly high frequency and capable of far weaker, but far more precise, manipulations! So intriguing. I say, my boy, if you survive this encounter perhaps you would allow me the pleasure of dissecting your brain?” Oswald stared up at Raze with glittering expectation shining from his eyes.

“Zat zoundz like zee most hackneyed jargon I have ever heard, Doctor. And of course you cannot operate on my brain! Are you ztark raving mad?! Sacrebleu, zee thingz I have to put up wiz. I don't even know why I am ztanding here juzt liztening to zis nonzenze.” Raze's voice seemed normal again. I disappointedly clicked my tongue.

“Well, I never! I'm sure they called the fusion between biological cells, mechanical parts, and computerized intelligence ‘hackneyed’ too! But then what happened? The nanite was created. Which is why you're alive today, albeit probably quite briefly, mind you!" Oswald snubbed his nose at the duke of flame.

I shook my head. The situation grew far too light hearted, far too quickly. I returned my attention to Raze, "You manipulated the tip of my rifle before I shot at you. You manipulate the tips of my blades to skim by you. You chose a small sword for its wobbly blade, and you manipulate the tip to curve around parries and dodges to strike your target in harmless spots to rile them up, blind them, and hide them from the truth of your ability. And for your fire trick..."

I thumbed behind me to the door, "it's all that sludge out there. Your telekinesis is so finite that you can manipulate small droplets of liquid as well. Like little bubbles, you dampen a given area with sludge. Then, you snap your fingers and slam dust particles together in the air like flint and steel. The friction is enough to ignite the fuel source, and the flame does the rest." I gestured to the piles of ashes that used to be Raze's subordinates.

"... How in zee world did you figure all zat out zo quickly?" His eyes widened. For the first time since I began combat with the flamboyant duke, I felt a sense of advantage.

"The strange feelings in my hands were far from subtle. That tipped me off to your psychokinesis. The fire part seemed logical to me when I thought about all the containers of sludge you store in those warehouses, but I was convinced of the theory when you kicked me and made that," I gestured to the dim black scorch marks marring the ceramic tile on the floor. They were the product of the flame Raze created when he kicked me from his presence; I had sailed across the room and landed in the fire he conjured at my projected destination.

"How does zat matter?" He asked.

"Simple. If you could truly control fire, why not just ignite my body in mid air when I had no control over my trajectory? Simply put, you require time to gather the droplets of sludge. You probably have a few barrels tucked away right outside the mansion or behind closed doors. I would be impressed if you psychokinetically carried sludge all the way from those warehouses, but it's not impossible, I guess," I shrugged

"Regardless, you can't properly aim the gathering of those sludge molecules when a target is moving. That's why you use those exaggerated hand gestures, like a magician fooling his audience. It draws attention away from what you're really doing." I grinned at him. The color drained from his face like an evaporating fog.

"Zat iz... mozt imprezzive. I truly undereztimated you. You are not dozile and foolizh like zee puppy. You are cunning and ruthlezz like zee wolf. But a wolf iz still a canine. And you will ztill die like one." Raze lifted his small sword so the thin blade bisected the view of his face with the same dramatic poise he used before our fight began. Though theatrical, it signified his weariness for talk and readiness for battle, "Knowing zee zecret and doing somezhing about it are two different zingz, Zhe-wolf."

My grin faded, and my brows furrowed. If he was aware of my discernment of his ability, then surely he understood that I detected the weakness of his implant? His left hand, which he held loosely above his head during our clash of steel and manipulated gracefully during his obscuring parlor trick, served as the focus for his psychokinetic powers. He utilized the imagery conducted by the motions of that hand and its fingers to guide his thought waves in order to achieve his desired results. Considering he no doubt understood I knew this fact, was it possible his left hand only served to amplify his abilities rather than as a necessity for their use?

I exhaled slowly. The cold draft seeping through the walls and windows nibbled at the few puncture wounds still decorating my body, but the most intense bite raced down my scorched right side with the brisk passing of chilled air. I noticeably winced. Raze's eyes squinted at the sight of my flinch, and with another pretentious "Engarde!" he dashed across the distance separating us.

His small sword gleamed in the luminescence atop the balcony as he poised to plunge it within my chest. I parried the blow, but the results from previous attempts repeated; the blade curved around my left dagger and pierced my pectoral just above my left breast. And when I thrust my right dagger toward his floating left palm, he simply pulled the blade's tip to the side with the force of his mind. I cried out in pain even as I began to understand the source of his confidence.

Even knowing the weakness to his finite psychokinesis changed nothing. I possessed no tool with which to counteract his abilities. Crelyos regarded Raze's capabilities with a melee weapon as unparalleled. That was before his unique nanite blossomed. Now, his level of skill was maddening. I clenched my teeth as he pulled the small sword free of its fleshy sheath. Though the pause in our combat allowed me to catch my breath, the dizziness caused by my blood loss failed to subside.

Despite all the analysis and information I gathered to defeat Raze and learn the next step in my journey, my defeat still seemed inevitable. My death seemed certain. I shook my head in an attempt to clear it of both my dizziness and frustration. I concentrated on my nanites and lowered my eyes to the ground; the neurons in my brain began firing bioelectric sparks at a target location.

No, I refused to leave this world without taking Bradich with me. I refused to fall because Raze's attacks blinded me with pain and frustration. Even if it meant activating that nanite, I would persevere. I would triumph no matter what it cost me. I stepped forward and tried to recall the last time I had activated *that* nanite.

But before any such memories bubbled to my surface thoughts, the color faded from my emerald eyes leaving only a pale green, and a sense of extreme apathy overcame my every thought and action. As my foot touched the ground, I felt the click of *that* nanite buzz to life within the folds of my frontal lobe. My world instantly dimmed to a foggy gray haze of numbers, probabilities, and calculations. Like a walking corpse, I felt that nanite strip every sense of humanity from me with crude efficiency.

File 18: Dousing the Duke of Flame

"Oh good heavens... she activated the nanite that cuts her pain receptors again. Damn it, Ihlia!" Oswald hissed from the base of the stairs.

Raze stared at me for a moment. I perceived his hesitation and surged forward. He thrust the tip of his small sword toward my chest in response. I understood his reasoning for avoiding an assault against a small target such as my head or neck. Even if he could wobble his small sword around my dagger, I was capable of swiveling my head to avoid the death blow with relative ease. His tactics involved poking and prodding the victim to the point of blind frustration, then finishing them in a fiery blaze.

Nonfatal strike, slight shift required. A voice that almost felt like another entity's floated through my head like an eerie whisper. The thoughts belonged to me but were detached and removed from me at the same time. I lifted my left dagger as though intending to swat his small sword away as in previous attempts, but instead I thrust it passed his extending arm toward his chest. The blade wobbled around an imaginary parry, and with his attention focused on piercing the nonfatal muscles in my breast, my dagger found its mark in his own. I simultaneously hooked the dagger in my right hand around toward his left ribs.

Raze's cries from being impaled in the chest shattered his concentration. The feeling in my right hand caused by his psychokinetic abilities still deterred the impalement, but the blade still managed to skim by his stomach and rend through his flesh, splattering his blood across the floor. He shoved his small sword deep into my chest, but my movements remained unhindered and my expression stoic. He staggered back a step to recuperate from his wounds, and his face contorted from the agony caused by my attacks.

Without pain receptors, Panacea acted sluggishly. The nano hub relied heavily on the information sent to the brain by medium of pain to quickly detect damage and dispatch nanites to the afflicted location. Without that pain, my wounds would remain in place far longer, and the blood loss would accumulate far more quickly.

In addition to stunting my healing, the nanite responsible for cutting my pain receptors also grossly distorted my sense of humanity. The boon of maintaining an unwavering assault in the face of extreme torture was questionably worth the price paid, but it was a feeling I never grew accustomed to in the scant few times I activated the implant. I lunged forward without mercy and renewed my attack. In the dim light, my daggers flashed like lightning, and Raze's howls seconds after the blades found their marks boomed like an accompanying clap of thunder.

Nonfatal strike, ignore. The dance continued with predictable results. *Right side parried, compensate next strike.* My every motion flowed with the perception of my Cognitive Accelerator. In my unfeeling state, I no longer required mental focus to maintain the slowed perception, I simply did. Or perhaps my mental focus could no longer be obscured by external sources. Regardless of the reason behind the phenomena, in my mind's eye, Raze possessed all the speed of a sloth.

Impact confirmed, press the assault. I suffered several wounds similar to those received during our first exchange, though without the accompanied flinches or sensory distractions, I managed to inflict worse wounds upon the duke.

"I do not underztand... how can zis be. It iz like you are not zee zame at all! Anzwer me, Zhe-wolf!" Raze gasped for air; with the climax of his angered cry, he gagged up a small blot of crimson which he spat on the floor. The flamboyant duke reeled backward to escape the threat posed by my lengthy daggers. Slowly, I knelt down. At my feet lay my leather trench coat. Its right half completely burned away, the charred remains of the lengthy black garb resembled half a vest more than a coat.

With a blank expression, I lifted the left portion of the frayed remains. After tucking the hilt of my left dagger firmly between my teeth, I shoved my left hand through the sleeve and adorned it despite its abysmal state. Raze's burning glare burrowed into me, but I felt nothing and tore a thin leather strip from the frays decorating the coat's right border.

As I placed either hand at the back of my neck, I scooped my ebon tresses from their prison beneath the collar of my coat. I used my free hand to bunch the flowing locks, still singed at the end from one of Raze's many bursts of flame, into a long ponytail. I calmly tied the leather band around the strip of hair to hold it in place and returned my dagger to my waiting grip.

"Raze..." I fastened my gaze on the duke of flame. Even the sound of my voice echoed like a cold vacuum devoid of humanity, "... I'll say it again. Give me any information you have regarding Bradich's whereabouts." I lowered both arms to my side and turned my daggers into a forward grip in my palms.

"Zat iz zo cute. You believe zat you have me on zee ropez. You forget about zis!" Raze leapt back and pressed his back to the wall as far from me as feasibly possible. He swirled his left hand in front of his face; he gestured more swiftly than usual and more akin to those he used when he set the floor aflame. Raze was gathering sludge quickly. Whether his hasty motions indicated a tactical maneuver or a sign of desperation, I was unable to decide.

The moment the sour, burning smell of sludge reached my nostrils I propelled myself forward. No sooner did my feet left the ground, than Raze turned his left hand toward my body with fingers pressed together for a quick snap.

My apathetic gaze never faltered even as the methodic thud of my boots hammered into the tile floor. Raze's lips twisted into a gnarled grin, “Too late, Zhe-wolf. Zis iz zee end.”

“I agree,” I responded plainly. As the muscles in his hand, in the sluggish manner in which I perceived them, drew his fingers together for the heralding crack, I tossed up my left arm encased in the remains of my trench coat. The click of his fingers and the synchronous roar of flames bathed my left forearm in golden light. With the sludge attached to various parts of my body, the fiery swathe twirled about my arm and blazed a trail along my back. With the passage of air intensified by my running, it only further provoked the flame's accelerated growth.

I felt nothing. With my pain receptors cut, not even the heat imposed its discomfort on me despite the flame's close proximity to my skin. I smelled the leather and burning flesh along my left arm as the clothes melted and fused with the fibers of my skin. I understood the significant damage racing across the left side of my back and torso as the fire rapidly pulled the moisture from my skin and marred the pallete of my flesh with crimson scorch marks. It failed to stop me or even give me pause. I rushed forward as a half-lit fireball.

Raze's eyes widened; he no doubt expected me to stop and writhe about in pain, consumed by the ruby sea burning away at my body. Instead, I thrust my left dagger straight toward his chest. The tug on the left side of my hand sent the dagger askew, accompanied by his confident shout, “Foolizh Zhe-wolf!” I simply barreled into him despite the edge of my dagger twisting harmlessly to the side. My flame engulfed elbow, instead, collided with the broad expanse of his pectoral muscles encased in elaborate garments. His expectations to swat me away and dust off a frayed thread or two quickly transformed.

Raze burst into flame with the ease of a cotton ball. The fire exploded like a bucket of red paint splashed onto a canvas. Robbed of his concentration, Raze failed to add new sludge to my burning body. Though the flame did not smolder, it maintained its hold only on my lithe frame's left side. Meanwhile, his ear piercing screams vibrated the walls and ceiling. The duke of flame's own bitter fire mercilessly consumed him. I kept my forearm pressed hard against his chest and burned with him as I pinned him to the wall. Amidst his incoherent shrieks, he managed to speak.

“How... iz zis... pozzible?!” He grabbed my arm, desperately trying to wriggle free of my grasp so he could roll about on the floor. As the flame enveloping my body traveled to my stomach, I reached up with my right hand and peeled the trench coat off my left side. The sickening squelch as it ripped layers of my flesh away elicited no reaction from me at all. As I finished tugging my left arm free, it hung at my side like a smoldering raw clump of charred flesh. One would hardly be able to discern it from a slab of well cooked meat. I stepped back, and Raze finally dropped to his knees and raked his fingers across his face as though trying to tear the fire from his body.

"The table," I monotonously responded.

"Zee...table?!" He howled and moaned, rolling about on the floor like a crazed animal.

"The sludge you were drinking when we walked in. It may be fit for consumption, but it's still quite flammable. When I tossed you on the table, it covered your shirt. It doesn't help that your frills encourage burning far more than leather or that your hair is long, flowing, and not pulled back. With all those fire hazards, I wonder if it's the world you really wanted to burn... or yourself."

By the time I finished my explanation, Raze succeeded in dousing the flames bathing his body. His charred figure lay at my feet; several charcoal patches marred his bald head, and the majority of his flesh resembled ashen flakes. Only small strips of burned, frayed cloth covered random parts of his body; as I stood over him watching, I could scarcely help but liken Raze to a half-cremated mummy. If not for Panacea, both of us would surely have died from our wounds. Raze no doubt would have died immediately whereas I would have perished later, so logically, I considered it my victory.

"Zee zludge on zee table... zee trench coat... zee hair band. You planned all of zis?... What zee hell are you, Zhe-wolf?" Raze's voice cracked and creaked like a smoker living prior to Panacea who went through three packs a day for forty years.

I stared down at Raze's feeble figure without remorse.

Sheathing both daggers at my hips, I reached behind me and gripped the stock of my hunting rifle. I tugged it from its strap and brought the tip of the muzzle to Raze's forehead. With a quick slide of the bolt action pin, I loaded a new round into the chamber. My vacant eyes offered the duke no comfort, but they seemed to provide an answer to his question. A pained smile quivered at one corner of his lips; perhaps he thought me a monster.

I slowly squeezed the trigger, but as the reverberating bang sent the round rifling from my firearm's tip, a strange sensation tugged at the tip of my gun. The bullet sailed clear over Raze and embedded itself in the decorative wall on the far side of the semi-destroyed ballroom. I glanced toward my rifle's end; Crelyos' biomechanical grip firmly clutched its tip. At the last moment, he had vaulted atop the balcony, grabbed the end of the gun, and yanked it up and away from the fallen duke of flame. My gaze drifted to him with stoic expectancy. I wanted an explanation.

My left hand, disfigured with hideous burns, gripped my dagger's hilt and slowly slid the blade from its sheath. A simple swipe would surely make Crelyos leap backward and relinquish his hold on my weapon. It was the logical course of action. I suddenly felt another's grip on my left hand. The firm but delicate hand of Doctor Oswald pressed down against my wrist, forcing my dagger gently back into its sheath with a soft whisper. As I swiveled my face toward the doctor, his free hand lifted and cupped my cheek with tenderness and genuine concern.

“Ihlia, snap out of it.” His words carried a power in them. It was like I sat in the darkness of my mind's eyes watching the events play out before me in sullen loneliness, but then Oswald appeared with a guiding light and beckoned me to follow him. My world's foggy haze lifted and the prickling sensation in my skin returned. I blinked a few times as the sweltering agony coursing through my body welled up at once. It felt like a giant flaming meteorite dropped straight onto my head. I cringed and cried out, gripping the grotesquely wounded left side of my figure with my more bearable, but still uncomfortably scorched, right hand. When I let my rifle go to accomplish this, Crelyos merely held it by its tip.

“How the hell are we supposed to get info out of him if you just off him? Damn, Ihlia. Think about these things.” Crelyos shook his head and shouldered my rifle for safekeeping. I laughed softly, painfully, under my breath and staggered toward Raze. His breath escaped him in ragged heaves, and his face contorted in a tortured expression. But Panacea already began the process of stitching his body together beneath his cocoon of black charcoal and raw flesh. I stepped one leg over the top of his body, hovering just above him while still cradling my left side.

“Last chance... Info on Bradich...” I grinned down at the defeated duke.

“Hmph, zhere iz nozhing you can do to make me zqueal, Zhe-wolf. I will not betray Zarge or Bradich.” He turned his head violently to the side.

“Hm, is that so? Suit yourself then.” I lowered atop him, my hips straddling his own. I took great care to press my every female contour, no matter how engrossed in wounds, against his body. I even flattened my chest against his and locked my legs against the sides of his hips.

“Ihlia! Good heavens, this is hardly the time...” Oswald gripped the bridge of his nose with two fingers and rubbed disappointedly.

“Whoa, girly, what the hell are you doin'?” Crelyos clamped his free hand across his eyes, though I noted he left a tiny slit between his pointer and middle finger from which he no doubt watched.

I pursed my lips and lowered my face slowly toward Raze's. His body stiffened with the rigidity of a steel beam. No doubt the excruciating pain of pressure against his burned body played a part in his reaction, but I suspected the true nature of his discomfort possessed far more practicality. At the last moment when my lips threatened to meld with his two cracked pieces of charcoal, he sat straight up. He shoved me from his body with a yelp that mixed the agony of his sudden movements with the terror of what almost transpired.

“Holy shit, woman. Get off me, that's so gross. What the fuck, man,” He cried out. His voice, his real voice, escaped him in a torrent of curses and unrefined murmurs. His manner of speech barely differed from that of Crelyos' during his angry tirades. Crelyos erupted into brazen laughter and leaned back over the rails. The floor below, littered with the blood and mangled corpses of many of Raze's subordinates, still held a small group of the shameless bandits confused by the events above them. Crelyos grinned and shouted down to them.

"Your boss just got whooped. I suggest you make yourselves scarce before bad things happen." Crelyos lifted his metallic right arm and clenched the steel digits into a fist. The fearful sound of the thugs racing for the door elicited another shameless guffaw from my ally. I shook my head and stepped over to Raze with a cat-like smile, "It's been a while for me, but I hope you'll be gentle." I tossed in a wink for good measure.

"Ok, ok, I get it. I'll talk. Look, it's like I told you. I don't deal directly with Bradich. I only deal with Sarge. From what I understand, Sarge is Bradich's right hand man. The military wasn't the only organization that knew about his knack for bringing out the best, or worst, in people. Harbinger is putting that to good use and gave Sarge complete authority over all his troops." Raze sat forward and, when he noticed I was not going to attempt molesting him again, relaxed, allowing his nanites to work on his body's burns.

"Troops? Are you trying to say that Harbinger has amassed some kind of military force, dear boy?" Oswald stepped forward and folded his arms across his chest.

"Something like that. It's more like an organization than a military. Think FBI rather than the army. They call themselves *E Pluribus Unum.* They got their peons, they got their top brass, and they got their special agents. Their special agents are like us... some of them got their hands on unique implants from somewhere, others have a unique skill set or are suffering minor hyped symptoms to cram a few more nanites into their brains. I hate to break it to you, well actually I don't, but I'm the lowest on the totem pole. Both in strength and influence," Raze glanced up in my direction.

I felt a sense of dread grip my chest like the icy fingers of death. If Raze was indeed the weakest and most incapable of Sarge's subordinates, then I was in trouble. Big trouble.

"You're the lowest? What? But you, me, and Sarge were closer than brothers! He shoulda put you way up there. That doesn't seem right at all." Crelyos shook his head.

"Crelyos, man. Sarge has changed. He's not the same guy we knew in the military. Hell, he's not even the same guy we ran around with as bandits right after the shit hit the fan. Something's changed him. Don't approach him expecting a high five or neck hug. He'll kill your ass. I'm warning you," Raze turned to the former soldier.

"What about the collection of hyped? It seems like you lads are working an around-the-clock operation just to take as many captive as possible. It hardly seems a profitable endeavor when you consider their radical instability and rabid disposition. They receive poor marks as test subjects and even worse as a directed force of arms. I am baffled. Shed some light, won't you dear boy?" Oswald stroked the scraggly beard hanging from his chin.

"Don't ask me, Doctor. I just do as I'm told. We collect as many hyped as possible and hold them in a warehouse until the end of the week. One of Sarge's agents comes and takes them away in a huge trailer. No one knows where they go, though. We got a quota; if we don't meet it then they cut our rations," Raze muttered a trailing tidbit under his breath, "... and my sludge supply."

"But why the charade? The guy destroys the world then starts gatherin' up all the crazies? It makes no sense. What could he be up to? I figured guys like him just loved to see things break and fall apart, but he's like a kid with tinker toys. He's blowin' shit up then tryin' to stitch it back together all different and shit." Obviously bemuddled, Crelyos scratched the top of his head.

Raze glanced left and right, theatrically examining his surroundings. When he leaned forward, his voice escaped him in a low hush, "I hear it's a new world project. Lots of research is going on in the background, and there are a lot of movers and shakers. Harbinger's got some brain he found working on stuff."

"What stuff?" Oswald asked.

"Hell if I know. Stuff. They're just rumors, but the whispers are everywhere. Not just with my men either. It could be one of those cliche 'guy destroys the world to rebuild it as he sees fit,' things. I don't know." Raze shrugged his shoulders.

"None of that matters. I'm going to kill him. If the world changes or gets destroyed as a consequence, so be it." I felt the bitter taste of hatred saturate my words as I spat them. I reached up and gripped my rifle. After snatching its length from Crelyos' metal hand, I returned the muzzle's aim to Raze's forehead, "You still haven't given us a location. I don't care where it is as long as it eventually leads us to Bradich."

"Calm down, girly. From what Raze's sayin', these guys are tough stuff. This opens up a whole new can of worms. This isn't just one man rootin' around in the pleasure of destroyin' the world; this is a group of killers with a set ambition. We gotta proceed with caution." Crelyos placed his fleshy left hand on my shoulder and offered a reassuring squeeze.

"Hmph. Northwest. Sarge has an installation in the area they used to call the state of Colorado. Bradich gave it to him; Harbinger had a real thing for Colorado before the Global Conflict. Apparently it was a really beautiful place. You might find Sarge there. If not, you'll at least find one of his top agents running the place." Raze staggered to his feet. The raw reds and ashen blacks peeled away; at the very least, the canvas of skin coating his body started resembling something similar to flesh.

"Thanks Raze, I knew somewhere in there you were

still your old self!" Crelyos walked up and slapped his left hand down atop the man's shoulder. Considering I endured similar agony from my burns and understood the two of us probably belonged in a burn ward somewhere, I offered Raze a sympathetic cringe. The former duke of flame screamed with a quivering voice and dropped to his knees once more; it surprised me that he resisted the urge to bawl outright.

"Agh, shut up, Crelyos. What do you know of my 'old self'? You, Sarge, everyone in the military. I hated all of you. Always looking over my shoulder when I wanted to be me, always worried what was at my back. Forced to put up pretenses and pretend to fit into what was considered a productive addition to the gene pool. You don't know my 'old self' any more than you know my current self!" Raze shouted, his voice full of angst.

"Hm? Productive addition to the gene pool? I thought you liked to do the dirty with other men." Crelyos arched a brow down at the curled up duke. Raze's gaze snapped up and his eyes widened.

"You guys knew?" Raze's lips quivered. I perceived a quaking change overtaking the charcoal man at our feet. For all the oozing hatred and bitterness Raze exuded in his every action, he looked hopefully up toward Crelyos as though the next words from his mouth would offer condemnation or salvation. Though clearly an adult, I perceived the broken man as nothing more than a conflicted teenager.

Crelyos arched his brow, "Of course we knew. It was pretty obvious. I mean, you avoided girls every time we went to bars. You stared at men out the corner of your eyes, you washed your hands every time you took a piss, you refused to eat bar nuts. Which, all that superstition about germs on those things is bullshit. They're delicious. Anyway, we'd be pretty stupid not to know. And you know what?"

Crelyos knelt down in front of his former comrade and placed a hand on top of his shoulder, "Those times you felt somethin' over your shoulder? That was us, man. Watchin' out for you like we always have. We knew there were ignorant bastards out there that might blame you and your tastes for the shit storm state of the world. But when you felt somethin' at your back, that was probably us trashin' some jackass that thought like that and dumping his ass in the garbage where it belonged."

"Why didn't you say... anything?" Raze's eyes misted. I stared at him with the same convoluted hodgepodge of emotional struggle that I offered Bojack in his time of despair. Intellectually, I understood the reason for his teary eyes. I understood the confusion, frustration, and relief washing over him. I remembered those feelings from my time spent with Donovan and Bradich before everything rotted right before my eyes. My heart failed to grasp the depth of it, and I found myself shaking my head.

"Why would we? Why did it matter? You were our brother in arms, a damn good soldier, and a better friend.

I actually hated wearin' our formal uniforms. They were stuffy and made my neck itch. Why didn't you ever say anything about that? Because it doesn't matter. It's just one characteristic of you; it doesn't define you, and it doesn't change how we felt about you. We were a team and the best there was. And that was the end of that." Crelyos nodded firmly.

His voice dipped low when he next spoke, "but you know... after listenin' to all that bullshit you said here tonight, I thought about punchin' you square in the jaw. You talk to Ihlia like she's not a person. You imprint all your woes on her like the choice she makes to fight for somethin' is the cause of all your bad luck. You want her to change to your idea of how someone should be who is grateful over somethin' dumb like being able to love a man. You're no better than all those people you hated, old friend." Crelyos stood.

"I..." Raze's voice quivered. I watched the revelation cascade atop his shoulders like a ton of bricks. Raze himself had placed all the pressure, all the intolerance, and all the pretenses upon himself in his tragic past. His emotions erupted from his chest, and he sobbed. He coiled up into a tiny ball, and tears freely flowed down his face. The flow of emotions washed away the burnt skin clinging to his healing body like the black spots fading from his soul. It seemed like a dramatic symbolism that represented the events far too accurately.

"Can we kill him now?" For the third time I placed my rifle against his forehead. This time, I slid the bolt action lever back to chamber a new round and pressed my finger against the trigger. Crelyos' hand found my shoulder a second time. Thrice he had interrupted my execution. As he applied pressure to my arm, I shot him an impatient glare.

“Ihlia...” Crelyos' voice trailed off with sympathetic evocation.

“He murdered his own men, took an entire town hostage, and tried to kill us. Did I mention he murdered his own men? He's just like Bradich. I'm not letting him out of here alive,” I grunted at the towering soldier staring down at me with pleading eyes.

“Look at him, Ihlia. He's a diva, that's all. He always has been. The men he betrayed were scum anyway; the town is safe; he didn't kill everyone in Loftsborough; and if people went around murderin' everyone that tried to kill them, we would be extinct,” Crelyos stated.

“What about Eugene?!” I glared at the former soldier. He lowered his head.

“It's the principle. It's betrayal. Those men trusted him, and he broke that.” I regained my resolve and shrugged Crelyos' hand from my shoulder. My finger coiled around the trigger.

Crelyos stepped in front of the barrel of my firearm, “I get it. Mete out punishment for traitors. I know I'm askin' you to be a hypocrite right now; I know I'm askin' you to go against somethin' you believe in real strongly. But please, Ihlia. For me. As a friend, will you just let this one go?" I never heard Crelyos beg before. The sound of his voice sent a tiny ripple through my chest near my heart.

"Get out of the way, Crelyos," I growled.

"I won't," He replied stubbornly.

Crelyos knew I would never fire on him. Part of me understood that I should have felt embarrassed and infuriated that the lumbering former soldier took advantage of my own distaste for betrayal. Most of me, the logical part of me, secretly applauded his strategy; it was another instance in which I questioned Crelyos' true tactical nature. Was he merely standing in front of my weapon as a desperate defense of his friend, or did he calculate that I would indeed never betray one of my allies? I furrowed my brows in frustration for a few seconds.

"It doesn't matter. Even if you guys don't kill me, Sarge or Bradich will once they find out I divulged so much information. I was resolved to die as soon as the She-wolf beat me." Raze sighed, apparently finished with his somber wails.

I grunted softly and returned my rifle to the strap across my back. Crelyos' lips curled skyward in a grateful smile. I closed my eyes, shook my head, and spun on my heel. When I opened my eyes, even the old codger stood there with a beaming look of relief and a dopey smile. I simultaneously felt victorious and defeated. My lips parted, and in a soft hush I whispered, “Fine. Not for him, but for you. Fine. Let's just get out of here. We have a lot of road to cover.”

“Thanks, Ihlia.” Crelyos whispered in return.

I stepped forward only a single step. The click of my boot against the tile floor sent a chain reaction racing up and down the entirety of my battered body. My vision blurred, and the voices of those around me faded into obscurity as though someone teleported them miles away. I lifted my right hand to my face as though grabbing my eyes might stabilize my vision. I felt the world tip upside down and soon found myself staring at the ceiling; the whipping wind blew cold at my back as I fell toward the ground completely sapped of strength.

File 19: After the Smolder

"Ihlia!" It was the second time I heard Crelyos sharply call my name, though it sounded like a distorted echo. I anticipated the uncomfortable smack of my battered body against the cold tile; I instead felt the warmth of a body. When I looked up, the former soldier encased his left arm around my waist like a pillar of unshakable support. I remained that way for a few seconds before standing upright.

"I'm fine," I muttered.

"You most certainly are not fine, young lady. Cutting those pain receptors was a terrible mistake! You have lost entirely too much blood. Panacea relies on those receptors to transfer information about wound locations, without pain your recovery nanite just has to stumble across them on its own. Good heavens, I am surprised you can even formulate thoughts let alone sentences," Oswald scolded in the background.

"You want me to carry you?" Crelyos inquired softly.

"No, I said I'm fine." I stepped away from his muscular physique and immediately felt my world spin again. As I stumbled back, my shoulder found his left arm, and the contact between his flesh and mine seemed to stabilize my world. I leaned against him and muttered, "Just let me borrow this arm for a bit."

"Affirmative," he chuckled beneath his breath.

Once outside the mansion, the sudden, rapid clicks of automatic weapons being primed for fire greeted us. A flood of artificial light seared our retinas and rendered us temporarily blind. The three of us hissed and tossed our hands in front of our faces as shields. In front of us, laying on the ground flat upon their stomachs, Raze's remaining minions were bound in iron chains clamped about their wrists and ankles. A solitary shadowy figure stepped forward into the illumination which I surmised to be vehicle headlights.

"Freeze!" The shout was conjured with a half authoritative voice painfully lacking in confidence.

"By Jove, don't shoot lads!" Oswald tossed his hands into the air; Crelyos, still supporting my unstable body, stood rigid. I was in far too poor a condition to offer anything more than a miserable groan. Raze slumped from the mansion behind us and nonchalantly tossed up his hands. As the apparent leader of the light show rushed forward, he immediately clamped Raze in bonds similar to the ones imprisoning his subordinates.

"Hey, who are you guys?" Crelyos shouted from behind the shield of his robotic arm with which he attempted to deflect the bright beams of light.

"I am Samson. I'm one of Loftsborough's men. We've

been trying to free ourselves from Raze's captivity so we can go see our families, but he works us like slaves and promises nothing. Our little rebellion operation has been in its planning phases for almost three months. But his men grossly outnumbered us, and with his pyrokinetic abilities, we just couldn't risk it. Then when we came back tonight from our usual hyped gathering, the base was in an uproar. We heard that Raze was being attacked and most of his brigands were in the mansion, so we decided to act. Are you the ones that attacked Raze?"

"Yeah, that's us," Crelyos responded.

"You did it all by yourselves? You took on his compound alone? That's insane. Where is your backup?" Samson's brown eyes widened to the size of electrocapacitor plates; he gestured behind him to the many men lining the dune buggies which they no doubt pilfered from Raze's warehouse and filled with his stores of sludge. The lights dimmed with Samson's signal.

"Backup? Hah. That's a laugh. We're all the backup we've got. Although this one doesn't do much," Crelyos gestured to Oswald, "You look pretty fierce. You want to replace him?"

"If you fought as well as you ran your mouth, Ihlia might not be on the verge of death. She's always pulling your weight," Oswald snuffed and shook his head. I thought I even heard him click his tongue.

"Oh? And I suppose you're just burstin' with helpful

combat maneuvers. If we ever encounter an enemy who can be talked to death, we'll throw you right on the front line, Fancypants," Crelyos boisterously laughed.

"You guys are... unbelievable. Men! Quick, load up the prisoners and the wounded mercenaries. Next we're going to go put an end to the thugs in Loftsborough and take back our city!" Samson called back with his hands cupped over his mouth. His fellow former captives raised their firearms in unison and unleashed a morale boosting cry.

"Ah, you see, we've already handled that affair as well. My associates and I dispatched the guard occupying Loftsborough before we arrived here to deal with Raze," Oswald puffed out his chest and nodded matter-of-factly.

"Wh..what?" Samson's eyes lit up like an ancient fireworks display. His relieved chuckles flooded my ears. With a quick spin on his heel, the resident of Loftsborough turned to his companions and raised his hands into the air, "They've liberated Loftsborough as well! Men, we can go home to our wives! To our children! This lot are heroes!" A few men dropped to their knees and wept, others leapt into the air with overjoyed screams, while still others marveled at the idea that we accomplished the feat we claimed without aid.

"No... please... not heroes," I whined softly. Heroes meant interacting with unknown people. It meant attention and inconvenience. Samson simply laughed as though I jested.

“Haha, let us take you back to town! You look like you could use a good rest!” Samson extended his hand toward Crelyos, who reached out with his cybernetic prosthetic and shamelessly shook it.

“Actually, if you could just drop us off at our buggy up the road,” Crelyos pointed, “we'll just follow you back ourselves.”

“That can certainly be arranged! Anything for you lot!” Samson laughed and led us to one of the procured buggies separate from Raze and his men. As the citizens loaded the prisoners into a heavily guarded buggy near the far end, Raze stopped in front of Crelyos and me. His gaze remained forward toward the dim prospects of his future. If Loftsborough decided not to outright execute him and his men, he would likely spend most of his remaining life in some holding cell or sold into slavery. That was assuming that Bradich's organization did not come after him in the meantime.

“Crelyos, She-wolf,” Raze's voice trailed off in a somber tone, “if there's anyone that belongs in that world of monsters, if there's anyone that can stop what they're planning to do, it's you two.” With those words, one of Samson's allies brutally hammered Raze in the back with the stock of his rifle. The harsh words, “Get a move on, thug!” escaped the lips of the nameless townsman. Still leaning against Crelyos' broad shoulder, I sluggishly lifted my gaze to his face. His eyes held a seemingly endless void of convoluted thoughts and emotions.

Perhaps he felt that if he had spoken up in regard to Raze's sexual preferences during their military days, the events might have turned out differently. Perhaps he believed that Smiles still resided somewhere deep inside the brigand's twisted personality and he longed to travel with him again or to offer him another chance. After a few moments, I nudged him to gain his attention. He looked down at me and replaced his conflicted expression with a dopey grin.

As we neared the gaudy paint and steel of one of Raze's vehicles, I stopped. An overwhelming chill crept up the base of my spine and settled against the back of my neck. I twisted as quickly as my condition allowed and glared toward the mountain ridges decorating the horizon beyond Raze's fortress. The dark clouds perpetually rolling across the cold wastelands faintly lit up as the hidden sun rose over the mountains behind the curtain of gray fallout. The dim light cast across the frigid, decrepit landscape failed to provide enough visibility to discern anything other than the jagged rocks shrouded in shadow.

"What's wrong, Ihlia?" Crelyos asked with a tilt of his head.

"I feel like... someone's watching us," I responded quietly.

"Like, right now?" Crelyos turned his gaze toward the same area as I. He squinted hard, trying to make out anything other than stone formations but to no avail.

“Yeah...” I replied reluctantly.

“Yeah...” He mocked me, “... that's quite enough danger and blood loss for you for one day. You're getting weird on me. Time for you to get some rest. Lots of it.” Crelyos planted his palm between my shoulder blades and shoved me into my seat in the dune buggy.

The concept of rest sank in like a double-edged sword. I craved nothing more than to traverse the landscape to old Colorado as swiftly as possible, but with my lids growing heavier with each passing moment and the burning pain tearing through my body, rest sounded like a viable alternative plan.

File 20: The Next Breadcrumb

My eyelids fluttered open to the golden hue of sunlight streaming beautifully through a nearby window. I pulled back the warm blanket and stepped from the soft bed. The freezing air immediately assaulted my bare skin; it reminded me that everything from the artificial light filtering through the tattered curtains to the synthetic bed and its blankets used to warm my body only imitated a long forgotten time of comfort and abundance. The reality, more frigid than the blistering breeze that penetrated Loftsborough's protective shell, was that our world all but perished during the Titan Crisis ten years ago. Three days had passed since the assault on Raze's desert fortress. Oswald, the old codger, had declared that he refused to budge from the city.

"For the last time, Panacea is no miracle. You need time for your accumulated deep tissue wounds and organ trauma to fully recover. Five days, minimum, and only after a thorough checkup," he had said. The citizens of Loftsborough kindly offered us Eugene's former domicile for the duration of our stay, but I already felt antsy.

I sauntered to the cracked, rusty-framed mirror in the corner of the room. My obsidian hair, long but haphazard, ended at the small bump of my spine a few inches above my rear. Singed frays tipped several strands, frays acquired from a snap of Raze's fingers. I lifted my bandaged left hand and slid aside the bangs shadowing my jade eyes. Aside from the tight, makeshift sports bra supporting the faint swell of my breasts, the practical, unremarkable undergarment hugging the slender curve of my hips, and the plethora of bandages encircling most of the rest of my flesh, I stood exposed in front of my murky reflection.

Wounds still busily healing and battle scars long since healed covered my sleek, athletic body; they remained testimonies to the doctor's passionate warnings regarding Panacea's lack of omnipotence. The scars decorated flesh that might otherwise have grown into immaculate, dainty skin if a different fate befell me than the path of war and combat. My mind, riddled with memories of death, violence, and loss, might have filled to the brim with recollections of life, laughter, and normality if not for that day of destiny in Yordleton when I was but thirteen.

And my heart, devoid of any deep emotions save burning hatred and the desire for vengeance, might have understood joy, camaraderie, and the inexplicable depth of love if not for the inevitable betrayal of my former leader, Bradich. I flattened my palm against its twin in the decrepit mirror. *"I wouldn't change a thing,"* I thought to myself with bittersweet reminiscence.

Shrill, excited cries echoed from the streets outside the room's single window framed with ripped curtains. I stepped to the baby blue rags and slid them aside enough to peer outside. From the second story of Eugene's home, I gazed across the city's central square. Once a barren metal plain with a giant stone crucifix glaring from its center, the open space had filled with the daily activities common among the cities sprinkled throughout our once great country.

Men and women exchanged goods and services along the perimeter of the imaginary circle forming the market; other citizens worked in the synthetic food processing plants tucked away in one corner of Loftsborough, and the children, the source of the shrill cries, pranced about in the streets while their parents worked. Those children not giggling and making merry remained indoors studying with one of their parents.

For whatever reason, some people believed keeping archaic knowledge alive would ultimately benefit humanity. Mathematics, engineering, philosophy, religion, literature, writing, and many other facets of education passed to America's youth only through the direct guidance of those parents who still valued academics. Most of the world, myself included, felt that the more pressing issue of survival far outweighed grade point averages.

Those trades still useful to human perseverance, namely nanite surgery, synthetic food production, scavenging, architecture, and combat, were far more easily shown than taught. Due to certain... hazards, many children would reach their early teenage years before tagging along with mommy or daddy to the production plants or on a scavenging mission. For better or worse, society functioned in such a manner.

A smile crept across my lips when I noticed Crelyos among the jovial children; they swarmed about him as though he was an enormous tree jutting from the city's metal saucer. His muscular arms outstretched, they served as massive limbs for a boy and girl to cling like monkeys to his right and left appendages respectively. Oswald had reapplied the synthetic flesh concealing his cybernetic arm's tubes and circuitry the day after our return to Loftsborough. Apparently, the latex material commonly served doctors such as the old codger in case of "oops" moments, so he kept plenty of the spray-on concoction available in his trailer.

The gaping grin on Crelyos' face suggested he possessed not a care in the world save the tykes clambering up and down his bulky physique. When he spun around, roaring playfully, the children shrieked and giggled, clinging to his body parts for what seemed like dear life. I unlatched the window and, with a gentle push, shoved it open to lean against the sill. My chin dropped against the flat of my palm and I planted my elbow on the frame.

I grinned at the spectacle of the lumbering blond mercenary; he pretended to double over from the weight of the children who took the opportunity to leap atop him with high-pitched shouts of, "get him!" or, "scrap pile!" The last one elicited a chuckle since most of those children had never heard of a "dog," much less seen one, but the myriad of scrap piles decorating cities and their outskirts caused the birth of a slightly altered form of the nostalgic slang, "dog pile."

I retreated into the dim room and adorned my outfit. Not one for much variety, I pulled on a new black tank top; tugged up a pair of multi-pocketed black cargo pants; slid my feet into a pair of black combat boots; and draped a fresh black trench coat of synthetic leather over my bandages. I flipped my hair over the collar of the coat, allowing it to spill across my back before reaching over to fasten my rifle strap across my shoulders and my dagger belt around my waist.

I rushed down the stairs as best as my injured body would allow; the faint thud of my feet against the stone stairs resounded until I reached the first floor dining area. Atop the table, a starch bar sat next to a small pile of vitamin and mineral pills resting atop a half-opened can of tuna. Next to the grandiose meal, a steel water canteen pinned a coarse piece of paper to the table. I lifted the paper, fashioned from a man-made material the molecular structure of which resembled old hemp plants, and glanced at the black sludge-based ink scribbled across it.

"Dear child, I cannot begin to illustrate the consequence of refusing to consume everything you see before you. Suffice to say the word ' unpleasant' fails to do it justice." I smiled and shook my head; in smaller, far uglier handwriting on the corner of the paper beneath Oswald's obvious warning, another message was written, "Yeah, girly. What Fancypants said." I chuckled.

As I consumed my tenderly prepared breakfast in silence, I reflected on Raze's words after his defeat during the fortress raid. *"I'm the lowest on the totem pole, both in strength and influence,"* he said.

I furrowed my brows at the thought of my own meekness. Individuals with abilities as potent as Raze's gathering at the feet of my former mercenary commander, I expected. More powerful individuals of high military rank, exceeding skill, and more potent augments flocking to my former mercenary commander, I did not. The very concept forced my lip beneath the clench of my teeth as I pondered the true depth of Bradich's capabilities, my limited understanding of them, and the goals he pursued.

Why? Why all the trouble, the ruse, the betrayal, the destruction of the world, and the formation of his organization? I sighed and downed the pills Oswald provided with the water housed in the canteen. As I stood, I sternly resolved myself. I refused to be disheartened by the staggering odds or my limited knowledge. If the odds stacked against me, I would cut them down. If the knowledge eluded me, I would wrangle it from Bradich's lackeys. If it cost me my life, I would avenge Donovan. If it took my last breath, I would drag Bradich into Death's black embrace with me.

I emerged from Eugene's home and purposefully moved through the crowds toward the town center. I simply followed the angelic laughs and melodious screams until I stumbled upon the squad of kids using Crelyos as a climbing post. I cocked to one side and placed my right hand atop my hip's curved swell. With an arched brow, I watched the former soldier until he noticed me, at which point he lifted a finger and cried, "Quick, munchkins, attack!"

The little ones paused in their frolicking to stare at me. With little hesitation, the small group of children scampered behind Crelyos with an orchestra of squeaks and whimpers. One child remained fearfully frozen in front of me; she stared at me with quivering knees as I knelt down in front of her. Our eyes locked, and I reached my hand toward her head to offer it a light pat. Tears instantly flooded the corners of her eyes, and she began sniffling. I jerked my hand away from her; sufficiently annoyed by her display, I stood and walked passed my ally with a brisk gait.

Behind me, I heard him offer the small girl words of reassurance, and with hands far gentler than mine, he ushered the children off to go play among themselves. My stride brought me to rest in front of the gaping charcoal hole driven into Loftsborough's town square. Though Samson and the others removed it, the barbed wire wrapped concrete pillar that toted the skeletal remains of Eugene still haunted my memories. As I stared at the empty space, a large hand found its way to my shoulder.

"Hey..." Crelyos' voice drifted from behind me.

"Even in Junction City, they never really liked me, so it's not that surprising," I responded without hesitation.

"You mean children? Haha, I guess it's those eyes of yours. You're not all that hard to read. Just lace every thought you might have with ‘Kill Bradich' and it pretty much sums you up. Kids, especially, pick up on those scary vibes pretty easy,” Crelyos sighed and stepped forward next to me; his eyes focused on the same area that haunted my memories. They must have haunted his as well.

“I suppose. It means everything to me, after all. Donovan wasn't just someone I loved; he was someone I was supposed to protect. And he was good to us - not just me, but all of us. Especially his brother Bradich. Why would you take away something so wonderful?” I clenched my fists at my sides and shook my head.

“Sometimes the beautiful and good things are the ones we want to hurt the most. When somethin' in front of you is good or beautiful, it sometimes makes you face all the bad and ugly in yourself. Some people can handle it. Other people can't and want to get rid of that beautiful thing no matter what.” Crelyos' explanation seemed convoluted, but more twisted was the fact that a large part of me understood the logic behind it.

“I've been meaning to ask you,” I interjected, “why did you not want to avenge Eugene? You were so angry when you found out Raze killed him. I thought I was going to have to hold you back long enough to get information out of him. Instead, you stopped me from putting an end to him. I just don't get it.”

Crelyos turned his gaze to the imitation sun gleaming from the center of Loftsborough's upper plate. A soft smile pulled up the corners of his lips, and he lifted and dropped his shoulders in a confused shrug.

"It's hard to explain," he said sadly, "Eugene was my friend, sure enough. But at one time, so was Raze. He turned rotten and sour and was the only one diggin' his own pit of despair without even realizin' it. But would killin' him bring back Eugene? Wherever Eugene is now, would it somehow make him happy? I dunno. I do know that the Raze I once knew, Smiles, is somewhere inside that idiot we captured. If there was a way to kill Raze without killin' Smiles, I'd be all for it. But if he dies, I lose two friends instead of just one. Haha, I've thought that for a while but actually sayin' it sounded really stupid, huh?" Crelyos laughed heartily and tipped his head in my direction.

"A little. It's idealism at its finest. You don't exact revenge to calm the dead, you do it to calm yourself," I pointed out with an almost vehement grunt.

"Really? Killin' people doesn't really calm me. In fact, I hate doin' it. Even those nameless thugs; thinkin' about it makes me sick." Crelyos lifted his right hand and stared at his open palm. I arched a brow at his statement.

"You do it liberally enough. In fact, you're one of the more efficient killing machines I've had the honor of working with." I crossed my arms as I recalled the various members of my squad during my days as a Bald Eagle. They were good, but Crelyos was in a league of his own.

“I'll pretend that wasn't a slap in the face.” The blond mercenary furrowed his brows and turned around toward the bunch of youngsters playing together in the distance.

His eyes softened, and he scratched the back of his head nervously, “It's them. I mean, if you think about it, the people that survived the Titan Crisis already made their choices. Most of ‘em went rotten. It sucks, but it's true. Guys that rape, steal, and kill are everywhere, and there's no system of law to protect those little guys. They haven't had the chance to choose yet, and it's not like they're goin' from a world of plenty to a terrible war to a global catastrophe.”

“This world is all they know, so it's kind of their world now. We're the old generation just holdin' onto it until they're old enough to choose. If the only thing left I can do is bloody these hands for their sake, then that's what I gotta do. I hate killin', but I hate the thought of someone takin' the choices away from those kids even more. If I have to choose, I'll bear the disgust of dirty hands any day.”

I smiled at the overgrown teddy bear. “I hate arguing with you. I always lose,” I muttered under my breath. That strange vibration touched my chest again; it fluttered through my torso like a splash of warm water. I turned to watch the children as well.

“What was that? You say somethin'?” Crelyos nudged me with his elbow.

“I said this sappy stuff is the kind of stuff you usually blabber on about when you're drunk. Isn't it a bit too early for that?” I rammed my fist into his rib and playfully twisted. His face lit up, alarmed, and he swatted at my hand.

“Ow, ow, ow! What the hell, girly!” Crelyos laughed between mock grunts, “The tavern around here has some really nice sludge. Where do you think I go every night? I've slowly been stockin' up my supply for when we head off to Colorado, too. What do you say we drink the night away tonight? For old time's sake, just you and me.” He reached down and curled his left hand around my slender wrist. As he pried my fist from his ribs, I smirked.

“That's fine. I need to talk to Oswald first. Raze, too, for that matter. We know that we're going northwest to Colorado, but we don't know exactly where or what to look for when we get there,” I shrugged and snatched my wrist from his iron grip.

“Yeah, I guess that info would be helpful. We can't just roam around an entire state lookin' for somethin' suspicious, and I don't really know the landscape all that well once you talk about goin' beyond Texas.” Crelyos folded his arms over his chest.

“You sure you want to come? You could just head back to Junction City and reclaim your seat at the bar there.” I glanced over at him. For some reason, a heavy lump hung on my chest, and its destination depended entirely on his next words. Either the weight would lift, or it would sink deep into my stomach. It was a strange feeling, but somewhere I understood that I wished for him to accompany me.

“I thought about it. But Sarge is involved now; I can't just leave things the way they are. He was my squad leader, I gotta find out why he's doin' this. Why someone like him would follow someone like Harbinger blows my mind.” Crelyos shook his head, “Besides, we both know you'd get dead without me. I can't let you have all the fun.”

“I think I'd do just fine. But...” I looked up at the mercenary and his dopey grin, “I'm glad you'll be there all the same. It means a lot.”

“You got it, girly.” Crelyos lifted a finger and pointed at one of the strangely shaped buildings a few houses to the right of Mayor Trumark's home. “That's the tavern. I'll see ya there when they turn that giant light in the sky off.”

“I've been wondering about that. Ever since we got back it seems they turn it off at night and on during the day. When we got here before, when it was Raze's Haven, it was night and the thing was burning bright. What gives?” I stared up at the enormous incandescent hemisphere illuminating Loftsborough.

“Apparently keepin' it lit all day and night was Raze's order. It represents fire, so, you know how that goes. The citizens use it to mimic the cycles of day and night, so they turn it off when the outside world goes from the gray of day to the black of night. Plus, keepin' it on all the time must consume a hell of a lot of sludge," Crelyos noted.

He turned slowly in place and surveyed the various buildings cluttering the city, "I just wonder if they ever plan on demolishin' and reconstructin' it all. Raze had control of this place for a year, when he got here he had all the buildin's torn down and rebuilt into some weird abstract architecture. There's no uniformity, the houses all look like somethin' out of a weird paintin'." A frown touched Crelyos' lips. I hypothesized that my ally's frown indicated his general distaste for what Raze considered art. It coaxed a chuckle from me.

"Well I'm going to go talk to Raze. I'll see you tonight, big guy," I offered Crelyos a faint slap against his shoulder before traversing the town square toward Trumark's house.

The large two story building to the right of Trumark's home reminded me of the tavern in Junction City. During the day, it was a desolate building the cracks and doors of which whistled like a haunted house with the passing of the faintest chill breeze, but when night fell it would stand as the only beacon of light in the entire town. The noises that erupted from a lively tavern were unlike any in the world. The thought painted a genuine smile on my lips.

To the left of Trumark's residence, however, stood a drafty stone building. Its simple design suggested a hasty construction; within the confines of that building, lining the walls of the first floor; the first basement; the second basement; and so on, steel cages and built-in cells framed with stone and iron formed Loftsborough's makeshift prison. Under normal circumstances, it was likely a mere temporary punishment for citizens who broke Trumark's laws. I surmised that Raze and his subordinates, however, were in for an extended stay.

I entered the prison. Dust caked the rocky walls, and the floors, smudged with streaks of blood and sludge, smelled stale; the prison must have seen many years without use. I remembered that during the year of his occupation, Raze sent all offenders to the upper plate to fend for themselves against freezing winds. I simply failed to comprehend why Crelyos believed even an ounce of humanity existed in the duke of flame, much less enough to warrant sparing his life.

The entire building functioned without electricity. With no generators to power lamps or light fixtures, the only illumination in the musty building stemmed from the lanterns that lined the wall in an efficient array. The sludge housed within the metal casing fed the flickering flames dancing behind glass. To the left of the doorway, a single guard sat at a stone desk facing the row of ironclad cells against the back wall. Directly across the room, a flight of stairs led down to subsequent basement levels of the establishment. In the grand architecture of Loftsborough, those basement levels actually cut into the city's lower plate, and the metal saucer formed a natural architecture for the walls and ceiling in the lower levels.

The guard nodded to me with passing recognition. He seemed uneasy. I glanced to his waist; a ring of rusty keys loosely hung around a loop in his belt. My eyes darted from the keys to the sludge-filled torches lining the walls. Finally, I stared at the cell in the far left corner of the room. Behind the thick iron bars, a small cot fit neatly against the back wall. Raze sat completely still atop its uncomfortable surface. His eyes, crystalline blue shards housing an intense sharpness that rivaled his small sword's, stared forward at the guard who anxiously kept watch. I strolled in front of the duke of flame's quarters and placed my hands on my hips.

"Raze," I glared at him with cold eyes.

"She-wolf," He mocked my tone but failed to take his eyes off the nervous guard.

"I need more information. Colorado was a big place. Crelyos and I aren't familiar with the territory. We need more to go on." I shifted my weight to one leg; my body rocked slowly in front of his eyes. Perhaps subconsciously, I attempted to alleviate a bit of the guard's unease, though I instinctively knew he possessed little cause for fear.

"You do, don't you?" A smile briefly passed across his face like a bolt of lightning in a cloud: there one moment, gone the next.

"Are you going to tell me or not? I have little patience for games and even less for seeing your face." My brows furrowed involuntarily. Raze, though healed through Panacea's efforts, retained the scars of our exchange. His bald head, once coated in lush strands of beautiful golden hair, gleamed after the tongues of his own fire consumed his illustrious locks.

Without his hair and in normal clothing, Raze looked like any other passerby one might meet on the streets. The only difference lay in those eyes of his; their pure icy hue belied his tainted, frozen heart. Perhaps the true source of my rage stemmed from the possibility that I was merely looking into a mirror similar to the one in Eugene's house. Did I perceive the frigid depths of his murderous heart within those frozen eyes, or did their shimmering surface reflect the monster hiding within me?

“I assume the doctor has maps? The coordinates are 38 degrees 44 minutes 45 seconds north latitude, 104 degrees 47 minutes 6 seconds west longitude. Crelyos should recognize those coordinates, it used to be an old military installation way before the Global Conflict. Before we got all enlightened and shit, too,” Raze quickly recited.

“If that gorgeous pea-brain doesn't remember or you don't have any maps, just keep following the road north-northwest until you reach a small town called Uriel. It's nearby. Ask around, do some tracking, I don't know. Stop bothering me,” Raze dismissively waved his hand.

I memorized the coordinates and directions and ignored the remainder of his rant. Without uttering a farewell, I spun on my heel and began for the door. Another quick glance to the keys attached to the oblivious guard's belt and the sludge-fueled torches gave me pause. I knew Oswald and Crelyos explained the dangerous capabilities of the duke of flame to Samson during our journey back to Loftsborough, yet there he sat surrounded by potential tools due to stupidity or negligence. Despite his ability to use finite psychokinesis to orchestrate an escape, Raze remained peacefully locked away in his cell. Why?

"I have nowhere to go anymore. My men are all but wiped out, the organization will kill me if they find me, and I have a lot to think about anyway. Don't even ask," Raze piped up after watching me take notice of the variety of small, dangerous objects littering the prison house. Perhaps he possessed telepathy as well, but it was more likely I failed to properly conceal my concern. Then again, I never attempted to do so.

"Hmph," I responded and continued from the dank structure that served as Raze's confines.

File 21: Oswald's Checkup

I spent the majority of the day meandering through the crowds bustling through Loftsborough's central plaza. Though my eyes roved the established shops for items of worth, my vacant gaze would likely have skimmed by the best items due to my wandering thoughts. Unable to reconcile Crelyos' logic regarding his two friends, Eugene and Raze, I dwelt upon the circumstances surrounding my quest for revenge.

After pledging my allegiance to the Bald Eagles, Bradich and the unit became more than mere bosom buddies. They replaced my family who died in the hyped attack on Yordleton. Larz, my sniping mentor, and the other members of the company grew closer to me than my own parents. We sang together, ate together, laughed, cried, and bled together.

I gritted my teeth when I imagined their faces blank, their eyes rolled into the backs of their heads, and pin-point accurate bullet wounds in each of their foreheads. Thankfully, Larz perished a year prior to Bradich's scheme. As Bradich's closest friend, Larz would have been most devastated by the betrayal. When I reminisced on my former leader's twisted face as he waltzed off into the desert rain after taking my second family away from me, my vision blurred from my unbridled rage.

"Ihlia! Hey, I've been calling you for like five minutes." The sound of a vaguely familiar voice snapped me from the dark hole of my own memories. I placed my thumb and finger against my eyes and gave them a good rub before glancing over to behold the face of Samson. A sigh escaped my lips.

"What is it, Samson?" I asked in a less than patient tone.

"Uh... did I interrupt something?" Circumstances prevented me from properly discerning his appearance the first time we met, but after a second gleaning, I realized his countenance was fairly easy on the eyes. He stood taller than I, an easy feat to be sure, at six feet even. He kept his head shaved; small stubs of brown hair cleanly jutted from his scalp. His surgical scar, a wide crescent stretching across the side of his head, afforded his buzz cut a bit of character. His dark brown eyes were soft but piercing, and his posture indicated a strong muscle frame and moderate combat training he likely obtained after the Titan Crisis.

In light of his exploits at Raze's fortress, Trumark offered Samson a position as the town's top mercenary. It was a guardsman's position at best, but it came with good pay, nice perks, and a snappy uniform, if one could call clothes a small cut above normal "snappy." I teasingly grinned at him.

"Ah, my apologies, Officer Samson. What can I do for you this evening?" I offered him a mock salute.

"Oh, stop it. I'm here on unofficial business. It's Doctor Oswald, he's looking for you. He said he'll be outside of town at the dune buggy; whatever that means," Samson shrugged.

"Got it, thanks, captain," I laughed jokingly between pursed lips.

"Ugh, whatever. I gotta get back to work. Have a nice day, ma'am." Samson offered me a salute far more serious than the one I displayed. I grinned and nodded; as Samson disappeared into the crowds of people, I turned in the direction of the elevator that would take me down from Loftsborough and into the surrounding deserts. The old codger's need to speak to me was quite conducive to the pressing matters I needed to discuss with him. Namely, I needed him to confirm or shatter my desperate hope that he possessed old maps of America.

The drawn out ride down the elevator shaft drew memories of the laboratory in Cairo, Egypt, to the forefront of my thoughts. I furrowed my brows in frustrated recollection. During that fateful mission, I rode down a similar elevator, albeit smoother in its descent, alongside Bradich and his brother, Donovan. Our jokes and teases served as intermittent breaks from the weary silence back then. Donovan's research on nanite personalities consumed him, and Bradich offered him as much support as his unscientific mind could muster. Their bond seemed unshakeable back then.

I clenched my fist only to be jarred yet again from my

trip down memory lane by the mechanical hiss of the elevator reaching its destination. I stepped from the rusty sliding gate and traversed the length of the bridge hovering mere feet above churning quicksand. The blistering wind tore through the flat landscape and peppered the exposed portions of my flesh with cold nips. In the distance, the deep gray light filtering through rolling fallout clouds faded as the sun sank beneath the horizon.

On a small, dusty plateau atop a ridge sat our little group's dune buggy. The attached trailer leaned precariously close to the edge of the cliff. Though steep, walking up its side proved only a minor challenge. I ascended the short distance to the top of the outcrop; a few pieces of rubble rolled harmlessly down the rocky surface when I finally reached the apex. I stepped into the back of the trailer following the sounds of a micro-drill and the flashes of electric sparks. Hunched over an impromptu desk, Oswald busily labored over the same project to which he dedicated his life: nanites.

“Ah, Ihlia. Do come in. I take it Samson was able to convey my message with little difficulty? Excellent, excellent.” Oswald's hand lifted from his work to wave me to a chair he prepared in the center of the trailer. Its partially reclined position immediately sent off red flags; I folded my arms beneath my breasts. Assumedly, the old codger felt my burning glare since he halted his work completely and spun around in his stool. “What, dear child?” He attempted to mock my stare.

"You want to slice me open again," I stated matter-of-factly.

"Yes, that is the point of summoning you. I will also offer to give you that checkup I promised. If your body is indeed ready for more potentially fatal action, then we can be on our way tomorrow. That's a day earlier than I promised was the minimum required time for your recovery! Not a bad bargain, if I do say so. Which I do." The doctor playfully depressed the trigger of his mechanical drill in two quick successions. It whistled at me. I made a face.

I sighed, shook my head, and removed the rifle from my back; after leaning it against the chair, I took a seat and began bunching up my flowing strands of hair near the back of my head. Oswald's firm hands took the job from me, tying off the strands of hair and folding them over my shoulders until the first few layers parted to reveal the stubble against the bulbous rear of my skull. I heard him shuffling about on his wheeled stool behind me, but I remained facing the trailer's exit. After a few moments, I felt the sharp pinch of a hypodermic needle.

The fluid Oswald injected into my brain always afflicted my senses with a powerful disorientation. He claimed it was a common drug used to inhibit the reaction of Panacea while simultaneously serving as an anesthetic. That way, an incision made would not simply close due to the nanites' speedy recovery process. The operations felt like daydreams to me. I existed in an interim state between conscious and unconscious, and it usually led to random rants. The old codger likely dealt with it often with his patients, since his only responses for the majority of my ramblings consisted of, “M'hm, yes, of course, dear, okay.”

“Are you... going to add... another nanite?” The flip-flopping vision between my right and left eye as they struggled, and failed, to coordinate their droops offered me interesting shifts in the distorted scenery. My question was met with a brief pause; the doctor was obviously thinking.

“Well I'm uncertain at this point, dear child. I'll need to take a look inside first, see how your activity is holding up with the other nanites clustered atop your neocortex,” Oswald chuckled as though he created some obscure pun which only he might have understood. Even the high pitched scream of the whirring surgical blade akin to a buzz saw coaxed only a subtle groan from the back of my throat, or perhaps I groaned at the doctor's poor taste in jokes. I decided to debate it later.

As the grinding vibrations performed by my old friend chipped away at the back of my head, I felt the patch of skull covering Oswald's preferred operation sight jar loose. The tender, careful hands of the doctor removed any necessary sections, and the suction of tubes to keep stray blood at bay changed the trailer's serene quiet into a mechanical madhouse.

I felt the wire which synchronously served as the link-up to my brain and the camera to guide Oswald's machinations feed into the moderately sized hole left by my absent patch of scalp. The sound of the doctor's holocomputer humming to life and the beep of the keys depressed by his skilled fingertips provided a soothing lullaby as I drifted in and out of awareness. I knew the routine; the doctor would input my real name, a fancy word for a secret password, and obtain a schematic of my brain detailing my every neurological trait ranging from my number of implants to their purpose and original designer.

The data, stored in its entirety through a medium known as the New Neural Network, or N-3, provided Oswald with a road map to my augments every capability. The N-3 itself was one of humanity's great accomplishments. An entirely new intranet designed to completely replace the World Wide Web, the N-3 became a sensation upon its introduction in the early 2200's to accommodate the massive influx of neurotech data. With the Internet too prone to hackers, the N-3 implemented a series of high security walls with no proverbial backdoor. Either you possessed someone's true name and could access their files, or you did not and were out of luck.

“Hm, it seems your cortical folds are still responding well. Every time I look at your brain it amazes me, so much is going on here! If we could just unlock its secrets...” Oswald's voice suggested one of his infamous scientific rants.

“Doc...” The distressed droning of my voice like a sick child calling for its parent tugged him from his blabbering.

"All right, all right. Well, everything looks remarkable as always. So I will add one more implant to test the limitations of your brain's innate adaptability. Just sit still for one moment... Goodness, I guess you haven't much choice, do you, dear child?" Oswald chortled. If the pursuit of vengeance against Bradich failed to end my life, the old codger's quips were sure to do the job.

As always, I lost any sense of discernible time. The annoyance of Oswald's jokes faded to mumbled obscurity. It began as fragmented pieces of audio stimulus I recognized, but by the climax of the nanite's installation when the Panacea anesthetic reached its prime, Oswald sounded as though he spoke through a scratchy broken microphone with the volume set to "muffled."

I felt my lips move several times over the course of the operation, though I remained unaware as to what words passed between them. My reality consisted of several worlds overlapping one another; some possessed shades of gray, others were blotchy colors running together like streaks of rain down a window. At least, my eyes fed that information back to my drugged brain, or perhaps my drugged brain deciphered that information and sent it back to my eyes. Whichever organ was the culprit, I wished for them both to shut the hell up.

"...and we're done!" The doctor's voice jarred me from my stupor like a buzzing alarm clock. My eyes shot wide open; the dim surroundings in the trailer remained unchanged as though I merely blinked and the action slipped my mind. If so, it was one hell of a blink. The nervous tempo of my heart would have offered a jack-rabbit's competition. I recognized a familiar sensation combing through my hair, and the rapid pitter-patter in my chest began to slow. The breath I held in the back of my throat finally hissed from between my lips in a relieved exhale.

As was his ritual, Oswald sat behind me after stitching my scalp together; guided by his hand, a plastic brush combed through my lengthy hair which we messily bunched together at the procedure's beginning. No matter his excitement for science, Oswald never neglected to brush my hair after a surgery throughout all ten years I knew him. It soothed me from the jitters of my reawakening, and the gesture served as one of respect to Donovan, whose love for my hair remained one of my fondest memories.

"How long was I out?" I murmured with a drowsy lull.

"Long enough to blabber the coordinates in Colorado... about an hour," Oswald laughed softly.

I lifted my hand blindly over my head. As though reading my mind on cue, Oswald reached over, snatched up a set of maps from his table, and planted them in my outstretched palm. I unfurled them in my lap while the old codger finished brushing my strands of midnight. Oswald had marked the coordinates just below the center of the box denoting the border to the old state of Colorado; I could scarcely remember a time that such borders were not utterly trivial.

“Raze said it's an old military base,” I commented.

"Hm, well I suppose we'll see when we get there." Oswald stood and maneuvered to my anterior. A few moments later, and he beamed a bright light into my eyes. The doctor followed through with his promise to thoroughly inspect me. Whether or not I measured up to his standard of health in order to continue our journey was another matter. As I examined the maps and nonchalantly offered the old doctor my limbs and appendages when he motioned for them, Oswald's throat released ponderous sounds of, “Hmmm...” and “M'hm...”

“So what's the damage?” I glanced up from my map examination.

Oswald sighed and placed his tools on the nearby table, “Well, so be it. We should be all right to depart on the morrow. Your brain, your nanite adaptation, and even the efficiency of your nanites... everything about you is most remarkable, after all.” Oswald rubbed the wiry extension of his beard.

“I see, As long as it means getting to Bradich sooner, I'll take it as a compliment.” I stood from the doctor's operating chair. The sudden rush of blood flooding my head and the faint throb at the back of my skull sent me staggering to one side. I placed my fingers atop Oswald's table to steady myself. Oswald placed his hand on my shoulder.

"You might be feeling a bit under the weather, take it slow. That serum is quite potent. I've nearly perfected the concoction since the trial run at Raze's fortress! Haha!" Oswald kept his arm extended in the air in a gentlemanly offer. I felt my knees ready to crumble beneath my own weight, so I accepted.

"Ugh. That stuff really kicks," I grinned and steadied myself.

"But of course. I made it, after all. By the way, I took the liberty of removing your bandages. I see little need for them anymore," The doctor replied matter-of-factly.

As he assisted my struggling attempts to move, Oswald snapped his fingers as though an important fact suddenly dawned on him, "Ah, that's right! Your new implant! After careful consideration regarding your Cognitive Accelerator, I have been wracking my brain over building an implant capable of..."

"Doc, no offense, but I think I'm going to hurl. I need some fresh air... later, ok?" I lifted my hand to halt his rampant speech about nanites. His words sounded like little more than a garbled foreign language in my current state, anyway. My body swayed to and fro with my erratic gait toward the trailer's mouth; as I stepped into the wastelands, the wind's cold sting promptly greeted me.

“Ihlia, your Panacea is still a touch impeded! Don't wander too far, dear child! The effect won't completely subside for several hours! Stay out of trouble and head straight to the city!” Oswald's arduous warnings received a dismissive wave from my right hand as I trudged out into the barren wastelands of Old Texas. A smile touched my lips as I recalled similar warnings after each operation the doctor performed. Even the first time I met him when he arrived at the Cairo laboratory site to assist Donovan with his research, the first words he directed at me were exclamations of caution regarding an electrcocapacitor plate with which I was, obliviously, acting far too friendly.

Some time amid my regard for Crelyos, Raze, and Oswald, my thoughts involuntarily drifted to the past. As my mind cleared in the crisp frozen desert surrounding the area of Loftsborough, I sighed at the power a vivid memory possessed on the frail human psyche. I understood the triviality of dwelling on the past and the folly of allowing it to affect my emotional state, but my heart sank anyway.

Not one for empty “what if” or “maybe if I...” thoughts, I snapped myself from my fanciful daydreams and glanced around. Where the hell was Loftsborough? I spun on my heel and buzzed my vision enhancing augment to life. With acute telescopic vision I swept the horizon in a full three hundred sixty degrees to no avail. My concern for Loftsborough's location suddenly faded. Where the hell was I?

I rigorously shook my head. "What the hell is in that stuff, Doc?" I muttered under my breath. I knew not how long my mind drifted through the realms of irrelevant recollection, nor did I know the direction in which I apparently meandered after escaping the stuffy confines of the old codger's trailer. Without a sense of bearing and with the darkness of night looming overhead, I quickly surveyed the surrounding landscape for an alternate means of assessing my situation. Considering the curvature of the earth's horizon impeded the full capabilities of my vision augment, my first order of business seemed clear; I required higher ground.

The dusty wastelands of the desert region of Old Texas truly became an eerie display at the onset of dusk. The gray rocks, stripped of minerals and serving as empty, jagged testimonies to the desolation of the Titan Crisis, were painted with a mixture of blacks and purples as the luminescence of the moon filtered through the perpetual fallout rolling overhead. The sky, a volatile soup of clouds grumbling with thunder and flashing with the occasional streak of lightning, hung over the area like bad breath.

The sour scents of dirt, rust, and sulfur blew in on the whistling breeze, and as the climax to the foreboding landscape, the only hopeful hill mountainous enough to provide a bird's eye view of the area was nestled at the far end of a valley formed by steep jagged cliffs erupting from the ground like a rocky ribcage not far from my location. *"Perfect..."* I sarcastically thought.

File 22: The Lonely Little Girl

The nameless valley formed the beginning of a series of small mountain chains which progressively grew taller and more numerous in lieu of the warped environment. Even from my position almost half a mile away, I saw gaping maws that formed the entrances to caves and tunnels no doubt worming through the earth like a labyrinth. As I approached the shadowy cliffs curling up around the valley, I noted two things: First, the cliffs looked infinitely smaller from a half a mile away, and second, at least a dozen openings peppered the ridges down the length of the valley. At the end of the ravine, taunting me like a checkered finish line, a mountainous hill swelled up like a pimple.

Its surface, far smoother than the daggers which formed the surrounding cliffs, lifted high overhead before emptying into the mountain chains behind it. At the apex of the hill, discerning my whereabouts and the necessary course to ensure my safe return to Loftsborough would have been a breeze. Unfortunately, at the hill's base, framed by its bulbous ascension, a cave far larger than any of the foreboding maws dotting the sides of the valley stood with all the inviting allure of sudden dismemberment. The gentle crunch of my first footstep displaced long dormant rocks in the valley and sent a tingle up the length of my spine. It felt like the Reaper's icy, beckoning fingers guided my path.

“Come on, everything's okay. Just one. more. step,” the imaginary voice cooed as a bolt of lightning struck one of the distant mountain peaks.

I paused and kicked on all my sensory augments. A laughing bystander might have called it paranoia; I called it preparation. Though the winds tore through the ribcage shaped valley and kicked clouds of dust against the jagged rocks, the blacks and greens of my night vision in tandem with my telescopic sight afforded me careful surveillance of its nooks and crannies. That surveillance, however, only lasted a second.

Unfortunately, for all my preparedness I failed to factor in the effect of Oswald's serum. A sharp pain suddenly cut through my skull, and I instinctively deactivated all my nanites and clutched my head; the pain subsided. Apparently, the serum did not merely inhibit the capabilities of Panacea. It was a side effect the doctor would no doubt be interested in knowing... if I ever returned to inform him.

As I recovered from the sting that pinched my brain, I slammed my back against the rough wall that formed the towering ridge to my right. I inched through the shadows with my ultimate destination of the tall hill constantly in my sights. Each footstep increased the sensation of dread swelling up in my chest. Time felt like a snail creeping along the threads of existence with no purpose other than to torment me.

As I neared the median, the realization sank in that I

crossed the threshold of no return. If something sinister dwelt within the caves along the ridge, I was in deep, "Shit!" I cried out in a hushed whisper as a fist-sized rock tumbled down the side of the stone wall right next to my shoulder. A quick glance up revealed foreboding darkness until a brief flash of lightning illuminated a great, big, scary "nothing."

I released the breath caught in my throat as a relieved sigh. When I returned my gaze to the distant hill, I caught sight of a faint sheen of white among the black rocks decorating the valley. I clutched my head and prepared for the same intense pain from before as I activated my vision augment. Surprisingly, the buzz occurred normally, and I painlessly opened my eyes to zoom in on the strange heap in the middle of the valley. Perhaps the serum's effects were random? Or perhaps the number of augments activated at one time was the source of the pain? I ceased my inner debate as the shape and definition of the lump became clear. It was a pile of human bones.

I immediately propelled myself to action. My hands clutched the jagged stones of the wall, and I hoisted myself vertically along its surface. Within moments I sat perched atop one of the small ridges that housed one of the many cave entrances along the ribcage valley. With faintly labored breath, I slid my backside against the wall formed by the cave's jutting lip and peered around the corner in the direction of the rotten white bones. Without the eternally hidden sun's ability to bleach it, the skeleton retained a grotesquely moist appearance no doubt accentuated by the occasional rainfall. Circumstances afforded me little time to hypothesize; in the direction of the hill, sudden ear-piercing screeches drowned out the howling winds.

Three figures staggered from one of the many smaller openings at the base of the cliffs a few feet from the enormous cave. With my telescopic sight still active, I honed in on the event. Three hyped moved with twitching rage across the valley in the direction of the rounded cave. The depth of their affliction lent them an appearance far more akin to mythical beasts than humans. Their leathery skin and deformed muscles defined their misshapen husks; their solid black eyes were endless voids exchanging information through quick, twitchy glances incapable of deep thought.

As their hunched figures clambered across boulders and over rocks with the creepy agility of lizards, one of the three dropped to his hands and knees and began howling in incoherent agony. He was injured; upon closer examination with my enhanced vision, his leg was horribly mangled. Panacea had long since healed the wound, but with no one to properly set the bone, it had healed in a terribly misshapen manner. The hyped's two pack mates encircled him with a slow gait and grunted intermittently. After a few moments they both reached down, grabbed each of the fallen hyped's arms, and dragged him into the open. A few more hyped curiously poked their heads from the enormous cave at the bottom of the hill. My hill; at least, the hill I needed to ascend. *"Great,"* I thought to myself as I watched the scene play out before me, *"a whole pack of 'em."*

After a few more moments of the injured hyped's protesting cries and a brief exchange of stares from his friends, the two healthy afflicted grabbed fist sized stones and excitedly screamed at the sky. They descended upon their pack mate with feral ferocity. His tortured screams intensified as they relentlessly bludgeoned his body to pieces. For the healthy members of the fickle pack, the weakened hyped would provide food and entertainment. That became evident when the curious hyped from the cave began excitedly hooting and yelping in response to the violence that took place before them. They dragged the bits of their meal into their den; I shook my head.

A bulbous, dark shape suddenly cut in front of my enhanced vision and obstructed my view of the brutal display. I deactivated my augment in time to behold another hyped shooting from the cave which I used as a lean-to. Across the valley, a second large hyped emerged from another cave; both of them turned their dark eyes toward the spectacle they had just missed. I almost squeaked, but at the last moment I spun in a quick retreat and planted the small of my back against the wall separating the hyped and me. Unfortunately, the force sent a stone rolling down the cliff's side with a few undesired clicks and clacks as it smashed against the rocks. I cursed under my breath.

From my position, completely bathed in the wall's shadows, the shift in the nearby hyped's attention was audible. He released a quick grunt; I heard his knuckles rap the ground as he crept toward my hiding place to investigate the noise. I slid my hands across my hips and clutched the pommels of my long daggers.

The monster's hideous face peeked over the lip formed by the wall that separated us. I stared into the endless darkness of his hellish eyes, but he only sniffed and stared down over the edge of the cliff. My breath caught in my chest; should I strike quickly and prepare for combat against the other hyped? Without the full use of my nanites, I felt a twinge of uncertainty, and that uncertainty sent tremors down my hands. The frightening prospect of becoming the pack's next exciting meal did not help matters.

Just as the hyped prepared to turn and face me completely, he growled and snapped his head back in the other direction. He glanced to the second hyped that emerged from the cave across the valley; the two nodded at one another and began creeping down the walls through the shadows. Their trek carried them toward the giant cave at the bottom of the hill. I pushed the tense breath swollen in my chest out of my lungs with the force of a hurricane. When I leaned around the wall to look back down the valley's length, my jaw dropped.

A small girl stood in the center of the valley just in front of the enormous hill. Her hair possessed length similar to mine, but it was a vibrant sheen of blond draped in loose curly waves along her back and rear. A white, dirt-smudged gown hung from her tiny body. She could not have exceeded the age of ten.

She rubbed her bare, blistered feet together as though using one to scratch the itch of the other. Her eyes, a deep sea blue-green, peered with confusion along the valley and back toward the cave. Clutched in a strangling embrace, an odd bear doll constructed of cloth, synthetic cotton, and machinery dangled in front of her torso. She seemed for all the world like a little lost angel. Lost indeed; how did a girl like that stumble out of an intricate cave system right near a hyped pack's den?!

I shot my eyes to the two creeping hyped moving down the cliff's shadows toward their unassuming prey. “Damn it, little girl, run!” I hissed and began moving as well. The girl's head tipped to one side as though instinctively responding to a stimulus. Perhaps she heard something from inside the cave? I did not doubt the hyped inside were quite enjoying the feast of their comrade; surely their sloppy eating made a bit of noise. Good, it meant she might run with wild abandon from the cave of monstrous humans and in my direction. It would certainly make intercepting the two stray hyped easier.

“That's it, little one. There are bad things in there, just come this way,” I coaxed under my breath as I leapt from plateau to plateau, always descending toward the ground when possible. The two hyped leisurely took their time. No doubt they wished to ensure they did not betray their presence; an easy meal tasted far better than one that required immense effort, after all. I paused for a moment. Though I remained several hundred feet from the small child, I swore for a moment that her eyes met mine through the dark obscurity of the valley. Suddenly, she gasped softly as though she recognized the two pursuing hyped and bolted... straight for the cave.

I vaulted from the last of the jutting lips that marked the caves of the ribcage valley and shouted after her, "No! Not that way!"

It was too late; even if she heard me, her small frame had already vanished into the darkness. I started running. My cry reverberated through the valley like a cannon, and the two hyped pursuing the small girl snapped their attention to me. Their slobbering mouths dropped open hungrily, and they released nearly identical screeches before rocketing in my direction. My eyes never left the cave entrance. I unsheathed my twin daggers and spun the left into a reverse grip in my palm. "Little girl... little girl... little girl!"

I failed to understand the reason for my desperation. It was one girl; why did she matter so much? Perhaps the scared, uncertain look on her face reminded me of myself as I stood in Yordleton at thirteen. Maybe the innocent gleam that sparkled in those glistening blue-green eyes represented a last hope for decent children to turn into decent adults. But while I failed to understand my own reasons, I understood that I would carve my way through an army of those afflicted assholes if it meant getting to her before they did.

The first hyped and I collided. He stood at least a foot taller than I, so the only way to reach the necessary height to inflict true damage was to jump. I hated jumping. As his arms closed in to entangle me, I drove my heel against the extended ball of his knee and propelled myself up. Reluctant to activate my Supersoldier implant, I instead stabbed my left dagger straight down into his trapezius and tugged myself skyward.

I lifted my right dagger, still pointing outward from my grip, in an uppercut motion into the underside of his jaw. The bloodied crunch as its length penetrated his lower jaw, upper jaw, and even his brain through his sinus cavity ensured his demise. My feet came to rest on either of his shoulders at the pinnacle of my vertical leap. As his hulking form descended and his eyes rolled into the back of his head, his partner appeared behind him intent on accomplishing what his pack mate could not.

I easily culled my blades from the body as I rode it down, and when the second hyped reached the point where his arms stretched forward to grapple me from my perch, I hopped over the top of his head. *"There's no time to deal with these guys!"* I thought vehemently. When my feet touched the ground, I curled into a ball and rolled forward. The gathered momentum carried me into a sprint when the moment I jerked upright. I ignored the ravenous roars pursuing me from behind and bolted through the gaping hole in the hillside.

The darkness saturating the tunnel seemed like tendrils designed for the sole purpose of impeding my progress. A dim light danced across the walls as I rounded a curve in the cavern. When the tunnel opened into an enormous room dotted with random fires consuming various items strewn about the cave, the pack of hyped, covered in the blood of the injured ally they slew, stood in complete stillness staring at the lonely little girl in white.

Hyped were insane; psychosis did not begin to describe their affliction. However, to call them primitive or stupid would be a tricky mistake. While they certainly succumbed to base instincts, shunned society, and sought to destroy everything that moved, they often displayed questionable traits when left to their own devices.

If they truly killed or destroyed with reckless abandon, why did the hyped occasionally form a pack such as the one that huddled in the cave? If their knowledge degraded to primitive understanding, why did they retain the ability to create fires or cohesive hunting groups? Their mere survival in the harsh wastes of the ruined world attested to their capabilities. That being said, when faced with the solid black eyes of a hyperaugmented, humanity was the farthest word from one's lips.

The seven hyped in the small confines of the cave and the one in close pursuit outnumbered me, and with my nanites malfunctioning because of Oswald's experimental serum, they likely outclassed me as well. I decided to take the risk, and with a buzzing click my Cognitive Accelerator spun to life. What I witnessed in that moment engraved itself in my core forever.

The apparent pack leader, characterized by his ridiculous height and girth compared to the other hyped, stood erect in front of the tiny girl in the white gown.

With his hand extended, he placed his fingers against the small child's cheek. She stared up with an innocent smile and stood on her tip toes reaching her fragile hand toward his face, all while clutching her toy bear in her other arm. The remaining hyped stood calm and silent, both of which I found utterly preposterous. As I witnessed the surreal scene play out before me like dramatized theater, the black swirls of bestial demeanor within the leader's eyes flickered. For a moment, he looked human.

Then everything went to shit. The hyped behind me exploded into the groundbreaking gathering; with the sluggish manner with which I perceived my surroundings, I heard the discordant roar burst from his throat like a popping bubble. The heads of the other hyped twisted toward me; I kicked into a dash straight toward the naive child. My pursuer dove to grab my ankles, but I escaped his grasp in the knick of time. The sap-like movements of the cave dwellers began in unison; they parted their lips to roar and lashed out to strike me or grapple me from my dedicated path. The slow, methodical manner in which the leader's eyes reverted to their enraged hatred sent shivers along my spine.

When he fully regressed, he furrowed his brows and curled his fingers, still in close proximity to the girl's cheek, into a murderous fist. Finally, the child recognized her situation; with a shrill cry, she curled into a ball and lifted her toy bear over her head to shield her from the oncoming battery. Two fists from different hyped swung in wide hooks toward my face, one on my left and one on my right. I dropped to the ground in an old fashioned baseball slide and drew my leg back when the motion reached its climax. Once my slide carried me to the hyped leader, I stomped my foot into the side of his knee; the flow of inertia did most of my work for me and bent his leg at a completely unnatural angle.

The bone's crunch reverberated synchronously with the hyped's tormented howl. He instinctively dropped to his broken limb; I planted both my hands on the dusty ground and quickly pushed to my feet. I threw a quick spin kick against his temple. The force sent his body careening to the side and left me standing like a stubborn bulwark between the small girl and the pack of crazed afflicted. I fluidly stepped forward and sheathed my right dagger; the pack leader, who recovered from the blow I delivered to his head, limped forward and clenched his fist with every intention of pummeling my chest into oblivion. Considering his hyperaugmented state, taking such a blow would be tantamount to standing in front of an oncoming train.

But I maintained activation of my Cognitive Accelerator, and the injured hyped moved with all the swiftness of a snail; it left me plenty of time to react. I reached back with my free right hand to clutch the stock of my rifle. My eyes widened when the motion ended with my hand clenched in an empty fist. In the brief moment I possessed as the brute's fist sailed toward my sternum, my memories flashed to the operating chair tucked away in Oswald's trailer. I remembered setting my rifle in a lean against it, but I did not remember picking it back up.

"Damn it Oswald... what the hell is in that stuff?" I thought with frustrated conviction. To leave my father's rifle behind, a part of me as inseparable as a limb, and to travel several hours aimlessly through the desert without realizing its absence was a mistake I never imagined I would make. And of all the rotten times to make it...

The hyped's fist crushed into my chest, instantly shattering my sternum and several of my ribs. I regretted my mistake with, quite literally, every bone in my body. I sailed back through the air with a pained scream; the trauma when my back cracked against the stone wall next to the little girl snapped me from the effects of my Cognitive Accelerator. I gasped for air, desperately trying to work my diaphragm. I wanted nothing more than to fill my crinkled lungs with the cold air to quell the fire raging inside my entire upper torso.

It was to no avail, nor did Panacea begin working on my injuries. *"Ihlia, your Panacea is still a touch impeded!... The effect won't completely subside for several hours! Stay out of trouble..."* Oswald's warning annoyingly echoed in my mind, but pain remained the most prominent sensation coursing through me. The small child's quivering whimpers heralded the certain end reaching for us like the Reaper's cackling mockery.

"See? I told you, I told you just one more step," he seemed to say through his grinning, bony jaws.

I grunted with stubborn refusal embedded in every cell of my body. I swiftly gripped the hilt of my right dagger and flung it with lethal precision, despite my battered torso, from its sheath toward the leader's forehead. At the same time, my arm encircled the tiny waist of the child at my left, and with a painful cry I pushed from the wall of the cave and sprinted toward its deepest recesses. My dagger penetrated the hyped leader's skull with a loud thwack, and as we passed by his felled body, I could have sworn I witnessed the small girl sob and reach for the felled brute with unnerving sympathy.

The rest of the hyped remained in pursuit even as I located an escape. Fortunately, the back of the cave possessed a tunnel leading into the extensive cave network running beneath the mountains behind the hill. Also fortunately, an extraordinarily narrow passage formed the tunnel's opening which, I asserted with all the certainty one might derive from a quick size-up, was far too narrow for the hyped beasts to pursue us. Unfortunately, the pitch black interior of the tunnel offered as much danger as it did rescue, and if the tunnel's shape betrayed its geometric design, the child and I were in for a steep drop.

Without my rifle and with only a single dagger, I dove, with the little girl under my arm, into the foreboding abyss that presented itself as our only salvation. The descent seemed uneventful in the first few seconds, but just as I clenched my arm around the small child and placed my free hand on the back of her neck to protect her from injury, the first impact sent a shock wave through my ribs. The girl remained unharmed in my protective embrace as we bounced down the tunnel, but I was not so lucky.

The slope at which the tunnel dipped caused a series of bone splintering slams which sent our bodies rolling and twisting through the air with each bounce off the jagged stones and stalagmites. Each somersault inflicted intense sensations of agony on my entire body. But through some miracle, I kept the small girl, still clutching my chest for dear life, atop me during each of our abrupt collisions. When the tumble ended and gravity ejected us from the tunnel, the two second free fall sent my thoughts racing to my comrades in Loftsborough.

Oswald would be finding my rifle right about then with an "Oh bother..." to accompany his unfortunate find. Crelyos, the blond brute, would be sitting in the tavern downing bottles of sludge and waiting for me to waltz in and offer him a slap on the shoulder. As the breeze of our descent streamed through my hair and kissed the tortured injuries ravaging my body, I clutched the small girl tighter to my breasts and grit my teeth in preparation. The last thought that raced through my mind before the cracking impact sent absolute darkness to overtake me... was of Donovan.

File 23: The Bald Eagles

The darkness became a haze, the haze slowly morphed into vague shapes accompanied by muffled voices, and the shapes emerged as clear images of familiar people sitting attentively around a campfire. I stood directly behind a female; her mid length black hair dangled between her shoulder blades, and the militant outfit she wore accentuated the unlady-like manner in which she sat atop a thick wooden log.

A black tank top left a small strip of flesh exposed just above her waist. A pair of camouflaged cargo pants clung to the swell of her hips, and the legs of her pants trailed down and tucked into her black combat boots. With both her legs spread and her elbows draped casually over her knees, she emanated a distinct air of masculinity. Her voice lifted as the first clear sound to tickle my ears.

"Bradich, sir, with all due respect, why do we need to go overseas to Cairo? It's a dangerous hot spot, has been since the Global Conflict started. There are attacks there almost daily." She spoke in a soft voice that exuded her youth. She could not have been older than sixteen. More importantly than that, however, she mentioned the name Bradich. My head jerked in the direction she spoke. From the shadows just outside the flame's reach, my former commander emerged. With his voluminous brown hair cascading down his shoulders and his strong but slim frame standing firm above the group of faces I almost recognized, I gradually pieced together the situation.

"A dream? Or perhaps I'm dead..." I thought to myself. As I thought carefully, I recalled protesting against our deployment to Cairo in just such a fashion over ten years ago. I glanced down at the militant youth with obsidian hair; an unnatural blur concealed of her facade in inky obscurity. I supposed it made sense; after all, I would hardly be able to recall the nuances of my expressions considering I never actually beheld my own face. Despite desiring nothing more than to leap across the fire pit and choke the life from the Bradich of my memories, I stood silent.

"Do you know why there are daily attacks on Cairo, Ihlia? Aside from the philosophical implications of humanity's base desire to destroy, that is." Bradich's lips twisted into a challenging smile. I shook my head; Bradich's ever-fanciful jargon tangled my thoughts more than once during my teenage years. The young me lifted her thumb to her chin; I watched her vacuum her lower lip between her teeth and chew.

"Don't think too hard about it, he's just trying to get into your head," I spoke aloud. My surreal voice echoed like a watery ripple. Even as the words escaped my lips and my hand reached down to touch the shoulder of my former self, she remained unaware and simply shook her head.

"No, sir, I do not," she responded.

“Well after the N-3 launched, and after the massive quantity of neurotech data filled libraries' worth of space, several laboratories dedicated to facilitating nanite research sprang up all over the globe. Of them, none are more advanced than the laboratory in Cairo. My brother believes he's on the verge of a breakthrough that will change the way we see nanites forever. I think it's idealistic dribble, but he's paying us well to guard him. And I am his brother, after all. I suppose I owe my flesh and blood at least that.” Bradich tapped the underside of his chin as though pondering the true extent to which he would go for the sake of his sibling.

Despite Bradich's overwhelming love for money and the crude manner with which he rationalized the world, he always seemed driven by some pseudo-spiritual search of self. Older members of the Bald Eagles once informed me that such thoughts consumed him long before I ever joined their ranks. Around campfires when the jests grew stale and the old stories became boring, Bradich often proposed existential and soul wrenching questions to excite our crew.

“What do you think the nature of our consciousness is? Are we just clusters of atoms with advanced neurons and an overdeveloped brain? Is there something more for us that waits for us after we die?” Such questions were common from our fearless leader.

Typically, they ended with passive interest and jokes regarding the implications “overdeveloped” might have for an imaginary attractive woman and how the men would love nothing more than to "cluster her atoms," but Bradich occasionally succeeded in provoking deep discussion among his soldiers. I rarely offered more than an exaggerated roll of my eyes to either the imaginary women or the deep discussions. Neither piqued my interests at that age, nor as I grew older for that matter. The thought of guarding Donovan, however, piqued my younger version's interest by quite a gracious margin.

"So it is an escort mission for Donovan?" My younger self barely contained her excitement. Her allies around the crackling fire immediately saw through her attempts to maintain a gruff mercenary's tone. A chorus of laughter bombarded the mercenary encampment. Though the blurred censor over my younger self's face concealed the emotional creases, I distinctly recalled the overwhelming flame that rosied my cheeks during my comrades' guffawing.

I had known my ruse proved futile as much as they had known of my unbridled excitement. Even I released soft laughter at my younger self's obvious embarrassment, and as the cool night air tossed about our clothes and kissed our skin, I glanced at the faces of each member of our family. Starting from my younger version's left and moving in a wide circle, I recalled the tight knit mercenary group: the Bald Eagles.

Shandi, the only other female in our squadron, served as our communications master during missions. No one assembled information on holocomputers or in their head as efficiently as she. Watching her curly red hair and freckled face illuminated by a blue screen was a treat my job rarely afforded me, but once in a while, Bradich assigned me to set up my kill zone over our forward operations base. And our forward operations base always housed the beautiful Shandi.

During those times, I often caught sight of the glint of streaming data as it raced down the holo screen and reflected off Shandi's rich brown eyes. When it came to processing and reassembling the data for surveillance and tactical prompts, our comms master's fingers moved like liquid tendrils and her voice donned the precision of a surgeon. Bradich credited Shandi with the success of our operations and safe return of our squad more than once. Each time, with a proud flip of her crimson curls, she lavished the praise.

With an ample bust, slender waist, and womanly swell to her hips, the auburn-haired southern belle was the object of desire for the company's male majority. Shandi, despite constant vies for her affection, remained steadfast to a single claim: “Sorry, sug', I already got my sights on someone else. You're a might sweet to think of me, though.”

The man who struck Shandi's fancy was none other than our leader. Anyone in the company for more than a week heard the line, and anyone that survived more than a month quickly pieced the puzzle together and learned of Shandi's undying affection for Bradich. The only person painfully unaware of her unwavering love and devotion was Bradich himself. For whatever reason, Shandi never mustered the courage to actually profess her love. At least I thought a lack of courage stopped her at the time. Only later would I learn how grossly mistaken I had been. Despite never professing her feelings for Bradich, however, Shandi's love for him never once faltered. Not even unto her dying breath.

To her left sat Jace, a rough cut ex-soldier who styled his hair in a typical brown crew cut and kept his facial hair trimmed to a manly stubble. A man almost as full of complaints as vices, Jace constantly grumbled about the direction in which Bradich took our company, but only when he took a break from gambling, drinking, chewing tobacco, or paying for a night with a town girl to join us around a camp fire. The occurrence was marked with rarity. No job paid well enough, and every job was too dangerous. Like a self-appointed big brother, however, anyone besides him that spoke ill of our commander received a sturdy right hook and hateful, tobacco-scented threats.

Jace's quiet, croaking voice reflected his constant chewing habit interrupted only by the occasional spit. More often than not, he sported a black leather vest and a pair of camouflaged cargo pants tucked into a pair of thick green boots. His weapon of choice, an automatic assault rifle outfitted with enough flashy lights and high tech upgrades to power a small city, remained at his side at all times. As one of our support guns, Jace accompanied front line operations.

Further down, I watched Downy laugh nervously as he

drew pictures in the dirt with a stick. Downy remained an enigma to most of us. His coke-bottle eyeglasses, as best as we could guess, corrected his lackluster vision. It seemed senseless to wear glasses with the existence of vision nanites that could enhance normal eyesight to the pinnacle of human limitations, and that did not even cover the various telescopic, or "super vision," nanites on the market for relatively cheap prices. Around his head, Downy wore a red bandana that kept unruly black hair messily feathered back against his head. His long nose offset his slender face, and I swore I never saw a single strand of facial hair touch his lip or chin. As the squad's tech engineer, if one needed a computer hacked or a security door blown, Downy was the man for the job.

Bit sat alone on his own log; this was largely because Bit's massive body nearly consumed the space of an entire log. The enormous man rarely spoke during most of our friendly exchanges. His hair, braided in tight cornrows, raced back along his dark head. His black skin bulged with giant muscles that coated his entire body like a suit of armor. Of course, carrying around a one hundred and fifty pound Vulcan minigun like a satchel tended to require gratuitous strength. Scars covered the giant's midnight skin as a testimony to his constant battle experience; more often than not, Bit led our charges and covered our retreats.

On the opposite side of our makeshift circle directly to Bradich's right and left sat the twins, Flint and Steele, respectively. Their hair swept back across their scalps like golden fields of wheat, and their bright green eyes flitted about their surroundings with passive interest. We knew as much about them as we knew about Downy. Flint and Steele were neither their real names nor their given names; they were nicknames Bradich branded on them in light of their special talents, namely their tendency to burn things down or blow them to pieces with remarkable efficiency. As our demolitions experts, Flint and Steele's expertise ranged from well-placed C-4 charges to masterful grenade throws and handheld nuclear detonations. In addition to their fantastic knowledge of explosives, they possessed the cliche, creepy, silent-twin-communication thing. Thankfully, I never heard them finish one another's sentences.

Gunther, Welsch, and Loxley completed our core group. Those three were inseparable. As former battle buddies in the military, their competitions tended to escalate quickly. Often they competed with a basic kill count during our hairier operations, but their lust for a definitive "better man" extended even to daily routines. They competed to see whose stream of urine arched the highest and landed the farthest away, whose charm might win him the heart of a naive bar patron, and even who could flirt with Shandi the longest before she slapped the shit out of him.

Gunther, with his jet black hair, piercing green eyes and Persian features, stood as the most handsome of the three. However, his uncouth nature often betrayed his sterling looks. Loxley's blond hair and blue eyes framed an unremarkable face that belied a charismatic and manipulative personality. Despite Gunther's stellar facade and exotic allure, it was often Loxley who won the competitions for the fair, drunken maidens during their courtship games. Most of the men joked that his silver tongue could wrest the panties from a nun. Welsch, a run-of-the-mill brunette with blue eyes and a strong jaw, always seemed caught in the middle of Gunther and Loxley. In fact, Welsch seldom seriously participated in the competitive games among the three. I often wondered what the result might have been had he exerted any effort.

When the troubling trio set aside their testosterone contests, they served as the crew's fill-in foot soldiers. If Flint and Steele needed an armed escort, they provided it. If Bit and Jace needed extra guns to spearhead an assault, they provided it. If our forward command base required heavy guard for Shandi's sake, they provided it. Whatever Bradich told them to do, they took care of it.

With myself as the company sniper included among the lot and our fearless leader standing stalwart at the helm of command, it meant eleven total Eagles soaring from one dangerous nest to the next seeking fortune and excitement wherever it was to be found. During larger operations, Bradich often employed temporary freelance mercenaries to add beef to our ranks, but the eleven of us comprised the core of the Bald Eagles. Aside from the death of Larz a year before the Titan Crisis, that number remained unchanged in all the years of my service under Bradich Lesfort... until *that* day.

"We leave for Cairo tomorrow. We stay until Doctor Lesfort no longer requires our assistance, until we return to America together or, obviously, until we die. A small militia is stationed throughout the city with a heavy concentration of manpower on the nanite facility. It's not much, as the city is nearly in ruins, but the militia will provide backup in case of an emergency. As Ihlia pointed out, there are attacks on the city and facility almost daily, from ground assaults to air raids, so this is not going to be pretty. The pay, however, is substantial, and the cause is acceptable," Bradich spoke with a commanding air after the boisterous laughter brought on by my former self's girlish embarrassment died down.

"Acceptable cause... you mean just cause it's your brother, we gotta go above and beyond our normal call," Jace grumbled from his position in front of the flickering orange and red campfire.

"Oh, shut up, Jace," Gunther annoyedly cried toward the tobacco chewing ex-soldier.

"What'd you say, pretty boy? I'll hop this fire and make your face look like Bit's left ass cheek," Jace stood and shot a wad of spit from his mouth into the hissing flames.

"Enough," Bit snapped at the two. After considering his girth, they both sealed their lips and hastily dropped their rears onto their respective logs.

"I won't lie, Jace, that did seal the deal. But it's not just because he's my brother; it just so happens my brother is also one of the most renowned nanite researchers and surgeons in the field. His current theories and experiments are secretly sanctioned by the U.S. government. If we aid in a major nanite breakthrough, it could be big. We could be rich and famous beyond our wildest dreams," Bradich replied, glancing toward the starry heavens with ambitious tenacity.

"Sug', if the government is so interested in this here little project of his, how come they don't send their armies to back him up?" Shandi cocked her head to one side as she posed our leader a valid inquiry, to which the rest of us nodded our heads.

"Good point, it's because they don't want to draw more attention to it than necessary. Donovan might be onto something big, we don't know, but the big wigs don't want to hang a flashing neon sign out that points to the lab and says 'Hey, over here,' so it's being treated as a private investigation. That's where we come in," Bradich gestured to our group.

"Privateers hire mercenary companies all the time. The Nanite Research Dome in Cairo may be controlled by the Free Alliance, but it rests in a hot zone constantly assaulted by the Union and the French. Thus far the Free Alliance military and the Cairo militia have worked together to keep the borders safe and the territory in our hands, but if we advertise a breakthrough in neurotech, they're likely to turn up the heat. Even if we succeed in holding The Nanite Research Dome for the Free Alliance, precious tools and research data may be lost or corrupted because of a heated skirmish," Bradich finished and leaned back against one of our nearby jeeps.

The Free Alliance referred to the United States of America and any of the countries that fought under her banner. Japan, England, the Soviets, South America, and much of Africa, including Egypt, joined the Free Alliance at various stages of the Global Conflict. Their poster-boy motto was "Free nanite information and distribution to the world, fight terror, and secure prosperity for the peoples of the free world." Most people knew their real goal was to police nanite distribution and keep as many combat nanites out of the black market as possible. Still, their motto sounded nice. Historically speaking, it always did.

The Union consisted of the "great evils" of the world; Spain, China, Korea, Vietnam, most of the European nations, and the parts of Africa that refused to join the Free Alliance made up their strongest military forces. If they possessed a motto, it probably involved killing as many of America's soldiers as possible. While their goals were probably similar to the Free Alliance's true agenda, they failed to wrap it up in a pretty public relations slogan. A part of me respected them for their honesty. That respect did not stay my trigger finger when a Union soldier threatened one of my comrades, but respect surely counted for something, right?

As for the rest of the world, most of them adopted a "we're not joining, but if you bother us you can bet your ass we'll fight," mentality. The French were the only exception. As the world's dominant military force with super soldiers far outclassing any other country's and military nanites years ahead of their competition's, the

French remained their own force throughout the entire conflict.

Their only brothers-in-arms, Canada, provided them with support; logistics; forward bases of operations against the United States; and the occasional military unit. Despite the foothold against America they gained from Canada, France attacked other countries of the Free Alliance, the Union, and neutral territories almost indiscriminately. Most people never truly grasped their goals in the Global Conflict, and they never released an official statement for their unbiased aggression. Perhaps they simply grew tired of ancient mythological cracks and jokes regarding their alleged cowardice in a bygone age?

"So keep it tight, keep it clean," Bit nodded and folded his arms across his massive barrel chest.

"And blow the fuck out of anyone that tries to mess with the doc," laughed the twins.

"Exactly. So party hard tonight, gentlemen. Tomorrow we put our game faces on," Bradich stated with stern affirmation.

The night's merriment in preparation for the operation's start kicked off with sludge and Bradich's disappearance into the simple tent he set up on the outskirts of our camp. To my former self's left, Shandi trained her dreamy gaze on the commander's retreating backside. My younger version leaned over and gripped her sleeve; after offering it a firm tug, the younger Ihlia whispered up toward the ginger belle fiercely, “Pst, Shandi. Can I talk to you?”

It took a few moments to receive recognition, but the red haired beauty eventually shook her head and glanced down toward my young self, “Hm, Sug'? Did you say somethin'?”

The young Ihlia leapt from her log and tugged Shandi off into the night far from the crackling fire, the blustering laughter, and the eavesdropping ears of the Eagles. When she was confident the other squad members partied far out of ear shot, Ihlia began pacing nervously across the squeaky, moist grass. Every few trips in front of the busty belle, Ihlia halted and turned with mouth agape as though to utter something, only to release a frustrated sigh and return to pacing.

Shandi quirked a brow, “Darlin', what has got you more nervous than a cow at a slaughterhouse? Calm down, Sug', you know you can talk to me.” Shandi gripped Ihlia's shoulders when she passed by again and turned the teenager toward her. Shandi replaced my mother, in a way, during my long years as a mercenary. As a fellow woman, the crimson haired comms master refused to allow me to grow up without a strong influence of femininity. In addition, she helped me through some of the messier, more confusing years of puberty. The young Ihlia sighed softly to calm her nerves.

“How do I get Donovan's attention this time? What do I say to him? It's been almost a year since I saw him, and we were still so messed up after Larz died that we barely had anything to say. Should I be aggressive? Or maybe I should try to stay nonchalant. I don't want him to think I'm some prattling school girl, but I want him to know I'm here, and in front of him. I mean..." Ihlia stammered.

I felt an embarrassed heat creep up my neck; even if it was my dream sequence or hellish afterlife, recalling the nervous explosion I dumped on Shandi shamed me so bad that I slapped my opened palm atop my face just watching it. I split apart my first and second finger to watch my stammering younger self from between the slit.

"Whoa, Sug'! Honey, you need to calm down. You're squealin' like a stuck pig, and I can't make heads or tails of what you're sayin'." Shandi cupped the young Ihlia's cheeks and brushed both thumbs beneath her eyes in an attempt to soothe her.

"Oh no, you're right! I'm acting like a baby!" Ihlia groaned and sank to her derriere on the grass, simultaneously covering her face with her open palms. Her whine escaped her like the troubled teenager she was, "I'll never get him to see me as a woman no matter how old I get! Why'd I have to be born so late?! Just a few years earlier! Why not just a few years?!"

I watched Shandi smile at the downtrodden version of my former self. As she sat her well-endowed curvatures next to the young Ihlia's, she placed an arm around the young girl's shoulders and tugged her into a soft embrace. She cooed her words like a reassuring mother hen calming her chick, "Now baby, that's just nonsense. Look at you. Why, when we first found you I remember you standin' in the rain cryin' your precious little eyeballs out. You were a pretty little thing that could barely fill a child's nightgown. Now look at you! A beautiful, buxom, shinin' jewel of a young lady that any man would be a fool to overlook!" Shandi puffed up the ample swell of her chest as though she felt proud that her guidance and presence helped mold me.

"You deserve to feel proud..." I whispered in the echoing voice my dream-like state afforded me. I knelt down and threw my intangible arms around the southern belle; as I expected, they drifted through her body like a ghost's. I did not care.

"Buxom..." My former self repeated plainly. The young Ihlia stared at Shandi's chest, pumped outward with the forceful arch of her back, and sighed. She smiled a smile interlaced with mixed emotions of relief and disappointment then retorted, "Those are what I'd call buxom, Shandi. Wanna trade?"

"Oh, please, child. You're making mountains out of mole hills," Shandi dismissively waved her hand.

"Psht, I wish!" The young Ihlia playfully hissed back and gripped her own modestly sized breasts as though comparing them to Shandi's. The two ladies laughed, and I joined them even as I sat with my ethereal arms draped around Shandi's neck.

"Now, baby, I need to ask you something important." Shandi maneuvered until she sat directly in front of the young Ihlia. She took hold of my former self's hands with her own, and she clutched them tightly. "Do you want Donovan, or do you love Donovan?"

I crossed my arms and sat next to the two figments from my past. I watched my former self tip her head in absolute confusion, but I understood her muddled expression even through her face's censored blur.

"Both? Can't I want him and love him?" Ihlia laced her question with desperate anticipation, as though she knew the answer would not be one she desired but one she needed to hear.

"Not always, Sug'. I'm here for you, so whatever you want is what I'll help you get. If you want that man, then I know some sure fired ways of workin' what you got to get him. By the end of the mission, you could bet your bottom dollar he'd be putty in the palm of your hand. But if you love him..." Shandi painfully furrowed her brows, "if you love him, things don't always quite work out like you might want, darlin'."

"What do you mean? If I love him I can't be with him?" The young Ihlia leaned forward.

"Heavens no, that's not what I meant, Sug'. It's just... as a woman, if you love a man, you need to support him as a man. Men are amazin' things. They're weak when they can be, strong when they have to be, and completely helpless the rest of the time. And there ain't nothin' on this earth with more power over a man than a woman," Shandi giggled.

"When a man is bein' a man and tryin' to move and shake the world, it's real easy to distract him and take him for your own. But I don't think that's love, baby. You gotta support what your man is tryin' to do, even if that means feelin' lonely and cold in a tent by yourself some nights." Shandi smiled a sad smile. While I knew her gems of wisdom helped her cope with the reality of her own situation, the younger Ihlia perceived her words as advice from the lips of the wisest love guru on the planet. I chuckled softly at my own young naivety.

"So if I tell you that I love him, what are you going to tell me to do?" Ihlia lowered her head.

"Show him you can stand by his side, darlin'. When he turns around lookin' for someone to be there in the darkness, make sure you're the first one he sees. When he stumbles, help pick him back up. Oh, but don't make it obvious you're doin' that. Men got that pride thing," Shandi giggled. "You have to share in his victories and failures, and when no one else will believe in him, Sug', you believe in him."

"Will it be like that forever?" Ihlia's voice echoed a sense of bitter sweetness.

"Hard to tell, baby. I'm really only tellin' you my point of view based on my experiences. But I can tell you what

I believe. I believe that one day, in the middle of chasin' his dream and makin' a mark on this here world, a man will realize what's really important is the people closest to him. Then, you'll be able to share those dreams together," Shandi longingly looked up at the stars.

"It's not somethin' you can force, darlin', but you can't just sit around and wait for it forever either. So long as you follow that gorgeous heart of yours and listen to it real close, you'll know when the time comes to put yourself out there." Shandi cupped my younger self's cheeks and gently lifted the young Ihlia's face toward the sky.

"Is that why you haven't said anything to Bradich about how you feel about him?" Ihlia inquired.

"That's right, Sug'. I'm livin' my own advice for better or worse. I won't lie, there are many nights I think it's the worst thing I ever decided to do. Some nights I wish I didn't love him no more. But then when I see him smile after a big mission or watch that passionate gleam flicker in his eyes when he negotiates a new contract, I just can't help myself," Shandi smiled. "Not to mention, I never seen anyone as handsome carryin' a gun as that man."

"Shandi..." The young Ihlia droned.

"What, Sug'? I'm a mercenary, not a princess. Watchin' him mow down the enemy at the front lines is what drew me to him in the first place. Mm, that man." Shandi blushed as her mind clearly ventured into a fantasy land;

no doubt she and Bradich stood back to back atop a hill against all odds professing their undying love to one another as they slew advancing droves of enemies.

"Oh, Shandi..." I laughed and shook my head.

"I tell you what, darlin'. Your birthday is comin' up soon, right? It'll probably happen in Cairo durin' our mission. We'll doll you up on your birthday; that way he'll at least see you as a woman. After that you can decide what to do with the advice I gave you, m'kay baby?" Shandi brushed her fingers back through the young Ihlia's obsidian hair. My younger self nodded and shifted positions until she sat directly next to the red headed beauty.

The two continued chatting in the grass beneath the star-strewn sky. The glow of the fire at their backs and the distant laughter of the men enjoying their alcohol and rambunctious activities faded first. As I sat in front of my fond memories, their voices distorted and the issues they addressed during their nonchalant conversation fell into the recesses of darkness creeping across the world I remembered like a whispering plague.

File 24: Cairo

"Ihlia, Bit says there's an enemy engineer at twelve o'clock relative to the facility; he also says that engineer is setting up an automated chain gun nest. If he finishes programming the AI, the entire north perimeter will be pinned down. Take him out." Shandi's voice scratched through a communications bead embedded in my younger self's ear.

The sixteen-year-old girl, prone on her stomach atop a nest on the roof of the Nanite Research Dome, stared down the length of her sniper rifle with her telescopic vision nanite dilating and expanding her pupils like lenses. The green hue of her night vision implant illuminated the darkness of Cairo's desert oasis. As the warm night breeze blew the exposed pieces of her hair in thin wisps behind her, she swiftly guided the muzzle of her rifle to the position Shandi mentioned.

I stood next to my younger self and sighed. Panacea, a night vision nanite, and a vision augment made up my three threshold-abiding implants at the time Cairo's mission took place. Those implants best suited my task as the company sniper, and I still remained blissfully unaware of my special ability to limitlessly load my brain with nanites back then.

"Understood," Ihlia responded and trained her rifle's

maw on the assaulting soldier who frantically worked to establish the chain gun nest. A blue holo screen extended from the or portable holocom cuffed around his wrists. The enemy engineer intended to set up a pivoting Vulcan with pre-programmed targeting algorithms that would decipher friend from foe. Ihlia intended to make sure that never happened.

Heavy cloth covered his entire body to protect his skin from the grinding sand blasted from the desert floor by violent winds. Given his attire, the young Ihlia barely discerned the engineer from any one of the locals. The thick turban pulled down over his head and the flowing scarf concealing his lower face left only a small slit visible near his eyes, but one thing betrayed him. His pale skin gleamed brightly in the green night vision onset by Ihlia's nanite. He was European, a Union soldier.

Three soldiers, obviously the engineer's comrades, guarded the technician as he busily punched the buttons of blue light projected by his holocom. Aside from the four soldiers setting up the Vulcan, a small contingency unit of troops kept a constant hail of suppression fire on Bit and the militia on the northern border of the facility. With their backs against the metal barricades constructed for the compound's defense, they were all but pinned already.

The Union soldiers continued hastily programming their automated Vulcan to waylay the militia and Ihlia's fellow Eagles along the northern perimeter, but they were little more than a forward suppression unit. Farther beyond the small squad, my former self and I noted several squads of soldiers racing down the dunes toward the compound. The chain gun, no doubt installed to cover the larger squads' advance, simply posed too great a threat to remain operational, at least under their control.

"Shandi, where's Downy?" The young Ihlia depressed the lobe of her ear to activate the communication bead wedged within it.

"He's setting up a couple of Sentinels on the western border with Welsch and Loxley. The militia is thin there, and the enemy activity is getting heavy on that side," she replied.

Ihlia, and by proxy I, heard several digital beeps as Shandi's fingers worked their magic. On the other side of the comm bead, she rapidly depressed glowing, holographic keys to process massive quantities of data within seconds.

"Sentinels? Bradich authorized their use? That's some heavy artillery," My former self seemed surprised, if only a little.

"You know the commander. He takes a contract seriously, Sug'." Shandi's grin was almost auditory.

"Tell Downy to hurry up and head to the north perimeter. Bit and our northern forces might be overrun even if they don't get that turret down. But..." My younger version's words cut through the night but Shandi interrupted.

“But if Downy can hack the turret after you take out their engineer and Bit covers him, then we'll have ourselves a chain gun to mow them suckers down like an overgrown lawn! That's a might smart, I'll send him over. You just take out that technician, baby.” Shandi's voice maintained its southern drawl, but her annunciation rang out as sharp as my daggers.

My younger self grinned and surveyed the eastern front. Ihlia watched as Downy touched his ear to better hear the orders from our comms master; his mysteriously dopey smile widened. He pushed on his ear and uttered a word of affirmation before sprinting across the combat zone's sandy hills toward Bit and the suppressed militia. The metallic clanks of his programmed Sentinels buzzing to life heralded his departure from the western front, and I returned my sights to the northern perimeter just as the cacophonous explosions of the Sentinels' cannons shook the night.

As Downy approached the site, he slid across the sand and slammed his back into the metal barricade next to Bit. The two exchanged a few words, Bit nodded, and they both pressed their comm bead to signal to our comms master that they were in position.

“Ihlia, they're ready to charge the nest with the militia forces. Take out the technician first, and as much of the forward unit as possible to cover their assault,” Shandi beeped over my comm bead.

“Roger that, Shandi.” My younger self locked her iron sights and night vision on the engineer. At the trough of her exhale, she squeezed the trigger.

A resounding crack propelled the first shot from her rifle. After a mere second, the technician jolted back as though struck with a furious blow. Blood pooled from his forehead, and he dropped to the ground, dead. His comrades flew into action; their assault rifles nervously swept in every direction as they hurriedly sought their mysterious attacker. By the time they surmised the possibility of a long distance sniper, Bit issued a deep, guttural command to charge.

A blaze of gunfire lit up the night sky along the northern perimeter. I almost heard the high-pitched whistle of Bit's portable minigun as he trotted forward into the surprised unit of enemies. With the militia behind him and Downy bringing up the rear with a pistol, their sudden retaliation left their enemies in disarray. The Union soldiers scattered for cover. Most of them ducked into a trench they had hastily carved during their advance, but a single man stood from the trench with a green bulb gripped in his palm. My former self noted the small digital red numbers bleep onto a miniature screen on the side of the device. The Union soldier was preparing to toss a nuclear pulse grenade.

Nicknamed a “Little Kid” as a jab at the ancient “Fat Boy,” the nuclear pulse grenade functioned similarly to an old fashioned hand grenade but with a blast radius several times larger and with enough heat to partially flash-melt steel and stone. After activating the timer, a simple flick of a switch-cover and the depression of a red button activated the chemical mixture.

Once in motion, shutting off a Little Kid is impossible. My younger self waited until the flash of the red digits began their countdown and the enemy drew his arm back to prepare the toss. The moment the Union soldier's arm fully extended back, Ihlia put a bullet in his forehead. The Little Kid dropped into the trench with the startled soldiers, and after a brief pause to lament their fate, the majority of the unit scrambled from the trench to escape the blast radius of the micro-nuke.

Of course, as they emerged from their protective pit, high caliber rounds squealing from Bit's minigun and the milita's assault weaponry thwacked into their chests and heads, sending them straight to a dirt nap. To choose between instant vaporization or a body riddled with holes as a final destination seemed a cruel fate, indeed. Such was war, however. My younger self kept her calm even through the dull explosions booming on all sides of the facility.

"Damn, I was a clever little brat," I grinned as I stood, an incorporeal witness to my past, and watched Bit and Downy secure the rotating Vulcan turret. With Downy on the task, it was a matter of moments before the high caliber automatic sentry gun hummed to life and turned on the advancing enemy squadrons.

I looked down at the young Ihlia. Tendrils of her

obsidian hair haphazardly poked through a heavy cloth encircling her face and head; the cloth protected her skin from the shearing sands carried by voracious gusts of wind. To blend into the building's metallic hue and the darkness of the war-torn Cairo, Ihlia sported dark gray combat attire similar to what she always wore. Similar to what I wore, too, save the color. I remembered the frustration caused by the cloth that obscured the young Ihlia's vision, but I also remembered that Cairo's unpredictable weather required it.

Over the course of two hundred years or so, the climate in Egypt gradually shifted. While still a desert, seasons closer to those experienced by a temperate region emerged. Compared to the old data of the area, where measurements of rain barely topped millimeters and temperatures rarely dropped below fifty degrees Fahrenheit, the colder seasons recorded temperatures as low as forty-two degrees, and during the winter months, rainfall occurred a few days more often than historically documented. Scientists speculated that within a few more centuries, Egypt may have been the center of a lush forest.

Of course, that was not to be. In the distance, Egypt's ruins from the cities of Cairo and Giza to the ancient pyramids offered a grim perspective on humanity's artistic preservation... or lack thereof. When the war started and Egypt became a forefront in nanite research, assaulting parties paid little heed to the seventh wonder of the world or its surrounding cities. Missiles and artillery reduced the sphinx and the towering pyramids it guarded to piles of rubble during the struggle to capture the territory, and the constant bombardment from the Union and the French reduced the city to dust. Only a faint resemblance to the area's former glory, a few military bases, and the Nanite Research Domes remained.

"Good work, Ihlia, but now is no time to get all lax-a-daisy. Jace and Gunther on the western border are under fire from a Hoverbuster. It's dropping in soldiers and spraying tons of lead on our boys. See if you can't ground it," Shandi urgently commanded.

As the young Ihlia swiveled to bring her iron sights and telescopic vision on the western perimeter, the distant whine of an aircraft engine drifted to her from across the desert. The Hoverbuster, a nickname for a science jargon numbered hover aircraft, reigned over the skies as an aerial juggernaut.

With the capacity to transport over one hundred soldiers for deployment or extraction, in addition to its ability to maintain altitude through various energy-efficient, antigravity propulsion systems, the Hoverbuster took the stage as an advanced transport carrier replacing helicopters. But its capabilities did not stop at simply transportation; with several electromagnetically charged rail guns and cannons, the Hoverbuster basically sported an entire fleet's artillery in a single ship.

"Where are the twins? I'm sure they have a rocket launcher or missile somewhere that could bring that bird down." Ihlia pressed down her comm bead.

“They're at the southern perimeter finishing preparations on a mine field. The southern border is quiet, but we need a detection system and deterrent against possible flanking maneuvers,” Shandi responded.

“All right, but this is going be tough. Those cockpit shutters are almost impenetrable; the pilots run the entire monster from holocoms on the inside. They don't even need to see, so no glass either,” My younger version began rummaging through a satchel at her side.

“So you can't do it, honey?” Shandi sounded concerned.

“I said almost impenetrable,” The young Ihlia chuckled and tugged a pair of bullets and a metal wrist band resembling a bracelet from her bag. After clamping the wrist band on, she pressed a few buttons on the metallic accessory before it beeped to life. I crossed my arms and watched on as my young self chambered one of the new rounds into her father's rifle.

A blue holocom screen sprouted from the device; its flickering blue emanations formed a hazy panel that floated roughly a foot above Ihlia's wrist. Her free hand moved like lightning and “grabbed” the blue light, shifting the illusory screen to hover above a part of the bracelet more conducive to her hand's position when holding her rifle. I still remembered how much I detested using that piece of equipment. Since the blue lights flickered and glinted, even if only a little, a good chance existed they would betray the young Ihlia's position to an enemy sniper. Just such a mistake sent Larz to his dirt nap a year prior. A situation as dire as the one that night, however, qualified as a viable exception.

The young Ihlia pressed a few holographic buttons floating under the blue screen; as it flickered and shifted, it showed her the world as though filtered through a piece of blue glass. Various nodes and indicators appeared on the screen when it drifted over programmed points of interest. Ihlia quickly maneuvered her hand to her firing position against her father's rifle. When Ihlia moved her hand the blue display, by her careful design, came to rest atop the rifle as though taking the place of a telescopic sight. A smile touched her lips as she aimed the cross hairs at the Hoverbuster in the distance, in particular on the thick metal cockpit shutters.

The blue screen beeped several times; the indicators drifting across the screen computed, analyzed, and displayed the thicker and thinner points in the Hoverbuster's metal hull, but more importantly, it used highly advanced sensors to scan the aircraft's interior. With an x-ray overlay, the metallic covering faded, and two human skeletons appeared on the screen.

Their limbs moved purposefully, and their fingers danced across various empty spaces my younger self surmised to be holocom consoles that remained undetected by her x-ray scanner. With the pilot and co-pilot in clear view, the penetration of the metallic shutters remained the only obstacle in her mission. But with her specially developed ammunition, she intended to rectify that conundrum as well. The dense osmium- and iridium-based alloys comprising the core of her rifle rounds were perfect for extreme penetration. In fact, aside from material constructed of solid diamond or the same osmium and iridium she used, most other practical barricades stood little chance of stopping the extremely hard and dense ammunition.

Just as the enemy soldiers began repelling from the side of the Hoverbuster, Ihlia fired a round at the pilot on the "safe" side of the metal hull; the brutal thunk jarred the aircraft in its entirety, and the pilot's skull exploded inside the cockpit. The co-pilot scrambled to react to the tragedy, but Ihlia abruptly halted his attempts to salvage the situation when she put the second osmiridium round into his face. Once the two operators slept soundly, and eternally, on the metal floor, the aircraft quickly spiraled out of control with a distinct whine. The impact likely killed many of the reinforcement soldiers, but those who survived met with the ferocious charge of Jace, Gunther, and a large platoon of Cairo's local military.

"The Hoverbuster's down, Shandi. Looks like Jace and Gunther will clean up," The young Ihlia said with a quick press of her ear lobe. As Shandi buzzed back a response, Ihlia deactivated and pocketed her portable holocom bracelet.

"Understood, Ihlia. Mighty fine work, Sug'. Looks like them Union boys will be packin' soon. Keep providin' support until they go on the retreat and things quiet down, ok?" Shandi's voice lost its sense of urgency. She sounded more like her calm, gentle southern belle self.

"You got it," Ihlia grinned and returned to her iron sights. Such was her life, such was the life of a Bald Eagle. My life, before it was snatched from me. *"If only it could have stayed like that forever..."* I sighed.

—

Once again the darkness swept through my consciousness and tore me from the blazing battlefield to a few days following the eventful skirmish. During a quiet period in which Bradich commanded our company to rest and allow the militia to handle perimeter security, our entire unit gathered in the common quarters of the Nanite Research Dome. Used by the scientists of the facility to relax between experimentation, socialize with one another during a reprieve, and consume their meals when they remembered to do so, the common quarters possessed a bar top, several tables, a few beds, and various holocoms and television sets for entertainment and N-3 access.

When the Bald Eagles meandered in and made it their roost, the sophisticated air of relaxation akin to a restaurant swiftly degraded to the ruckus of a bar or lounge. Cigarette smoke wafted through the air; mugs of sludge littered the bar top; and arm wrestling, card games, and messy plates filled the tables strewn about the room. After a short time, finding one of the researchers in the common quarters became as difficult as finding a virgin in a brothel.

“I don't think I can go through with it...” My younger self whined to Shandi, who meticulously spread blush on the young Ihlia's pale cheeks. At a table of their own, far cleaner than those of their male comrades, Shandi painted various shades and colors of makeup across my younger version's girlish countenance. I lifted a hand to my lips and chuckled as I watched the transaction, and though the face of the young Ihlia remained blurry to my ghostly vision, I remembered the sensation of Shandi applying cosmetics to the contours and curves of my facade.

“Sug', all you're doin' is goin' to say hello. Ain't nothin' wrong with that. I'm just makin' sure you look fabulous when you do. Now come on, hold still, baby. You're makin' this a might harder than it needs to be,” Shandi giggled. The young Ihlia released a defeated sigh and nodded. As Shandi placed the finishing touches on my teenage version's cosmetic makeover, she emitted a dreamy exhale.

“Oh, Sug', you look gorgeous. There ain't no way he won't notice you now!” Shandi clasped her hands in front of her face and giggled excitedly. As she puckered her lips and blew softly across Ihlia's eyes to dry the makeup, I smiled at the memory.

Finally, Shandi leaned back, gripped a small porcelain-framed mirror, and placed it before Ihlia's eyes. The moment the reflective glass crossed her vision, her face illuminated and the censor blur vanished like a veil pulled back from the head of a bride. I stared at each detail of my face; every crevice and beautiful color Shandi created popped with the same subtlety and grace she exuded, herself.

"That's me?" Ihlia whispered in disbelief.

"M'hm. That's you, baby doll," Shandi whispered back, "now go say hello to that man you got your eyes on."

Ihlia smiled and stood. The blur drifted across my former self's face once more, but a smile remained on both corners of my lips. The young Ihlia gulped down several deep breaths to prepare herself for her meeting with Donovan, but a shrill whistle suddenly interrupted her ritual.

"Whoo, look at what we have here! Our little sniper's all dolled up!" Gunther stepped forward and examined Ihlia with extreme scrutiny. I looked over to see Welsch laughing under his breath; he and Loxley stood and found their places at Gunther's left and right. Their chorus of cat-calls and whistles froze Ihlia in place. I furrowed my brows and glanced around the rest of the room.

The twins preoccupied themselves with a television program that featured over the top explosions, Bit and Jace chugged a pair of mugs filled with a sludge so black it might have made Crelyos cringe, and Downy sat at the bar on a stool, drawing random patterns in his food with his fork; he occasionally shot a glance at my former version's face only to snap his attention back to his food with an incoherent murmur and flushed cheeks.

My former self grinned, despite the deep crimson stain splashed across her face. She placed both hands on her hips and cocked her shoulder to one side. “Yeah? So I'm dolled up. I'll still put a bullet between your eyes if you don't back off!” Ihlia's voice cracked as she chuckled. I knew, as an omniscient witness to my own dream and memory, that my younger version's threat and laughter served as little more than a ruse to conceal the utter embarrassment and the nerve-racking fear that she looked strange or unnatural. The men, however, failed to pick up on those insecurities.

“Oooh, watch out Loxley and Welsch, she'll hit you in the eyes with her deadly mascara sniping skills!” The crude Persian-featured mercenary laughed heartily. Welsch shook his head and chuckled under his breath again, while Loxley merely placed a finger against the tip of his chin as though processing the information in front of him like a holocom. Small tears pooled at the corners of Ihlia's eyes. Still, she maintained her quaking grin; her dedication to hide the vulnerability she felt coaxed pity from me.

“You scum o' the earth!” Shandi's voice rose up like a roaring fire. She launched a swift right hook through the air that landed square against Gunther's jaw. The crude, handsome devil staggered into a nearby table and smashed through it.

“What gives?!” Gunther shot up and rubbed his jaw; his flickering eyes focused on Shandi with a combination of fear and confusion. “We were just having a bit of fun! It's not like she's seriously...” A sharp elbow from Loxley interrupted Gunther's words. The nudge snapped the pretty boy's attention back to the young Ihlia, whose chest heaved rapidly as she attempted to quell the urge to cry.

“... Oh. Look, Ihlia, we're sorry. We didn't mean anything by it. I thought it was a gag or something, it's out of character for you. Man, what am I trying to say here...” Gunther fumbled with his words, but Loxley stepped forward and placed his hand on the young Ihlia's shoulder.

“What he's trying to say, Ihlia, is that he had no idea how to react when he saw how beautiful you were. We're used to your normal beauty, the pretty face without makeup and the strong loyal comrade that exhibits utter radiance in everything she does. Now that you have makeup on, the effect is just too much for a simple mind like Gunther's. Please forgive him, he just doesn't know how to talk to gorgeous women.” Loxley's smile, which swept the hearts from the chests of many a maiden, worked its magic yet again as the young Ihlia's lips relaxed into a natural smile.

“Thanks, guys...” She said. Loxley nodded his head in the direction of the door, and Ihlia bounded off with the intention of greeting Donovan as a woman rather than just a mercenary.

“That's too risky. It may not work; I will fix this world my way!” As Ihlia approached the door to the office in which Donovan took up residence for the duration of his research expedition, the unusual sound of Bradich's infuriated voice exploded into the hallway. My younger self's fist, a mere inch from rapping the metal door to announce her presence, paused at the outburst. With widened eyes, Ihlia stepped back into the hallway. The conversation escalated quickly.

“Brother, you sound insane. I'm offering you a viable alternative. I understand you've become jaded since the Global Conflict, you've always been sensitive to things like this, but what you're proposing is downright evil.” Donovan's soft methodic voice echoed from the office. It was as though Donovan sought to remain the voice of reason during the exchange.

“Evil? I never thought I'd hear the word from a scientific mind like yours. I have no intention of going about things so indirectly. I will force humanity to become more than what it is.” Bradich's voice dripped with a venomous depth which young Ihlia never heard until that night. I never forgot it since that night.

“Run in, Ihlia. Just run in and kill him now. You can end all this before it ever begins!” I shouted with unbridled aggravation.

“Brother, it is not the job of the enlightened to force humanity forward. We present the truth and allow those with the power to think to decide for themselves. This is why I'm urging you to rethink your stance on my proposal." Donovan earnestly pleaded; Ihlia continued eavesdropping.

"Your proposal involves showcasing research data and making slow steps toward a potential future. But I assure you, brother, if things continue the way they are the world won't last long enough for your future to manifest!" Bradich fumed. I remembered the abrupt shock I experienced as a young teenager listening to the commander's demeanor steadily decay during his debate with Donovan. Then, I feared a family feud might lead to a rift separating the brothers. As I experienced it in hindsight, it sounded like the raving madness of a man pushed over the edge.

"Have faith," Donovan sighed.

"Faith? Faith in what? Your science? Human nature? Surely, you're the one who's insane," Bradich growled.

"I see, so there's just no convincing you. At least give me just a little time before you carry out your nefarious plot, then, brother. The end of this mission. If I can't show you hopeful results from my science by the end of this trip, I'll give up," Donovan's voice escaped him, defeated.

"Fine. You have until we return to America to show me something solid. Not theoretical, brother, solid. Are we done then? I have an appointment I must keep," Bradich retorted; the electronic door clicked and wooshed open.

As Bradich stormed from the office, he halted to stare at the cosmetically enhanced young Ihlia. The commander lifted a single brow skyward, but he offered my younger version a brief grin and continued down the hall back toward the rest of the Bald Eagles. Ihlia stared after him for a few moments before turning her gaze to the doorway which quickly filled with the broad shoulders of Bradich's brother, Doctor Donovan Lesfort. His white laboratory coat flowed about his body, and he shoved both his hands in his pockets. A cigarette hung loosely from the soft clutches of his lips.

“Hm? Ihlia? It's been a while! My, how you've grown.” The doctor approached within mere inches of my nervous young self. When Ihlia parted her lips, I envisioned she desired to provide a sensual, seductive greeting with the allure to capture even the hardest heart. Instead, what poured from her mouth was a series of embarrassing stammers and stutters.

“Well... I, um, I see. Yeah, it has been... a while. I've grown for a year since you last saw me!” Ihlia blurted.

“Uhm, quite so. I mean, since it's been a year since we last saw one another, I would assume as much my dear, hahaha!” Donovan laughed and pulled a lung full of smoke from his cigarette. Likely, the doctor assumed my stammering was a simple sarcastic jest. At the time, however, I tried my utmost to appear as sincere as possible. And I failed, miserably.

“Yes, yes I suppose... um, that's right, ehehe...” Ihlia's

voice quivered; she twirled a strand of hair around her finger and frantically searched for something to say. When it finally hit her, she abruptly shouted, “Ah, what were you two fighting about? It seemed important!”

“Hm? Oh, yes, Bradich and I. It's just a difference in opinion. We're both looking for ways to make the world a better place. Each of us thinks the other's methods are a bit twisted or, in his case, he thinks mine are inefficient as well as twisted. I'm sure I'll get through to him in time, though. In time...” Donovan stepped forward and ran his fingers through Ihlia's silken, obsidian locks. I smiled as I watched.

“Kiss me or something, you dunce...” How I wished Donovan acted so crudely at that time. Alas, much like Cairo becoming a temperate forest, it simply was not meant to be.

“You really have become so beautiful, Ihlia. So very beautiful. Especially this hair... I love how long and lush it is. I see you and it brings me just a little peace from the constant stress of my work. Thank you.” Donovan and Ihlia maintained their locked gazes for several moments; eventually, however, Donovan stepped away from her.

“Alas, even a small break could mean the difference between people living and dying, between happiness and sorrow. If you'll excuse me, my dear,” Donovan smiled. The depth of his wise brown eyes penetrated the young Ihlia's, and I remembered the thrum that rattled my chest as I witnessed it.

Donovan shouldered the burdens of the world. The doctor felt the pain of the dwindling global population; he understood the men and women burdened by the war and sought to rectify the world's problems alone. He worked tirelessly, and as he did, I thought of little more than how to make him fall in love with me. The young Ihlia's face contorted with disgusted self-loathing.

As Donovan turned down the hallway in the opposite direction from his brother, my younger self stared at his back until he disappeared into the dark corridors of the Nanite Research Dome. I, too, watched him vanish down the hall.

"Oh Donovan... why didn't I realize in that moment... what was to come?" I sighed synchronously with my younger version. After a few moments of silent thought, Ihlia turned and walked back to the common quarters. The slow gait she adopted offered her plenty of time to think. By the time she reached the dim doorway of the common quarters, Ihlia remembered Shandi's advice and resolved herself.

"Surprise!" As the sixteen-year-old girl crossed the threshold of the room, a spray of confetti launched toward her from every direction. The Bald Eagles, in their entirety, leapt from various hiding places to shout. Despite the grave nature of the mission, each of Ihlia's comrades donned a festive attitude.

Even Bit, the normally stoic dark warrior, painted a wide smile across his face and wore a pointed party hat.

The twins tossed miniature explosives into the air that burst forth streamers and fragrant smokes. Jace balanced a cake atop a large platter on his palm. Gunther's, Welsch's, and Loxley's hands formed cylindrical cups around their mouths. Their apparent competition of who possessed the loudest shout vibrated the room's metal walls.

Shandi stood in the center of common quarters with a gentle smile and her hands clasped together excitedly, and Bradich leaned against a shadowy corner on the far end of the room. Despite his obvious fluster from the passionate conversation with his brother, his reassuring smile calmed my younger self. The warmth that flooded me as I remembered the surprise party might have brought tears to my eyes if they were capable of crying any longer. My younger version, unlike me, possessed the ability to cry rather well, and she exercised that ability with the happiest tears I remembered crying in my life.

“But...” Ihlia whimpered as she rushed forward to throw herself into her comrades' embraces, “my birthday's not for a few more days!”

File 25: Want or Love?

"I know it's not much, Sug', but we decided to throw your party early to surprise you!" Shandi giggled softly as the young Ihlia dove into her arms.

Ihlia's allies had lavishly decorated the room. The colorful array of balloons, streamers, and paper mache struck me as fairly juvenile in my dreamlike recollection. To the young Ihlia, however, the collection of party favors and sentiment behind her allies' premature surprise party touched the most vulnerable places in her emotional vault. As my former self buried her face into Shandi's massive bosom, the other members of the Bald Eagles offered various gestures of affection befitting their personalities.

Jace placed the cake on the nearest table; with a gruff motion that belied an earnest show of camaraderie which only he could accomplish, the tobacco chewing mercenary gripped the top of the young Ihlia's scalp and offered her head a patronizing rub as if to say "'atta girl! Happy Birthday!" When Ihlia glanced up at him from the safety of Shandi's embrace, she offered him a playfully annoyed face; in return, he lifted the blue plastic cup clutched in his free hand and spit a healthy brown stream of saliva into it.

"Touching, Jace. What is she, twelve? Let me show you

how it's done." Loxley swatted the vulgar mercenary's hand from Ihlia's head and gingerly cupped her fingertips in his. "To the stunning young sharpshooter's seventeenth birthday." As he commemorated the moment, Loxley lifted my younger version's hand and placed his lips tenderly against the back of her knuckles.

"Oh, sure, that's classy. What is this, the twentieth century?" Gunther mocked the condescending tone Loxley had offered Jace and sauntered to Shandi before draping his arm around her shoulder. Gunther slowly, sneakily lowered his hand dangerously close to the round swell of the auburn-haired belle's right breast. My younger version lifted her head and clamped her pearly whites atop one of his roaming digits. The mercenary yelped, uncertain of what exactly transpired, and snatched his hand into a cradle formed by its twin.

"Ow, Ihlia! What the hell was that for?" Gunther puckered his lips; as he cursed under his breath, he gently blew across the teeth marks that burned his right hand with a throbbing, fiery pain.

"Sug', you're lucky Ihlia bit you. If you actually touched me, I'd have done much worse," Shandi grinned and tossed Ihlia a grateful wink.

"Fuck, that stings," Gunther's words faded into mumbled obscurity.

Welsch stepped up and offered Ihlia a light slap against the center of her shoulders, "Grats, Ihlia. You've survived seventeen years, here's to hoping you got a few more in ya." Welsch and Ihlia exchanged jovial laughter.

"Wait, if she's only seventeen does that mean she's not legal yet?" Gunther ignored his pulsing hand to pursue knowledge which struck him as infinitely more important.

"Depends on where you're at," Loxley responded in a blatant fashion.

"And how many of us you think you can go through to get to her," Bit added with almost fatherly regard.

"Aw, man, so she's still off limits? We can't bang her?" Gunther pried the issue with a nonchalant undertone. Ihlia and Shandi simultaneously shot him glares infused with the damning chill of death incarnate.

"Haha, he said 'bang'..." The twins guffawed in unison, exchanging glances and mischievous smirks at their inward correlation between the sexual innuendo and the explosives they loved.

"What makes you think I'd want whatever you're carrying, anyway?" My younger version stepped back from Shandi and crossed her arms across the humbly budding swell of her breasts.

"Aw, come on, I'm clean," Gunther laughed. The entire room echoed with a resonating "Riiight..."

As the gathering of my former allies rumbled with dirty jokes and light-hearted laughter, Ihlia felt a soft tap on her right shoulder. She whirled about to face the passive request for her attention, and her gaze fell upon the downcast countenance of Downy.

"H-here, this is f-for you. H-happy B-birthday," Downy stammered. Within an extended hand covered in a fingerless leather glove, the quiet tech engineer offered Ihlia a single, mostly white flower. A splash of crimson painted one side of the gorgeous petals. "I f-found it during our last s-skirmish. It's a d-desert flower, so it's p-pretty rare."

"Thanks, Downy! Wait, what's this bit of red here?" Ihlia tenderly retrieved the flower from Downy's grip and twirled the green stem between her thumb and forefinger. The petals spun in a delicate dance within the young sniper's fingers.

"Probably blood. It was near an enemy's corpse," Downy stated in a blatant matter-of-fact manner. The young Ihlia blinked at him a few times, likely alarmed by the lack of his usual stammer.

"Oh, well, um, thank you very much!" Ihlia chuckled under her breath.

The evening sun eventually sank behind the desert sands, and the darkness of night encroached on the celebration. Bradich remained motionless in the corner with his back planted firmly against the wall the entire time. Though night brought darkness to the desert oasis, the perpetual shadow lingering over the commander's facade had been in place long before the moon rose over the sandy hills. In the midst of the festivities, Ihlia stopped and stared at her leader with a perplexed expression. She tossed a quick glance to Shandi; though the buxom belle managed to maintain an air of happiness, she occasionally cut a worried stare at the man she loved.

My younger self and I synchronously sighed. Ihlia sighed at the distress of her motherly figure; I sighed with the knowledge that Bradich's abysmal countenance remained rooted in a problem far beyond the scope of the party or even the mission in Cairo. If the young Ihlia possessed my knowledge, then perhaps the events destined to transpire would have concluded differently. *"If only I had known..."* I frowned.

"Bradich, sir... Are you okay?" The young Ihlia bent forward at the waist in front of her commander and lifted her head so that she might lock eyes with his downcast gaze.

As I beheld his twisted, gnarled expression, I understood the thoughts racing through his mind. His brain busily worked to justify his rationale, and his heart hardened to steel his mettle for the act of treason he prepared to commit. There was no other way to explain it, but there was no way to convey it to the young Ihlia, either. Though I perceived the imminent danger to those I loved, Ihlia spent her concern on the very perpetrator fated to strip her of her second family, her second chance at happiness.

"Are any of us truly "okay'? I wonder..." Bradich's dismal features, frozen in a misty, contemplative state, suddenly honed their negativity on the young Ihlia like a focused beam. His eyes, deep brown voids seemingly consuming everything around them, locked onto Ihlia's.

"We turned a simple silicon-based material into a micro super computer capable of solving the world's problems with a few simple cuts. Yet as in ancient history, no matter how far we come, we turn everything good and pure that we get our grimy hands on into a tool of destruction. Why?" Bradich's rampant fiery rant ended with a question that took my younger version aback.

It felt like a plea, as though the commander begged the young sniper to offer him a word or statement to redeem the humanity he perceived; he wanted her to save him from the decision I knew he would soon make and to which everyone else was utterly oblivious.

"Sir?..." Ihlia's response, a combination of a shocked statement and confused question, escaped her after a brief moment of hesitation.

"Do you know why I became a mercenary? Why I started the Bald Eagles?" Bradich stood erect, uncrossed his arms, and took a step toward my younger self.

"Now! Take out your daggers and plunge them into his forehead! He's so close, just do it, do it please!" I

screamed at the young Ihlia.

"I believe it was for excitement, to see the world, and to make your mark on history," Ihlia recited it like an answer to a midterm. Bradich, still standing in the shadow that painted his frame in foreboding darkness, sighed and shook his head.

"I could have done many different things to fulfill those goals. I started the Bald Eagles to help put an end to conflict. My abilities, my knack for strategy, my contacts, and my capability in direct combat are things with which I was born. But they are things which I believe are unnecessary in this world. We need to understand one another, we need to be able to connect with other human beings on the deepest levels of our spiritual selves. War, fighting, struggles, they need to go away," Bradich replied calmly.

"But, sir, that doesn't make sense. You're fighting and killing to stop fighting and killing? You excel at war, yet you wish to erase it? Even if you make a mark on history and find your place in society that way, at best you'd be remembered as a necessary evil, and at worst just one of the many obscure groups of violent antagonists that impeded the very path you think humanity needs to take," Ihlia's response elicited a wide-eyed blink from the mercenary commander.

My younger self rarely felt it necessary to engage in meaningless theoretical jargon, but her concern for Bradich's mental welfare outweighed her sense of triviality. Bradich seemed pleased; perhaps he always wished to engage in such a conversation with the young Ihlia but never obtained the opportunity until then.

“Perhaps it doesn't make sense. In fact, that is part of the conundrum I face even now. I decided long ago that, if necessary, I could become the evil the world requires to dig itself from the hole it's fallen into. If history forgets me, or vilifies me, then such is preferable to doing nothing at all or struggling in futility to change the world with more passive tactics,” he turned his gaze down the hall toward Donovan's office and narrowed his eyes.

“I want the world to connect; I want our higher sense of spirituality to branch off into each individual that we might be unable to harm one another without harming ourselves.” Bradich stretched his arms out as though to offer his ideology an all-encompassing embrace.

“So, like a hive mind? In your ideal reality, we would all think the same. We would all be connected through our thoughts and possess no individuality or different opinions. Creativity would vanish; arts, crafts, inspiration, and unique tastes would disappear. Is that cost worth it?” My young version tipped her head to the side in thought.

“You're thinking too small. I want us to connect in mind, spirit, and body. It's not that individual thought would disappear as to be eradicated through tyranny, it would disappear because it is no longer needed. We are all one, and in our unity we could reach the stars and beyond. As things evolve, their unnecessary parts disappear. I believe this can apply spiritually as well," Bradich looked up to the ceiling as though staring through it to the stars above us.

"This thing you call individuality, is it really so important? What benefit has it given us? I can certainly name a list of negative consequences. Can you offer me solid, empirical examples of the benefits to alleged individuality?" The inflection in Bradich's voice echoed from his lips like a haunting melody peaking in tempo. He was enjoying the conversation.

"I suppose not. But must all good things be quantified or observed empirically?" Ihlia posed.

"Are those things worth the countless lives lost to the hatred birthed from differing opinions? If humans were capable of standing on different viewpoints, different opinions, and tolerating one another's stance in a calm, rational, reasonable manner then I might agree," Bradich's calm rapidly deteriorated.

"But they don't! Humans allow their emotions to interfere with their reason; they allow their opinions to transform into hatred and act on that hatred to bring harm to one another over the course of years until they can't even remember why they're murdering in the first place!" Bradich stepped forward into the light with each vehement spew of his impassioned argument.

His eyes flickered wildly, harboring a pent up rage for

the state of the world which I did not remember beholding as I stood before him those ten years ago. My former self took a step back; her fearful expression snapped Bradich from his rampage.

“I'm sorry... See? Even I get too heated sometimes. Imagine if I acted on that,” He laughed and stepped forward. He placed a soft kiss against the center of the young Ihlia's forehead.

“Sir?” Ihlia asked, confused and slightly shaken.

“Enjoy the party, Ihlia.” Bradich slunk from the corner and found refuge among his subordinates. It was as though the life of the party walked through the group; boisterous shouts of praise and excitement rose up from the murmurs and revived the festivities. Shandi smiled and rushed to Bradich's side with a cup of punch. When he gripped it, his hand lingered atop hers for a few seconds longer than was necessary to secure his drink; their eyes met and Shandi's lit up like the stars in the sky, while Bradich's seemed to ponder the very nature of her wonderment. I shook my head and frowned; the young Ihlia shook her head and smiled.

“Hey, Bradich!” Ihlia called out across the room. The bustle of my comrades quieted as though a vacuum sucked the noise from the air. Ihlia placed a single hand on her hip and nodded at her commander, “Aren't you going to wish me a happy birthday?”

Bradich placed the cup to his lips and tipped his head

back; as the cool liquid quenched an obvious thirst which he had apparently suppressed during his sullen contemplation, the wily glint in his eyes intensified. He was obviously preparing a quip. When he finally finished drinking, Bradich tossed the empty plastic cup playfully at the young Ihlia's face.

“It's not your birthday, yet,” he said.

—

As the hours passed and the night became late, Ihlia retreated to the restroom in the middle of her own party. When she stood in front of the mirror, my former self beheld the glamorous beauty which Shandi had painted across her face with the experience of a cosmetic guru.

I smiled. *“You look all right, kid. You look all right,”* The words that echoed from the ghost-voice to which I grew accustomed synched up with the squeaky hinge of the door as Shandi swung it open and marched into the bathroom.

“Sug', Donovan just arrived at the party! He was lookin' for you! What are you doin' hidin' away in here, baby? Come on!” Shandi motioned furiously.

The young Ihlia smiled and turned to the mirror once again. The dark mascara accenting Ihlia's eyes brought them to life in a vibrant emerald glow. Her lips, normally thin and dull, appeared full, lush, and colorful beneath a masterful coating of ruby lipstick. Her pale cheeks exuded a rosy imitation of a blushing face, and the entire artistic pallet rested upon an expertly applied foundation that brought the makeup to life.

“Sug'? What's the hold up?” Shandi tilted her head to the side and sauntered behind Ihlia; as she placed both hands on my younger version's shoulders, Ihlia offered her a bittersweet mile.

“Why is Donovan looking for me?” Ihlia inquired.

“Oh, I don't know, honey. I think, maybe, someone raved about how pretty you got and how the party was to celebrate your birthday and stuff. Someone may have hinted, with a mighty fine dose of discretion, mind you, that a certain someone might have dolled up specifically to get a certain doctor's attention,” Shandi giggled.

“What?! Shandi!...” Ihlia droned with despair, “Why?”

“Because, baby. You did somethin' for me. You pulled Bradich out of that there darkness when I couldn't even talk to him. None of us could; we were all too afraid to approach him. Even me, and I love that man,” Shandi smiled sadly and lowered her chin atop the young Ihlia's shoulder. The two women stared at one another through their reflections with loving adoration.

Ihlia placed her hand atop Shandi's. “I just saw you were worried about him. Thought I could help.”

“I know, Sug'. And considerin' how disgruntled you looked when you came back down that hall, I think it's safe to assume your talk with Donovan didn't quite go as planned,” Shandi arched a brow.

“Ugh, I stammered like a school girl. I could hardly think, let alone form words properly. It was horrible. Did I really look that depressed?” Ihlia winced her features into a face that resembled a child preparing for a vaccination.

“Darlin', you looked like someone just told you the world was endin'. I almost cried for you.” Shandi laced her arms around Ihlia's waist from behind in a comforting hug. “But you know what, Sug'? I'm pretty good at readin' people like him. He may be a doctor, but he's still a man. And he is most certainly open to the idea of you.”

“I can sense it. Just a few bats of those long lashes and a few flirtatious moves, and he just might seek your embrace to take the sting out of his stressful research. If you want him, baby, just talk to him. Trust me. The chemistry is at work here. I can feel it! Go on, go talk to him!” Shandi tugged at my younger version's waist.

“Hang on,” Ihlia stammered between soft chuckles. She twisted the knob atop the sink, and as the water gushed from the silver faucet, my former self cupped her hands beneath the stream and filled the bowl formed by her palms with a miniature lake of the cool liquid.

With a swift and sudden motion, Ihlia splashed the cold

water across her face and vigorously rubbed away the beautiful artistry Shandi had afforded her. After a few repetitions, Ihlia stood and stared at the faded cosmetics. The remaining makeup was smudged and running, and the phantom of her plain features peeked through the colors that represented Ihlia, the woman.

"Honey, why?" Shandi questioned with a slight touch of sadness.

"Because, Shandi. I don't want him. I love him," Ihlia responded with a passionate, sorrowful longing.

Shandi and I smiled at the same time. As I watched the scene in the ladies' room of the Nanite Research Dome play out, I felt a heaviness in my chest. Sadness? I understood the possibility that the memory conjured forth those dormant feelings, but I still felt dissociated from the emotion itself.

Shandi's eyes filled with tears. As they spilled over her cheeks and dripped from the bottom of her pretty chin, she removed a cloth and a small case. A strange chemical concoction filled one of the case's many compartments.

"That's my girl," she sobbed as she went to work blotting away the faux beauty covering Ihlia's face, "but you'll need more than water to wash away this stuff completely!"

Ihlia's methodical footsteps carried her back to the lobby of the Nanite Research Dome's common quarters.

With the late night, or early morning depending on one's perspective, hours quieting the festivities to a murmur, the Bald Eagles had migrated from the innocent tang of party punch to the harder sludge-based beverages powerful enough to overcome Panacea and inebriate them.

Downy and Welsch slept soundly on nearby cots; Gunther and Loxley sat at a table with their downturned faces smashed against its wooden surface. Their hands loosely dangled next to the chairs in which they slumped with improper posture, and bottles of rancid liquor remained clutched in either of their unconscious grips. Ihlia shook her head; she correctly guessed that the two passed out during a drinking contest.

Bit sat calmly on a less-than-comfortable stool with one of his trademark cigars smoldering between his lips; he fixed his unwavering gaze on the flickering television screen hanging from a nearby wall. Jace, Flint, and Steele lay in a strewn heap across the floor; Jace snored soundly, and the twins murmured incoherently about explosions and blast radiuses in their sleep. I smiled along with my former self as we reminisced on the various misadventures experienced with our unsightly crew of cutthroats. But while the young Ihlia's thoughts widened the grin on her face with their conclusion, that same conclusion erased my smile and left only the bitter taste of hatred and anger on my scowling lips.

The largest cluster of still-conscious bodies circled a table sitting near the common quarter's exit. Bradich and

Donovan sat in chairs on opposing sides of the table, and a second scientist stood directly behind the object of the young Ihlia's affections. I recognized him as a ten-years-younger version of Oswald, but to my young self he was nothing more than a snide doctor.

Consistent with my own version of Oswald, his younger self possessed a shiny bald head. His wiry brown sideburns descended the length of his cheeks and wrapped around his chin in a bristly beard. His facade harbored a stoicism devoid of any joy one might take in life as though someone had robbed all emotion straight off his face. A pair of thin, pretentious glasses rested on the bridge of his nose. And as we did with Downy, the young Ihlia and I questioned the need for vision assistance from external sources. While one might have argued that, with only three safe nanite slots, other implants took precedence over a sensory implant to correct eyesight, what attribute trumped the importance of correcting faulty sensory organs?

Oswald stood in an immaculate posture with his hands shoved in his khaki pants pockets. The bend of his elbow forced the tails of his white laboratory coat to pool loosely at the backs of his thighs, and with a black tie neatly tied around his neck and a pair of shiny black shoes encasing his feet, Oswald looked more professional than most of the scientists running around the sweltering facility. After a few weeks of the scorching midday temperatures, most of the researchers adopted a less strict code of attire with the exception, of course, of their laboratory coats. No researcher ever went without it. It was as though the white flowing garb represented everything it meant to be a scientist in the field.

While Oswald's clean-cut uniform represented a look of professionalism, the young Ihlia immediately attributed it to some baseless, imaginary rookie quality Oswald must have possessed. She figured that within a week's time, the uppity scientist would look more disheveled. Unfortunately, that theory would never be put to the test.

“This again, brother? I already told you, I have no intention of subscribing to your methods. Nanite technology is what got us into this mess in the first place. Sure, it started benign, but now nanites are the leading cause of the development of advanced weapons. Weapons that kill people. Your research will lead to nothing different.” Bradich furrowed his brows and defiantly crossed his arms over his chest as he leaned back in his chosen chair.

“I'm not asking you to endorse my research this time. I just need you to uphold your contract. This is Doctor Oswald; he flew in from the states a week ago to assist me with my research. We're at the cliff's edge on a major breakthrough, but I require some test samples from a nearby laboratory. The only catch is they're too busy to accommodate a privateer, so we have to go pick them up ourselves,” Donovan defensively explained.

“It's only about thirty miles to the labs just beyond Giza where the samples are located. I just need an escort. Anti-nanite local terrorists, Union forces, and the French have many forward recon units and bases of operations hidden along the ruins that used to be this fair city." Donovan's hands, folded atop one another with his elbows standing erect on the tabletop, obscured the lower extremities of his face as he calmly explained the situation. The wisps of smoke that drifted over the top of his hand suggested a cigarette hung between his lips.

I remembered the thoughts and emotions that overtook me back then. Like a stroke of fate, an opportunity presented itself for the young Ihlia to take her place at Donovan's side as a supporter of his work and beliefs. As Bradich tiredly rubbed the annoyed creases in his face, my younger version stepped forward to join the conversation.

"I'll go," she stated matter-of-factly. The heads of the three men twisted toward Ihlia when her gait brought her to rest at the table's side between the brothers. With her face alight, Ihlia crossed her arms beneath her breasts and exuded confidence.

"Ihlia?" Donovan's eyes twinkled for a moment. Neither my younger version nor my adult version fully understood the faint gleam emanating from his deep brown eyes. Behind him, Doctor Oswald regarded the young Ihlia with passing scrutiny but remained silent. Donovan's gaze slowly veered back to his brother's; the object of Ihlia's affection seemed to hide a smile of victory as he stared at Bradich from across the table.

"I was just telling Bradich here that you'd help me if I

asked. With your vision nanites and expertise in marksmanship, I'd feel safest with you in the jeep to pick off any assailants before they ever endanger the doctor and me," Donovan nodded like a researcher whose hypothesis passed experimentation with expected results.

"You sure, Ihlia? The trip will be dangerous," Bradich scratched his chin and offered my younger version a concerned glance.

"I'm sure, sir. And with all due respect, and perhaps it's not my place, but you should support your brother's research a little more. He's trying to change the world just like you are. I think you two stand a lot to gain by working together; your solutions don't have to be mutually exclusive. Whatever those are, exactly..." Ihlia trailed off as she realized that in her attempts to impress Donovan, she spoke on a topic with which she was not entirely familiar.

"You're right, Ihlia. That's not your place," Bradich narrowed his eyes into a cautionary glare that indicated almost certain punishment had my former version pressed the issue.

"Hold on now, as your employer I'd like to hear this," Donovan lifted a hand to silence Bradich.

The commander intensified his glare and snapped it to his brother. After a brief moment of silence, Bradich's voice escaped him as a guttural growl might leave the maw of a territorial predator, "Sorry, boss. Your contract clearly states I am in charge of my soldiers. You have enlisted our assistance, but you may not deal with any of the mercenaries save me. If you attempt to circumvent my authority over the Eagles again, your contract will be null and void."

Bradich was serious. In all my years as an Eagle, Bradich nullified a contract exactly one time. An ally of the United States hired our group to assist them in an assault on a Union base. Our job was to create a diversion to ease the Free Alliance's attack. To do this, the contractor ordered Bradich to disguise our group as raiders and lay waste to a village of civilians. The idea was to have the Union soldiers respond and for the Free Alliance to ambush them when they arrived. Needless to say, Bradich kindly instructed our employer to "fuck off."

"My apologies, Bradich," Donovan recognized the serious tone with which his brother spoke, as well, and backed off the issue.

"You're dismissed, Ihlia. Report to the garage at 0600," Bradich nodded my younger version off to bed.

Back in the special quarters provided to her given her female gender, Ihlia began removing articles of clothing. As she slid the dark gray pants from her hips and sat atop her cot, my younger self thought at length on her situation. She had succeeded in showing Donovan support for his research, and in time she intended to show him her support for his goal in its broader sense.

Ihlia failed to understand Bradich's objections to the concept of using nanite research to propel the world into a new age of prosperity hopefully devoid of war and conflict. As she wondered, she lifted the tight tank top that simultaneously served as a sports bra to support her growing breasts. The black material obscured her vision, and she felt the warm night air kiss her bare flesh. Suddenly, the sound of a brief knock on her door stopped her motion completely.

"Ihlia, are you awake?" The sound of Donovan's voice on the other side of the door might have sent the young girl's heart into an excited pitter-patter. Instead, no sooner than the two swift knocks and brief question escaped the doctor on the other side of the door, he depressed the button and the door hissed ajar.

Ihlia's eyes, covered by the half-lifted shirt concealing her face like a curtain, widened to the size of electrocapacitor plates in the darkness. A shrill cry escaped her, and Ihlia shoved the tank top back down across her breasts and fervently yanked the cot's blanket across the simple black bikini-cut underwear contoured to her budding young hips.

The scarlet fire that raced across her cheeks represented both irritation and embarrassment. With a startled and angry face, she shot her gaze to the offending doctor who stood rigid in the open doorway to her quarters. His bottom jaw dropped, and the cigarette that hung loosely from his bottom lip dropped to the floor like a burning tear drop. The doctor coughed and turned his back after a moment of surprised silence.

"Ah, ahem. Yes, well, forgive me. I keep forgetting that uh... there are more than just men here. I mean, not that you remind me of a man. In fact, I don't know quite what I mean, there are plenty of female scientists here too. I would never just walk in on them, so I don't know what... Hm, ahem, well, I apologize. H-how are you tonight, Ihlia?" Donovan stammered. As he stood with his back to my younger self, he laced either of his hands together behind his back and began rocking nervously from his heels to his toes.

"I hope you'll knock first from now on. You scared the living hell out of me!" Ihlia exclaimed, "I'm okay, Doctor. What can I do for you, tonight?" Though the young Ihlia managed to feign maturity and calmness with her voice, her chest pounded as though war drums had replaced her heartbeat's subtle thud.

"I just wanted to say thank you. I didn't realize that you understood or grasped what was really going on. You're so young, I mean. I feel like I patronized you earlier when I gave you that uninformative explanation about the argument Bradich and I got into," Donovan scratched the back of his head.

"See, we both think this world needs to change. There are not enough resources or humans to sustain this kind of global murder; that might have worked three hundred years ago, but it just can't go on like this much longer. We've both felt this way since we were kids. As we grew up, our opinions on how to go about it changed. Bradich feels he needs to become the villain. To fight it with his hands until the war is over and the innocent aren't suffering. A direct approach," Donovan explained.

"And you believe in the passive approach?" Ihlia inquired.

"Not passive, exactly, but rather we need to make humanity more intelligent. If we capitalize on the wonderful discovery and implementation of nanites, the problems will work themselves out once people understand that the violence solves nothing. We may have solved petty issues like global starvation and the energy crisis, and our information and lab technology have taken leaps and bounds, but all that serves nothing if we use that information and those advancements to bring harm to others." A hint of despair saturated Donovan's voice. Ihlia sensed that though the doctor believed in his ideas, he recognized that the chance of their execution, at least as perfectly as he envisioned, would be far easier said than done.

"So, Bradich fires guns and you research nanites, both trying to save the world," Ihlia mused.

"Precisely. Is that strange or wrong?" Donovan tilted his head to one side and turned around to face the younger version of myself. The young Ihlia and I laughed at the same time.

"It's not that. I just figured you two were these highly

sophisticated older men with deep complicated reasons for everything you did. I felt like I was years from even scratching the surface. But now..." Ihlia stood and allowed the blanket to slip from her hips like the curtain of her embarrassment. She stood close to the doctor with a new sense of understanding; for the first time since she knew Donovan, she felt she could face him as an equal: as a woman.

"Now I see you two are just a couple of kids that never let go of your dreams. I can just see both of you with superhero capes. Super Brain and Machinegun Man off to save the day," Ihlia giggled.

Donovan chuckled beneath his breath and tipped his head down toward my former self. As the two locked eyes, the mist of pretenses and restraint seemed to clear away like a dispersing morning fog. Ihlia slowly raised onto her tip-toes toward the doctor.

But just when her racing heartbeat threatened to leap from the confines of her chest and their lips drew close, Donovan placed his hand on her shoulder. His breath escaped him in ragged puffs, and wanton fantasies gleamed in his eyes. But the hand he placed on her shoulder was not inviting; it stopped her motion. Ihlia forced a smile and placed her hand atop his own.

"Um, yes, quite. I also wanted you to know not to be so hard on my brother. You see, despite his attitude, Bradich is quite supportive of my research. He disagrees with my approach, but he is earnest to see if I can prove him wrong. I daresay he wants me to. He does not like to kill, and while he's willing to paint himself the villain in history if it means making the world a better place, it is certainly not his ideal ending," Donovan took a step back.

Ihlia tipped her head down. The dark shadow of her bangs concealed the glistening sadness that threatened to tear up her emerald eyes. I remembered that sadness as I watched her, though it felt disconnected and far from me like a piece of a memory.

It was the sadness of realization; at that moment, Ihlia realized that quelling her desire for girlish recognition and some love-story relationship would take time and an overwhelming amount of willpower. It was not Donovan or Bradich who she was years from understanding; it was her own heart. Unfortunately, as the living testament to her story's harrowing conclusion, I knew such an understanding would never come.

After a few seconds of reflection, Ihlia turned her sad smile toward Donovan after ensuring her eyes would not betray her true feelings. "How can you be so sure, Doctor? He may just be doing this for the money or something."

"Hm, well actually, he's not getting any. The contract entails no monetary transaction between Bradich and me. I simply don't have the funds as a privateer to hire a mercenary group as renowned as the Bald Eagles. Bradich's doing this for free." Donovan shoved his hands in his pockets. In the dim light cast by the hallways, Ihlia noted a blush streaked across his face. At the very least, my younger version took solace in the fact that she aroused the good doctor. However, after hearing that Bradich would receive no pay for the excursion, her bittersweet expression transformed to one of shock.

"No money? But he promised the men good pay for this! It's not like him to lie and stiff them out of good money! They'll string him up alive if they find out!" My former self cupped a hand over her mouth at the thought of her allies and their shattered trust in the commander. In particular, Jace would string Bradich up alive if he flew all the way out to Egypt only to return to America empty handed.

"Ah, yes, I believe he's paying you all out of his own pocket. He pretends I'm paying a large sum, then divides that sum amongst himself and the men. The amount he promised to divide among you all, he intends to simply pay out of his private stash. Not only is he not getting paid, he's actually giving money to ensure my research. I cannot, will not, let that generosity and belief in me go to waste," Donovan's resolve grew; it was as though the doctor understood Bradich's sacrifice all the more after verbalizing it.

"Why are you telling me this?" Ihlia quirked a brow at the man she loved.

"I'm not sure exactly," Donovan scratched the back of his head as he searched for a way to express his thoughts and feelings.

"I think, perhaps, I trust you. Maybe it's the way you look at me or the aura you exude when we're together, but I feel soothed by your presence. When I said that just seeing your beautiful face takes the stress off my constant work, I was not deceiving you," Donovan's blush returned in force.

Ihlia smiled a large, genuine smile and lunged at the doctor with wild abandon. She threw her arms around his waist, and as she sank into his body and pressed her tank top clad breasts against his upper abdomen, she buried her face into his chest just beneath his chin.

"I-Ihlia!" Donovan exclaimed, surprised. However, as the warm feeling of the scantily clad Ihlia sank against him, Donovan's left arm encircled her slender shoulders and his right hand moved to brush through her hair and massage her scalp. His fingers found the curved scar at the bulb on the back of her head and he paused, "Ah, how is your latest nanite treating you? It's been almost a year since I gave you night vision, as per your request."

"So far so good. Both the nanites you've given me have helped me save my comrades countless times. I can't thank you enough, and I won't let anyone else inside me," Ihlia retorted with a gentle sigh.

The doctor coughed and his hand ceased its motions. When Ihlia realized how her words escaped her, she buried her face in the doctor's chest even harder. "T-that's not how I meant! I mean in my head; no one else can perform nanite surgery on me but you. That's all."

“Indeed,” Donovan laughed, “perhaps before the mission's conclusion you would like for me to perform a quick checkup? Make sure everything is operating properly?” Donovan's eyes flickered to the wall in the back of my former version's room where a digital holoclock displayed the time as two in the morning.

His demeanor changed to one a touch more frantic, and he hastily turned to exit Ihlia's quarters, “Ah! But you must sleep, and I must make a few calls before the operation tomorrow. I shall see you in four hours, then, my dear?” Donovan chuckled and offered Ihlia a wave with the back of his hand.

“A checkup would be great. And Donovan?” As Donovan escaped into the light-flooded corridor outside Ihlia's room, he turned his head back with a casual “Hm?” Ihlia once more clung to him, though this time from behind his back. She looped her arms around to the front of his stomach and pressed her entire body against his backside. Ihlia gently laid her cheek against the area between his shoulder blades. “I believe in you, too. If there's anything I can do to help. Anything...” Ihlia cooed softly.

“I understand,” Donovan replied with a gentle whisper. As my younger version relinquished him, he disappeared down the hall, but his head periodically swiveled to behold Ihlia's half-dressed figure standing in front of the doorway. Once the object of her affection vanished, Ihlia fell atop her cot and slept the next four hours away more soundly than she ever had in her entire life.

File 26: The Giza Expedition

As the dream-state shifted, and darkness again encroached on my senses, I seriously wondered if the dream, in fact, was my horrifying afterlife. The idea that I experienced a dream so vivid struck me as surreal. Whatever forces dictated my subconscious state afforded me little time to contemplate it, however, before a new scene rippled into view.

My former self nervously fidgeted in front of an elevator designed to descend into the lower garage level of the complex. A dreadful sensation overwhelmed me. Every scene, every passing moment, led closer and closer to the horrifying end that set everything into motion. And I knew it was coming. Ihlia criss-crossed her arms over her chest as she awaited the two scientists she would be escorting to the nearby Giza facility. To her surprise, the only two figures that approached belonged to Donovan and Bradich.

"Sir? What brings you here this morning? And where is that Doctor Oswald?" The young Ihlia inquired with a standard salute to her commander. Bradich rubbed his temples and nodded in response to Ihlia's salute.

"I'm going with you. I simply can't let my company sniper go alone; you might not come back to me," Bradich droned. He briskly walked passed my younger self to the elevator's panel. As he pressed a few of the buttons necessary to start the machine, Donovan elbowed him and laughed before turning toward the young Ihlia.

"Good morning, young lady. Despite his tone, my brother is actually quite worried about you. There've been reports of heavy activity near Giza as of late. Oh, and don't worry about Oswald. I'd wager he's already in the garage making adjustments to the jeep. That's just how he is, always has his mind in the clouds and his nose buried in anything scientific or mechanical," Donovan laughed.

The descent in the high tech elevator full of flashing lights and quiet hisses passed with refreshing banter. Ihlia smiled between the two men who towered at least a head above her. The idle chat and occasional joke passing between the brothers calmed her nerves, but as the elevator neared the end of its journey, the clean shiny metal interior briefly transformed into the decrepit elevator in Loftsborough. Though only for an instant, I saw the sparks and frayed wires hanging loosely from the rusty cage that screeched in protest with every inch it moved.

I remembered riding the elevator down to meet Oswald in Loftsborough and seeing the image of Egypt's pristine elevator and the enjoyable times shared with the two brothers. Now that I found myself imprisoned in my past, the post-apocalyptic world decided to interject images like a jealous lover. I shook my head; as neither the young Ihlia nor the Lesforts reacted to the brief scenery change, I chalked it up to irony.

“Hey Oswald! If you don't hurry up, my contract is going to end before you even get that thing cranked!” Donovan shouted toward the jeep when the doors of the elevator parted. A thin metal arm extending from the vehicle's frame propped open its hood, and hovering over the various mechanical parts, Oswald tinkered with the vehicle's innards as surely as Donovan predicted. When we approached, Donovan's colleague popped his head from the side of the machine and nodded in our direction.

“Tosh,” he dismissively waved his hand in response to Donovan's accusation. No sooner did we reach the vehicle, than Oswald slammed the hood shut with a reverberating thunk and glanced at his watch. “By Jove, exactly as I hypothesized with a margin of error of only ten seconds. You arrived almost exactly when I predicted. Were you just ten seconds longer, I'd have started this confounded, stone-age contraption too. Now enough complaining; we have sand to put behind us.”

Though it was the first time I ever heard him speak, he directed his words toward Donovan. The doctor was the only person to whom Oswald offered any regard. The four of us took our places in the sludge-powered jeep, and Oswald pressed a few buttons before flipping the ignition switch. The engine roared to life, and Ihlia retrieved the rifle strapped to her back.

My younger version closed her eyes and concentrated, and the subtle click of the nanites in her brain brought her telescopic vision nanite to life. The thick metallic door in front of us hissed; the electromagnetic system kicked into high gear to pull apart the barrier. As the slit in the middle of the garage door widened, the red lights and ascending concrete led the way to the surface upon which Cairo's ruins stood in the midst of an oasis.

Oswald floored it. The jeep's powerful engine revved with an escalating hum and propelled us up the tunnel in the research dome's basement. The steep slope leading to the surface ended in a second enormous metal portal similar to the first. The circular lock in the door's center clanked open as the electric pulses went to work. The burning rays of the desert sun that filtered through the expanding slit cast a beacon of light on the road that measured the width of the door as we raced along the corridor.

"Brother, is he planning on slowing down at all? I mean, the door is still opening. If we hit it at these speeds..." Bradich expressed mild concern. When he glanced over to his brother, Donovan, the doctor clamped his eyes shut. Bradich's jaw dropped.

"No, brother, he's not planning to slow down at all. And just for the record, Oswald, I really hate you," Donovan laced his response with a sense of accustomed dread.

"I am aware," Oswald responded.

The jeep's velocity reached its maximum and shot through the door like a ballistic missile. As the wheels lost their connection to the ground and the jeep sailed through the air, the young Ihlia yelped with excitement and released a torrent of laughter. The vehicle slammed into the ground, and the jeep bounced a few times before the tires gripped the sandy dunes and it sped off into the desert. As Ihlia's laughter died into soft giggles, Oswald grinned and clicked his tongue.

"Well, how disappointing," he stated in earnest.

"Disappointing? What are you talking about, were you trying to kill us?" Donovan cried out from the passenger seat next to the doctor. In the rear seat next to mine, directly behind Oswald, Bradich sat shaking his head.

"Of course not, Donovan, but there were at least six inches of space on either side of the vehicle when we launched through the opening. That means I waited too long to reach maximum velocity," Oswald chortled beneath his breath.

When Ihlia finally ceased her amused giggling, she stood and leaned back against the bar that formed the safety frame at the top of the jeep. Her enhanced vision adjusted like the buzzing extension and retraction of a camera lens with a zoom feature, and she swept the area for threats. The roaring breeze that combed sand through her hair forced the lot of them to shout when speaking, and Ihlia did not intend to remain silent.

"So, Donovan said your name is Doctor Oswald, but is that your first name or your last name?" Ihlia called out across the space that separated them.

Several seconds of silence passed; Donovan sighed and leaned back to stare up at the younger version of myself. “Don't mind him, Ihlia. He's a sour puss that just hates anyone who uses a gun, especially soldiers and mercenaries,” Donovan asserted.

“That simply isn't true, Donovan. I also hate children, irrational thinking, and, quite recently, deserts. It just so happens your friends tend to fall into one... or more... of those categories,” Oswald cut a glance to the young Ihlia.

Roughly twenty minutes passed without incident in the back of the jeep. After discovering Oswald's innate disdain for mercenaries and an assortment of other characteristics, the young Ihlia abandoned her attempts to strike conversation with the bald old codger. Bradich and my younger version exchanged glances when the group tore passed the decrepit pyramids and obliterated sphinx. As the jeep kicked a stream of glistening sand behind the tires, Ihlia pondered the quiet solitude of the expansive desert.

Something felt wrong; in Ihlia's experience, when something seemed too good to be true, that was likely the case. Nothing existed between the Nanite Research Dome and the laboratories supposedly housing Donovan's data samples. No allied militia scouts, no enemy recon units, no wandering nomads, nothing obstructed the path to the doctors' destination. Indeed, the young sniper felt very wrong, and she perceived that her commander noticed it as well.

"The laboratory... why is it such a hazy memory?" I asked myself as the jeep came to a halt in front of the only pristine structure in a twenty mile radius. I watched the young Ihlia and her commander vault over the jeep doors while Donovan and Oswald hastily, but normally, exited the vehicle. The two mercenaries rushed to the laboratory's entrance and knelt down.

In front of the enormous electronic doors, four of the Egyptian militia, likely stationed as the laboratory's guards, lay dead. Ihlia and Bradich swiftly readied their weapons and crouched in preparation for tactical maneuvering. They stalked the immediate area for threats, and the two scientists checked the fallen soldiers for vitals. When Ihlia and Bradich returned to the laboratory entrance, the scientists shook their heads. Bradich glanced at the corpses.

"Gunshots. Two to the chest, one to the medulla oblongata; these were professionals. It has to be either Union or the French. We should leave. Those corpses are still fairly fresh, and if the lab's been compromised, we'll have to report it and get the Free Alliance to send an operation unit to reclaim it. We can't go in there like this; it's too dangerous," Bradich stated and immediately began the trek to the parked jeep.

"We can't go back now, brother! If the lab's been compromised there may still be important research data and samples inside! If we go back now, the enemy will take them, and all the work we've done up until now will be lost!" Donovan exclaimed as he marched after his retreating brother. Oswald shoved his hands in his pockets and watched the display while I awaited Bradich's official order.

"Donovan, I'm not endangering our lives for samples and research data. There will be other opportunities. Ihlia, let's go, we're moving out," Bradich twirled his hands in the air, a motion he used to communicate "let's wrap it up, boys."

The young Ihlia loved Donovan, but she considered Bradich's orders absolute. She took that oath as one of his mercenaries. On his command, she trotted across the sand toward the vehicle with her rifle at the ready.

"What about our contract?!" Donovan shouted.

"Contract, brother? Are you talking about the contract that we have?" Bradich turned, lurched forward into his brother's face, and glared him down with scornful eyes. As their gazes exchanged emotions their words never could, Donovan finally released an exasperated sigh and adjusted his coat with a snap of his wrists.

"Very well, brother. I'll go alone. Take Oswald and Ihlia back, and await my return at the research dome." Without allowing an interjection, Donovan turned and dashed into the laboratory. Oswald shook his head silently and turned on his heel.

"Actually, mercenaries, I'm going as well. Perhaps, to you, violence and killing are more important than the research that might usher in a peaceful solution. But to dense thinkers like us, it's more precious than life itself. We'll be fine, you two run along home now." Oswald vanished into the darkness after his colleague.

"Sir..." Ihlia's crooning drone as she directed her attention to Bradich insinuated a deep rooted longing to follow them. "... this is your chance to show your brother you really do support what he's doing."

Only the fury in Bradich's frustrated pacing topped the brooding anger in his silence; he marched back and forth across the desert sands contemplating his next action. "Son of a bitch. Alright then, Ihlia. We go in, we keep it tight. Get the data, get the hell out. Keep the VIPs safe and don't get killed, is that understood?"

"Sir!" My former self snapped up a salute.

The young Ihlia and her commander entered the facility with their weapons pressed tightly to their shoulders and their chosen nanites buzzing with activity, but they stopped when they witnessed Donovan and Oswald checking the vitals of another pair of militia guards. Just as those outside in the desert sun, the bodies had been shot thrice. The two shots in the chest rendered the targets immobile, and as they struggled to stand while Panacea worked on their wounds, a final shot through the medulla oblongata terminated their lives. As Bradich previously stated, the killers were professionals.

"Brother, stop messing around. If we're going to do

this, we go in, get whatever's still here, avoid the enemy if we can, and get out. Assume all casualties are fatalities, understand?" Bradich's words turned the two scientists from their endeavor.

"See? I believe I'll collect on that bet when we return, old friend," Oswald grinned at Donovan.

"You mean 'if' we return, Oswald," Donovan's tone reflected his concern.

I remembered Oswald informing me later, during one of the many ten years we traveled together following the Cairo incident, that the two bet on whether or not we would actually leave them. Apparently, Oswald was the victor, but Donovan never paid him the money. He never got the chance.

As the group progressed swiftly and silently through the facility, they stepped over many similar bodies with a cause of death identical to their comrades'. Bradich and Ihlia moved with purposeful steps with their hips set tactically low and their conditioned legs keeping them in perpetual motion. The two scientists jogged down the metal corridors as quietly as possible just to keep up with the two mercenaries. The metallic smell of blood mingled with the scent of steel, disinfectant, and wiring. Though the commander and my former self experienced the scent and remained unaffected by its repugnant odor, the two doctors held their sleeves tight against their nostrils to filter the smell. It offered them little relief.

“There! That's the laboratory with the specimens I need!” Donovan hissed as we approached a large, electronically sealed metal door. Bradich and Ihlia turned to cover the rear, and Donovan set to work punching in numbers and providing his retina for a swift scan. When the door slid open and the group shuffled through into the laboratory, the young sniper beheld a single eye gawking up at her from the ground. Unfortunately, it possessed no socket.

“I think someone beat us here,” Ihlia mentioned as the door clicked shut behind them.

Donovan and Oswald immediately set themselves into motion. Their fingers flew across various data pads and holocom keyboards with inhuman speed and precision. Bradich and Ihlia, after ensuring the room held no surprises in wait to ambush the group, shouldered their weapons. Ihlia's gaze roamed around with passive interest; she was intent on learning as much about Donovan's line of work as possible that she might support his research better. Her curiosity led her to a humming cylinder tucked away in the corner of the room. As her hand extended toward it, a voice arose from one of the holocom terminals.

“I wouldn't if I were you, Ihlia,” Oswald calmly stated. His voice carried subtle concern, but despite his uncanny knowledge that Ihlia attempted to toy with a dangerous object, the doctor never even looked away from his work.

“Even back then, huh? How does he always do that.

And why... does this seem so familiar, but not... it is my dream sequence, I should understand what's going on, but I feel this has been..." I spoke aloud in the quivering ghost-voice that fate ordained for me.

"That's an electrocapacitor plate. If you touch it and it's been damaged in anyway and any of the components are exposed, not even Panacea will save you from the electric shock your body will take," Oswald continued.

"I thought you didn't like us mercenaries, Doc? Wouldn't you have rather seen me fried to a crisp?" Ihlia retorted.

"Hmph. The two of you came back for us despite there being no logical reason to do so. I hate that kind irrational thought more than anything. But I think if you had abandoned us, I would have hated you a lot more. In short, maybe you two aren't so bad. But don't let it go to your head. I still have yet to definitively conclude that hypothesis," Oswald peeked over his shoulder and offered the young Ihlia a grin.

"Oswald, no time. Download the program. I've got everything I need from my end," Donovan turned and began removing hardware components from the holocom station at which he worked.

"Yes, I've almost finished, calm down," Oswald nonchalantly responded. "You're always such a worrisome fellow. It's not like the place is about to explode."

An infinitesimally soft beep barely reached the edge of Ihlia's hearing. She instinctively glanced in the direction of the phantom noise with an understandable “hm?” As Ihlia carefully maneuvered around the electrocapacitor plate, a tiny black box rested atop a pair of yellow cylinders fastened to the allegedly dangerous machine. The digital display of the black box clearly portrayed a timer counting down from five minutes.

“Bradich, sir! Explosives! The facility is rigged to blow!” The young sniper snapped her head toward the commander, who rushed over to take a look. The two scientists, without skipping a beat, continued the finishing touches on their data collection.

“Shit. It's a small explosive, but it'll take out this room and the nearby area. If they've got the whole place rigged then we don't have much time. These bombs don't pack much punch alone, but you never set one by itself. Ever. Donovan, Oswald, hurry up we have to get out of here.” Bradich hastily rushed to the door.

“Conventional explosives. I wonder why they simply did not initialize the reactor self-destruct sequence. That explosion would vaporize the surrounding area far more efficiently and leave far less mess in its wake. How thoughtless,” Oswald mused.

“Reactor self-destruct sequence?” Bradich looked toward his brother.

“All laboratories have them these days. Research data

in the field of nanites is more precious than all the wealth you could imagine. If a laboratory is compromised, overloading the reactors guarantees that any on-site data is lost. We don't put the data on the N-3 until we're sure of its use and have it mapped out properly. While in its research phases like the labs in Egypt, it's all classified. Privateer or not, if you're caught uploading data to the N-3, it's grounds for immediate execution." Donovan pressed a few more buttons; a series of beeping noises and symbols flashed across the holocom terminal at which he worked.

"What are the chances they've done that as well as set the structural explosives?" Bradich asked impatiently.

"Slim," responded Oswald, "the reactor explosion would be more than sufficient to demolish the immediate area. It won't blow things up a mile away, but the chain reaction is designed to wipe the lab and all its research from the face of the earth. There's no need for structural charges when you do that. I would assume they did not possess the proper initialization codes to do it themselves and killed everyone in the lab before forcefully acquiring them."

"They must have swept in, took the place by storm, copied the data, then set the charges. Although it makes little sense; the encryption to obtain a laboratory's data is no more complicated than the initialization sequence to self-destruct the reactors. Something is terribly off," Oswald's rambles did not cease him from pressing the final few keys on his own designated holocom terminal.

“We can worry about that later! There's no time!” Donovan called out as the holocom beeps ended in a flashing symbol. The holocom hissed, and the blue projection image vanished. “Excellent! We're done! All right, let's get out of here!”

“Right, move out! Ihlia, cover the rear, I'll take point. Donovan, get this door open. We're operating on a fixed time limit here, let's go, go, go!” Bradich motioned like a trained military commander with his free hand. His other kept his assault rifle tucked beneath his armpit.

The scene became hazy for me as I watched the group rush through the laboratory the same direction in which they entered. The walls cracked in my mind, and the details blurred in a mosaic of uncertainty. As the light threatened to fade and darkness encroached my fuzzy vision, I prepared for another transition jump. Instead, the images I perceived in my dream state snapped into focus at the last minute.

I watched as the scene played out in slow motion in front of me. *“I don't remember any of this... how am I seeing it?”* I wondered as I watched Bradich wave his arms in a giant windmill motion, urging us to exit the facility. He stood at the door with his red face flustered and his lips parted to release a scream which I failed to discern.

As I spun to behold the two doctors and the young Ihlia bringing up the rear behind them, a massive explosion rocked the corridor walls surrounding us from deep within the structure. Like a game of dominoes, one blast followed another and the blustering cacophony began bringing down metal, rock, and dirt all around the group.

The young sniper glanced up as she reached the final stretch of the collapsing corridor. The fiery bubbles protruding from the walls and ceiling obliterated the structural integrity of the facility, and Ihlia realized that at their current pace the three of them would not only fall short of the exit, but they would not even reach the frantically waving Bradich.

Ihlia's lips moved. Though I heard no sound, my ability to read those lips combined with the distant memory I seemed to be recalling elicited the words from my ghostly voice, *"I believe you can change this world, Donovan."*

As her lips closed and a smile tugged at each corner of her mouth, Ihlia increased her speed to its maximum and shoved both palms into the scientists' backs. The jarring blow propelled them forward through the exit just as the facility collapsed around her. As the darkness closed in, Bradich lunged back toward my former self with the name, "Ihlia!" roaring from his lips.

"If only you died that way, Bradich, and ended my memories of you with that concern. The concern of the mercenary leader I remember..." I murmured as the complex fell atop the two mercenaries and darkness engulfed all.

File 27: Happy Birthday, Ihlia

I remembered what happened next all too well. Ihlia stirred from a state of unconsciousness to the sound of a computerized voice echoing through the compound.

"Reactor self-destruct sequence initiated. Meltdown in... ten minutes... all personnel please report to the evacuation site." The robotic voice possessed a condescending calm. The drowsy Ihlia might have experienced a chill if not for her gross mental faculties.

As I appeared next to my former self, I watched her rise from a high-tech medical table. The action snapped various tubes and sensors from her body. Clad in nothing more than a typical hospital gown, the young Ihlia stumbled through the darkness. Only the dim blue glow of holocoms and rotating red lights mounted on the walls like twisted crimson lighthouses illuminated her surroundings.

"Ugh... my head. What happened?" Ihlia rubbed her forehead and approached what seemed to be the only entrance or exit to her quarters. She pressed the button on the panel, and the door hissed open. Ihlia stepped into the corridor outside her containment room and looked around. With her mind still foggy, she struggled to recognize her whereabouts or discern the nature of what transpired. For a moment, she forgot her identity and even the last memory that led to her predicament. The sight of a scientist's corpse laying on the floor in front of her, however, instantly cleared her head.

The shock of the researcher's body jarred her memories loose, and the jigsaw puzzle of events pieced themselves together. She reasoned that Bradich, Oswald, Donovan, and she must have barely escaped the collapsing facility near Giza, but then why the hospital gown and strange computer voice of doom? As her thoughts raced in an attempted to conjure the truth, an acute pain ripped through her brain; she dropped to her knees and clawed at the sides of her head in agony. The pain eventually subsided, and she decided to forego thinking too hard in favor of keeping the mind rending agony at bay.

My younger version moved along the hallway straight in front of her, gripping the wall to support her as she staggered through the facility. Her journey carried her to a familiar door, and after she instinctively pressed another button, the door swished open. As she stepped into the dim room lit only by the whirling scarlet lights, she paused. The room vividly mapped by her brain struck her as familiar, though she remained unable to discern why until she beheld the bodies.

"... The Eagles?" She stammered. The large black husk of Bit sat in a heap against a nearby wall. His forehead seeped blood and pieces of his brain; behind him, a splatter of his crimson life force painted the wall a few feet above the back of his head. With the trick played by the flashing lights, the blood appeared midnight in color, and a small trail smeared down the wall until it reached Bit's position on the ground. After a bullet had blown through his brain, Bit had slammed into the wall and slid down to his final resting place.

“Bit...” Ihlia called out softly and placed a hand over her quivering lips.

Ihlia realized she stood in the middle of the common quarters of the Nanite Research Dome back in Cairo. Though unable to grasp the interim existence between Giza and the research dome, she understood that something went horribly wrong.

“Insurgents? We were attacked?” She glanced around frantically for signs of an enemy; though if one appeared while she drunkenly meandered around in a hospital gown, she was in for a world of hurt. But as she swept the room for enemies, she instead found the bodies of more of her comrades. Downy, Gunther, Flint, Steele, and Welsch all lay in random mortified positions in the common quarters.

Downy's body lay on top of the bar; he must have flown back onto it after taking a bullet in the brain. His red headband rested in lopsided disarray across his face, and terror gripped his frozen expression. Gunther found his eternal rest among innumerable broken bottles of sludge lining the back wall of the bar. Welsch hung limp on the bar next to Downy with his arms spread wide and his face contorted in pain. Only the twins wore a peaceful expression in their demise; in a pair of cots on one side of the room, single bullet wounds had burrowed through the center of their foreheads while they slept.

Ihlia's eyes glistened, and her body quivered as she fell to her knees. I failed to understand why I perceived her facial expressions despite not knowing them first hand, but her shocked face and confused brain worked in tandem in an attempt to process the information flooding her senses. It was to no avail. Ihlia doubled over and vomited in between a symphony of distraught screams joined by a chorus of wails. But not a single tear dripped from her eyes. Not a single tear would drip from those eyes ever again.

The robotic voice interrupted her grief, “Reactor self-destruct sequence initiated. Meltdown in... seven minutes... all personnel please report to the evacuation site.” Ihlia raised her face and, with quaking legs, forced herself to stand. She hobbled back to the entrance and gripped the wall for support. As she escaped the room that seemed more like a nightmarish hell than a common quarters, she whispered, “I'll make them pay. I'll make whoever did this pay. I'll never, ever forgive them, and I'll never, ever forget you guys... it wasn't... it's not supposed to be this way...”

Her stumbling figure worked toward the facility's entrance; at least, she headed in the direction in which she remembered it. The whole way, her weakened body stepped over and around various fallen personnel. Littered with corpses ranging from militia guards to civilian researchers, a bloody path of death stretched before Ihlia like a paved road. In the final stretch leading to Cairo's desert oasis, the distant sound of thunder meshed with a streaming tip-tap of rain. Though more common than in generations past, precipitation in the deserts of Egypt was still a rarity often treated as an omen by the locals.

"To think the sky would cry for my friends when I could not..." I stared at the grief-struck Ihlia. For some reason, her tear ducts produced nothing, nor did the grotesque scenery succeed in driving her young mind into shock. Ihlia approached the corner to the final hallway, and another familiar figure lay face up on the ground with a bullet in his head; from the corner of his mouth a mixture of blood and tobacco seeped down his cheek.

"Not you, too, Jace..." Ihlia sighed sadly.

As the final hallway stretched out before her, Ihlia's eyes found Loxley in the same position as the rest of her comrades except his face lay downward in a pool of his own blood. Ihlia's mind began twisting and she felt her mentality fracturing beneath the sorrow her emotions could not process. She lifted her hand to her skull and cried out in pain, agony, and what she believed to be intense sadness. Her incoherent noise stopped when she heard a southern drawl at the end of the path.

"Bradich, I don't understand... Sug'." Though the voice strained to release the gurgled words, it undeniably belonged to Shandi. As Ihlia stared down the length of the corridor, a pair of figures stood against the dark backdrop of the rainy night. The water streaks and occasional lightning flashes decorated the horizon like a retelling of her childhood in Yordleton. Ihlia's eyes widened when she witnessed Shandi's frame lifted from the ground by the powerful hand of their fearless commander. Bradich's tight clench around the southern belle's shirt forced her to struggle for air.

"Now you'll see, little one. Now you'll understand why you should have listened to me... He's the one you can never forgive. He's the one who takes them all away!" I screamed at my former self as she stared helplessly at the scene in front of her. The words caught in her throat when she parted her lips, and her hand quivered furiously as she reached out to the woman that took her mother's place in her heart for so many years. "Shandi..." she managed to squeak.

"You don't have to do this, baby. You never... had to do this. We would have gladly given... our lives... if you asked. But not like this, Sug', not like this... please. Don't you know, baby, how much we loved you? Don't you know how much I lov—" *Bang.*

The loud sound of gunfire cut Shandi's sentence short and her head jerked back. The sentence she waited her entire life to say, the sentence that she sacrificed so much to one day be able to profess, was taken from her by the very man to whom she wished to say it. Bradich's free hand clutched a pistol, and as the tip smoked and the crimson-haired belle crumpled lifelessly to the floor, the commander sighed sadly, "I know, Shandi. I've always known."

Unable to suppress it anymore, Ihlia and I screamed in unison. The powerful yell reverberated against the walls and snapped Bradich's attention to us from his position seconds away from the exit, seconds away from the rare stormy night of the desert.

"Hm? Ah, Ihlia." Bradich meandered back down the hall toward my younger version. Still in a state of emotional and physical ineptitude, Ihlia shakily leaned back against the corridor wall. "I was wondering where they put you. I wanted to thank you. You, my brother, you were both right all along. They're the key. The nanites, Ihlia, the nanites are the key. I understand now after that little nap of ours. I know what I have to do. And you know what? It involves both my plan and my brother's."

"Bradich... How could you? We all trusted you! Shandi loved you! How can you do this as the commander of the Bald Eagles?" Ihlia cried out defiantly.

"It is precisely because I am the commander of the Eagles that I must do this. I am sorry it must be this way, but I would rather this happen than for you to suffer. Like this, I can ensure that your transition to the next life is swift and painless. I cannot guarantee that in the times to come, so I am merely doing what a responsible commander should. Perhaps on some plane of existence at some time in the stream of the cosmos, you will understand and forgive me." Each word brought Bradich a step closer to Ihlia.

Unlike my former self, the commander seemed completely in control of his body and unaffected by the "long nap," as he so delicately phrased it.

"Bradich, I just don't understand..." Ihlia's words, laced with anguish, escaped her as the commander placed the hot barrel of the pistol against her forehead; it was the same pistol that murdered the entire complex.

"You'll pay for this. I'll make you suffer worse than you made them suffer. I swear, I will end you," I growled as I watched. The muzzle of the gun rested in the exact spot on which Bradich offered his kiss during Ihlia's surprise party.

"Rest well, Ihlia." Bradich pulled the trigger. The echoing click of the empty chamber drowned every other sound from the young Ihlia's mind. Bradich's lower eyelid twitched and a grin pulled at one corner of his mouth.

"My, my. I thought for sure I properly calculated the number of rounds I would need to set all the Eagles free." Bradich lifted the gun and tapped its tip against the side of his head repeatedly. "Is it fate? Perhaps coincidence or chance? I cannot be sure."

"Ihlia!" The distant echo of a familiar voice drifted through the corridors. Given its labored state, a high probability existed it belonged to one of the facility's researchers, and given the number of researchers acquainted with her name, Ihlia assumed it to be either Oswald or Donovan. My younger version stared at Bradich with an unchanging bewildered expression wrought with sadness; he stood and pondered the nature of his gun's empty chamber when the time arrived for Ihlia's "salvation."

"I see. Then I shall follow the strings the cosmos sets before me. Unfortunately, Ihlia, you shall remain a caged bird. If you experience pain and suffering, don't blame me. Blame fate. Radical action is needed for radical change. I understand that now; it only gets harder from here, my young friend." Bradich turned and stepped over the corpses of his former allies toward the facility's exit.

"When next you hear of me, it shall be as the harbinger of the true age. The harbinger of the final stage of human evolution. Harbinger, I like it. Harbinger..." The slender figure of the Bald Eagles' former commander paused one last time at the mouth of the tunnel.

He turned his head back, and with a gnarled grin he shouted, "By the way..."

"Happy birthday, Ihlia," a flash of lightning and crack of thunder accompanied his words.

The robotic voice echoed over the intercom system immediately after Bradich's twisted words. "Reactor self-destruct sequence initiated. Meltdown in... three minutes... all personnel please report to the evacuation site."

As Bradich faded into the night, a sudden pressure on Ihlia's shoulder snapped her from her bemuddled daze. “Ihlia! Quickly, snap out of it! We have to get out of here! This way!” Oswald, the living Oswald, stared down at the young Ihlia with impatience creasing his face. As he tugged my former version to her feet and dashed in the opposite direction of the facility's obvious exit, Oswald muttered a wish under his breath; he wished he never mentioned the existence of the reactor overload sequence so arbitrarily.

The soft tapping of Ihlia's and Oswald's feet as they raced down the twisted halls of the Nanite Research Dome bounced unnoticed off the walls and ceiling. The shock of what transpired threatened to keep Ihlia in an inattentive stupor the entirety of their escape. At least it would have, if not for the soft thud of fists on the glass of a nearby door the two passed on their escape route. Ihlia's eyes drifted lazily toward the circular window at the top of the steel door and caught sight of her beloved's distraught face; he desperately slammed his closed fists repeatedly against the transparent material.

“Donovan!” Ihlia wriggled from Oswald's grip and lunged at the door. Relieved to see the object of her affection alive, Ihlia busily worked to press the button responsible for opening the door. A grinding hiss and fiery sparks ended in nothing and dashed Ihlia's relief across the jagged rocks of reality yet again. Oswald finally stepped forward to the door next to Ihlia and examined the panel. After pressing a few buttons and avoiding a few more dangerous sparks flying from the electronic keypad, Oswald shook his head.

"It's no good, Bradich must have destroyed the panel altogether. Donovan was working on his brother's recovery in that room after the accident, as I was working on you in the other room. After the alarm went off for the self-destruct I went to see if I could override it, but it was too late. Now this... blast it, Bradich. What are you thinking?" Oswald gripped the metallic plate covering the panel and forced it open. After a few wire crosses, a green indicator appeared above the electronic panel. "There, we should be able to manually push the door open now." Oswald gripped the metal grooves on the inside of the door and pulled. It only took him a few tries to realize the door simply would not move. "Oh no, it's jammed."

The robotic voice interrupted their contemplation. "Reactor self-destruct sequence initiated. Meltdown in... two minutes... all personnel please report to the evacuation site." On the other side of the door, Donovan stared at the younger me longingly. His face, contorted with terror, anger, and sadness cried out to Ihlia from behind the glass. He narrowed his eyes in a dark rage at his colleague, Oswald. He gestured to the young Ihlia and nodded with resolve, shouting something that neither of them could hear.

"I see. Fine, then, Donovan. I'll take care of her. I promise." Oswald softly placed a hand atop Ihlia's head. Donovan's face dropped, and he hopelessly beat his fists against the glass a few more times. Oswald tugged my younger version's arm, "Come on, Ihlia. We have to get out of here; the whole place is going to blow."

"No!" My younger self screamed violently. "I'm not going to leave him! Move out of the way! Donovan!" Ihlia gripped the metal door in the grooves Oswald recently abandoned. With one foot propped against the lip of the wall, the young sniper heaved and tugged until the bones in her fingers cracked. Oswald wrapped his arms around her waist and pried her from her endeavor.

"Ihlia! What good is it to die as well?! This is the kind of irrational thought I cannot stand! If we die, no one can tell this story! No one can warn the populace, no one can exact revenge on Bradich!" Oswald forcefully dragged the young Ihlia away from the door. As he raced down the hall toward his apparent escape route, his ears filled with the name "Donovan," as Ihlia screamed it relentlessly.

Within a moment, the doctor and his human cargo burst into the basement garage. Given the unreliability of the elevator, Oswald opted to rush down the winding stairs. He shoved Ihlia into the jeep's rear seat once they reached the basement and sprinted to the titanic electromagnetic door. After quickly working his magic on the nearby manual override terminal, the sealing mechanism unlocked with a loud click.

As the vibrating hiss of the gigantic door slid open from the center, Oswald leapt into the driver seat of his vehicle and brought it to life just as the slit in the door appeared and the robotic voice echoed overhead, "Reactor self-destruct sequence initiated. Meltdown in... one minute and counting... all personnel please report to the evacuation site."

"Come on, come on baby, go!" Oswald whispered passionately and hammered the accelerator against the floor. The roar of the engine and squeal of the tires rocketed the vehicle through the first steel frame. The long tunnel, alight with the spinning red lights that signaled the impending doom of the Nanite Research Dome, seemed endless in the crucial moments that followed.

"Reactor self-destruct sequence initiated. Meltdown in... thirty seconds and counting."

Ihlia remained detached and stoic sprawled across the back seats. In her mind, perhaps the young Ihlia felt a quick death in the heat of the vaporized research laboratory would be preferable to her continued existence. Oswald shifted gears, and the rainy night filled with a gentle breeze. Lightning streaked the distant sky that appeared through the tiny slit in the second electromagnetic door as it groaned open.

"Reactor self-destruct sequence initiated. Meltdown in... ten seconds and counting." The robotic voice began the eminent countdown; as "nine" rang out overhead Oswald shifted the vehicle into its final gear.

By the time "eight" crooned from the computerized

voice, the jeep sailed overhead through the desert sky. As soon as the gripping tires hit the moist dirt, they screeched, and the jeep bolted into the darkness. Another transition overtook my senses, but rather than the dark distortion of my perception, the blinding light of the exploding facility consumed everything.

When my blurred vision returned, Ihlia stood next to Oswald in the hammering rain atop a large dune a few miles from Cairo's newest crater. Oswald's hands remained in the pockets of his khaki slacks, and as he stared at the desolation of the former research laboratory, a deep sigh passed between his lips. He walked with a tired gait to the trunk of the jeep and lifted popped it open. Ihlia glanced over as he removed her belongings. In his hands rested her typical attire, her twin daggers, and her father's hunting rifle.

"I saved these, Ihlia. I know I'm a genius, but this is some impressive handiwork even for someone of my intellectual caliber. Why I..." His voice trailed off as he stared at my younger version's face. Sadness furrowed his brows, and he stepped forward. He wrapped his arms around the young Ihlia's shoulders, and as he squeezed her in a tight embrace, she tilted her face up toward the heavens.

The shock slowly dissipated from my former self; the capacity for happiness and sadness seemed to vaporize like the facility had only moments prior, and Ihlia's emerald eyes that seemed to glisten with the shock of the events slowly narrowed with hateful determination. Even as her face remained tucked away against Oswald's shoulder, the burning desire for vengeance distorted her beautiful features and hardened them with the callousness I recognized as my own.

As the rain fell in sheets on the pair atop the desert dunes, I stared up at the heavens along with the young Ihlia. I watched the dark clouds tumble overhead, and a single wet droplet rolled down my upturned cheek. I rapidly blinked, surprised; until that point, the sensation of touch eluded me. I continued staring, and a second moist drop splashed on the opposite side of my face. I noticed that the dark clouds of the night sky churned perpetually, but as their darkness consumed my vision, the shape of a face protruded from the cloud cover. It looked like the face of an angel.

"So, I died after all," I thought to myself.

"You're not dead, silly," a tender young voice spoke from the void that blanketed my world. My eyes snapped open for what felt like the first time in days. The inky black surroundings smelled of sulfur and stagnance, and the distant sound of water droplets falling against protruding stone tickled my ears. The angelic face from the clouds hovered above me; the face, however, was quite real and belonged to the small girl I rescued from the hyped. A steady stream of tears cascaded down the young girl's cheeks before splashing softly against my face.

I realized the droplets of rain I perceived hitting me in

my dreams were actually the tears of the small girl. Slowly, I understood that I lay at the bottom of the long cylindrical drop into which I cast the child and myself. Slowly, I understood that the impact from the fall rendered me unconscious, and slowly, I understood that my head rested safely on the girl's tiny thighs. After we collided with the cavern floor, the girl must have placed my head in her lap as I slept.

“So it would seem. I guess I'll count myself lucky, then.” I lifted a hand and rubbed my forehead. Though the girl giggled, her stifled laugh occurred between the pitiful sound of her sniffling. I glanced up at her and offered the child a gentle smile. “I'm sorry, I must have worried you. But there's no need to cry anymore. I'm just fine.”

“Hm? Oh, it's not that.” The child rubbed the tears from her eyes and sniffled once again.

“Then what's the matter?” I asked, confused.

“It's your dream,” she responded sympathetically, “it was just so sad...”

File 28: Elsa Friis

"My dream? I don't understand..." Despite the numbing haze sweeping across my brain like a fog, I locked gaze with the small girl's. Her long locks of blonde cascaded over her shoulders like waves and framed her pretty white face as she stared down at me. Her small mouth maintained a gentle smile even while the sound of her sniffles betrayed that she still sat on the verge of tears. With moderate effort, I clenched my abdominal muscles and lifted my head from her lap; once I found myself in an upright position, I twisted until I settled next to her.

"Yeah, your dream. What happened to that man? The man named Bradich? And what happened to Donovan? Did he... die?" The small child shifted; as she drew her legs against her chest and wrapped her arms tightly around her knees, I noticed the heavy white mist of her breath pouring from her lips with each of her labored exhales.

The caverns in which we sat likely never saw the gray of day. As such, an icy cold gripped us tighter even than the frigid world above. With a heavy sigh, I removed my large leather trench coat and draped it over the girl's shoulders. Despite what many believed to be "too little clothing," each of my garments possessed state-of-the-art insulation designed specifically by Oswald to trap and reflect body heat. Besides, in a world where ninety percent of whatever encountered you imagined you dead or wondered what they might gain from your corpse, the cold quickly descended the priority list of concerns. I doubted the child had learned that harsh lesson yet, though.

"There, that should warm you up. So was I talking in my sleep or something?" I arched a brow as she questioned the nature of my past. Though the question left my lips as a light-hearted retort, my suspicions mounted when she paused. Her questions seemed quite detailed, far more so than any troubled sleep mumbles justified.

"Thank you, it does feel very warm!" The child gripped the corner of the coat's collar and twisted the material between her left hand's tiny fingers. Her right arm perpetually clutched her semi-soft, semi-mechanical toy bear against her armpit. As she idly twisted the coat, I garnered that her long pause indicated her attempt to find a way to explain herself. After a few seconds of palpable quiet, she finally spoke, "You weren't exactly talking. Just thinking very loudly. And why does ninety percent of everything want you dead, Ms. Ihlia?"

She read my thoughts like an open book fanned out on a table before her. Stunned, I sat wondering how much of my dream she perceived in great detail and how much filtered through in a vague haze. I attempted my best poker face and glanced down at her. She lowered her sea blue-green eyes to the cold, dark, and stony ground. I doubted she actually made anything out in the pitch black of the frozen cavern, but the action elicited a small grin from one corner of my mouth all the same. Was she shy?

“I'm not shy, but people think I'm weird when they find out,” she protested as soon as the thought crossed my mind. Her fingers stopped twirling the material of my coat and she glanced directly up at me for the first time since my awakening.

“I don't like that look people give me, that's all.” She stated calmly.

Seconds later, her eyes lit up like the stars no longer strewn across the night sky, “Oh, wow! Your eyes are glowing a little! That's so cool, how did you do that?” She giggled fervently.

“Hm? Oh, you mean my night vision. You know, once upon a time animals called cats used to roam the earth. There were big ones and small ones, and most of them had glowing eyes at night too. It helped them see better. It's the same as that.” I sounded like a babbling idiot to myself, but as I locked my eyes with the small girl's, her excitement deepened into genuine interest. I laughed and shook my head, “So, what's your name little miss telepath?”

“I'm Elsa, Elsa Friis. And this!” She held up the cyborg-teddy-bear, “this is Magnolia! Richter made her for me! Isn't she so cute?” With a satisfied hum, Elsa coiled the small, apparently female, bear into a tight embrace against her tiny chest. After a few seconds, she lifted her small finger and pointed it directly between my glowing eyes, "Oh, and I'm not a telepath. Richter and the doctor talked about it once. They said telepaths can talk to people with their minds, but no matter how hard I try nobody hears what I think. I can only hear what they think and feel what they feel."

"So, closer to an empath? But I didn't think an empath heard people's thoughts. That's very strange, and not a very useful nanite either." I pressed a finger against the tip of my chin in thought. The applications for a thought transmission and reception nanite would have been impressive, but a one way radio that also received the dead weight of emotions and sensations? Why in the world would someone afflict the poor child with such torture?

"Yeah, that's what they said too. Empath; I dunno, whatever it is I hear things people think and feel what they feel." Elsa held her toy bear by its arms and imitated the motion of it walking across the cavern floor.

"Well you shouldn't listen to people's thoughts and emotions without permission, you know. You should only use it when you absolutely need it." I flattened my palms against the chilly stone ground behind me. As I glanced down toward the young Elsa, I watched her eyes widen to the size of electrocapacitor plates.

"You know how to turn it off?!" She exclaimed. "Tell me, please!" Elsa's small hands wrapped around the circumference of my forearm. The small child tugged as though she begged me to share some information that eluded her. I stared at her in amazement. Not only did an individual infect her with a situationally useful nanite but proceeded thereafter to neglect instructing her on its use? Or perhaps Elsa's medulla oblongata housed the implant? I did not wish to even frighten myself with the idea; surely, no one possessed that cruel a heart.

"So, you don't know?" Elsa perceived my pondering thoughts, and her giddy anticipation waned in the face of disappointing reality. "What's a medulla whatever and why would it be cruel if an implant is there? Is that bad?" Elsa slowly retracted her grip on my forearm and doodled random patterns across Magnolia's head with her fingertip. The frown on her face spoke volumes of her fear that she was somehow different in a terrible way.

"The medulla oblongata makes your heart beat and makes you breathe, it does the things you don't have to think about. It's hard to explain. If you have a nanite like yours there, it means only the part of your brain you can't control could turn it off. I doubt that's the case, though, it likely just has a special way to think about it to activate or deactivate it," I pointed out.

"It's true I don't know how, though. Only the person that gave you the implant would know how to turn it on and off. Each one works a little differently, you see. But don't ever be afraid just because you're different. There's absolutely nothing wrong with you, Elsa. In fact, that uniqueness makes you special." I inwardly groaned at the hackneyed warm and fuzzy nonsense I spouted. Surely, even a child of Elsa's age found the words to be empty and contrite despite the sincerity with which I spoke them. I stole a glance at her; the radiant gleam on her face, complimented by her wide vibrant smile, informed me of the mistake in my assumptions.

"You can read my thoughts?! You knew I was afraid!" She beamed.

"Well, no, not exactly. I'm good at analysis that's all. I take the evidence of my surroundings and piece together logical, reasonable answers that might fit a given circumstance. Your posture, the way you turned your eyes away, and the somber tone in your voice suggested apprehension. Since that apprehension followed one of my thoughts, I logically concluded your fear of being branded different or bad," I explained.

When the last words escaped my lips and I stared down at the young Elsa, I watched her features contort into a bemuddled mess. After a few seconds, she erupted into a fit of giggles.

"Well thank you, Ms. Ihlia. You hear that, Magnolia? I'm special!" Elsa placed both hands beneath the arms of her cyborg teddy and tossed it gently into the air. As it descended into her waiting arms, she enveloped it in a tight hug. I grinned and stood, wiping the grime and muck that collected on my backside during my involuntary nap. The insufferable dampness of the cavern caused the bits of dirt to cling all the more stubbornly to my rear, and my endeavor to brush it off did little to stifle

Elsa's amused giggling.

“So, you think this is funny, hm?” I placed my hands on my hips.

“Yep!” Elsa thrust Magnolia toward me and wiggled her about as though taunting me. I waited patiently for the girl's laughter to subside.

Elsa's cybernetic bear looked handcrafted. The majority of its body consisted of a synthetic black fuzzy material resembling old cotton. Its face housed a single beady obsidian eye on its left side; on its right, a metallic plate coated the entire half of its head, and a glassy red eye dotted the plate's center. I questioned the creator's knowledge of animal anatomy since the right half of Magnolia's face lacked an ear.

Its red cybernetic eye gleamed in the darkness like a crimson slit, though it merely looked like a brightly shining green through the filter of my night vision. The teddy's mix of cuddly and scary concluded with a pair of metal arms and fluffy legs; surprisingly, the arms accurately resembled those typically associated with a toy bear. I half expected to see giant gnarled claws protruding from the metal limbs, but instead, they ended in smooth rounded bumps typical of a teddy.

“Elsa, we should find our way back to the surface. Do you know how long I was out?” I assayed our surroundings. The distinct acidic compounds that saturated most bodies of water sent an overpowering sulfuric smell to assault my nostrils. To our left, a stagnant underground lake encompassed the majority of the space offered by the cavern floor. That explained the smell.

The cavern in which we temporarily resided expanded like an enormous dome hollowed from the heart of one of the mountains. Stalagmites erupted from the ground like an array of spikes whittled down over the years by the water droplets falling from the stalactites haphazardly jutting from the ceiling. In fact, the small clearing of relatively smooth stone on which Elsa and I fell was the only patch of ground not covered with hazardous stone teeth or a lake in which we would have likely drowned. As I assessed the area for a feasible escape, Elsa interrupted my thoughts.

"Hours? I think. I'm not very good at tracking time. It was a little while, though." Elsa offered me a soft apologetic smile from her position on the cold ground.

"Hours, huh? You must be tired. We should probably get you to a safe place so you can sleep. Well, let's go, little one." I nodded my head in the direction of a path on the far end of the cavernous maw. The rocky ascension, while jagged and steep, seemed like the only logical path to take given our circumstances. When several seconds passed and Elsa remained seated, I crossed my arms and stared at her expectantly.

"Um, Ms. Ihlia?" She began fiddling with the single fuzzy ear of her teddy bear.

“You can just call me Ihlia, little one. What's wrong?” I retorted and took a step in her direction.

“I can't feel my legs very well. Your head was heavy.” She lifted Magnolia to cover her face, but not before a crimson hue of embarrassment splashed across her cheeks. Though with the filter on my vision, they just looked a touch darker than the rest of her pretty pale skin. I laughed under my breath before extending my hand to the small child. When she finally shifted her bear aside enough to gaze up at me with one of her large, captivating eyes, a smile tugged at the corner of her mouth at the sight of my offered hand.

She placed her delicate palm atop mine, and I encircled my fingers around her dainty appendage. The realization of the true extent of her frailty struck me in that moment, and I furrowed my brows as I tugged the small girl to her feet. It took a few moments for her to steady her wobbly legs, but soon our footsteps carried us toward the winding path carved into the depths of the mountain. Hopefully, the dark tunnel would lead us to an exit.

“You mentioned a man named Richter made the bear for you; is that your father?” I asked as we weaved and bobbed between the razor teeth protruding from the cavern floor.

“No, but he takes care of me when he's not being a mean jerk. Is being frail a bad thing, Ihlia?” Elsa clutched the draping trench coat I laid over her shoulders tighter around her slender frame. The question she tacked on to the end of her explanation jarred me from my train of thought. Growing accustomed to her ability to perceive my thoughts as clearly as I perceived her words would be difficult. I tapped the bottom of my chin as we reached the base of the sharp incline of our ascension, the point at which I knew our difficulties would begin.

"I'm sorry, I don't do it on purpose," She whispered in response to my thoughts and coiled deeper into my black coat for warmth. I shook my head.

"It's not your problem, little one, it's mine. You have no reason to apologize. Also, you shouldn't confuse frailty with weakness. Your body is frail because it is young, but look at you. With bare feet you walk along jagged rocks, and for hours you sat attentively with my heavy head in your lap while I slept. You are quite strong and sturdy in your own ways, Elsa. I'm just not used to your telepathy, or with people asking so many questions," I replied.

When the last words escaped my lips, I planted a foot against the steep hill that served as our route through the mountain interior. I used a free hand to grip one of the many stalagmites rising from the ground and utilized it as a brace. Though unnecessary, it allowed an easier time working up the incline.

"So, do people stop asking questions when they grow up?" Elsa followed at my heel along the sharply rising trail. While she failed to remain completely erect as we scaled the slope, simply dropping forward onto one of her hands and using it for balance proved sufficient. She likely may have expedited the process had she abandoned Magnolia or planted it on the grimy rocks in order to use her right hand in addition to her left, but like a mother protecting its young, Elsa kept her teddy bear tucked safely beneath her right arm.

"I suppose they do, to an extent. Eventually you gain enough knowledge that questioning every small thing becomes unnecessary," I replied.

"How much knowledge is enough?" Elsa grunted in between labored motions that carried her along the pattern left in the wake of my stride.

"I suppose it varies from person to person," I casually tossed her an answer as I neared the top of the dark slope. When the ground leveled and allowed for an easier trek, I turned to face the small child who busily clambered up the slick damp rocks with her hand and feet. I extended my hand in her direction when she neared the apex of the slope.

"Well, then I guess I'll ask questions forever!" She exclaimed as she took hold of my hand with her nimble fingers. "Because I want to know everything!" She giggled as I tugged her up the remainder of the stone hill; as her petite figure stood in front of mine, a faint twitch widened my eyes if only by a small margin.

Once in a while, an adult receives a lesson from the innocent truths of a child. Such was the case, as I quickly concluded that apathy, pride, and stubbornness, rather than knowledge and experience, were the culprits responsible for shutting the mouths of people as they grew older. When an issue presented itself to which I lacked knowledge, I either drew an assumption from a related topic that closely matched the issue or decided the information simply was not worth possessing.

After all, I subconsciously derived, I had survived to said point without that information, what usefulness might it have offered that it did not before? Thus, rather than part my lips and pose a question, I remained silent and went about my life. I offered Elsa a pleased smile. As she read my thoughts and reciprocated my grin, I bent down and spoke softly, "That's a very good trait to have. Don't forget those words, because once you think you know everything, that's all you're ever going to know."

"Yes, ma'am!" Elsa exclaimed.

The trail continued winding and twisting through the darkness. The ceiling dropped significantly at the peak of the incline, so much so that if I stood atop my toes and reached with all my might, my fingertips would have scraped along the cavern's gritty roof. The deeper into the tunnel the trail went, the more cluttered and threatening the jagged spikes from the ceiling, floor, and even the walls became. Elsa clutched the back of my charcoal tank-top; I realized that my night vision did little to assist her own eyesight. While the extensive hours in the darkness likely tailored her natural sight to make out basic shapes and details at short distances, Elsa was essentially blind. I chuckled.

“Don't worry, I can see perfectly,” I assured her.

“'Kay.” She nodded and pressed closer to me.

As various spikes became more numerous during our journey through the cave's tight confines, it eventually became necessary to duck and weave through the protrusions that obstructed our path. After almost an hour, the narrow passage constantly pressed our bodies against some form of sharp object. We slowly inched forward, and the growing sound of crinkling cloth tickled my ears. When I glanced back, the end of my trench coat which Elsa donned as her own lay frayed as it slid across the ground's rocky protuberances.

I curled the corner of my lips into a smile, and Elsa paused in her struggles to wedge her tiny body between the stalagmites and offered me a beaming smile. I reached forward to place my hand atop her head, but as my fingers brushed the tips of her hair, the image of the girl from Loftsborough flashed in my mind. Her sniffling face and streaming tears had embodied her fear at the thought of my scary hands patting her head; the memory sufficiently convinced me to snatch my hand back, though I did offer Elsa a reassuring grin.

“Why was she crying? Was she hurt?” Elsa asked as we resumed our painstaking squeeze through the tiny slits the cave's teeth afforded us.

“No, just afraid of me,” I responded plainly.

“Why?” Elsa tipped her head to one side in a display of confused curiosity. The action knocked the side of her forehead against one of the bulky sides of a stalagmite. The young girl inwardly hissed and rubbed at the small red mark that formed.

“I'm not sure. My friend Crelyos says it's because I only think about murder and vengeance; apparently, kids can feel that,” I grunted as the space between rock formations and jagged points thinned to almost impassable widths. Finally, through a small horizontal space dividing a row of stalagmites and stalactites jutting from the cavern like the teeth lining the jaws of a monster, I noticed a cavernous opening.

I bent my body and arched my back to maneuver through the minuscule opening. The action accidentally drew my hand sharply across one of the rock tips; I hissed in pain as the tooth tore a gash through my palm. By the time I glanced down at the open wound, Panacea's busy kneading had already finished sealing the tissue. It meant Panacea, and likely my other implants, fully returned to operational status; Oswald's horrible experimental serum must have finally worn off.

Once on the other side of the imposing shards of stone, I extended my hand for Elsa's sake. The small girl stared at the scrape across my hand as it finished healing. She seemed hesitant, though I knew not if her hesitation stemmed from touching the area with a former wound or the fear of acquiring one of her own if she misstepped while crossing through the frightful stone jaws. I offered her a reassuring nod, and after a moment of glancing between my hand and my face, she curled her tiny fingers into mine and began the arduous process of shifting between whatever spaces the horizontal slit allowed. With my assistance, her endeavor concluded more favorably than mine; Elsa emerged unharmed on the cavernous side of the constricting tunnel.

"Maybe a little... but it's not scary," Elsa mused as she stepped across a small puddle of shimmering water and into the new cavern's expanse. When I turned to follow, a blinding glare of burning white light seared my eyes and forced me to draw my hand in front of my face to ease the sudden agony. Instinctively, I deactivated the implant responsible for the green and white filter. When the pain subsided and my eyes fluttered open, I stared into a scene one might swear leapt from the very canvas of a beautiful painting.

The cavernous dome in which we stood possessed a body of water similar to the one before it, though far smaller and tucked away in a single corner. The stalagmites and stalactites lined the outskirts of the opening in an array that barely seemed natural, and the majority of the protrusions, from the teeth lining the walls to those scattered across the floor, glistened and shimmered from the source of my eyes' previous pain: a stream of dim gray light pouring in from a hole in the ceiling.

The closest thing to daylight for the world left in the wake of the Titan Crisis, the gray that streamed through the perpetually rumbling fallout clouds struck the surface of the water and bounced off it onto the nearby rock formations. The quartz-like composition of the stones accentuated the sparse light and splashed the refracted patterns in a dazzling hodgepodge across the dark cave. With the soft blue glow sparkling from the still water as the final touch, the display was the most intense source of natural colors and gorgeous scenery I had seen since the world's end.

"It's just really sad," Elsa finished her previous thought, "are you sure they aren't crying because they're sad for you?" The small girl maintained her conversation with me, but her eyes lit up like Loftsborough's sun at the sight of nature's artistry painted before her. I heard the wonder in her voice and instantly knew it to be attributed to the cavern.

"I'm not sure which would be worse, now that you put it that way," I laughed and stepped in front of her. The soft drips of moisture cascading down the various jutting rocks to the ground in tiny puddles added a pleasant ambiant sound to the cavern's visual beauty. As I approached the body of water tucked away on one side of the cavern, I dropped down and scooped up some of the cold liquid in my palm. The plain taste of the water belied its irradiated nature, but thankfully, Panacea allowed for the harmless digestion of virtually any substance.

Radioactive food and water posed little threat, and even bacteria infested consumables rarely possessed the sheer strength required to overcome the virtual cure-all nanite.

While disease and sickness in the wastelands of the world's end were not completely unheard of, the instances that emerged fell into the classification of superstitious rarity, and since Panacea's invention, the death toll for pathogenic infection dropped to virtually zero.

From my squatted position, I surveyed the area for an exit. Given the hole in the cavern roof, I assumed my choice to take the steep, winding path through the heart of the mountain was, in fact, correct. Though many smaller pathways led from the cavern's interior, only three sloped upward toward the surface at first glance. The sound of a small voice grunting drew me from my thoughts; when I glanced over, Elsa sat on her knees next to me and busily scooped water into her mouth with her free hand. When she finished and released a refreshed "ahh," I stood and walked toward the first of the three potential paths to the surface. With my left hand, I placed my finger within the confines of my ear as tightly as I was able, and with my right I cupped my uncovered ear and activated my auditory enhancement.

Like thundering footsteps, I clearly perceived the distant sound of water droplets echoing through the tunnel deep in the cave. I kept my hands in their position and moved to the next vertical incline; a similar result reached my sensitive hearing. When I finally reached the third pathway that spiraled up through the mountain, I heard it. Though faint in the distance, the sound of whistling wind flowed down the tunnel and tickled the innermost parts of my ear; I found our ticket out of the mountain's belly.

"You found a way out! Yay!" Elsa tossed Magnolia into the air a couple of times while she climbed to her feet. The small child with pretty blonde hair and beautiful sea-green eyes danced around me in her tattered white gown like a mischievous, giggling sprite. I grinned when she clutched my right hand in her grasp and rigorously tugged us toward the path.

"Come on, come on!" She shouted. Most people probably found the innocent emotions that emanated from her like an aura to be fervently contagious. Even I, with my limited ability to comprehend the depth of any emotion save my rancor for Bradich, felt the smallest twinkle of excitement as I watched her dance about in the dazzling cavern.

"All right, all right, little one." I shook my head as we started down the path toward the hopeful exit of the dark mountains. Before we escaped the dim light of the cavernous dome, I glanced back once more at the stream of daylight that filtered through the opening in the cave ceiling. If the illuminated gray was any indicator of the time, it was well into the morning. Considering our misadventure culminated with our perilous fall through the darkness in the middle of the previous night, I marveled at the fortitude of the small child.

"A few hours indeed," I thought to myself, *"you took care of me the whole night. Just how tough are you, little one?"* For once, Elsa remained silent despite the overbearing volume with which I projected my thoughts. I stepped forward in front of her and closed my hand

around hers; as the darkness of the tunnel enveloped our sight, I reactivated my night vision augment.

The path spiraled up in a general forward direction. Though keeping a bearing on the cardinal directions proved a difficult task, the direction of the dim gray color streaming through the previous cavern's ceiling suggested we traveled south. The trek to avoid protruding rock formations and jagged surfaces seemed far easier than through the previous tunnel. And after a solid half hour of monotonous hiking, a vibrant white glare similar to the one in the second cavern seared my sensitive night vision and forced me to put it to sleep.

The hole containing the whistling winds and draft of cold air, albeit warmer than the stale air of the cave, loomed overhead at the far end of the tunnel. With the various large rocks and assortment of rubble, the climb to the opening appeared relatively easy, but the steep rise necessitated a climb nonetheless. I glanced down toward Elsa and pressed a finger to my lips before whispering, “I'll go first. You wait here until I make sure it's safe, okay?” Elsa nodded and wrapped both her small arms around her cybernetic bear.

I slowly slid my remaining dagger free of its sheath and crept quietly toward the rock face. With my extensive training as an infiltrator and sniper, the grime beneath my feet issued absolutely no sound during my cautious steps. I clamped my teeth around the hilt of my dagger when I reached the wall and carefully positioned my hands atop the sturdiest stones. Like a panther, I stalked vertically toward the opening. No pebbles shifted, no gravel crunched, and no rocks or stones clanked together. I was a wraith in the darkness.

I neared our target exit and paused to activate my auditory and olfactory enhancements. The smell of sulfur, rust, and blood that saturated the entire world rushed to assail my nose. The stale odor of stone and decay that the howling winds carried reminded me that the world had long since died, and all the elements of such a world sought nothing more than the death of those things which desperately clung to the mockery of life that remained.

The sharp, shrill sound of the wind suggested my altitude increased since my reckless dash through the ribcage valley, but the sound that alarmed me most drifted down from outside the exit. At its peak performance in a quiet room, the auditory enhancing nanite Oswald implanted in me detected sounds as faint as breathing without care taken to conceal them, and in extremely favorable circumstances, even the sound of a human heartbeat fell within the range of the implant's detection.

The noise that found its way through the whispering winds and howling sky sounded like a wire or string creaking as someone strained to draw it taut. The soft crunch of an unknown hard substance followed it, but after a few seconds, the noise ceased and utter silence enveloped the wastelands. If an intelligent being lay in wait at the source of the audible disturbance, they were good. Really good. The lack of breathing sounds, the quietness that kept their heartbeat from detection, and the overall lack of movement served to conceal them well. If not for my auditory enhancement, my chances of detecting them would have been nonexistent. I slowly poked my head from the crevice to locate the source of the noise.

The cool wind tore through my hair, whipping it back like a dark, billowing curtain. As my eyes cleared the rim of the opening, I quickly scanned the area in the general direction of the noise but discovered only the extensive rocky surface of the mountainside coated in rocky debris. The only glaring object seemingly out of place, an enormous boulder, jutted from the side of the mountain roughly twenty feet from my location. I glared at it intently and gingerly placed my fingertips into the shifting gravel that covered the broad incline of the mountain.

I glanced down at the loose stones and noted the precarious danger of maneuvering across the ground. If a hyped or bandit lay in wait behind the boulder, the slightest shift or sound in the stone would prove fatal to me. It also meant that the slightest movement from behind their giant barricade would prove fatal to them. *"Great,"* I thought to myself, *"a game of chicken."*

File 29: Richter Sarkany

The seconds passed like decades, and the howling wind provided the only backdrop music for the stubborn confrontation with my unknown assailant. I coiled my legs against the stone in preparation for my moment. A shift in wind direction signaled the end of our stalemate as it blew a few loose stones down the side of the mountain. The first tap of their smooth surfaces against their fellow stones propelled me to action.

I launched myself from the hole like a pouncing predator and sped toward the boulder; at the same time, I reclaimed my dagger from between my clenched teeth. The moment my feet collided with the ground, a humanoid figure spun from the cover of the enormous rock. I quickly hummed my Cognitive Accelerator to life; a sense of relief washed over me when the augment operated properly and caused me no pain or discomfort from Oswald's atrocious serum.

The figure before me was more than merely humanoid, it was a human male. At a height of roughly five feet and ten inches, the man stood with good posture and a stoic expression. His brown hair clung to his scalp in braided cornrows, but their long ends spiraled down the back of his neck in stylish tendrils; they extended just beyond the toned curve of his trapezius muscles. His eyes glistened a pale blue color reminded me of mist wafting from the top of dry ice.

A dirty, greasy white sleeveless shirt tightly hugged his middle; the tight fabric displayed his sleek but toned muscles even through the synthetic material. A large pair of tool belts hung loosely at his waist; the black material criss-crossed directly at his front and, I assumed, once more at his rear. It offered the illusion of a giant “x” draped around his hips. A pair of tight, dark green trousers tucked into a pair of lightweight black boots, but the most shocking features of his ensemble rested on his arms and back.

A large quiver made of some leathery material extended from his back between his shoulders; within its confines several thick black stakes protruded like arrows, though they lacked fletching and were unlike any arrow I had ever seen. Upon his right hip, a smaller quiver slanted forward and attached to the flashy “x” tool belt clad to his waist; it housed more of those metallic stakes. The outside of his right calf possessed the smallest and last of the quivers, and within that vertical container, slightly smaller black rods fanned out more evenly than the clutter of stakes in the other two quivers.

The most startling piece of his gear, however, formed a thick shell that ran down the length of his arms. Starting at either of his shoulders, a pair of metal contraptions added a significant bulk to his appearance. The apparatuses looked like extended gauntlets from a full suit of armor. They lent him a far more imposing stature than he otherwise would have possessed, but I surmised with a quick assessment that those gauntlets offered him more than aesthetic intimidation.

The material resembled an extremely dense alloy; in fact, at a glance it seemed close in appearance to one of my osmiridium bullets. Though osmium and iridium had become far more abundant on the planet since my time with the Eagles, I doubted he comprised the mechanical gauntlets entirely of such a substance. If so, however, the resourcefulness of the stranger bordered a level equivalent to military organizations at the height of civilization.

The gauntlets hissed slowly, in my mind's perception, as gears and various moving parts lined the joints and the areas covering the stranger's muscles. The machines ended in glove-like extensions that coated the man's fingers with rough, blocky metal digits. The right metal appendage clenched a stake between the pointer and middle finger and drew its indented surface taut against a bowstring that the stranger clenched in his augmented grip.

The wire creaked and groaned as the power behind the metal gauntlets bent the sleek bow back into a strained arch. The metallic left limb held the bow steady despite the unfathomable strain placed upon it. The base of the bow looked like a strange carbon based material resembling a cross between the malleability of soft wood and the absolute hardness of osmiridium. Its ornate design suggested great detail had been placed in its creation, and the deep shimmering black color provided a nice finishing touch to its threatening appearance.

The man's eyes never blinked nor altered their glare in my direction, and as his armored fingers released the wire holding back his black stake, I slid to my knees and arched my back to allow the projectile ample clearance to pass over my body. The thunderous sound of the wire snapping into place as it launched the stake forward struck me first. The powerful wind that passed over my torso as the metallic arrow cut through the air above my body like a ballistic missile struck me second, but my eyes did not widen until the stake slammed into the earth just shy of the cavern entrance.

The powerful impact launched several stones and a cloud of dirt into the air like a bomb explosion. Though the monstrous collision seemed like an explosion, a quick glance revealed the small hole where the stake drove through solid rock and the crater that formed around it. The arrow simply hit with enough force to shake the very ground it struck. I decided that one of those high velocity projectiles striking any part of my body simply seemed inconducive with my desire to live.

The stranger lifted his arm to tug another bolt free of its quiver, and in that moment I deactivated my Cognitive Accelerator and launched myself forward. With a swift twist, I drew back my leg and drove it against the center of the stranger's chest; the force catapulted his body down the glacis; when he struck the ground, rocks rattled and clanked down the gentle slope like a miniature avalanche.

The man proved surprisingly agile; he utilized the momentum my kick provided to roll backward and plant his feet into the shifting rubble, effectively surfing down the avalanche itself. Despite his continued slide, the stranger drew one of the smaller bolts from the quiver on his calf and nocked it. The powerful hiss of his machine arms indicated the raw power needed to draw the bow; I hypothesized normal human muscle could not have accomplished the feat.

The bow's groaning black body bent on its ends to accommodate the drawn wire as the mechanical power of the stranger's other arm held it in place. The beautiful design allowed a unique bow, virtually incapable of being fired by human hands, to work in tandem with technological advancements. It created a weapon just as deadly as conventional firearms but with far more versatility. I decided to admire his handiwork later, even if that meant admiring it while staring down at his corpse.

I lunged down the slope and flipped my remaining long dagger into a reverse grip. As my feet struggled to keep balance while I pursued the assailant down the mountain, his bolt struck the ground in front of me. When the thin stake impacted the ground a few feet away, it exploded bits of dirt and rubble into the air as before. I furrowed my brows, confused; I assumed the man possessed remarkable marksmanship to choose a weapon as specialized as the bow and arrow. His harmless, ineffective shot, however, left me startlingly disappointed at his terrible aim. Then the dust settled.

I stared at the stake's point of impact as I sped toward it. A faint red light flashed where the man's shot had embedded his stake. As I neared the area in question, a soft interval of electronic beeps sent red flags waving like wildfires in my head.

"Are you serious?" I exclaimed as I drove my legs into the ground and activated my Supersoldier nanite; taking a page from Al, I utilized it to stimulate the muscle fibers in my legs and increased the speed of my sprint. Though my raw speed certainly paled in comparison to the late crime lord's, it successfully whipped me through the air fast enough to put the blinking stake behind my agile frame. "Who the hell uses bombs in arr—" The cacophonous kaboom cut my words short.

My body sailed through the air with explosive pressure at my back, but the stranger must have failed to calculate the sharp increase in my speed when he fired his special stake. His eyes widened when I rocketed into him with flames licking at my backside. No doubt he expected the explosion to blow me into tiny pieces and scatter me to the wind. I did not even attempt to lessen the impact of our bodies; I slammed into him with a headlong tackle. As we tumbled and slid down the glacis, the rocks around us which may have been stagnant for decades shifted loose. The dirt and stone ebbed and flowed like a raging gray sea.

Finally, we rammed with a deafening thud into one of the many boulders protruding from the mountain's face. The cloud of dust that burst up in all directions briefly concealed us, but it did nothing to stifle a shrill voice's scream, a scream which the wind carried down to us from the boulder several feet up the hill. It was the original boulder which the stranger hid behind to ambush Elsa and I. The voice belonged to Elsa and immediately drew my, and surprisingly the stranger's, attention.

"Richter, Ihlia, stop it!" Elsa screamed as she clutched Magnolia in her right arm at the top of the enormous rock.

"You know her?" The stranger asked bluntly.

"You know him?" I asked bluntly and synchronously with the stranger.

When the dust settled, we stood pressed against the flat surface of the boulder into which we tumbled. My left shoulder faithfully supported my weight as it rested against the rocky surface; I faced the man Elsa referred to as Richter, forcefully shoving the bladed edge of my long dagger uncomfortably against the side of his neck. When I applied enough pressure to make my "point," I felt an equal application of pressure against the base of my skull. Richter held his black bow's body in his left hand as before, but the wire no longer faced the stranger ready for him to nock an arrow.

Instead, Richter pulled the wire taut against the back of my neck with fatal implications. If he used the strength in his right mechanical gauntlet to push my body backward, the pressure assured that the wire would pass through my neck like a knife through butter. The idea of my head rolling down the hill without my body seemed unappealing to me, so I drew my knife away from Richter's throat at Elsa's behest. The stranger followed suit, and the two of us stepped back to assess one another.

"Name's Ihlia, Ihlia Lorando," I said as I sheathed my long dagger.

"Richter, Richter Sarkany," he responded plainly. After staring at me for a few seconds, he tugged a cigarette from behind his ear and placed the filter between his lips. A steel lighter provided fire, and within a few seconds puffs of gray smoke wafted from his lips as he took gratuitous drags from the formerly fatal narcotic. Without another word, Richter marched up the slope toward Elsa and her cyborg teddy.

"How many times have I told you that you can't just shoot people whenever you want! This is why I run away! You don't listen!" Elsa clambered down from the boulder and began fervently wagging her finger at the significantly taller male. Richter simply drew a few more shots of nicotine from his burning cigarette and stared at her.

"How did you find me anyway?" Elsa stammered, seemingly embarrassed.

Richter placed a finger against the metal plate that served as the right side of Magnolia's face. When he finished exhaling his rings of smoke into the air, he responded in a matter-of-fact manner, “Tracking device.”

Elsa gasped and clutched Magnolia tight to her chest; her words escaped her between half-hearted whimpers as she stroked the cyborg bear's head, “Oh Magnolia, what has he done to you?”

“A tracking device and an archaic weapon with more stopping power than most advanced weaponry even after the advent of neurotech. I'd wager that even if a human being naturally possessed the physical prowess to draw that bow, the tensile strength of the wire would slice clean through their fingers before the composite body actually bent,” I relaxed and caught my breath.

“So you have those' things on your arms. They give you both the power and hardness you need, but their mechanical design looks unfathomably complicated. Just who the hell are you, anyway?” I analyzed the man called Richter from head to toe. From all accounts, I perceived him as a normal human with a smoking habit. Something in those foggy blue eyes, however, assured me that something very special lay beneath his surface. After a few moments of silence and three puffs of his cigarette, Richter finally dignified my question with a response; he shrugged.

“Even with a tracking device, we've only been out here about a day. Are you going to tell me you flew across the desert in some advanced airship, too?” I jested.

“Hm? Actually a town is close by! Lofts something.

Richter and I have been camping near there for almost a week now. It should still be close by, anyway, we didn't go that far'" Elsa interjected and swiveled her head to and fro seeking some manner of bearing with which she could direct our attention to Loftsborough. My ears perked and I offered her a hopeful glance.

"Do you know what direction it's in?" I asked; the idea of the old codger and the drunken former soldier worrying for my safety stirred a warm yet sickening sensation in the pit of my stomach. Returning to the city to nonchalantly explain away my brief absence ranked among my immediate priorities.

"Um'" Elsa trailed off, but the uncertain twists of her body and hesitant twirls of her head answered my question long before her words.

With wisps of smoke blowing into the dim gray afternoon from the tip of his cigarette, Richter thumbed in the direction of the glacis' peak. I offered him a silent nod, and we started up the hill. The heavy crunch of our boots sinking into the loose stones on the mountainside were joined by the sudden, less imposing, pitter patter of Elsa's bare feet as she rushed after us.

"Wait for me!" She cried out in her desperate struggle to ascend the pebble strewn incline. For the short duration of the hike, Elsa recounted the events of our fateful adventure with passionate abandon. I grinned at her enthusiasm.

“So if you two are in such close proximity to Loftsborough, why not take up temporary residence there? Even if you only plan to stay for a few nights, it is bound to be more hospitable than the wastes,” I turned my gaze to Richter. My question silenced the excited little girl long enough for Richter to answer. As in most cases, that proved to be a surprisingly long wait; Richter took a few final drags from his cigarette and lackadaisically tipped his head in my direction.

“People and I don't usually get along well,” He stated as he removed the smoldering filter from between his lips.

“Really? You're a bit quiet, but I actually find it endearing. I certainly don't see why anyone would dislike you.” I pondered the idea of Richter roaming silently through the crowds in Loftsborough's markets. Aside from the occasional accidental nudge from a passerby, the only person I saw truly drawing attention to him was Elsa with her jovial spirit and kind-hearted disposition.

“Don't know if they do or not, but'” Richter drew the last bit of consumable tobacco from the end of the smoking stick and tossed its remains on the ground in front of him. His boot fell harshly atop the burning ember to snuff the dying flame completely out of existence. In perfect synchronization with his rough stomp, Richter continued, “I definitely dislike most of them.”

His words served to exhale the last of the smoke from his lungs into the crisp, cool wind. The action in its entirety sent my brow arching skyward. The act of snuffing out a cigarette usually pertained to the idea of preventing an out of control fire, but what, I wondered to myself, threatened to burn in the rocky wasteland? I laughed under my breath and surmised the action stemmed from habit rather than reason. Elsa detected my thoughts and giggled, too.

We rounded the top of the hill that jutted from the side of the mountain like a cancerous growth. The rotund peak offered an extensive view of the surrounding area, and I marveled at the distance Elsa and I traveled within the network of caves inside the mountain itself. As I peered to my right between jagged rocky peaks, I noticed the smaller zit of a hill I targeted in my original plan to gain a vantage point; I also noticed the valley of rib shaped rocks and cliffside caves that extended beyond it.

The vantage point, while significantly less, would have served my intent as well as the current bulge on which we stood. With the furious wind tossing my obsidian strands of hair in a wild fan behind me, I cast my gaze forward into the unforgiving wasteland. I drew my jaw into a concerned clench and widened my eyes at what I saw.

Loftsborough lay far in the distance situated above the churning quicksands which I distinguished even from the few miles separating us from the city. The bright glow of the artificial sun that beamed from the slits in Loftsboroughs clam-like protective plates illuminated it for miles. At first glance, the city appeared normal, but as my enhanced telescopic sight awakened, I noticed several sources of light which did not belong to the peaceful city.

Several fiery spotlights projected from twin aircraft that hovered just above the city. The imposing lights, an entirely different hue and intensity than the warm glow of the artificial sun, penetrated the city's protective slit like searchlights. I recognized the aircraft. Hoverbusters. Though long antiquated with patches of rust and attachments that provided more flair than function, the aircraft definitely ranked among those constructed and operated by highly trained military personnel.

"The city's in trouble' it must be Bradich!" I exclaimed between clenched teeth; I curled my hands into fists and leapt down the hill in Loftsborough's direction. I resisted my natural urge to steady myself among the shifting rocks that slid around my feet like miniature surfboards and maintained my balance as their speedy descent carried me down the hill. *"Crelyos, Oswald, hold on. I'm on my way!"*

File 30: Loftsborough's Hero

The cold wind swept my hair back as I sprinted across the rocky desert. The long miles between the peak of the rounded hill and the looming city of Loftsborough extracted their toll on my endurance even with the assistance of my neurotech. The furious stomp of my boots into loose rocks and lifeless sand joined the exhausted huffs of my labored exhales like a lonely chorus in the midday gray.

By the time I reached the rocky plateau housing our dune buggy, I glistened with a steady stream of perspiration. I wasted no time; my sprint's momentum carried me up the steep hill with relative ease, and as I hopped into the back of the old geezer's trailer, I scanned the dim confines for Oswald or, at the very least, my rifle. When I found neither, I kicked the side of the trailer in frustration; I cursed between my heavy breaths before hopping from the trailer and gazing toward the city.

In the distance, one of the two Hoverbusters floating near Loftsborough buzzed with activity. The blue lights denoting the antigravity propulsion system twisted to send it along a horizontal path, but those lights intermittently flickered and dimmed. A strange sputter emanated from the engines like that of an antique automobile. It testified to the armored aircraft's age and state of decay. However, despite its decrepit condition, the Hoverbuster streaked through the sky toward the horizon. Upon careful scrutiny, I realized its flickering blue thrusters carried it in the direction of Raze's ransacked fortress.

After swallowing a few more gulps of precious air, I bounded off toward the towering city. My mind raced with thoughts regarding the intruders as the bridge's metal grating clinked methodically beneath my heavy footfalls. The silver intercom at the bridge's end seemed infinitely farther away during my hectic dash than any of the times I casually strolled up to it. I finally reached it and smashed my thumb into its button with relentless fervor. An eternity passed before the intercom quietly beeped on the other end. Though distorted by the crackle of faulty wiring and ancient electricity, a frantic voice finally escaped the speaker. I recognized the voice; it belonged to Samson.

"Who goes there? State your name and business! Now is not the time for visitors!" Samson's command carried a concerned but authoritative tone. No doubt the head mercenary desired no outside refugees to become caught in the city's conflict, but I questioned his logic considering any sane visitor would toss one glance at the Hoverbuster floating near Loftsborough and quickly conclude that another location might provide more hospitable lodging.

"Samson, it's me. What's going on? Why is there a Hoverbuster here?" I called through the intercom while swallowing gulps of air.

"Ihlia?! Thank goodness! Oswald and Crelyos have been worried sick! Ah, but now's not the time! You call those things Hoverbusters? They're monsters. Our guns couldn't do anything to that thick hull, and the onboard weapons nearly annihilated the city guard! There are several dead and even more wounded! Some guy calling himself Sarge swung in through the slit between the plates with a small army and demanded we give him Raze! It's madness in here!" The authority in Samson's voice gave way to panic as he accounted for the sudden invasion of Bradich's minions.

"Sarge? Send the elevator down, quick, Samson. What are their numbers? Where's Crelyos and Oswald? I need more details of the situation." As my blood settled and the cold winds kissed my glistening skin, I shivered. I regretted rushing headlong into danger without first snatching my coat from Elsa. The elevator screeched to a halt at the base of the bridge, and as I stepped into the cage's confines, Samson's voice scratched through the intercom attached to box's metal wall.

"They have about twenty foot soldiers. They're all rank and file and follow the Sarge guy's orders explicitly. They look really professional and intimidating," Samson spoke quickly. His voice dropped to a whisper; undoubtedly he sought to prevent detection.

"Twenty... Have they injured or taken any of the city hostage? What about the second Hoverbuster? Where did it go? You sound quiet, are you in danger? Don't compromise yourself!" I hissed. With my body temperature stabilizing thanks to a racial adaptation to the cold which the Titan Crisis forced all humans to develop, my shivering ceased.

"No hostages yet. The second Hoverbuster had a... I don't even know how to describe it. It was a little old man riding some kind of enormous beast. Sarge told them to go collect the hyped that we left in Raze's fortress, so they took off. I still have men there so I'm not too concerned; the old man didn't even take any of the soldiers with him. I'm fine, but this Sarge guy has two lieutenants or something, he calls them the Storm Duo. They're patrolling and keeping everyone in line; they haven't found me yet, but man they're scary as shit. Their powers are—" Samson's quiet words erupted into a shocked cry, and the buzzing intercom system suddenly exploded in a rain of sparks before dying altogether.

Though the mechanical device ceased functioning, Samson's surprised scream of anguish reached my ears from the watch tower above. A few quiet seconds passed, and with a jarring jolt, the screeching elevator halted in the middle of its ascension. I shot my gaze skyward toward the open hole at the climb's apex; one by one the lights clicked off starting from the uppermost point and rapidly descending. Engulfed in the darkness of the elevator shaft, I flicked on my night vision augment.

"Samson? Samson, come in! Answer me, Samson!" I desperately rapped my knuckles across the silver intercom box hoping for a response. Naught but silence met me in the lonely confines of the cage. My long obsidian tresses that normally trailed neatly across my back draped around my face like a curtain as I hung my head. I knew the harsh reality of invasion, and I knew the kind of people associated with Bradich. I knew Samson's heart had likely ceased beating, but normal feelings of sympathy or grief failed to find their way to my heart. In their place, a fire crackled like a fanned ember; my curtain of hair did not conceal any expression of sadness, it concealed an expression drowned in wrath.

A crackling from a far more tangible source interrupted my brooding rage. When I looked up, my night vision revealed a woman standing on the edge of the elevator shaft several feet above me. The crackling emanated from her; vines of lightning embraced her almost as tightly as her clothing. A sleek black leather bodysuit hugged her modest curves. Inky black hair sat atop her head in a carefully planned assortment of spikes. Their glossy texture suggested some applied gel kept them erect.

Her odd hairstyle reminded me of porcupine spines, and though they protruded wildly from the back of her scalp, a small gap ran between them and the several strands that she clumped into bangs and hung in the front of her face like antennae of varying lengths. The bald valley in the middle of her skull no doubt housed her surgical scar. The thin slits of her black eyes belied her far eastern heritage; her slender bone structure and high cheek bones vividly complimented that theory.

Given Panacea served as the staple first implant for any living human, it stood to reason that in order to function as a lieutenant in Sarge's squad, her other two nanites needed to go beyond the scope of normality. If her second optional augment resembled her first in any manner, she passed the intimidation test with flying colors. As she stood ominously over the elevator opening with a menacing expression painted across her thin face, bright cracks of electrical current spread from her fingertips and palms like spider webs hanging between tree branches.

My eyes widened; to make matters worse, she tightly clasped the hilt of a well-honed, expertly crafted katana. Her twisting currents of electricity ominously raced down the slender blade's edge. I presumed that though the display filtered through my night vision as an assortment of dark greens and bright whites, the actual energy likely adopted an imposing yet impressive blue. The vacant stare on her face indicated she possessed no night vision of her own; instead, she merely stared down at my general area with a menacing glare. She slowly lifted her head until her eyes, flickering with her dancing sparks, suggestively rested upon the thick cord supporting the giant cage in which I stood. I immediately leapt to action.

A quick hum set my Cognitive Accelerator into motion, and as the electrifying female drew back her katana with the poise of a master swordswoman, I pressed my palm fiercely against the roof to pop off one of the grated metal tiles on the elevator's ceiling. Her blade arched through the air like a bolt of lightning just as my hands gripped the lip of the opening I created. As I worked to hoist myself to the roof, I felt the cage wrench and groan around me.

I glanced up in time to see the female's back turned on the elevator shaft; the tense chord wriggled freely through the air like a squirming worm as it descended through the darkness toward me. The jolting lurch warned me that the box on which I hung had begun its destructive free fall. I swiftly finished hoisting my body through the hole I created and planted both feet firmly against the roof. With my legs in mind, I activated my Supersoldier nanite to aid my jump as I leapt from the cage at the last moment.

The screeching sparks beneath me as the cage scraped against the walls reminded me that I might have joined its fate. Instead, I clenched the indented groove that housed one of the shaft's many light fixtures. With my chest and abs flattened against the vertical tunnel walls, I searched with my dangling feet for a fixture close enough to gain a foothold but grunted when my endeavor left me empty... footed.

I furrowed my slender brows with determination; after clenching my abdominal muscles to fold my lower torso up toward my chest, I drove both feet into the wall. A deep inhale and a second of concentration activated my Supersoldier enhancement again. Targeting the muscles in my thighs, I vaulted off the wall like a coiled spring. A quick calculation allowed me to properly distribute the power I needed to ascend to the next light fixture and the horizontal power I needed to reach it on the other side of the elevator shaft.

In midair, I twisted my body to face the opposing wall

and extended my hands instinctively. My fingers slid into the groove with little difficulty, and I immediately clenched the muscles in my upper body to stabilize my weight as I hung down from my new precarious perch several feet above my previous one. A quick glance up informed me that a significant investment of time and effort would be required to reach the shaft's apex.

I ground my teeth together; I possessed an abundance of effort, but time was an unaffordable luxury. Circumstances left me with only one logical course of action; I needed to double my efforts. I shot through the elevator shaft with immense exertion, bounding from fixture to fixture. When my hands finally gripped the edge of the shaft, I swiftly hoisted myself into the city. I used the momentum of my ascension to roll to an upright squat, and as I settled into my alert crouch on the city's surface, I immediately drew my dagger from its sheath on my hip.

A quick survey revealed little more than the quiet whistle of the wind passing through the metal lips of the city's protective plates. My night vision provided enough illumination to discern the city's entrance in the darkness, and though the immediate area lacked any enemies I could see, I remained vigilant. My thoughts fleetingly drifted to the question of how one might exit Loftsborough with the elevator destroyed, but I decided more pressing issues warranted my attention and crept quickly to the elevator watchtower.

It did not take long for my green and white filtered

vision to detect the fallen body of Loftsborough's recently appointed head mercenary. I rushed to his side and knelt beside him; cupping the back of his head in the palm of my free hand, I lifted him to a half seated position and examined his injuries. A crusted stream of blood trailed from the corner of his mouth to his chin. He used one hand to cover two wounds directly atop his chest over his lungs; it was obviously caused by a blade impalement, but aside from the smudge of charred crimson that stained his palm, the wounds bled very little, if at all.

As I worked to analyze my initial theories regarding the nature and purpose of the attack, Samson's free hand shot up and encircled my wrist in a vice grip. His throat worked to swallow air, but I doubted he succeeded considering the pained look on his face.

“Ih-Ihlia... I... It hurts,” Samson's hoarse whisper expelled air far more quickly than he inhaled it. At first I did not understand; Samson's chest heaved rapidly and I clearly heard him suck the air into his lungs. Unfortunately, he exhaled it just as quickly and I soon understood the nature of his doom. Either the woman that stabbed Samson did not understand the nature of her ability, or she was a cruel, demonic human being.

“Samson, you're going to die. That woman stabbed you in the lungs and used her electrical abilities to superheat the area. She fried your alveoli. No matter how much you breathe, you're not losing any carbon dioxide and you're not getting any oxygen,” I frowned.

“I'm sure your nanites are working desperately, but something as delicate and finite as repairing the tiny sacs in your lungs is going to take too long, especially since without oxygen your brain will shut down. If your brain shuts down, Panacea will stop working. This is going to be a long death, Samson... I'm sorry, I don't know what to say.” I placed my hand atop his and gazed down into his tormented face. Samson's shaky fingertips wrapped around my hand, dagger and all, and drew it slowly toward his own neck.

“It... hurts. You talk... too much. End...” The last word that escaped him sounded like a crackling squeak, as though Samson just swallowed a piece of burning coal and washed it down with a healthy dose of helium. I repositioned the tip of my dagger against the side of his neck; the point indented his skin directly near his brain stem.

“Understood,” I responded plainly and tensed the muscles in my arm, driving the dagger through Samson's flesh. His body jerked one final time before falling completely limp in my arms; I stood and shoved my dagger into its sheath on my hip. I found myself secretly grateful that I left Elsa behind. For that small child, witnessing the emotions and thoughts of a dying man would have assuredly caused her immense grief.

As I thought back to the hazy memory of the young girl reaching out and sobbing for the hyped warrior when I slew him, I briefly wondered what she felt or heard in the minds of those psychotic afflicted. Unfortunately, I needed to place my musing on hold and focus on the situation at hand.

As I crouched and prepared to exit the elevator tower with stealthy haste, I offered one last glance to Samson's corpse. *"Rest well,"* I thought to myself.

File 31: Out of the Frying Pan...

The artificial incandescence emanating from the city's various light sources painted a painful glare on my night vision augment as I neared the archway that led to the city's central square. I deactivated the the nanite and flattened my back against the large stone arch. I cautiously peered around the corner into the city square while clicking my telescopic sight and auditory enhancement to life. As the lenses of my pupils dilated and constricted to adjust to various bright or dim details from extreme distances, I slowly scanned the immediate vicinity.

The market seemed to be the focal point of the invasion; a small group of ten soldiers stood in perfect rows and columns and occupied a large portion of the central square. The rigid nature of their stance indicated strict military training, and their uniforms certainly appeared to match the feel of an armed military. Their faces from the tips of their noses down to the dips above their collar bones were concealed by skin-tight, black latex masks resembling the lower half of balaclava.

From the tallest man located in the back corner to the shortest at the front, the soldiers' eyes radiated a sense of focus and resolve. If any of the men still possessed hair, the thin strips barely poked down from underneath dark black berets. A silver emblem embossed the center of the berets. I clenched my lower lip between my teeth; rage slowly clouded my head when I recognized the symbol as the same one used to denote our mercenary group many years before.

An eagle, presumably a bald eagle, spread its wings across the circular emboss. Its head faced its left wing, and a giant striped shield rested across its chest. At the base of the emblem, the phrase “E Pluribus Unum” shimmered in a far lighter metal. In fact, the phrase almost glowed like white light from the decoration itself. Bradich once told me the letters belonged to a dead language, and formed the words “Out of many, One,” but I considered most of his historical myth more amusing than informative and disregarded it.

Thick black vests covered the soldiers' heavy uniforms; various tints of gray peppered their attire which, I assumed, helped conceal them in the rocky terrain that covered most of the planet. Also, unlike Raze's minions, most of the imposing gentlemen standing at attention possessed firearms. From semi-automatic machine guns to six-shot revolvers, at least half the men secured some form of gun on their shoulders, in their hands, or strapped to their hips. That certainly raised the stakes of the game.

At the head of the entourage of ten soldiers stood a slender, well toned man towering at least six feet three inches. His well-defined biceps and triceps popped since he stood with both arms folded just beneath his chest. The same black beret sported by his soldiers rested atop his head, though small copper strands of hair jutted from the sides and down his forehead. A thin steel necklace hung around his neck and fell between the ridge dividing his pectorals.

Other than the beret, the man at the front of the troops donned far different raiment than his troops. A green tank top hugged his shoulders and chest before tucking into a pair of dark, forest-green camouflaged pants held at his waist by a simple black belt. Twin thick black combat boots rested on either of the man's feet to complete his ensemble. An intricate tattoo that began at the tops of his shoulders and raced down either of his arms decorated his pale skin in a bright blue tribal pattern.

From my position, even with my telescopic sight, I detected no weaponry on his person; though when marching with an escort as large as that man possessed, weapons might have been a bit overkill. The stranger's steel blue eyes stared forward at Mayor Trumark, the large congregation of Loftsborough's citizens standing behind him, and Crelyos' bulky figure standing next to the mayor. Crelyos clenched his fists so tightly that I feared he might cut into his palm or break his prosthetic limb.

"Reasonable? Oh goodness young ones these days... What do you mean be reasonable? You drop into my city like it's a terrorist warehouse, wave your guns around, start making demands, and then tell me to be reasonable when I refuse them?!" Mayor Trumark's dusty-old-man-voice reached my heightened auditory sense from across the football field's length that separated us. Disdain and irritation saturated his tone.

"Let us consider the options, Mayor. Either you release Raze and his subordinates to my care, or I take him by force with no guarantee that the citizens of your fair city will remain unharmed. Which sounds more reasonable to you?" The man with his arms folded replied with an eerie calm that unsettled me even more than Raze's eccentric accent.

"Sarge, stop ignoring me! I asked you a question! Why are you working for Bradich? Do you know what he's done to the world? Do you know how many people died?" Crelyos stepped forward; his frustrated shouts echoed with little regard to the conversation transpiring between the mayor and the sleek-muscled man he identified as Sarge.

"In due time, Crelyos. Right now I am negotiating the release of one of my comrades," Sarge unfolded his right arm and lifted it in a halting gesture toward the blond mercenary. I arched a single brow at the spectacle playing out like dramatic choreography.

The sound of heavy thuds snapped my attention from the conversation to the path leading to the archway against which I hid. The methodic intervals of the thuds indicated marching footfalls; it was a patrol. I swung my partially exposed torso back into the shadows and flattened my back against the stone. The footsteps drew nearer, so I softened the sounds of my breathing and ordered my muscles to remain absolutely still. With my head turned toward the archway's opening, I watched as one of Sarge's men, clad in the same balaclava as his comrades, marched through the arch mere feet to my left side. His eyes ardently swept the area.

"Please spin left..." I thought to myself as he began the turn to head back into the city square. If the soldier's heel spun him to the right, his gaze would inadvertently fall upon my hiding place, but a swift spin to the left would leave me safe from detection. As luck would have it, the soldier drew back his left foot and pivoted upon it, twisting his body to the left before marching hastily back into the city to continue his patrol.

"Come now, Mayor Trumark. My proposal is more than generous. Not only will I rid Loftsborough of Raze and his brigands, but I will not so much as turn over one of the many loose stones scattered about your city." Sarge continued his conversation with Trumark. When I glanced back around the corner of the arch, Sarge failed to offer Crelyos even passing recognition during his negotiation with Loftsborough's leader.

"You know what, Sarge? It doesn't matter what Trumark says, I'm not letting you take Raze! He told us what would happen if your organization got their hands on him, and I won't allow him to be killed. He deserves the chance to change his ways and go back to being his old self!" Crelyos stepped between the mayor and Sarge. The copper-haired military leader finally acknowledged Crelyos' presence with an aggravated glare.

"Is that so? A word of advice, Crelyos. Do not stand in my way. I have orders. I will kill you if I must." Sarge slowly unfolded his arms and brought his hands to his sides. I detected a brief tension in his core; Sarge was ready to fight, if necessary, in order to complete his objective.

A white coat's sudden flutter in the distance drew my attention from the two former military men. A hundred feet from Eugene's mansion, Oswald stood among a few of the town's citizens. Aside from the mass gathered behind the mayor in the town center, small pockets of bystanders crowded the outskirts of the city square curiously murmuring to one another about the events displayed before them.

I leaned out a little farther from behind the arch; though the action increased my risk of detection, it allowed me to quickly calculate the number of hostiles occupying Loftsborough. Four clusters of citizens stood littered about the outskirts of the city; each possessed its own pair of armed guards who stood with imposing stature at the crowd's left and right. Other than the patrolling soldier with whom I almost became far too familiar, six men marched in specific intervals around the central square. Adding to that number the ten men at sharp attention behind Sarge, I concluded the enemy forces numbered at approximately twenty five. That was five more than Samson mentioned. I needed my rifle; I needed to reach Oswald.

I gripped the dagger at my hip and slowly slid it from

its sheath. The smooth whisper of steel gliding across synthetic leather traveled to my ears like a subtle breeze. As the methodic thud of boots clicking against the steel ground tickled my hearing a second time, I pressed my back against the wall once again. This time, however, my dagger readily waited in my right hand.

Like clockwork, Sarge's patrol stepped through the archway and scanned the darkness that encompassed the elevator shaft and its command tower. Either the soldier possessed a night vision augment, or he simply watched for motion in the inky blackness. Either way, whatever vision he possessed soon ceased functioning at all. As before, the man drew his left foot back to pivot; he intended to return to his patrol along the city's outskirts with no incident to report. Unfortunately, we were in disagreement on how we envisioned the next five seconds to proceed. As he twisted his body and brought his broad back into full view, I spun from my concealed position and tossed my left hand around his face. His body's natural turn brought his mouth securely against my palm as I finished my spin and came to rest with my chest securely pressed against his back. Before his lips uttered even a muffled cry, I drew the sharpened edge of my long dagger across his wind pipe. A hiss of air and gurgle of blood escaped the unfortunate patrolman, but even that ended quickly when the same motion that drew my blade across his throat brought its tip to rest against the back of his skull. A firm push with my right hand and a pull with my left sent the dagger crunching through bone and into the portion of his brain housing his restorative nanite.

His body twitched against me for a few seconds before falling limp; my legs tensed to support the additional weight when his corpse dropped against my chest. I swiftly yanked my dagger from the back of his head, and after returning it to its sheath, I wrapped my arms in a tight embrace around his chest and dragged him into the nearby shadows. After properly tucking away his body, I carefully crept back to the archway and took a deep breath. The distant conversation between my comrade and his former commander echoed in the back of my mind. Though my senses remained piqued through the activation of my nanites, I focused my concentration solely on infiltrating the city. I slowly peered around the corner and surveyed the patrols.

Once certain that darting into the city square would not compromise me, I turned the corner of the archway. I kept low and drifted through the shadows that Loftsborough's abstract architecture provided, traversing the city's perimeter like a purposeful specter. I encountered my first obstacle at one of the larger houses decorating the town square. The tall home likely belonged to one of the "wealthier" scavengers of Loftsborough, and it offered an impressive vantage point at its peak. A large, flat area crowned the building and simultaneously served as its terrace. The owner probably ventured to the roof to admire the view and soak up the faux rays cast by the city's glaring artificial sun.

Unfortunately, as I recognized its tactical boons so did Sarge's soldiers Sarge's. A single man stood alert atop the structure; his domineering gaze cast an overwatch across much of the city square, and he patrolled the perimeter of the rooftop in a steady, well-trained pattern. I annoyedly sighed at the difficulty of the infiltration and glanced back toward the archway from which I emerged. It would certainly only be a matter of time before the patrols were due to report, and with the efficiency of the unit, a patrol or two failing to report likely meant "game over" for anyone brazen enough to challenge Sarge's outfit.

"Bring it on," I thought.

When the guard briefly shifted his attention to one of the other sectors of the city square, I made my move. I fluttered in utter silence across the steel ground, and within seconds I pressed my back against the wall of the house. I shifted around the corners until I reached the side of the building opposite Sarge and the large group of soldiers. The chill breeze from the slit between the city's metal plates cooled the parts of my flesh not covered by my black tank top or cargo pants. But there was no time for shivering.

I steadied my breath and glanced up to assess my options. A window, situated roughly five feet below the square lining of the roof, piqued my interest. It likely belonged to a makeshift attic directly below the roof itself. I glanced to the nearby door leading into the domicile; the idea of maneuvering through the unknown territory of the home and finding the attic, while plausible, struck me as risky endeavor, not to mention a waste of time. Instead, I enhanced the muscles in my arms and legs with my Supersoldier implant and gripped the various abstract protrusions which riddled the exterior wall.

With the trained silence of an assassin, I scaled the building, and upon reaching the window I desired, I quietly slid it open and hopped inside. The attic's musty metallic odor filled my nostrils and suggested its owner rarely used it even when Loftsborough was not facing one of its many crises. If the pungent smell nearly overpowered me, I possessed little time before the wind carried the smell to the vigilant guard a mere five feet above the cavity in which I stood.

I swiftly hooked the back of my legs on either side of the window sill and sat with my back facing the chill air outside; I spread my thighs far enough apart to properly brace myself, and after taking one final deep breath, I arched my back until I hung upside down from the window itself. I once more drew my lengthened knife from its home at my waist, and as my hair spilled like an ink waterfall toward the ground, I began tapping the blade of the dagger in set intervals against the building's metal plates.

The resounding rings reminded me of clinking coins, and not much time passed before the sound's intended effect bore fruit. "Huh?" I heard my target's curious grunt high above me. His heavy footsteps carried him to the edge of his patrol perimeter; no doubt he intended to peer over the edge and confirm some mundane source responsible for the noise, release a sigh of relief, and return to his post until the occupation of Loftsborough concluded and he could return home with his platoon to enjoy a round of sludge. As with the previous guard, I disagreed with the course of those events, and I considered myself to be rather persuasive.

No sooner did the soldier's head peer over the side of the building than I tightened the muscles in my abdomen and curled upward with the motion of a hanging sit-up. After transferring the momentum from my core to my shoulder, and eventually the extension of my arm, I launched the dagger with practiced expertise directly toward his forehead. The “thwack” as the blade sank into his skull was quickly followed by the whoosh of his lifeless body toppling over the roof's edge.

I desired as little compromise as possible, and the loud thud of a body as it fell several stories to the ground struck me as an unacceptable risk of detection. With my core muscles clenched and my body virtually horizontal, I steeled myself for the impact of his descent. My extended arms encircled him, but the force behind his fall broke the firm domination my abdomen possessed over gravity. My body forcefully arched back into an upside down vertical mess.

Even with my Supersoldier augment, my physical strength barely equated to that of a normal human bodybuilder. Others with naturally strong frames or an exceedingly advanced nanite possessed near superhuman levels of physical prowess. People like Crelyos, for example. In the moment when I strained to keep my legs hooked to the window and grunted under the stress of the dead soldier's body weighing me down, I envied those bastards.

"Buddy, you need to go on a diet," I thought to myself as I struggled to draw his figure flush with my own. Without the dangling weight, the curl of my abdomen with augmented muscles proved just strong enough to fold the two of us into the attic with a sit-up I would assuredly never forget. Once inside, I retrieved my long dagger from the front of his skull and shoved it through his medulla oblongata to ensure his expiration.

After sheathing the weapon, I glanced out the window toward Eugene's mansion and Oswald standing mere feet from its protective confines. I descended to the ground and resumed my stealthy endeavor. The remaining distance proved uneventful, as the number of guards thinned the further from the heart of the occupation I traveled. The one or two that may have proved threatening simply lacked the expert attention needed to detect my movements. Within a few moments, I pressed my back against the rear wall of Eugene's home.

I slowly twisted around the corner and grabbed a tiny pebble from one of the building's loose stone components. I took careful aim and drew my arm back with every intention of beaming the tiny rock straight into the back of Oswald's head. A gentle toss likely would have sufficed, but the idea of causing him mild physical discomfort provided me with a great sense of justice in lieu of the nightmare I endured thanks to his experimental let's-kill-Ihlia serum. Unfortunately, the moment I lifted my hand to practice my fastball pitching technique against the old codger, he extended his hand behind him and motioned exotically to inform me of his keen awareness of my presence.

"How the hell does he do that? Honestly..." I thought to myself as I coiled back into the shadow of our temporary abode.

I assumed Oswald turned to head in my direction, for the sound of one of the nearby guards erupted sharply, "Hey, old man, where do you think you're going? Get back here with the rest of the trash!" The voice was well-trained. It possessed the illusion of a serious threat and the authoritative depth of a command one naturally desired to obey; of course, that only applied to weak-willed civilian types. Oswald was many things, weak-willed was not one of them.

The old codger's voice rose up immediately with a calm but logical exposition. It possessed all the points and evidence needed to convince a rational mind of its validity. The topic, unfortunately, made me slam my palm into my face, an action which accompanied my aggravated sigh.

"Good brutish captor, might I remind you that even we trash have necessary bodily functions to which we must attend? Given my age, my prostate tends to flare up. When it does, it creates a powerful need to urinate. Unless you are suggesting that I expel my urine on you or another innocent bystander, I suggest you allow me time to do my business." Oswald's matter-of-fact tone left the sentry speechless for a few seconds, but eventually he fired off a rebuttal.

"W-well, uh. Look, there's a bucket. Take that bucket and go over there somewhere, but make sure that I can see you! No funny business!" Though my position prevented me from witnessing the spectacle, I assumed the bewildered guard struggled to make sense of Oswald's long-winded explanation for the simple need to piss. When he finally decided to avoid making heads or tails of the speech, he caved in and gestured somewhere remote but in visual range for the good doctor to expel his "liquid."

"You dare to have me urinate in front of so many? Including women and small children? You are a fiend, sir, but I can respect the compromise. I shall walk over to the corner of this building so that only you can see me. I shan't be but a moment," Oswald responded.

The brief moment when Oswald lifted the alleged bucket created a small scrape; the old codger's approaching footsteps soon followed the sound, and I assumed he had conveniently chosen my location to perform his business. Sure enough, the towering figure of my longtime friend and nanite surgeon appeared. I prepared to speak, but the sound of the doctor's trousers unzipping completely changed the words that hissed from my lips in a furious whisper.

"I thought that was just a ruse to get over here! What do

you think you're doing?!" I exclaimed quietly.

"A ruse? Think of it more like fortuitous coincidence. Now, more importantly, where have you been?" Oswald's stern whisper belied his apparent concern. The idea that Oswald worried for my safety might have brought a smile to my lips in less dire circumstances.

"No time for that, Doc. Where's my rifle?" I glanced in the doctor's direction. My gaze met with the sight of the good doctor fishing through his trousers. I immediately twisted my head in the opposite direction just in time to avoid the sight of Oswald's liquid expulsion. Turning my head offered little refuge from the sound, however, and I made a distinct mental note to do something horrible to the old codger later as punishment.

"Ahh. Oh, yes, your rifle. It's up in your room, of course. I could scarce believe that you left it in my trailer when you went out; you had me worried something terrible, you know," Oswald whispered.

I moved to ascend the side of Eugene's home long before Oswald finished speaking. I needed to reach the top floor, enter through one of the windows, and retrieve my sniper rifle. It so happened that with my room at the apex of the late Eugene's mansion, retrieving my rifle and finding an excellent sniper's nest coincided. Upon witnessing my swift action, Oswald whispered, "You're not thinking of doing anything rash, are you? There are a great number of soldiers in Sarge's employ, and they are merely here to retrieve Raze and their hyped. I fail to see the logic of interrupting their endeavor."

"There is none, but Crelyos wanted Raze alive. If anyone is going to kill Raze, it's going to be me. Besides, you know that lug Crelyos will do something stupid to protect his old comrade. He could be injured or killed," I responded plainly.

"Hmm?" Oswald laced his inflection with accusation. When I heard the sound of his zipper enclosing his business, I glanced down to see one of his brows arched curiously.

"What?" I fired back with subconscious indignation, briefly pausing in the middle of my ascent.

"Oh, nothing. I didn't think you worried about someone so much. Especially with your quest for revenge superseding all other emotions and thought," Oswald drenched his tone in sarcasm. I felt my face flush, though discerning if the source of the heat stemmed from anger or embarrassment proved impossible.

"I'm not worried about him! I just need him to be healthy if he's going with us so he doesn't slow us down! Besides, his fighting talent and nanite are both very useful, so we need him," I snapped back and resumed my climb up the back of the house.

"Yes, of course. What was I thinking?" Oswald responded with a soft chuckle beneath his breath.

The sound of the disgruntled guard interrupted our conversation. “Hey, you've been over there long enough. Get back here.” Oswald offered the guard a dismissive remark regarding the brutish captor's impatience, promptly grabbed his bucket, and trotted back to the group of hostages.

I muttered a few things beneath my breath regarding Oswald's obvious sarcastic replies to my perfectly reasonable explanations. While I scaled the wall, I bit my lower lip and tacked another note onto my compiled list to make sure I extracted an extra horrible revenge on the old codger to quell my irritation. Inside the familiar territory of my room, I found my rifle propped neatly against the bed and slowly encircled my fingers around its lengthy barrel. The sensation felt like regaining a lost limb. I sighed with relief before searching for the various boxes of ammunition I stored for safekeeping.

Once I tucked a few bullets neatly away into my deep cargo pockets, I knelt down in front of the window from which I used to watch Crelyos play merrily with children during a more peaceful time. I might have been amazed at how quickly the dark clouds of conflict shadowed peaceful days if not for occupational experience. Unfortunately time made the best teacher, so I understood all too well. That was simply how the world worked.

Careful not to extend the muzzle of the rifle out the window itself, I activated my telescopic sight nanite and surveyed the small box of visible environment that comprised my kill zone. Crelyos and Sarge continued arguing, though the distance between them shortened with every one of Crelyos' obscene hand gestures and annoyed roars. Despite the blond mercenary's slow advances, Sarge remained unphased and unintimidated. He stood his ground. Though I half-expected as much from someone of Sarge's stature and experience, it still surprised me a little to see him completely unaffected by Crelyos' daunting physique.

With my new vantage point, I beheld two slender figures far to Sarge's left that stood out from the rest of his entourage. One of them belonged to the woman that nearly dropped me down the elevator shaft with her flashy swordplay. The figure standing next to her looked identical to her in every respect save one. He was male.

The male portion of the duo wore his hair in a similar style to his counterpart, and like his counterpart, he donned sleek leather that hugged the contours of his body. He appeared frail, so much so that even his skinny body resembled the woman's. He possessed neither the large muscular frame of Crelyos, nor the chiseled muscles that covered Sarge's figure. Instead, he looked for all the world like a woman with a small pectorals. If not for the clearly defined Adam's apple and square shape of his jaw, I would have chalked him up as a flat-chested female.

"Crelyos, you're always writing checks your ass can't cash. I will ask you one more time to step aside. I will take Raze, I will leave, and you can go back to your blissfully ignorant existence. If you refuse, you will suffer the consequences." Sarge lifted one of his hands in front of his face. He drew his thumb and forefinger together as though he prepared to snap his fingers.

"You can do whatever you want to me. I'll die before I let you take Raze," Crelyos dropped into his fighting stance. With his fists clenched and his shoulders parted, the blond mercenary was no more than ten seconds from leaping wildly into combat with total disregard for any form of strategy. Normally, the action drew an endearing smile from my lips. This time, however, something seemed horribly amiss. Crelyos misunderstood a very important piece of information; I felt it. If I understood Sarge's character as I expected I did, the situation was about to go from bad to worse.

"That's exactly what I'm talking about, Crelyos. Ignorance. Who said anything about doing something to you? We're old comrades, you and I. I don't want to hurt you. At least, not your body. Men, take aim. Women and children first. Fire on my command." The soldiers standing in rank and file drew their assorted firearms and took aim on the crowd standing behind Crelyos. The small children, already sniffling and shaking, clung to their corresponding families and released fearful cries. The women gasped and screamed while coiling down around their young offspring.

The hesitant men stepped forward to shield their women; their valor was impressive. In fact, of all those involved in the horrifying threat, only Crelyos froze in his tracks. The color drained from his face, and the very muscles in his legs quaked beneath his weight. As I feared, Crelyos still saw Sarge as the gracious commander with whom he served in the military. The idea that Sarge became a ruthless thug in Bradich's employ failed to register, but I watched with a concerned furrow in my brow as the reality opened up before him.

"Sarge... you wouldn't. You can't involve innocent people. This has nothing to do with them! Fight me like a man!" Crelyos stammered.

"That's ineffective. I'm sure I could obliterate you, but I told you, I don't want to harm you. You have so much to learn about the world. I've always felt I needed to teach you more than anyone else that served under my command. You're like some naive child that thinks everyone in the world is going to operate on your sense of values and morals. It's infuriating," Sarge growled. "Regardless, the bottom line is I have a job to do and I will take any course of action required to fulfill that job. It's just a bonus that I'll be able to open your eyes and fulfill my mission in one fell swoop. Remember, Crelyos, the blood of these innocents is on your hands. I hope the life of one man is worth the blood of so many. Ready, men! Aim!"

Though Sarge's words rang harsh, I secretly agreed with him. Crelyos colored his world with his sense of valor and personal code. Unlike Sarge, who apparently felt very strongly about destroying that code, I felt an inexplicable desire to protect it.

I trained the tip of my rifle on Sarge's temple in perfect

timing with his command for his men to aim. I felt as though, for a moment, I stood among his ranks taking aim with them despite our significantly different targets. Sarge's fingers grew tense; I anticipated his snap, the snap that served as the death sentence carried out by a merciless executioner. It would herald a unanimous cry of suffering throughout Loftsborough. But in that moment right before he prepared to dispatch the many lives gathered in the city square, I squeezed my trigger.

File 32: ...and into the Fire.

My shoulders jerked back with the recoil of the shot within the small confines of the room. Though the rumble shook the bed and echoed across the walls, nothing garnered my attention more than what happened at my bullet's destination. The shot approached the stalwart commander of Loftsborough's invading forces with pinpoint accuracy, but it curved.

Though I lacked the wherewithal to activate my Cognitive Accelerator, I clearly watched the bullet's trajectory rapidly deteriorate as it approached Sarge. By the time it struck a solid surface, a gulf of several feet separated the man's head and the bullet as it ricocheted off the city's metal ground with a high-pitched whine.

"Not finite telekinesis again... but how did he know I was firing? Is it impulse?" I inwardly groaned. Whatever the cause, Sarge stood alive and well in wake of the shot. With a quick jerk of his neck, Sarge's eyes locked onto my relative position with the trained skill I expected from a soldier of his caliber.

"Nomeiko, Izuma, the window!" Sarge lifted a hand and pointed toward the very floor of the very building from which I sniped. The twins wordlessly responded with the swiftness of a serpent's strike. The woman sprinted across the city square like lightning, synchronously drawing her blade as she reached the midpoint between her starting position and my nest. Her twin trailed behind at a noticeably slower pace, though not unimpressive in its own right.

In addition to earning Sarge's attention, the group of soldiers with readied rifles seemed shockingly distracted, too. Crelyos took advantage of the opportunity and leapt to action... literally. The bulging muscles in his legs propelled him forward into the midst of the boggled troops standing in rank and file, and at the apex of his mighty bound, the former soldier released a booming roar and drew back his right arm. Though I expected my blond comrade to perform a recklessly courageous feat at any given moment, that expectation did not prevent my surprise. Instead of engaging the lot in ferocious and bloody combat, Crelyos rammed his humming right arm into the ground in the dead center of Sarge's army. The metal groaned and creaked for a split second before exploding into near microscopic fragments like dust glittering in Loftsborough's artificial sunlight.

The dome of chaff easily compared in radius to the explosion of a "Little Kid," and the chorus of alarmed and desperate cries in the wake of Crelyos's Harmonic Resonance certainly resembled the final shouts of a Little Kid's victims. As the metallic dust plumed into a cloud, it cast a sparkling fog around an enormous crater in Loftsborough's central square. The shocked sounds of Sarge's troops transformed into elongated howls which drowned in the blustering gusts of wind whipping through the city.

Crelyos had used his nanite to punch a giant hole clean through Loftsborough's bottom. Considering the immense thickness of the steel used to craft the town's shell, my eyes understandably widened at the prospect of his Harmonic Resonance possessing enough force to simulate the impact of a ballistic missile. It also stood to reason that the source of the droning screams belonged to the various soldiers as they plummeted to an untimely demise into churning quicksand several hundred feet below the city's new gaping wound, but where were Crelyos and Sarge?

The initial blast from Crelyos' impact provided enough of a diversion for the people gathered in the city square to disperse. Mayor Trumark ushered them into their homes or the nearest available shelter, but not before their uproarious panic created a symphony of surprised gasps and horrified screams. Like their steadily rising cries, a faint but firm twinge of panic slowly built in the pit of my stomach. I frantically sought to pierce my gaze through the blot of chaff but to no avail. In the midst of my search, a different glint far outside the chaff cloud's radius caught my attention.

It belonged to one of Sarge's men; a sniper sat poised atop one of the many homes in the city square. The lens of his telescopic sight reflected stray beams of light from Loftsborough's large incandescent sun. He busily swept his rifle to and fro probably searching for the same person as I, but I conjectured he sought Crelyos for completely different and wholly unacceptable reasons. I instinctively drew my rifle up and placed the iron sights between his eyes using my augmented vision.

I slid the bolt action back to eject the shell from my wasted shot against Sarge; I reloaded a new round, exhaled calmly, and steadied my hands before offering a gentle squeeze to my weapon's trigger. The soldier's head shot back as though it ripped clean off his shoulders, and after a gratuitous spray of blood, he crumpled lifelessly to the ground. The familiar action of taking down an enemy sniper eerily calmed my nerves, and when I returned my enhanced sight to the settling dust cloud, a most relieving sight waited to greet me.

The two former soldiers hung from the enormous crater as though their lives depended on their grip, and in all likelihood, they did. Crelyos swayed at the base of the hole where several straggling soldiers clutched at jagged metal for dear life. One by one, their holds faltered, and they issued their final cries during their drop into the merciless sea of sand. The backlash from Crelyos's Harmonic Resonance had torn the skin-colored latex from his cybernetic arm until only a few scant strips remained in an eerie pattern. The limb's metal grip clutched the razor sharp surface of the crater he had created.

Sarge's arms hung over the top of the crater on the still-flat surface of Loftsborough's ground; he clutched at the metal plates which made up the city floor. Though the surface was sheer, for some reason Sarge managed to effortlessly maintain his hold on the flat metal plates. It took only a few seconds for the seasoned commander to draw himself up from Crelyos' hole, and by the time my blond comrade joined him on the city floor, Sarge already stood as composed as ever with his arms folded over his chest.

The moment I confirmed Crelyos' safety, a figure darkened my window. The katana-bearing woman crouched atop the sill with a stoic expression painted on her thin face. Though she possessed enviable exotic beauty, she offered me little time to admire her. I released my father's hunting rifle and blurred my hands to my waist to grip the hilt of my remaining dagger; her hand flashed to her side with equivalent speed. No, she was faster. She lunged into the room and snatched her katana from its scabbard in a blinding swipe.

I lifted my dagger in the nick of time and caught the silvery edge of her blade with a sharp clang. As I stared at her emotionless visage for a second, a vicious pain suddenly streaked through my midsection like fire. A spray of blood splashed from a fresh gash across my stomach, and in the seconds that followed, I quickly put the pieces of the puzzle together. In the time it took me to raise my dagger, she had swung not merely once but twice! Her speed left me dazed but not nearly as much as the crippling shock that coursed through me in the next instant.

Her katana sparked with the snaking blue electrical veins I perceived when I first beheld her. As the blade connected with my flesh and a second time with my extended dagger, the pulses of arching lightning coursed through my body and sent me into violent convulsions.

My legs quaked, and my hands clenched into useless heaps of rigid flesh. My lack of flexibility in light of the electric pulses provided the sleek fighter ample time to deliver a powerful spinning back kick to the center of my chest. When her heel thudded against my sternum, the blow launched me into the window on the opposite side of the room. My shoulder blades shattered the half-open glass frame, and I stared at the olive-skinned beauty who stalked toward me like a cat toying with its prey.

Though I regained control of my body, my muscles continued twitching intermittently; the electric shock she emitted was no laughing matter, and its effects partially extended even after contact. I crawled out the shattered window frame and grabbed the roof's protruding overhang, and with a firm push off the sill, I rolled onto its subtle incline. The cold breeze tore through my hair and against my healing wound with a vicious chill. As I backed away from the roof's edge, the sound of footsteps behind me quickly diverted my attention.

The male half of the alleged Storm Duo rushed at me with the purposeful motions of a trained fighter. Unlike his sister, however, his movements barely surpassed human limitations and his muscles operated with easy-to-read normality. Without so much as activating my Cognitive Accelerator, I swiveled to the outside to avoid his right hook. As his arm passed next to my left ear, I brought my left fist up into his diaphragm. His forward momentum and the propulsion behind my augmented muscles caused my fist to thud into his chest with a boisterous crack. Shakily, the man sank to his knees, and

I stepped forward to drive my dagger through his skull.

Unfortunately, as soon as my first step collided with the metallic roof, my vision blurred. A queasiness built in the pit of my stomach, and I soon found myself applying extraordinary effort to merely remain standing. My empty left hand shot to my forehead; I plastered my palm across my eye as though applying pressure might stop the world from spinning in front of me.

Eventually, I succumbed to the dizziness and dropped to a single knee to keep from toppling over in atop the glacis formed by the roof's slope. Though the man remained doubled over a few feet from my location, I could not even stand under the effects of such intense vertigo, let alone finish him. The light clack of boot heels slowly approached from behind; the female had joined us atop the roof, though I doubted she intended to join us for midday sunbathing or friendly gossip.

"Izuma, do not interfere again. I do not need your meager assistance or your half-assed nanite." The woman stepped forward and placed her boot against my shoulder. She applied pressure, and I toppled to the side with a confused groan. The young man she called Izuma finally recovered from the severe blow I dealt him enough to struggle to his feet. He bowed his head solemnly and took a few steps away from me and the woman.

"As... you wish... big sister," He responded between sputters and coughs.

"You may be feeling a bit under the weather. You shouldn't have let my brother get so close to you, I'm afraid," The woman grinned and sent a swift kick into the nearly-sealed gash on my stomach that she inflicted back in my temporary quarters.

I grunted and protectively curled inward to the best of my ability. It felt as though an oncoming train had barreled into me. Considering the only damage I suffered stemmed from the woman's katana and electric shock, I grew more confused the more my mind dwelt on it. It took several seconds for my assailant's words to fully sink into my disoriented brain. Close to me?

"Why... is that?" I stammered.

"Nomeiko... Sis, is it really necessary to divulge? Just kill her, as per our orders," Izuma spoke up after fully regaining his composure.

"Quiet, useless brother. The order was to eliminate the sniper, and eliminate her I shall. I want to see what kind of pain I can inflict on her, first, though," Nomeiko responded harshly, and as she returned her attention to me from her apparently "useless" brother, she placed the tip of her katana just above the metal roof and channeled her electrical abilities through the blade.

The hot, blue light sparked and cracked as the bolts jumped from the tip of her sword to the roof; they discharged harmlessly over the expanse of metal, but they were still powerful enough that I felt a faint buzz against my cheek and exposed midriff. Either the charge she emitted lacked the power to injure, or the surface area of the metal roof extended too far for the charge to carry.

"Impressive... but I know that trick... already," I groaned.

"Indeed. As you can probably guess, my nanite converts my bioelectric field, which is a chemical process, into an actual electromagnetic field. In addition to revving up the power a lot, it allows me far more control over the currents than the normal involuntary functions they serve. My brother's nanite, however, is a bit more complicated." Nomeiko scraped the tip of her blade across the metal rooftop; an ear piercing screech resounded.

When she spoke, her lips curled into a devious grin, "His nanite produces and manipulates sound waves. More specifically, the vibrations responsible for sound waves."

"Boring, heard that one already, too. That crater down there wasn't from the city spontaneously exploding. My ally, Crelyos, matches up harmonic resonance frequencies instantly and disintegrates the objects using vibratory waves," I strained to form the words, but at the very least, my voice recovered enough that I could speak without dramatic coughs and groans. Still, I was far from a condition worthy of standing or fighting back. I needed to keep her talking a little longer.

“So that's what that was. See, brother? Why can't you be more useful, like the guy who's about to die down there?” Nomeiko quirked a condescending brow at her brother, who stood silently with his head bowed. She giggled sadistically beneath her breath and returned her gaze to me, “Unfortunately, my brother's nanite works a bit differently. He uses preset vibration frequencies which he consciously controls. At their lowest frequency, they can cause tremors on surfaces or in bodies. At their highest frequencies, however... well, you're suffering those effects now.”

“I'll give you a hint: it directly affects the eardrums and sense of orientation. Just a quick pass of his hand and whoosh, he can turn your world upside down!” Nomeiko's giggles perfectly belied the pleasure she derived in the torture of others.

“I see, so it doesn't matter if he actually hits your or not. As long as he gets close, his nanites will take care of the rest,” I finished the line of thought and glanced toward the submissive Izuma.

His head, still bowed in avid respect to his older sister, lifted only faintly until his narrow eyes met mine. It lasted a brief instant before he returned to staring at the rooftop, but in the second our eyes locked, I perceived his grave concern and anxious spirit. He confirmed my suspicions when next he spoke, interrupting his sister's cruel laughter and sword scrapes.

“Sis... she'll be functional soon. Something's off about

her; I don't trust this feeling. Please hurry and kill her so we can go back to Commander Sarge's side!" The desperation in his tone leaked like a dripping faucet. I might have offered a passing grin if not for the poker face I fought to maintain throughout the experience. Izuma's worrisome emotions were quite justified.

"Just a few more seconds..." I thought to myself.

"Hm? You're awfully demanding today, brother dearest. Commander Sarge needs our help about as much as I need yours. Although..." Nomeiko folded one arm across her underdeveloped chest and gripped her opposite elbow with her free hand.

From our vantage point on the roof, her gaze swept out over the central square of Loftsborough as though she worked to hastily analyze the crater formed by my blonde comrade. I twisted from my position on the ground and followed her stare. When she spoke again, her tone possessed an acute curiosity, "Although I wonder what kind of side effects a destructive force like that must have. Surely it takes its toll on him somehow."

"His right arm," I rebutted.

I began testing my stability by swiveling my head back and forth; when my vision moved from the sky to the city square without the accompanying vertigo, I released a relieved sigh. When I stopped, my gaze rested on Crelyos still engaged in combat in the city square. The strips of false flesh that hung from his prosthetic arm had vanished completely, and he used his fully revealed cybernetic limb to make short work of the remaining stragglers in Sarge's platoon.

The few guards which I failed to exterminate during my infiltration fired at the former soldier from afar, but Crelyos used his metal arm to cover his vitals as he closed the distance to each of them. I witnessed one attempt to swerve behind one of the buildings for cover; he obviously failed to understand the nature of Crelyos' ability from his former display. No sooner did the soldier think himself safe with his back pressed against one of Loftsborough's odd buildings than the corner of the structure exploded in a spray of infinitesimal metal fragments.

Crelyos cleaved through the building with a single punch and continued the blow through to the unfortunate soldier's back. Though the soldier cried out in pain and his back snapped with a deafening crunch, Crelyos did not activate his Harmonic Resonance. Or, perhaps, he could not? After careful thought, I deduced that the Harmonic Resonance probably could not activate in rapid succession. After blasting the wall to pieces, it needed a small window of time before reactivating. But how long was that time? Two seconds? Three? Even longer?

To my surprise, Sarge remained inert through the entire ordeal. As Crelyos ducked and weaved from one soldier to the next and eliminated them, the copper-headed commander stood silently in his original position. He maintained his folded arms, and I could have sworn an amused grin touched one corner of his mouth as he watched his own men fall to Crelyos' unbridled rampage. What was his game?

I glanced up at Nomeiko, who still seemed confused with my limited explanation. Even as she watched Crelyos obliterate the men around him using only his cybernetic right arm, she failed to piece together my words. I hardly blamed her; I spent many years next to the blond mercenary without so much as suspecting he even possessed a faux limb, let alone discerned its secrets.

"The Harmonic Resonance has a backlash effect. When he used it before the Titan Crisis, the backlash completely disintegrated his arm, shoulder, and part of his chest in addition to the object he punched. His metal replacement is designed to absorb the backlash effect so that doesn't happen again." I despised divulging so much information to the twins, but I needed a believable excuse to continue the conversation.

"Besides," I thought to myself, *"I have no intention of letting them leave here alive, anyway."*

Nomeiko placed a hand against her mouth and drew in a sharp inhale. My brow twitched involuntarily because I understood, deep in my gut, that her gasp dripped with the same sadistic sarcasm she exuded in all her actions. A few seconds followed, and my instinct proved correct when she erupted into robust laughter. I gritted my teeth and flattened my palm against the metal roof with palpable anticipation. “What's so funny?” I nearly growled.

“Oh, nothing. Just... the chances of your little friend's survival went from slim, to none. He can't even lay a finger on Sarge with that kind of ability.” Nomeiko sauntered back to my location and gripped a fistful of my long raven locks in her free hand. The force she exerted as she dragged me toward the roof's edge threatened to rip the hair from my scalp.

I clenched my teeth and grunted until she stopped; her paltry upper body strength barely allowed her to lift the upper half of my body into the air. As she forced my face in Crelyos' direction, Nomeiko stepped forward into a half-lunge and held the position. Her back bent and she lowered the elbow of the left hand she used to grip my hair atop her extended knee. Her long katana stretched out, and she pressed the tip flush against the back of my neck. “Let's watch, shall we?”

File 33: A Hopeless Battle

"Sarge, looks like it's going to be man to man after all!" The glint in Crelyos' eyes radiated his daunting excitement. With his metal limb embedded in a partially disintegrated soldier, Crelyos squared off in front of his former commander. As the deceased soldier slid from Crelyos's prosthetic limb to the ground with a disgusting squelch, the blond mercenary took up his trademark stance that resembled a cross between trained martial arts and good, old-fashioned street brawling.

Sarge quickly scanned the surrounding area; to my surprise, his eyes flitted over the locations where the soldiers I dispatched might have emerged had they lived. His attention to detail was more than impressive. A smile touched his lips, and the copper-haired commander unfolded his arms and took up his own stance, drawing both his arms wide away from his sides with his palms opened and turned toward Loftsborough's metal floor.

I twitched against Nomeiko's blade; Sarge's combat stance was unlike any I had ever seen. When he spoke, his words left him with the calm resolve of a seasoned combat veteran. "It seems your sniper friend helped you more than I thought. Very well, Crelyos. It pains me to fight one of my former comrades, but if that is what it will take to crush your spirit, then so be it. I *will* fulfill my orders."

"Get ready, Sarge! I'm not the same green piece of shit you left all those years ago!" Crelyos charged forward and drew back his left arm; he sent his fist sailing through the air toward Sarge's jaw. I activated my Cognitive Accelerator to view the fight in slow motion, and I noted that the slate blue eyes of Crelyos' former commander effortlessly followed the punch throughout its entire swing. Instead of a large unnecessary motion, Sarge waited until Crelyos' knuckles threatened to scrape his jaw before twisting his head and body to match the flow of the punch. Crelyos' lips twisted into a premature smile the moment he believed his blow would connect.

Under that misconception, the blond mercenary threw his entire weight into the attack. Sarge spun on his heel with the force of a tornado at the exact moment Crelyos passed the point of no return, and he stumbled forward through empty air. Using the centrifugal force of his spin, Sarge forcefully drove his elbow into the back of Crelyos's neck with an expert hip twist. I marveled at the lack of any wasted movement on Sarge's part and the unfaltering confidence with which he allowed Crelyos the illusion of success. Even with my Cognitive Accelerator, I was unsure I possessed the nerves to maintain such a ruse for that long before enacting countermeasures.

I snapped my perception of motion to normal; Crelyos stumbled forward with an agonized cry. As he dropped to his hands and knees with stunned groans and bloodshot eyes, his hand lifted to rub at the painful knot forming at the base of his skull. Sarge stepped forward and drove a combat boot swiftly into Crelyos' ribcage; the kick provided enough force to lift the bulky blond from the steel floor, but as he rolled with the momentum of the strike, Crelyos growled and leapt to his feet.

Crelyos entered his typical frenzy, throwing blow after blow in Sarge's direction. With each attack, Sarge waited until the last conceivable moment and slid aside. His nerves of steel were astounding, but his acute perception surprised me more. He smiled with pleasure when Crelyos did not throw his entire center of balance off during any of the strikes that followed his unfortunate first. Somehow, Crelyos understood that Sarge had taken advantage of his imbalance and learned from that single incident. Crelyos' intelligence and cunning played far less a part in his adaptation than one of his attributes of which I was already keenly aware; apparently, so was Sarge.

“I see your combat instincts are as sharp as ever. Throw everything you got at someone more experienced than you, and the result is pain and discomfort. Very good.” Sarge's words floated through the air with the same fluid tempo he displayed as he danced around Crelyos' flailing limbs. But what startled me most as a witness to the display was that Crelyos' attacks, even when filtered through my analytical discernment, possessed very few flaws.

His punches, knees, and kicks from his natural flesh limbs, while wild and lacking finesse, cut through the air with pinpoint precision, blinding speed, and properly trained technique. In fact, given Crelyos' natural instinct to evolve and grow over the course of a fight, every subsequent blow that rocketed from my blond comrade escalated in efficiency and expertise at an alarming and impressive rate.

Unfortunately, with each stage of evolution, Sarge increased the level of experience he displayed by a margin exactly what I might consider “one step ahead” of Crelyos. In each moment of prescience, when I believed Crelyos might strike his former commander down, Sarge twisted a fraction of a second faster or dipped in a new and effective direction to bypass Crelyos' entire attack. I watched the mix of horror and frustration creep across Crelyos' face like a deadly plague. Sarge was simply toying with him, and he knew it. We all knew it.

“You grow stronger the longer you fight someone. It's such a rare gift, that combat instinct of yours. However...” Sarge's voice trailed off. Crelyos roared and threw a brutal knee straight into Sarge's diaphragm. When the blow connected with an echoing “thwack” and Sarge doubled over, a glimmer of hope soothed some of the agony in my body. It quickly vanished, however, for as Crelyos drove his fleshy left hand down toward Sarge's temple to incapacitate his former commander, the man performed a feat similar to the one I witnessed in slow motion at the bout's start.

It seemed as though Crelyos' confidence in his victory encouraged him to give his punch the entirety of his force and weight. Such an action played heavily in Sarge's favor; he twisted with the energy of Crelyos' fist and spun into an upright position. At the end of the twirl, Sarge securely gripped Crelyos' left wrist. The copper-haired commander's right hand drew back with an open palm aimed high above Crelyos' extended elbow.

Sarge's words hung in the air like a bad punch-line, "... you're holding back and treating this like some kind of game or spar! When, I assure you," Sarge grunted as he hammered his open palm into Crelyos' joint. The resounding snap and blood-curdling scream that escaped my ally as Sarge turned his elbow inside-out rattled my core. It swallowed my glimmer of hope and redeposited all the agony in my body with compounded interest. Sarge finished his sentence as Crelyos lay writhing on the ground, his arm flopping about unnaturally, "it is no game and no spar. I'm serious. So long as you hold back that ability of yours, and that right arm, you will not beat me. When you get up, I will come at you to kill you; I suggest you do the same to me."

"Crelyos!" I instinctively screamed. In my concern, my body lurched forward on its own, but the tight grip on my hair and the dangerous depression of Nomeiko's sword against my neck made short work of my movements. The cry garnered my comrade's attention, however, and he lifted his sky blue eyes to my position atop the roof. His countenance darkened, and he rose to his knees and gestured toward me with a single metal finger.

"Sarge, let her go. She has nothing to do with this," Crelyos spoke calmly but with a foreboding sense of darkness laced in his voice. Despite my heightened auditory sense, I almost failed to distinguish his words.

"Not that speech again, Crelyos. She slaughtered quite a few of my men and made an attempt on my life. She'll be killed. So will you, if you do not back down. Last warning." Sarge returned to his strange combat stance and Crelyos fought to his feet. He slung his elbow back into a proper shape with a disgusting crunch, and Panacea began the tedious work of stitching the joint back together. Crelyos gritted his teeth.

"Not her, Sarge. If you hurt even one hair on her head, I'll rip you apart even if it's the last thing I do. Let her go." Despite the pain which no doubt sang through Crelyos' arm like an obese opera singer's vibrato, he resumed his own combat stance.

"Interesting. Tell you what, I'll issue the order for Nomeiko to release her with my dying breath. That is, of course, assuming you can defeat me. If not, she dies. I think those stakes should prove most..." Sarge abruptly ended his speech when Crelyos' left fist rocketed into his nose with enough force to concave his face.

The muffled, tortured cry that escaped Sarge's busted lips as his nose all but exploded beneath the force of Crelyos' punch echoed in my ears. The copper-haired commander staggered back several feet, and his head arched back so far I anticipated the sound of his snapping neck to join his echoing cry in my enhanced ears. Crelyos growled and followed up with a vicious front thrust kick into his former commander's stomach. Sarge's jaw dropped, and the sound of a dry heave escaped him as the force of Crelyos' blow drew his former commander into an involuntary curl. Crelyos carried through with the momentum of his kick; he drew his metallic right arm back and launched it skyward in a brutal uppercut that cleaved into Sarge's jaw.

The energy behind the strike was such that Sarge's hat sailed from the top of his head and he flew back, completely airborne, several yards. When Sarge's shoulders collided with Loftsborough's metal floor, he rolled backward and planted his feet firmly onto the ground to stabilize himself. From his crouched position with one hand slammed down on the city's steel ground, Sarge coughed and spat blood onto the town's lower plate.

"... I'll beat you, but I'll do it my way. I'm not your soldier now, and I don't take orders from you anymore." Crelyos slammed his flesh fist against his open metal palm.

"Hahaha," Sarge laughed and shakily rose to an erect position. Over the course of their brief dialog, Panacea already reversed much of the aesthetic damage caused by Crelyos' furious onslaught. The former commander drew the ball of his thumb across his nose and lips to wipe away a stray trail of blood; such an action also revealed his sinister grin.

"So she's worth enough to get serious... but not serious enough. You won't save her that way. A pity. I suppose to really make you angry, I need to go ahead and kill her then." Sarge lifted his hand and drew his fingers together with the intention of snapping them; as Nomeiko pressed her blade more firmly into my neck, I assumed she awaited the snap as a sign to carry out my execution.

"You're mistaken about two things," Crelyos held up two of his cybernetic digits. "One, I'm serious. If I have to use my nanite to blow your guts out to wake you up then, damn it, I will. I just wanted to give you the same fair warning you gave me. When you broke my arm, that could have easily been my neck. Cheeky hypocrite bastard, you held back too. So now we're even." Crelyos made an uppercut gesture with his metal right arm. I grinned from my "captive" position.

It was true; if Crelyos wished, he could have easily activated his nanite and turned his former commander's head into red sludge. Though I found his sense of honor endearing, I wondered if such an action might return to haunt him.

"And two," Crelyos grinned, "you're underestimating that girl up there. She's Junction City's top mercenary and the best damn fighter I know. I don't need to save her, and I'd be much more worried about Tweedle Dee and Tweedle Dumbass up there, if I were you."

My grin widened; his words served as the precious motivation and cue I needed to propel myself to action. I quickly reached up and gripped the buzzing wrist of my captor; I prepared myself for the debilitating shock. When the electrical buzz shot through me, I managed to withstand its effects long enough to swivel my head sideways and alleviate her katana's pressure against my neck. I clenched her wrist involuntarily as her electrical currents seized control of my muscles, and with a deep growl I drew my head down and forced the edge of her blade across the small handful of hair she tightly clutched in her fingers.

The obsidian wisps flew off into the cold breeze. I snatched my hand from her wrist and pressed my palms into the rooftop, freed from her grasp. Using the roof's edge as leverage, I lifted my hips, split my legs, and clamped them around her neck. Such an action became immensely easier considering her knelt position. The currents of electricity she kept flowing through her body worked to my advantage as they forced my muscles taut. I willed my convulsing body forward and activated my Supersoldier nanite.

With the tight clench of my thighs about Nomeiko's neck, the forceful momentum I gathered due to the roof's gentle incline, and the strength my Supersoldier nanite imparted on me, it took a matter of seconds to arch into a handstand with Nomeiko in tow. Not wishing to lose the power behind the movement, I continued the motion and toppled the two of us over the edge of the roof, but at the last moment, I gripped the roof's edge. The added resistance and introduction of gravity sharply snapped us down.

While my back collided forcefully against the building's wall, I released my grip on Nomeiko's neck at the peak velocity of the descent. She relinquished a surprised shout when her body plummeted like a wayward asteroid into Loftsborough's metal floor several stories below us. Without waiting for her grim impact, I flipped backward and landed safely atop the roof in a readied crouch.

"Sis!" Izuma shouted; the rapid tap of his boots hammered against the roof as he rushed toward our location. As my nerves settled and the sparks from Nomeiko's nanite wore off, I bolted passed Izuma to the location where I first collapsed to retrieve my dagger. I snatched the hilt of my blade up and spun into a combat stance facing Izuma who stood at the roof's edge.

"She's... not moving. You bitch!" Izuma turned and charged across the roof in my direction. In the distance, the sound of Crelyos and Sarge exchanging blows mingled with the howl of the wind whistling through Loftsborough's numerous openings.

Izuma drew back his right hand in preparation of a vertigo-inducing hook; I nonchalantly lifted my empty left hand and stepped toward him. His punch slammed into my waiting left palm, and I immediately clutched it in a tight grip. The vibrations emanating from his unique nanite sent chills up the length of my shoulder, but the further they traveled from their source, the more their effects harmlessly dispersed. Against his mind-altering, high frequency waves, I merely needed to intercept the blows before they approached my head.

He grunted and applied pressure behind the blow, as though he aimed to overpower my hold. His stance was flawless, and based on the force behind his strike, I surmised his training was far above adequate. In a regular military during a regular time, Izuma would have made a fine soldier despite his feeble build. But the times in which we lived were absurd, and normal exceptionality simply did not cut it.

Keeping Izuma's fist in a wide arch away from my head, I pulled his arm far to my left using the force he exerted and my own enhanced power. Synchronously, I flipped the dagger in my right hand into a reverse grip and sent a hard jab straight for his throat. Despite being tugged slightly off balance, Izuma lifted his left hand to parry my punch.

Though my body lacked the raw speed exhibited by Nomeiko or Al, in the eyes of those without speed augmentation, my swiftness knew no equal. Though Izuma's wrist caught mine, he only succeeded in lifting my fist from his throat to his face. My knuckles drove into the bridge of his nose with a satisfying crunch, and as his head jolted back and he released a stunned cry, I glanced over his shoulder toward the roof's edge. A familiar yet undesirable hand clenching a katana emerged over the rooftop's lip; Nomeiko heaved herself halfway atop the roof. Blood seeped from a rapidly healing wound in her forehead, but the scuffs covering her leather suit and the various bruises and dirt smudges informed me that her impact had not been very pleasant.

While Izuma sputtered and attempted to recover from the shocking blow to his face, I swiftly took hold of his outfit's collar. My feet left the ground in a guided jump, and I sailed over the top of his head; with my hands firmly clasped about his attire, the restriction snapped my body down directly behind him. I pressed my back flush to his and tugged myself forward, keeping a firm hold on his outfit. I clenched the muscles in my abdomen, and using the momentum I accumulated during my flip, I pulled Izuma up and over my back in a reverse shoulder toss that sent him flipping through the air with the power behind my augmented muscles.

At that precise moment, Nomeiko finished clambering to her feet atop the building. "You crazy bitch!" She shouted with disdain, "I'll make you suffer for th—" Her words stopped short as her brother's flying body collided with her. The Storm Duo careened off the rooftop, and though the prospect of watching Nomeiko slam harshly into the city's steel ground a second time amused me, I wasted none of the precious little time I acquired.

I sprinted to the roof's edge and placed the hilt of my dagger between my teeth. I hopped from the roof and simultaneously spun to face it; after gripping the rooftop's lip, I used it as an anchor to swing through the window into the room that previously served as my sniping nest. I gripped my rifle and chambered a fresh round before shifting toward the window.

"Those kids are good and well trained, but they're young and inexperienced. They swing about wildly and waste motions, and that girl is too caught up in causing pain." I mused to myself as I leaned from the window to

take aim at my two immobile targets below. Unfortunately, another jarring surprise lay in wait. Nomeiko's infuriated face awaited me below, but it stared at me from a closer distance than I anticipated when I leaned from the window. Somehow, in her unbridled rage, Nomeiko leapt like a spark of electricity from one protrusion of the building to another and reached the window far more quickly than her first climb back to the roof.

With the tip of her blade extended, Nomeiko attempted to impale my face during her rapid ascent; I barely ducked back into the room in time to avoid a lobotomy. Her slender body filled the window, and I instinctively lifted my rifle's underbelly to parry her oncoming assault. She brought the blade down in a diagonal slash aimed to bisect me from the right shoulder, down between the center of my breast's modest swell, to my left hip. She almost succeeded.

My father's rifle, which I carried with me for so long, split in half as the flawless katana sliced through it like it was a stick of butter. Though it failed to stop her cut completely, it succeeded in buffering it from potentially fatal to excruciatingly painful. My skin and clothes tore apart with a spray of blood as I staggered further back into the room.

With a hiss of pain, I dropped the two pieces of my father's rifle and released my jaw's hold on my dagger. It fell into my waiting right hand. Considering that my previous experience parrying her attacks ended with shocking amounts of pain, I instead opted to weave and dodge in the wake of her unrelenting assault. Unfortunately, she was just too fast for me to completely avoid her attacks, and as we danced around the room, more than one fissure opened up in my pale skin.

My muscles buckled beneath the coursing electricity with each consecutive blow she landed, and every spasm slowed my movements and increased the disparity in our speeds. A few times her blinding movements forced me to parry in order to protect my head and heart; I immediately regretted each of those times. The currents of lightning conducted between her metal blade and mine sent my body into spasms.

Speed; I needed speed more than anything, and not just the speed of thought I acquired during Cognitive Acceleration. Even if the jarring electrical shocks would not shake my concentration and deactivate the nanite, which they would, my mind's swift processing power meant little if my muscles lacked the raw ability to keep up with my opponent. I had always known the Cognitive Accelerator possessed such a weakness. While its applications in tactics and situational awareness provided a paramount advantage, the ability to utilize it in actual combat was inarguably limited.

As the clang of our blades met in rapid succession followed by several buzzes of swift electric discharge through my body, I found myself defensively pressed against a wall. The sight of her katana's tip stabbing toward my forehead seemed to slow time to a crawl even without the activation of my Cognitive Accelerator. If I died, my chances to kill Bradich died as well. If I died, I would never know why he betrayed us and killed everyone we ever loved. I could not die. I would not die.

My head snapped to the side at the last possible moment. Nomeiko's katana embedded itself in the metal wall with an audible whine, but as I expected the intense burst of speed to end and my head to pause in its rightful position just to the right of her sword, I surprised myself by staggering toward the opposite wall from the uncontrollable momentum caused by my simple head motion! Her head cocked to one side, and our gazes locked.

“What the hell was that? It was like some kind of piston rammed into the side of your head,” Nomeiko growled as she wriggled her blade from the wall.

“Hell if I know, I'm trying to figure it out myself.” I shook my head a few times hoping the motion would clear the strange haze that settled into my skull like an obscuring fog.

“You're a crazy old hag,” Nomeiko spat and dashed across the short distance to the wall which I used to steady myself. She dragged her katana behind her like a deadly steel tendril, and as she closed the gap separating us, she swung it in a blinding horizontal arch toward my neck.

Perhaps she grew tired of our game because her action

carried with it the clear intention of my decapitation. I knew as soon as her arm began the swing, I would no longer be able to visibly follow her movements as I could with lesser opponents. I needed to react immediately and focus on the muscles in her shoulders; I needed to concentrate and keep my cool. Deadly, flashing silver made that a little easier said than done, however.

As soon as the indention between her clavicle and shoulder twitched, I commanded my body to move. The fast-twitch muscle fibers responsible for swift jerky movements reacted to that command, and I forced my body to the floor in an impromptu crouch. As the blade sang over the top of my head, I noticed the same unfortunate event occurred in the partial second that passed between my crouch and Nomeiko's attack. My entire body rocketed to the ground as though being drawn to some invisible black hole in the floor.

Once I initiated my movement, I seemed to lose control over my body's momentum. The result, as before, was an over-the-top extravagant maneuver. It felt as though my own swiftness overwhelmed me, and I lost the ability to stop once I set myself in motion. By the time I planted both palms on the ground and regained control of my legs enough to stop my descent, I was glancing up at Nomeiko's bewildered face from a near prone position against the floor.

"What... what the hell are you doing all of a sudden? Stop wiggling around and just die already!" Nomeiko drew her blade back over her head. The force behind her preparation as she drew her muscles taut fluttered the short spikes of her styled black hair. I rapidly shoved my feet into the ground and propelled myself straight into her sternum with a blinding shoulder tackle. Not surprisingly, my body refused to stop once it collided with hers.

The two of us tumbled across the room with flailing limbs; as the painful sparks of her electricity passed through my body, I growled and struggled to regain control of my movements. By the time I succeeded, we had rammed into the metal frame of my temporary bed. Without a full range of motion, Nomeiko possessed little alternative than to ram her bony elbows and knees into various parts of my body. I retaliated with several quick wild blows that left the two of us grunting and groaning. Before long, the soft cover atop my bed wriggled its way between our writhing forms and entangled us.

"Blasted cotton contraption!" I growled to myself. After a second of thought, it dawned on me like a scientific "Eureka!" Though the material was not actually cotton, its synthetic properties imitated the extinct material almost perfectly!

I ceased my wild assault on Nomeiko and focused my energy on freeing myself from entanglement. When I emerged from the cotton-like tethers, I gripped the flailing end pieces like reins on a steed. The material worked as I expected; despite my connection with the lightning maiden, I felt no painful buzz or spark course through the insulating material. And with the weight of Nomeiko as an anchor, I was able to safely utilize the fluke burst of hyperspeed my body exhibited, and the consequential, uncontrollable flailing, to my advantage.

I felt the pressure of Nomeiko's body within the soft cocoon, and I immediately tugged the ends taut. With my Supersoldier augment still providing me increased strength and the new, freak occurrence of quickness, I yanked Nomeiko, sheets and all, from the bed and slammed her into the nearest wall with enough force to dent the steel and crack the stone.

Her cry echoed in time with the environment's destruction, but I offered her no time to lick her wounds. With another powerful heave I drew her body from the wall and slammed it hard into the ground. The process continued, with each strike leaving one of her bones broken or a piece of furniture destroyed. To my admiration, she kept her katana clenched firmly in her hand, and despite the amount of pressure I applied to her body by swinging her wildly about, I watched as she prepared to cut the blanket in which I ensnared her. I had no intention of allowing that to happen. With a final heave powered by my determined shout, I flung her cocoon encased body toward the window and released the sheets. She howled as she descended to the hard floor of Loftsborough for yet a third time.

I dropped to my knees and reached over to grip my dagger. Even the simple motion of extending my arm threatened to rip it from its socket since I was unable to keep from thrusting the limb out like a striking serpent. I sighed and slowly encircled my fingers around my knife.

Every motion I made required extensive thought to keep from moving too quickly lest I lose control. When I finally reached my feet, I exhaled a slow, methodic breath. But as soon as I felt a calm envelope me, the entire building violently groaned and shook; with the rumbling metal and stone cracking around me, I nearly lost my footing.

Within seconds the interior began falling apart; the steel sheets twisted, the giant stone blocks crumbled, and the floor sank under the weight of the rattling mansion. I fought to maintain balance and growled as several pieces of falling debris struck various parts of my body. As the definitive instant approached when the whining steel and cracking stone silenced for a split second before the structure's utter collapse, I bolted for the open window. I launched myself from the implosion; the dust and debris fell just behind my backside like sheets of rain.

In the distance, Crelyos and Sarge leapt and bounded around one another in vicious combat. Unfortunately for my blond comrade, Sarge's smile and lack of any significant wound indicated who possessed the advantage. Just before my situation recaptured my attention, I watched him easily lean back to avoid one of Crelyos' left-handed punches by a hair's breadth. Sarge quickly retaliated; he kicked Crelyos' knee inward and unleashed a torrent of blows that sent him sprawling across the ground.

I was in no better position, myself. As my body descended, I glanced down to see Izuma with his hands outstretched toward the dust and metal cloud that used to be Eugene's mansion. Though I assumed his low frequency vibrations to be strong, witnessing a person bring down an entire building with a mere touch still shocked me, but the worst sight approached from directly below. With bloodshot eyes seethed in rage, Nomeiko leapt through the air covered in bruises and blood with her blade pulled tight to her side.

Without the ability to change trajectory in midair, Nomeiko easily found her mark; she thrust her katana forward and impaled me. The sharp, cold steel contradicted the fiery electrical burst that coursed through my body as she plunged her sword through my chest. Thankfully, I managed to lift my dagger against the side of her blade to keep it from penetrating my heart or lungs, but it tore easily through the flesh near my shoulder. The force behind her airborne tackle as she brought her blade to bear slammed us both into the ruins of Eugene's mansion with a loud clatter and a puff of dust.

"Stupid bitch, I'll kill you!" Nomeiko brought her weight down upon her sword, shoving it clean through my body and into the steel ground beneath me. I clenched my teeth and fought the urge to spasm as my muscles convulsed with the bursts of electricity pumping through them. The pain threatened to tear my mind asunder. As the palpable sparks coursed across my teeth and singed the very tissue beneath my skin, I prepared to deactivate my pain receptors. A familiar voice drifted from an apparent hiding place behind one of the nearby buildings.

“Ihlia, dear child, if you do what I think you're thinking, I will not be responsible for the consequences!” Oswald emerged and, while keeping a safe distance, approached Eugene's destroyed manor.

“Who the hell is this geezer, you old hag?” Nomeiko twisted the blade in my chest and stood erect, glaring at Oswald as electricity coursed along her fingertips and weapon. “Look, old timer, get lost or get fried.”

“Oswald... it's no good... she's too fast...” I groaned between pulses of electricity. I lifted my bloodshot eyes to the old surgeon who stared at me with a mixture of earnest concern and genuine fear. I reached up to grip Nomeiko's blade and continued during a lull in the pain, “And besides...I'm randomly losing control of my own body... it must be a side effect of her electricity. Cutting those receptors... is the only way.”

“Hm? Oh! Ihlia, no! You're likely talking about the effects of your new nanite! I tried to tell you about it before you vanished into the wilderness!”

File 34: A Changed Man

“I've been trying to design a nanite to supplement your Cognitive Accelerator. What I came up with is roughly based off the technology you described in Al's nanite, and involves exciting your fast twitch muscle fibers in short bursts. The design is intrinsically different, however. Perhaps you're familiar with reflexes? Myotatic and polysynaptic reflexes and the like? No? Well, reflexes normally bypass our brain and respond directly to external stimulus using sensors in the muscles themselves!” Oswald exclaimed excitedly.

“They do this by firing impulses to the spinal cord; while your brain becomes aware of reflex movements, it does not control them. In this way you snatch your hand from hot fire or your foot off a sharp nail far faster than you would if you actually thought about doing so! The augment I implanted in you sets up a network of nanites to bridge the connection between those synapses, your spinal cord, and your brain! In other words, your voluntary muscle fibers, when you activate the nanite, can operate at the speed of your reflexes!”

“As a bonus, the nanites serving as the conduits excite the impulse rate at which your synapses fire by several hundred fold! Of course, a normal human being would not be able to control such movements. The brain is such a limited tool; after activating the nanite to stimulate the muscles hundreds of times faster than normal human reflexes, you would then need to reactivate it to stop that motion or redirect the energy; in short, to stop or change direction. Alas, humans cannot think so quickly. Oh, wait. You can. Haha!" Clearly, Oswald's speech spiraled into the realm of excitement he referred to as his "zone." I referred to it as his "ranting."

"Laymen's terms... you old codger. We're kind of... on a time crunch." I reached up and grabbed Nomeiko's wrist. Though she seemed to keep a curious ear open to the words of the good doctor, she maintained the force behind her painful blade twists. In fact, with a vehement growl she placed one of her boots atop my throat and began stepping down. As in all of her endeavors, she applied pressure slowly with the desire to inflict as much pain and discomfort as possible.

"Ah, right. To be frank, you do not have Al's super running speed. That nanite strains the muscles with voluntary electric impulses and destroys them by pushing them passed their limitations, thus taxing Panacea. You have quickness. Bursts of fast movement that capitalize on the body's synapses by bridging your voluntary and involuntary actions while multiplying them several hundred times their normal speed. Humans do not have the brain processing power to normally accommodate this, but during cognitive acceleration, you do," Oswald carefully explained.

"You should notice you move far closer to your normally perceived 'speed' during cognitive acceleration.

At least in terms of quick steps, jumps, or hand motions. The muscles can still be strained and overburdened if you overuse it, thus taxing Panacea, but it is a far more reliable nanite than Al's." Oswald pressed his spectacles up the bridge of his nose and nodded.

"So I have super speed... as long as I'm not trying to run..." I rolled my hips back and pressed the bottom of my combat boots against Nomeiko's chest. Despite the constant spasms caused by the electric current in my body, I was determined to get the psychotic sadist off me.

"You could... have just said that from... the start!" I roared and activated my new synapse enhancement. The muscles in my legs bolted out in a furious kick that, without being in a state of cognitive acceleration, sent Nomeiko whistling through the air and me chaotically rolling to my feet. As I stumbled forward into a crouch and planted my hands against a nearby distorted metal pillar to steady myself, the sound of Crelyos howling in agony averted my attention. I instantly enhanced my senses to better perceive the situation.

Sarge's fist drove into my comrade's spine like a drill. The fact that Sarge faced Crelyos' back implied the copper-haired commander somehow danced a complete one hundred and eighty degrees around my ally. Infuriated, Crelyos pivoted and drove his left fist toward Sarge's face, but due to the wide distance the blond mercenary needed to spin in order to reach him, Sarge followed Crelyos' entire motion with the passive interest of a bird-watcher.

In the last moment, Sarge dipped low and allowed the strike to pass directly over his bristly red hair. Using the recoil of his crouch, he then sent a crushing uppercut into Crelyos' jaw and followed it with a swift roundhouse to the side of his face. The overwhelming force behind his foot threatened to pop Crelyos' head from his shoulders, and I thought the sound of several cracking vertebrae reached my augmented ears as my ally slammed into a nearby building. Sarge finally glanced in my direction, and when his gaze averted to the Storm Duo, he shook his head with disappointed dismay. "Enough is enough," Sarge grimaced and pressed a finger to his ear. "Hoverbuster Alpha, this is Sarge. Punch a hole in this clam and prepare the ballistic missiles, I want scorched earth policy on this place. Torch it all."

"No!" Crelyos cried out, pulled himself off the building, and dashed toward Sarge, who turned to face him. The commander's eyes widened; though I was unable to discern if the misty gray saucers glistened with excitement or concern. For Crelyos' right metal arm cut through the air directly toward the copper-haired soldier, and it sang with the vibratory force of his Harmonic Resonance. Part of me felt relief that Crelyos put the safety of the town before his desire to save one old war buddy; another part of me felt a heart wrenching sadness knowing Crelyos likely hated the nanoseconds between his punch's launch and its connection more than any other moment in his life. Either way, Sarge would not survive.

At least, I thought that to be the case. I was sadly mistaken.

As Crelyos' deadly punch neared Sarge's face, he simply lifted his left hand directly in the trajectory of my comrade's cybernetic limb. The heavy thud of Crelyos' prosthetic rang out like a detonation, and Sarge's clothes billowed back with the shockwave created by the powerful impact. My jaw dropped, however, when Sarge stood in the wake of Crelyos' blow unscathed.

Did Crelyos hold back again? Was he simply unable to bring himself to kill an ally even if it meant the lives of hundreds of innocent bystanders? Upon closer inspection, I realized how far from the truth my hypothesis actually was. Crelyos' metal fist hovered almost an entire foot from Sarge's outstretched hand. The steadiness with which it vibrated in the air made it appear as though Crelyos struck some solid object, but the gap between his fist and Sarge's hand contained only empty space.

The cold bite of the whistling wind swept through the city as the only prominent sound. I was stunned and confused. Nomeiko used her katana as a brace and shakily stood; she parted her lips and unleashed a torrent of her trademark sadistic laughter.

“That's what I tried to tell you. He can't even touch the commander,” Nomeiko panted between her wicked chortles and shifted her weight to her feet. With a deep inhale, she readied her katana and sank into a battle stance in front of me.

“Psychokinesis? With enough force to stop a punch like Crelyos'? Why doesn't he just pick him up and throw him around like a rag doll with his mind, then?" I flipped my dagger into a reverse-grip and sank into my own typical combat stance.

"Psychokinesis? Sarge doesn't have psychokinesis. His nanites generate electromagnetic fields that respond in shape and power to his will. Repulsion, attraction, a dome, a line. He's mastered it," Nomeiko beamed proudly.

I had to hand it to Nomeiko, her unshakable loyalty to Sarge impressed me. She downright idolized him. Sarge's unique nanite certainly explained why my metallic bullet ricocheted off some invisible force field; if Sarge kept a basic electromagnetic field up around his body with enough strength, it would easily double as his own personal anti-bullet dome.

"That's why that giant dipshit doesn't stand a chance," Nomeiko continued, "because Commander Sarge has absolute control over metal! And in a world full of glistening steel and metal..." Nomeiko's countenance darkened, and a smile spread across her lips. Behind me, the metal debris left over from the collapsed mansion shook and rattled.

I glanced back in time to watch various steel beams and metal plates dislodge from the ruins. An inexplicable force tugged on the dagger in my hand, threatening to rip it from my fingertips. It took considerable effort to merely hold onto my weapon. Nomeiko's lips parted, and her words accompanied a proverbial, split second calm-before-the-storm that suddenly overtook the air, "... the entire world is his weapon."

The metal behind me snapped forward with the force of a locomotive. I instinctively activated my Cognitive Accelerator and Synapse Augment; no better time to test the doctor's invention than when a volley of deadly building guts were traveling through your location like a meteor shower. To my relieved surprise, I found the maneuvering transpired precisely as Oswald described.

While I marveled at how intricately the old codger understood my Cognitive Accelerator, I shifted to the left of a jetting steel beam and ducked beneath a tumbling metal panel. Though a faint sluggishness remained, for the most part my body moved as it did in my typically perceived sense of time and space. Everything around me, however, moved at a fraction of its actual velocity.

A grin touched one corner of my lips; in all my years of slowing down my perception of reality, I never felt so liberated. Every motion brought a sense of omnipresence, every twist of my head and dart of my eyes invoked a plethora of new information in nearly three hundred and sixty degrees. Before, my neck's range of motion limited my analytical processing power to the scope of vision I possessed at the time I activated the Cognitive Accelerator. Even swiveling my head took place at the pace of a sluggish crawl. But with the Synapse Augmentat, I understood my entire surroundings at any given moment in time. The elation nearly swallowed me whole.

To the naked eye, I must have blurred like a ghost between tiny debris particles and sheets of steel. When the river of rusty death passed, I deactivated the nanite combination and admired my muscle contractions by gazing at my palm as I opened and closed it. When I looked up, Nomeiko and Izuma's mouths hung open in amazed silence. I looked past them to Sarge.

His right hand extended in my direction, but I understood his palm actually targeted the metal behind me. That metal traveled with purpose across the expansive distance between where I stood near the Storm Duo and where he struggled with Crelyos. It perfectly demonstrated the degree of control he possessed. Crelyos struggled to draw back his right metal arm, but as he did, Sarge must have altered the polarity of his magnetic field. Rather than repulse Crelyos's prosthetic, he drew it torward him and angled his arm down; Crelyos's metal fist drove straight into the ground. With his left hand free, Sarge quickly returned to his strange combat stance in which both his arms hovered in the air several inches away from his sides. I soon understood why.

As it raced through the air toward Sarge, the debris changed its trajectory and began circling in a wide arch around Sarge's backside like a swirling storm of steel to his left hand. He precisely manipulated his limbs, and with his mysterious nanite, he lifted the metal into the air before slamming straight down atop Crelyos in a dome shape. I lurched forward; my brows furrowed with involuntary concern, and I felt the thump of my heart sink into the pit of my stomach.

“Crelyos!” I shouted before rushing in the direction of my fallen comrade and his new rival. Honor or no honor, man to man or not, I would not allow the stubborn fool to die!

“Not so fast, old hag!” The sound of crackling lightning and rushing wind passed in front of me. I immediately leapt to the right and barely avoided a vertical cut from Nomeiko's katana intent on removing a chunk from the left side of my body. As I twisted to face her, the rumbling sound of the metal refuse pile drew the attention of my peripherals. A mere few seconds passed, but the time felt like years. Finally, the metal exploded in a partially disintegrated cloud of glittering chaff. Crelyos emerged covered in wounds and seeping blood from every conceivable pore in his body. His chest heaved rapidly beneath his shredded clothes, and as he staggered from his painful prison, Crelyos glanced toward me and lifted his cybernetic thumb skyward.

“I'm fine... You have your own shit... to deal with. Stop trying to interfere... just mind your own damn business.” I thought that any one of his given words would surely be the last he sputtered before collapsing to a useless heap, but to my constant surprise and admiration, Crelyos regained his composure and assumed a fighting stance in front of Sarge.

“Unfortunately, time's up,” Sarge crossed his arms and turned to the city's east wall; in particular, his gaze fell upon the slit in Loftsborough's dome near the elevator tower. At precisely the moment he folded those arms, a powerful explosion tore open a gash in the city's protective plates. The pressure change sent a blast of wind roaring through the city; the elongated whistle drowned the sudden screams that emanated from within the houses where the citizens took refuge.

The noise bombarded my sensitive hearing; it sharply peaked like a screeching speaker before I shut down the augment to avoid injuring my ears. Meanwhile, the humming Hoverbuster engines joined the whipping wind in an overlay of ear-piercing noise. My long tendrils of hair sprayed about like black waves, and the piercing cold penetrated my skin as sharply as Nomeiko's katana.

"Sarge... don't do this!" Crelyos coughed both words and blood. The copper-haired commander sighed, shook his head, and stepped toward my blond comrade. With a wave of his hand in a downward direction, Crelyos' metal arm slammed into the city's steel floor. Unable to resist the force, Crelyos followed suit and found himself pinned beneath the electromagnetic force Sarge generated. Crelyos stared up at his former commander with a look of horror on his face. Sarge casually pressed his finger against his ear.

"Open fire." The Hoverbuster opted out of using its electromagnetic rail guns and instead launched conventional missiles from the craft's underbelly. The hiss of the ballistic warheads emanated from the carrier like a bell toll from the Reaper. Crelyos' face contorted in anguish as the homes near him exploded. The shrill screams of the innocents quickly escalated to a gruesome pitch, only to be extinguished in the merciless flames of the Hoverbuster's arsenal. So many homes filled with frightened families changed into a sea of fire in the blink of an eye. I shook my head.

"No... This can't be. Sarge, you couldn't have..." Crelyos whispered with a quaking voice. His metal arm creaked beneath Sarge's magnetic force, and his bloody and broken body tightened with fear, frustration, and heartbreak.

"I told you. It's on your hands, Crelyos. Take that with you to whatever life is after this one." With his free hand, Sarge willed one of the metal beams from the dome of debris into the air above Crelyos. After Crelyos blew it to pieces, it left one of the ends jagged and pointy. Sarge pointed that spear-like end at my blond comrade's head.

My heart tightened in my chest, my breath caught in my throat, and I abandoned all attention on Nomeiko; I focused solely on Sarge and Crelyos. Just as I prepared to dash toward the two men, a distinct sound fluttered through the wind: an audible "tink!" Sarge, Nomeiko, Izuma, and I all glanced back toward the source of the odd noise, the Hoverbuster. The high-tech aircraft carrier toppled to one side but quickly stabilized itself with a wobble. Whatever struck the Hoverbuster did so with enough force to jar its hovering despite the meek little "tink" that echoed from the hull.

"What do you mean you've been struck by an unknown projectile? I want a full interior scan, and I want it yesterday. Move it!" Sarge dropped the metal beam directly next to Crelyos' head and pressed his finger against his ear to issue his orders.

"A metal stake? A beeping ball? What the hell are you—" *Kaboom.* A huge chunk of the Hoverbuster exploded and fire erupted from the interior like an active volcano. The cry of the engines as the aircraft spiraled to the ground several hundred feet below widened all our eyes until the faint sound of a second explosion sent wafts of smoke drifting up through the desert sky.

"Damn it! Dr. Korenkov, how far out are you?" Sarge kept his finger to his ear and briskly walked away from Crelyos, who remained stunned on the ground with his eyes wide and his mouth agape. "Just outside? Did you round up the hyped at Raze's fortress? Good, we need immediate extraction. I think Loftsborough has some reinforcements." Sarge finished issuing orders and offered Crelyos one last brief glance before looking at the Storm Duo and waving his hand in a circle above his head. "We're bugging out, you two. Get a move on; I'm issuing an immediate retreat. That's an order."

"Well looks like you get lucky this time, old hag." Nomeiko drew her blade across her tongue as though enjoying the taste of my blood before she shoved it back in its scabbard. "Let's go, useless brother." The Storm Duo rushed off after their commander between houses ablaze with crackling flames. A quick glance at Crelyos' spiritually broken state propelled me to action, and I dashed after the fleeing trio.

"Not so fast, you three... I'm not letting you get away that easily!" I determined in my thoughts. The wall on the opposite end of Loftsborough exploded much like the first, and the Hoverbuster I witnessed fly into the distance upon my arrival to the city waited on the other side of the gaping hole. Sarge allowed his subordinates to pass and pointed his hand at Crelyos; a metallic groan echoed from Crelyos' metal arm, and Sarge lifted my blond comrade off the ground with the power of his unique nanite. Crelyos helplessly dangled in the air with downcast eyes.

Sarge cast a glance to me and flicked his wrist, launching Crelyos across the scene of destruction directly into my body. Logic demanded that I shift to the side and continue my pursuit. Something in my bosom, however, halted that action; instead, I dropped my dagger and widened my arms to accommodate him. When he collided with me, we both tumbled across the metal floor. At the end of our roll, my body pressed atop his own as we lay in a heap between several burning structures. I groaned and regained my senses before glancing down at Crelyos' glistening blue eyes. Such deep regret and guilt filled them that I immediately broke eye contact.

"This is all my fault... I should have..." Crelyos' voice cracked like a man's last sane words before succumbing to hyperaugmentation. But where a hyped's last words cracked with madness, Crelyos' words cracked with grief. The Hoverbuster's engines whirred in the distance, and Sarge and his subordinates disappeared into its belly. After the hulking metal vanished from the gaping hole like a phantom, Crelyos parted his lips to speak.

“Stop.” I pressed my hand firmly against his mouth. I could not assure him there was nothing more he could have done to prevent the tragedy; I could not even assure him that he bore no responsibility for its occurrence. However, despite the reality of what I could not do, I did not want to hear the next words he planned to utter in his state of self-loathing. After a few seconds, Crelyos gripped my wrist and removed my hand from his lips.

“Where is Oswald? I need to be stronger... I need a new nanite.” His voice changed, his eyes narrowed with furious rage, and for a moment, I felt as though I stared into a mirror that was ten years old.

File 35: A Cursed Destiny

The next day, the harrowing stench of decay and the stale chill of death swept through Loftsborough's ruins like an infection from the wastes. Though not absolutely obliterated, the city's devastation testified to the destruction Sarge's military force left in its wake. The miserable screams of the unfortunate citizenry consumed by the previous day's merciless fire rang fresh in my mind I stood in the wreckage of Eugene's mansion. I sifted through the rubble and bits of steel that Sarge neglected to draw toward him during his display of magnetic might. As I systematically searched the debris, Crelyos' horrified face and solemn words haunted me like an ironic case of foreshadowing.

"This is all my fault... I need to be stronger... I need a new nanite." The blond mercenary's words hung in the air even as I located the target of my search. I curled my fingers around the segregated pieces of my father's hunting rifle that hid among the rubble. I stared at the broken halves and wondered how closely my rifle represented Crelyos' emotional state. The whistling wind carried the sounds of the mourning city with its cold sting, and it drew me from my inward musings.

I stood erect and turned to face the carnage of Loftsborough; the surviving men and women busied themselves with the recovery and disposal of their fellow citizens' corpses all while sobbing and whimpering. Despite the faint glint of morning gray streaming through the gaping tears in the clam-like slit, Loftsborough's enormous central sun remained unlit. I assumed Trumark ordered its dousing to aid the town's grieving process. Nearby, the little old mayor directed human traffic with quaking hands. My eyes drifted to the charred, shattered remains of the central square. They settled upon the feature which stood out like a cotton ball in a pile of coal: the little white angel, Elsa.

In the middle of the scorched destruction, the small child stood with her feet angled in toward one another. She drew her arms tight around her cyborg teddy with which she never parted and hugged it to her chest. Her entire body shook as though overcome with an insurmountable chill, but I knew the tremors that raced along her frame stemmed from the incessant stream of tears pouring down her cheeks in a river of grief. She hung her head; her blond hair covered her face like a curtain concealing her empathetic tears. I sighed, shook my head, and approached the small child.

“Elsa...” I knelt down and set the pieces of my broken rifle on the ground in order to place my hands atop her shoulders.

“It's... not fair. These people are all... so sad. Why? Why is everyone dead?” Elsa's voice quivered synchronously with her sobs.

“That's why I told you that you didn't need to come. I

was only retrieving something. Mayor Trumark wants us to leave, so we'll be heading out soon. You could have waited for me with Oswald and Richter." I stood and twisted the upper half of my body to glance back at the mayor and his people.

To my surprise, while the townsfolk continued scurrying about with heavy hands and heavy hearts to collect their fallen, Mayor Trumark's wrinkled brow faced Elsa and me. He arched his sagging forehead; the old man's vacant algae colored eyes belied an undeniable conflict which no doubt raged within the pit of his bosom. Did the mayor regret commanding us to leave shortly after we aided in repelling Sarge's invasion? Or did he abhor our presence like a cancerous tumor that offered him nothing but grief since its first appearance?

"Neither," Elsa sniffled, "he feels pity for us..."

"Pity? I don't understand," I turned my gaze to the young girl who stared up at me with puffy eyes still holding the watery remnants of her sorrow.

"He thinks bad things will follow you everywhere," Elsa wiped her eyes on the back of Magnolia's head.

"He's probably right," I chuckled softly in an attempt to lighten the mood and take Elsa's thoughts off the grief and pain that undoubtedly invaded her telepathic mind.

It seemed hard to believe that the previous day, Loftsborough transitioned from a place of celebration to a stage of merciless battle before ending as a black charred stain in the middle of the desert. I recalled the confusion that ensued when a communication from the aircraft to Sarge foretold the enormous bird's destruction moments later.

I learned shortly afterward that, although at their own leisurely pace, Elsa and Richter had pursued me during my headlong dash to the city from the hilltop. When he reached Loftsborough, Richter promptly dispatched the Hoverbuster with one of the explosive stakes he kept in the miniature quiver on his right calf. The chaos inevitably led to Sarge and the Storm Duo's retreat, but I failed to understand the reason behind Richter's interference. As I pondered what the sleek archer stood to gain from rendering aid during my plight, I began toward the former elevator shaft with a slow gait. Elsa followed close behind.

"I made him! I told him if he didn't come, then I was gonna run away again!" Through her sniffles, Elsa chortled behind me when she perceived my thoughts. I grinned as we approached the edge of the long shaft newly fitted with a corded ladder. I slipped the pieces of my father's broken rifle into the belt housing my lone dagger and descended.

When I reached the bottom and glanced up, I noticed Elsa struggling to steady herself on the ladder's unsecure rungs. Despite her trouble with the swaying apparatus, she refused to relinquish or even reposition her embrace on the teddy bear. Elsa finally cleared the last few pliable rungs by hopping down with dramatic flair and a high-pitched “Hiyah!”

I waited patiently with my back against the nearby wall and my arms folded beneath my breasts. My leather trench coat groaned with my motions. I had retrieved it from the small girl shortly after she and Richter dramatic arrived in Loftsborough. Elsa giggled and bounded across the precarious bridge extending from the city's entrance. I followed.

Though the morning fallout rolled overhead in typical grim fashion, the distant smell of acid and soil gases tickled my nose. It would probably rain that day. As we traversed the short distance to Oswald's trailer, Elsa occupied herself with a gentle hum and a sprite skip. A sense of relief washed over me in light of her happier disposition; I assumed we had ventured too far from the city for the anguished cries of the citizens to reach the range of her telepathic nanite. She quickly informed me that I was mistaken.

“I can still hear them,” she chirped with a hidden sense of sadness emanating from her voice, “but it's just the feeling, not the thoughts. It's like a big pool of black poking the back of my chest. I'll be okay, though, I think those people will find happiness again one day.”

“I hope so, little one.” Without glancing back at the city, I ascended the short, steep hill on which Oswald's trailer rested behind our dune buggy.

Leaning against the wall with his arms crossed over his sleek pectorals, Richter stood with a cigarette tucked loosely between his lips. His bow hung in a tight fastening between his shoulder blades; its tip peeked over the top of his head. I did not see the mechanical contraptions which afforded his arms the strength to draw his otherworldly bow, but a pair of gaudy pauldrons took their place on his shoulders. I assumed with the proper stimulus, the metallic and mechanical parts would fold out like a segmented garage door to cover the entire length of his arms within seconds. So they were powerful, intimidating, and portable.

"How convenient," I thought to myself. I ended my journey at Richter's right side and pressed my back firmly against the trailer; I folded my arms across my stomach. From our vantage point, the two of us watched Elsa struggle to ascend the rocky slope with passive interest.

"Is the doctor still operating on Crelyos?" My gaze cut to the archer. At first, he only gently shrugged his shoulders in response.

"If you mean the big guy, then yeah I guess. I just met all of you crazies yesterday, and I'm awful with names." Without drawing the tar-stuffed stick from his lips, Richter hissed smoke from his nose and mouth with a sharp exhale.

"Yeah, that's him. I'm just worried. He's already got three implants. I tried to convince him not to get this procedure. But he's stubborn, and Oswald really wanted to get inside his head. What if four is too many for him?" I tipped my head back against the trailer and closed my eyes. My thoughts drifted to that giant blond lug and the zany doctor no doubt toying with his unique implant with the excitement of a child on his birthday.

"Four? One is too many." Richter tugged the remnants of his cigarette from his mouth and tossed it to the crusted earth. Surprised, I snapped open my eyes and raised a single brow at his remark. I lifted one of my hands and rapped my knuckles methodically atop one of his metal pauldrons.

"Cryptic words for someone that uses so much technology. Most of this stuff you can't even find anymore. The only difference between your technology and neurotech is the difference between hardware and software," I grinned. Richter's initial response involved a sluggish lift and drop of his shoulders. But a few seconds passed, and as I took note of his trend to shrug, he retorted.

"No, the difference is that I tell my equipment what to do. I made it with my own hands, and there is no chance that it will ever decide it doesn't like what I have to say, no matter how many tools I slap on my belt." Richter's words conveyed his disdain for neurotech effectively enough, so I decided to drop the issue.

"So, what, you have no nanites at all? How do you even survive?" I posed my inquiry with active interest; the prospect of someone surviving the apocalyptic events of the Titan Crisis and its ensuing fallout without Panacea baffled me.

“Unfortunately, when you're a kid you don't control what your parents put in you. I got Panacea, but that's it,” Richter tugged another stick of tobacco from his vest pocket and shoved the filtered end into his mouth. With a flick of a sludge-based open-flamed lighter, the tip took on the glowing hue of an ember.

“I see. So what do you two plan to do now?” I asked as I lowered my arms to my sides and made my best attempt at relaxing.

“We're... going with you... of course!” Between the sounds of her heavy breaths, Elsa interjected her intentions. The small girl finished clambering up the hill and stood before the two of us; with her body doubled over and her hands resting atop her slightly bent knees, Elsa swallowed gulps of air. Magnolia hung by its arm from the pinch created by the girl's right hand pressed against the ball of her knee. While her state of exhaustion amused me, her statement intrigued me far more.

Richter narrowed his eyes into a thin slit and glared down at the young child. When she perceived this, Elsa stood erect, crossed her arms, and glared right back at him. I glanced between the two with a grin painted on one corner of my mouth. After a few seconds, I stepped forward and squatted in front of the small child. Her attention shifted from a stubborn glare at her benefactor to a pleading gaze at me; I simply tilted my head to one side and reached up to ruffle her long blonde locks of hair.

"You sure? Where we're going is far away and fairly dangerous. There will be a lot of fighting and killing, and I can't guarantee your safety," I pointed out.

"Are you serious? She's just a kid. She's too young to be caught up in your bullshit," Richter interrupted with a condescending scowl.

"Really? I guess I never really thought about it..." I sincerely retorted. As Richter pointed out the girl's excessive youth, I allowed my gaze to travel up and down the height of her. I grew up among the Bald Eagles and matured with Shandi's help; through those experiences, I came to understand that the tragedy that occurred in Yordleton far exceeded normal events one might expect in the life of a young girl.

Intellectually, I knew that a girl that age typically involved herself with dolls and school rather than a life of learning combat and walking a tightrope on the edge of death, but the reality asserted itself with the same fervor Elsa asserted her will to travel with me. From an age not much older than the small child, I grew accustomed to the intimacy of battle and the Reaper's tango. So the concept that her age might somehow hinder her ability to make life-altering decisions eluded me on an intrinsic level.

"I'm not a child anymore, Richter! I can do what I want!" Elsa shouted defiantly; the flustered crimson that spread across her cheeks likely stemmed from her aggravation that Richter spoke of her as though she were not standing directly in front of him.

"The fact that you think you can do whatever you want makes you a child." Richter's voice never changed in pitch or volume; he spoke with a cold, piercing calm with all the penetrating power of one of his custom arrows.

"Elsa, Richter's right. It's really dangerous, and I don't want anyone getting hurt because of my vendetta," I placed my hands on her shoulders and stared into her pretty blue-green eyes.

Crelyos' face raced through my mind like a dune buggy. At first his lopsided grin and stubborn, endearing anger pervaded my thoughts, but as the images progressed to represent the time that passed since he accompanied me on my journey, those expressions contorted into rage, anguish, and deep sorrow. Much like Crelyos, the threat of Elsa experiencing irreversible emotional or mental trauma concerned me far more than the idea of any physical wound. "Why do you want to go with us so badly, anyway?"

"Because you're special too! And..." Elsa's initial statement escaped her in a passionate torrent of desperation, but she paused before speaking her latter words as though streaming them through some unseen filter. She tugged Magnolia up to her face to cover her quivering lips. Only the sad glint of her eyes peeked over the top of the cyborg teddy's head, and those sea-hewn oculars averted themselves from my gaze as though they might betray her embarrassment or grief. "...and I don't want to be alone anymore."

Her words knocked me on my proverbial ass. I creased my brows and stared back over my shoulder at Richter. At first, his mouth hung slightly agape to the point that his cigarette threatened to escape and plunge to the ground. After a few seconds, however, he drew his lips taut and inhaled a lung full of smoke. He closed his eyes then lifted and dropped his shoulders in a defeated shrug.

"I'll go pack our stuff," he sighed a combination of words and smoke.

"Oh, Richter, you're the best!" Elsa dashed up to Richter and threw her arms around his hips with wild abandon. As she giggled and nuzzled into his stomach, he scratched the back of his head in mock annoyance. The faint smile pulling at his lips, however, belied his satisfaction. I laughed under my breath.

The sound of Oswald's trailer doors clanking shut tore me from the sentimental moment, and as I shuffled to the back of the contraption, I arrived just in time to witness the doctor dust off his hands after sealing up the doors. I expected Crelyos to stumble from the doctor's makeshift operating room with the same overpowering disorientation I experienced, but instead, only Oswald emerged from the metal laboratory. I approached him with a concerned furrow marring my brows.

"So, are preparations complete for us to embark? We have much ground to cover," Oswald inquired nonchalantly. I cocked my hips to one side and pressed a single closed fist against the swell created by the stance. My position immediately provoked Oswald to cross his arms expectantly. His words rolled from his lips with the aggravation of a parent addressing a spoiled child, "What is it, dear child?"

"Don't 'are preparations complete,' me. How is Crelyos? Why isn't he leaping from the back of the trailer with a bottle of sludge in his hand swearing at you for your rough handling?" I gestured to the sealed door at Oswald's rear with obvious suspicion.

"Rough handling? Well I nev— Ihlia, when you underwent the procedure your wounds had all but recovered. The drunkard insisted I operate on him after that military fellow brought a house down on his head. He needs rest considering the extent of his injuries when I deactivated Panacea to perform the surgery, so I properly sedated him," Oswald nodded and pushed his glasses up the bridge of his nose.

"He'll be asleep for quite a while; besides I don't want him wandering off into the desert like a certain someone. Now, please calm down and explain to me why we are allowing these two strangers, one of which is a child, to accompany us on our journey? Ihlia, you know I hate children." Apparently Oswald heard the entire conversation through the trailer's thin metal walls. His stern gaze suggested he believed he succeeded in shifting from a defensive standpoint to an offensive one in our little argument.

"Things are getting more complicated, Oswald. We're dealing with an entire organization. Richter uses some pretty high tech gear, and I can vouch that he's a decent fighter. I mean, he took down a Hoverbuster! I hardly see the harm in having another able body along." Like a small rodent in a trap, I fell into a defensive explanation.

Despite my reasoning, the sound of Oswald's annoyance in his questions sounded far more like my usual self. Normally, I would express my gratitude for Richter's assistance then bid him and the young girl in tow a heartless farewell. Why did I feel so intent on the two strangers accompanying us? Was it the security of an extra fighter? *"Or perhaps..."* I thought to myself, glancing over at the pair.

Elsa still clung to Richter's waist, but her giddy expression had transformed. She buried herself into Richter in a shy attempt to hide herself from Oswald. He offered her absolutely no regard. Upon noticing my attention, Richter simply shrugged and pulled away from the young girl. He began through the desert in the direction of what I assumed to be their temporary abode. More than anything, however, I focused on Elsa.

"Where are you going?" Oswald called after the sleek archer. Richter paused and glanced over his shoulder.

"Like I said," Richter finished the last drag on his

cigarette and flicked the butt into the wind, "I'm going to pack our things."

"And what do you stand to gain from traveling with us? I can't say I trust someone who so easily adjusts his entire life around the whims of a small child or the requests of a stranger." Oswald's narrow gaze followed the aloof renegade even when he turned his back on us and started through the desert again.

"I have my reasons. I'm not acting selflessly; I have my own agenda," Ricther lifted his hand and offered a dismissive wave as he shrank into the horizon. The distant roll of thunder heralded the approaching rain that I smelled when Elsa and I left Loftsborough. Oswald adjusted his glasses with an annoyed sigh.

"And what of the child? I will grant you the logic of Richter's approval to our band; the technology on his shoulders most certainly predates the Titan Crisis. I myself am actually quite intrigued to find out where he acquired it. But this young girl named Elsa? She would certainly be nothing more than a hindrance. We should leave her in the care of Loftsborough's denizens." Oswald crossed his arms and stated his points with all the affection his scientific mind afforded him: none.

Upon Richter's disappearance, Elsa found a new hideaway behind me. She clutched the frayed ends of my synthetic leather trench coat and poked only a small portion of her face from around the swell of my hips in order to look upon Oswald. While most onlookers would surmise her gaze to be one of a normal, confused young child, I knew better. No doubt Oswald's mind fell under intense scrutiny by her telepathic nanite. I shuddered to think what the poor child discovered.

"Loftsborough's done so much for us already. They restocked our supplies and didn't try to kill us for bringing a miniature war to their town. I hardly think it's fair to thrust a child upon their already strained resources while they rebuild. Besides, I seriously doubt that Richter would approve. He takes care of her, so I'm fairly certain that wherever he goes, she goes," I responded; even I recognized my words were little more than excuses. Perhaps somewhere in the convoluted sea of my dormant emotions, I wanted Elsa nearby, though for the life of me I could not fathom why.

"Quite..." Oswald trailed off with an arched brow. He no doubt attempted to size up my intentions, but in the end he simply threw his hands in the air, defeated. A cryptic smile touched his lips, "Very well then, Ihlia. I pray you do not regret your decision. When Richter returns, we will load up his equipment and be on our way." The doctor shoved his hands into his coat and waltzed to the front of the dune buggy to tinker with the machinery.

Regret? I was far beyond experiencing regret. The wheels had already begun to turn. People died, a township burned to the ground, and an organization formed by the very man who destroyed the world undoubtedly marked us as kill-on-sight. I turned my face into the wind; its stinging cold carried the odor of destruction that I prepared to leave in my wake. Whatever fate lay ahead of us, it left no room for regret. Not anymore.

I glanced down at the young Elsa and grinned; she returned my glance and smiled.

38709783R00326

Made in the USA
Charleston, SC
13 February 2015